The
Helmingham Rose

Joan Hessayon

CORGI BOOKS

THE HELMINGHAM ROSE
A CORGI BOOK : 0 552 14535 1

First publication in Great Britain

PRINTING HISTORY
Corgi edition published 1997

3 5 7 9 10 8 6 4

Set in 10/11.4pt Plantin
by Phoenix Typesetting, Ilkley, West Yorkshire.

Corgi Books are published by Transworld Publishers,
61–63 Uxbridge Road, London W5 5SA,
a division of The Random House Group Ltd,
in Australia by Random House Australia (Pty) Ltd,
20 Alfred Street, Milsons Point, Sydney, NSW 2061, Australia,
and in New Zealand by Random House New Zealand Ltd,
18 Poland Road, Glenfield, Auckland 10, New Zealand
and in South Africa by Random House (Pty) Ltd,
Endulini, 5a Jubilee Road, Parktown 2193, South Africa.

Printed and bound in Great Britain by
Mackays of Chatham plc, Chatham, Kent

This book is for my grandchildren Ella Norris, Alex Gibbs, Georgia Norris and Theo Norris

My thanks to two friends of long standing, Constance Barry, for her initial researches, and Gillian Jackson for her careful reading of the manuscript.

Several people spent time with me, giving me information or sharing reminiscences about the real 1929 and life in real country houses. My thanks to Leonard Ratcliff, Daphne and Michael Dormer, and Roy Balaam.

Finally, my thanks to my editor, Diane Pearson, for her time, her knowledge and her friendship. In fact, the many friends I made while working on this book have made it a particularly happy project.

Foreword

Every novel has its source of inspiration and the stimulus for *The Helmingham Rose* was the real Helmingham Hall and its gardens in Suffolk. Many an artist must have reached for his paints on seeing it, while I'm sure that any novelist who beholds the moat, the drawbridges, the Tudor spires and the gardens must instantly think of a story to fit the setting. I chose the depression of 1929 for my story, but how different the real-life Helmingham Hall of today is from that bleak time. The beautiful interior is not open to the public, but on a Sunday afternoon in summer you can visit the exquisite and much praised, filmed and photographed gardens and breathe the heady scents of the many old fashioned roses growing there. It is famous for its roses, but the herbaceous borders are outstanding, and the vegetable beds provide a lesson for all gardeners. It has been said that house, park and gardens form a work of art and this I truly believe.

So much for reality. The reader should understand that my story is fiction and bears no resemblance to the real family which has owned it for five hundred years, nor to any other person living or dead who actually lived or worked at Helmingham. I am extremely grateful to The Lord and Lady Tollemache for allowing me to weave my tale of 1929 around their home, and for spending so much time in helping me to visualize what a typical estate of the period must have been like.

As the house is not open, I've not described the rooms as they actually are nor the real furniture, paintings or other objects. The paintings mentioned do exist but not at Helmingham. *Stuart Child*, for instance, is in a Turin museum.

I don't know who actually lives in the lodges. I used them in my story because they are very beautiful. I hope that everyone who lives on the estate and in the village will enjoy my 'alternative history'.

The Helmingham Rose described in the story is the real Felicia, a hybrid musk bred by the Reverend Joseph Pemberton at Havering-atte-Bower, Essex, introduced in 1928.

Rosie Cook, the gardener's wife, is not based on anyone who lived at Helmingham, but was inspired by Anne Bentall, the wife of Pemberton's gardener. She ran the gardens, and presumably the nursery, while her husband was away during the First World War. After Pemberton's death, she bred many roses, including Buff Beauty.

As ever I am grateful for the support of my husband, Dave, without whom I would never have discovered the wonderful world of gardening.

I am indebted to a number of people who have helped me with information and I'll start my thanks where I started my research, at the library of the Royal Horticultural Society. Dr Brent Elliott had no trouble in remembering relevant books on roses that had not been borrowed for forty years.

Richard Balfour, a former President of the Royal National Rose Society and worldwide authority on roses, gave me much needed advice about varieties.

The Royal National Rose Society does not have a large library at its home in St Albans, but the old Year

Books were a great help. Colonel Ken Grapes, its Secretary General, offered me every assistance. It's a pity this wonderful Society does not have more members and far more visitors. There is nothing more glorious, nor more British, than a large garden devoted to roses.

A few years ago, Lady Tollemache, who is a garden designer, devised a rose aid which makes it easier to peg down the large shrub roses than it was in 1929. The effect is wonderful, for each long rose stem arches down to the ground bearing blossom its entire length. Many of the roses at Helmingham are regularly pegged, and I don't know where else they can be seen treated in this way.

I am indebted to a new friend, Peter Wormell, for permission to use information from his unpublished work on British agriculture in the twenties. Few people nowadays can imagine how difficult things were for farmers and landowners at that time.

My legal advisor was Jonathan Long of Bankes Asheton, who gave me general advice to help me create a family and an estate. The details of the d'Avranche inheritance bear no relation to the Tollemache family.

Keith Gott, nurseryman, garden designer and former head gardener, gave me a great deal of background to the life of a professional gardener and some suggestions about what to include in Bill and Rosie's working lives.

My son-in-law, Chris Gibbs, provided me with information about country ways, particularly in regard to the threatened hedgerows.

My thanks to two friends of long standing, Constance Barry, for her initial researches, and Gillian Jackson for her careful reading of the manuscript.

Several people spent time with me, giving me information or sharing reminiscences about the real

1929 and life in real country houses. My thanks to Leonard Ratcliff, Daphne and Michael Dormer, and Roy Balaam.

Finally, my thanks to my editor, Diane Pearson, for her time, her knowledge and her friendship. In fact, the many friends I made while working on this book have made it a particularly happy project.

Chapter One

There had been no sign, no rainbow or tinkle of celestial bells to warn her that this day, Tuesday, February the twelfth, 1929, would be the one that would change her life for ever.

Joyce d'Avranche had risen in darkness, shivered into a black skirt and white blouse in front of the two-bar electric fire in her bedroom, then gulped half a cup of tea before leaving the flat for work. Eight hours spent taking shorthand dictation and typing letters for Manton and Company, Exporters, made her back ache. She spent the last half hour with one eye on the clock and her thoughts on dinner, and as a result had to retype Mr Manton's letter to Paris three times.

The half mile walk home to the King's Road in Chelsea was usually rather pleasant. At six o'clock in the evening there was that feeling of school having been let out, of the evening's excitements about to begin. The pubs were full, of course. Bowler hats and flat caps and the smell of damp wool, and that intangible sense of masculine camaraderie which always unnerved Joyce. Never having had a father or a brother, she viewed men with suspicion, reinforced by her mother's tales of male perfidy.

The newsagents were crowded. Joyce bought a quarter of liquorice allsorts and ate them greedily as she walked along. She never ate breakfast and seldom splashed out on more than a cup of coffee and a toasted teacake for lunch, because she knew she would eat well in the evening.

There were three flights of stairs and no lift in the mansion block. At last she put her key in the lock and opened the door, sniffing the air for cooking smells. 'I'm home!' she called, hopping around on one foot to remove an overshoe from the other one.

'In here! I'm in the sitting-room and I've got the cocktails ready,' answered Marsha. Her friend opened the sitting-room door. 'You must be frozen. It's so cold! And the damp! Back home when it gets cold, the weather's dry and crisp.' Marsha was an American from Kansas City, and everything about her from her rich brown hair to her rich mid-western drawl seemed exotic to Joyce.

Joyce picked her way through the maze of furniture to take her cocktail glass from Marsha who told her it was a pink lady. 'It's so snug in here. You do keep it terribly warm, Marsha. I'm glad your father is paying the electricity bill.'

The room was no more than five yards square, so the American had struggled to get all the new furniture into it; the moquette three-piece suite that didn't have a single spring poking through, the 'Tudor' oak dining table with bulbous legs, and the four dining chairs with brown rexine seats. The matching sideboard held candlesticks, magazines, bills, knitting in progress, a vase of artificial flowers and, for some reason, Marsha's best hat. And all this clutter had accumulated since the weekend, for Joyce tidied the flat each Saturday.

There was a glass-fronted display cabinet in the corner, crammed full of Marsha's treasures as well as Joyce's two modest heirlooms, a nest of tables, two pouffes, another table in front of the small windows and a standard lamp. There was a semi-circular hearth rug in front of the tiled fireplace, just as if there were a grate with coals that might burn the carpet, instead of an inset three-bar electric fire that regularly toasted their shins.

This was the most elegant lounge Joyce had ever sat in, and she was extremely grateful to Marsha and the Grissoms for allowing her to share the flat.

Mr and Mrs Grissom were wealthy Missourians who ran a thousand head of cattle, as well as owning the largest hardware store in Kansas City. In one of Marsha's confidential outbursts, she told Joyce that Daddy played the stock market and made more money in this way than he did with all his other business interests put together.

At twenty-five, she was three years older than Joyce, a good-natured young woman with a ready fund of sympathy who could turn strangers into good friends within an hour of meeting them. However, her parents had clearly found her a trial. She would not be told what to do, would not be corrected upon any point, and had turned down every young Missourian who took a romantic interest in her. She wanted, she told her parents one day when the quarrelling had been distressing to all, to live in Paris.

Mr Grissom's reply had been an unequivocal no. However, when it looked as if Marsha was going to be a spinster, in spite of her beauty and her father's wealth, the Grissoms, with four younger children to think about, answered an advertisement in a Kansas newspaper, and agreed to send her to a finishing school in Paris, France. Aunt Minnie was intending to go to Germany to see her brother and agreed to chaperon Marsha to the school.

Joyce's year of polishing had been achieved by courtesy of Lord d'Avranche, the head of the family, a man in his eighties whom she had never met. Her mother had died, and Joyce had written immediately to tell him that the wife of his long-departed nephew had passed away. For six weeks there was no reply, then a letter arrived to say that her tuition had been paid for one year

15

at Madame Puget's on the Rue de Gare, Paris. Joyce was to buy herself a ticket with the enclosed cheque and to arrive at the school on September the first. Excited, yet frightened, she had resigned from her clerical job, bought two new dresses and a snug rimless cloche, had travelled with trepidation to Paris and there met the uncritical friendliness of Marsha Grissom. It was truly the greatest good fortune in her young life.

They became firm friends immediately, drawn together by the coolness of the other girls, both British and American, who found Joyce too diffidently poor and Marsha too vibrantly rich. Marsha found in Joyce a good cause, a recipient of well-meant largesse, someone to protect from cutting remarks and tiny snubs.

At first Joyce thought she had nothing to give in return, but she quickly learned otherwise. Marsha, effusive and trusting, could not understand that dangers lurked on the Parisian streets. 'I've been dealing with the advances of rough ranch hands since I was fourteen,' she said once. 'Why do you suppose I can't handle Frenchmen?'

They had been at the school for less than a month when Marsha found a way to escape for half a day. She returned with tales of not one but two handsome men, quaint brasseries and a warming drink called grog. She thought she might have invited them to visit Madame Puget's, which would be disastrous. Unfortunately, Marsha could not remember exactly what she had or had not said. Most of America had been 'dry' for years, so the young American had no experience of alcohol. The following day, Marsha, with a headache, and Joyce, with gravel in a sock, had met the two Frenchmen. There followed a conversation conducted in childish French and basic English in which the men were given to understand that if they did not leave

Marsha alone, Joyce would hit them with the gravel-filled sock. This made them laugh, but they quickly departed.

'Why, I could have done that,' said Marsha. 'That's the way I would have treated a ranch hand that got out of line, but I thought Frenchmen were more sophisticated.'

'Yes,' laughed Joyce, teasing her, 'they are, because they've been to Paris, France.'

Joyce was beginning to understand why Marsha's Aunt Minnie had called her a handful. From that day forward, the two girls looked after each other. Marsha kept her friend in stockings without ladders; Joyce appraised the instant friendships, the exchange of flirtatious words between Marsha and young men seated perhaps as far as three tables away at pavement cafés. She also located missing earrings under the bed, plucked her friend's blouses from the floor or under the bed covers and ironed the georgette dress that was so short Marsha had trouble sitting down with dignity. The school year passed with terrifying speed. The girls learned how to be chic and how to tell a Manet from a Monet. They developed an appreciation of good food and an understanding of how little French they had learned at school. Marsha learned to cook; Joyce learned how to dress smartly – if only she could afford it.

Mr and Mrs Grissom arrived to convey their daughter back to Missouri, and Joyce tried to prepare herself for the loss of paradise: a return to a clerical job if she were lucky, terrifying unemployment if she were not. But the Grissoms, while hardly looking the part, turned out to be fairy godparents.

Marsha announced to everyone's surprise that she wanted to stay in Europe. She wanted to live in London, England, with her dear friend, Joyce. Why couldn't Daddy rent a flat so that she and Joyce could enjoy one more year together? Who knew what might come of it?

The Grissoms were not keen, until Marsha mentioned that Joyce was the great niece of Lord d'Avranche, and a most respectable young woman who was well connected. Exhibiting some of the naïvety that characterized their daughter, the Grissoms assumed that if Joyce were related to a lord, she must be a trustworthy companion and guide to English ways. At a loss as to how to control their eldest child, they thankfully took the girls to London and funded the furnishing of the flat. Mr Grissom paid the bulk of the rent and all of the electricity bill, and gave Marsha a generous allowance.

Joyce couldn't find a job immediately, and was in danger of becoming Marsha's pensioner for ever. She dared not think what might have happened to her if she had returned to London alone, but hated the loss of her independence. Fortunately, a very good post came her way. Hard working and efficient, Joyce received three guineas a week for her work at Manton's, and seemed to get along very well with the ten other members of the staff. Paradise had moved from France to England, but more was to come.

'Let me top you up,' said Marsha, approaching with the cocktail shaker. 'You look beat. Had a hard day at the salt mines?'

'As usual. Mr Montgomery stopped and talked to me for five minutes after work. He's so handsome.'

'Oh, who's he like?'

'Sort of Gary Cooper. So laconic, but English with it, you know. How was your day?'

Marsha made a face. 'Rotten. If it carries on like this, I might just get a job. Or I would if there was anything I could do. It's very boring without you during the day, Joyce. Why don't you quit? I'd look after you

and we could have some grand times. I went to the
Victoria and Albert Museum. A lecture on Egyptian
antiquities. You know, Daddy insists I send him a list
of the lectures and courses I'm taking each week. He
says I can't just lie around, because it's not right. But
you know me. I could stay in bed all day. The lecture
was very boring, but there was a gorgeous man in the
group who joined us half way through. Now, he was
your genuine Gary Cooper type. American, and he's
from the mid-west. Indiana. His name is Robert Trent.
You would have loved him. We struck up a conversation at lunchtime and I allowed him to take my
telephone number. Wasn't that wicked? But, well, an
American. What can be the harm?'

'None at all, unless he's a white slaver. I hope you
didn't give him your address.'

'Boy, do you think I'm stupid! Of course I didn't. Let
me just remind you, Joyce d'Avranche, that my meeting
people casually is how we've made all our friends.'

'Did he look rich?'

'No, darn it.' Marsha helped herself to another pink
lady. Joyce declined an offer of more. Her head was
beginning to spin. She needed food, not alcohol, having
had nothing but a cup of coffee and a digestive biscuit
this lunchtime. 'Crumpled suit,' continued Marsha, 'a
squashed fedora and his shirt points were frayed. Still,
it's a start. He might know the perfect sugar daddy, and
he would introduce me and we would fall in love,
and I'd invite Mr Trent to the wedding. Of course, he
would have to be the most delicious sugar daddy. I
would only marry a rich man for love.' She took a sip
of her drink. 'What shall we do tonight, honey? You
look in need of a little relaxation. A play? There's a Ben
Travers farce at the Aldwych. Or the movies. Ronald
Colman in *Bulldog Drummond*.'

Joyce adored Ronald Colman and daydreamed about

him quite a lot, but her finances were in a parlous state. She was down to her last five shillings and it was only Tuesday. Three guineas a week didn't go far when one was trying to keep pace with a wealthy, bored American.

'I'm really tired. Why don't you go? Ring up one of the gang and go with them.'

Marsha smiled sympathetically. 'Poor dear. Is money short? Really, you know you need never worry. My father wants you to have fun, too. Why, he said in his last letter that he's making heaps on the stock exchange. Things are hard in England, but the good old U S of A is booming. So let the good times roll!'

Joyce never held out for long. She told herself that one day she would repay every penny and that her financial embarrassment was only temporary, but in her heart she knew otherwise. The best Joyce d'Avranche could hope for was a good marriage to a professional man. Failing that, she might, at forty, become a private secretary and earn four or five pounds a week, instead of three guineas.

Marsha had prepared *boeuf en daube*, and the two girls ate greedily. Afterwards, Marsha rang the six friends she always called 'the gang' and suggested a midweek night out.

Instead of a quiet ninety minutes in the dark with Ronald Colman, Joyce and Marsha, together with Bunny and Freddie and George and Thelma and the brothers, Horace and Wilfred Brant, all went to the Palais for a noisy evening on the dance floor.

Bunny and Freddie were married; he sold shoes at Harrods. Marsha had met him when buying silver dance slippers. They lived in rented rooms in Maida Vale, but were always happy to travel to the West End if the outing was not too expensive. George and Thelma were having a fling, which Joyce thought was terribly naughty but rather glamorous. They were both in insurance. George had knocked on the door of their mansion flat. He had not sold them any insurance, but had been invited to a party Marsha had decided to give.

But before she ever laid eyes on Bunny and Freddie and George and Thelma, Marsha had entered Brant's hardware store off the King's Road and introduced herself to Mr Brant who was seated on a high stool with his jacket off and his white sleeves covered by black elasticated sleeve protectors. Her father owned a hardware store, she had assured him, and she missed being around the nails and pins, shoe polish and dusters.

Mr Brant, dazzled, offered her a position immediately, but Marsha worked for just one morning. She couldn't calculate in pounds, shillings and pence, leading Mr Brant to fear for the solvency of his business. By this time, she had become acquainted with his two bucked-toothed sons. Wilfred had bulging blue eyes, sunken cheeks and a rather high voice. Horace was fond of tight-waisted suits and spats. He slicked his brown hair back with cream and wore it an inch longer than his brother's, so that less of his scalp was showing below his ears. Horace made Marsha laugh with his biting comments.

On the following Saturday, Marsha and Joyce went dancing at the Palais with the brothers. The girls had been in London just four days but, as Marsha said, people had to make an effort to make friends or they might just spend all their time alone.

The two young women worked hard to provide a handsome buffet at their party, which was so successful, there were complaints from the neighbours. After that, the eight friends met regularly. Joyce, who had never had more than one friend at a time, found that she was part of a ready-made group into which she fitted quite easily. She dreaded the day when Marsha would head for home, and couldn't help wondering if the friends would want to know her without her lively companion.

At the Palais that night, Marsha, who loved to dance, spent most of the time on the dance floor with Wilfred. Bunny and Freddie also loved to dance, while Thelma and George took any excuse to put their arms around one another. Freddie danced once with Joyce, but as he always made improper suggestions to her when they were alone, she was happy not to dance with him a second time. This left her in the company of Horace who excused his refusal to dance on the fact that he had two left feet. Fortunately, he tended to be kind but distant when alone with her, because he was captivated by Marsha. A very gauche young man, he chose to express his tender feelings for the American by insulting her whenever possible.

'I suppose your father is a bootlegger, Marsha,' he shouted across their small table after the men had enjoyed too many drinks. 'All American men make their money bootlegging, don't they?'

Marsha giggled. 'Oh, he has booted a few legs or legged a few boots, but he's quite respectable now.'

Everybody laughed, and Joyce sighed with envy at such ready wit. She would not have known what to say to Horace. She never did. Marsha, on the other hand, never took offence because she always had the last word. And the men adored her.

Of approximately the same height as Joyce, she was rather more fleshed out. The full bust, tiny waist and rounded hips were anathema to young women who wished to look elegant in the current fashions, and Marsha often spoke of her envy of Joyce's boyish figure. Her thick brown hair with a slight curl in it was not best suited to a shingle, either. She was letting it grow out, a tiresome business. After three weeks she was able to cover the straight ends with a neat hairpiece precariously pinned at the nape of her neck.

She would roll her huge brown eyes and purse her bee sting lips while bemoaning her 'horrible looks', but Joyce doubted the sincerity of these remarks.

A young lady of restricted means needed something with which to congratulate herself, so it was with some satisfaction that she would look into her mirror at her own blue eyes, straight d'Avranche nose, and dark blond, side-parted hair with its effortlessly fashionable wind-blown bob, and feel slightly superior to her rich friend, at least in the matter of personal appearance.

'You'll never guess what we did the other evening,' said Wilfred. 'My brother is too cheeky for his own good.'

Horace smirked as they all urged Wilfred to tell them Horace's latest outrageous act. It seemed that the brothers had attended a film which was really too boring and stupid for words. They were about to leave when Horace accidentally dropped his unlit cigarette on the floor and, while retrieving it, noticed that the woman sitting next to him had removed her shoes. The cinema was almost entirely empty; the woman was asleep. Quick as lightning, Horace flung the shoes underneath the seats, down towards the screen. Wilfred, having no idea of this screamingly funny action, was surprised when Horace left his seat and moved several rows further down. He located the shoes and tossed them further along, and so eventually made sure that they were lying in a heap right next to the orchestra pit, although on this night there was no orchestra due to the fact that the film was a talkie.

When the work was done, Horace directed Wilfred to take seats in the very back row. There they stayed until the lights went up. What a scream! The poor woman spent absolute ages searching for her shoes.

How they laughed! They were nearly caught out and had to make a hasty exit.

The evening was fun and the fellows paid for the refreshments, but Joyce was sleepy long before the others wanted to leave.

The little flat was bitingly cold when they returned at half-past twelve. Joyce, knowing she had to be up early, was anxious for bed. Marsha, however, wanted to discuss the evening. The fire was switched on and Marsha embarked on an animated monologue about how absolutely right for Joyce would be Horace Brant, and it didn't matter a bit that he was not so very handsome, nor that he had a tendency for practical jokes. The important thing was that his father owned two hardware stores, and, honey, you couldn't do better than to be in hardware these days.

Joyce said Horace was too fast for his own good. Marsha was always picking out men for her, and they were always second-rate. She slumped down on the settee and leaned her head against the back, her half-closed eyes focusing on the mantlepiece where the clock said a quarter to one.

She blinked, jerking upright. 'Excuse me, Marsha, but is that a telegram for me tucked behind the clock?'

Marsha jumped up. 'Oh, I'm ever so sorry. It came this afternoon. I forgot all about it.' She retrieved it and handed it to Joyce.

The telegram was brief. 'From Lord d'Avranche's lawyer,' Joyce said as her eyes raced down the page.

'The one who paid for you to go to Madame Puget's? You look really strange. Is it bad news?'

Joyce took a deep breath, shaking her head in a vain attempt to stop the buzzing. No wonder she looked strange! The world was spinning madly and she had been thrown off to float out into space. For the rest of her life she would remember this moment of exhilaration. Years of poverty and hours of listening to her mother's bitter diatribes against her father's relatives faded into insignificance. In an instant, she discovered an abiding love for the family which had ignored her all her life.

Struggling for a sophisticated expression and a calm tone of voice, she drawled, 'I rather think I've had a spot of *good* news.' Edith Evans could not have delivered the line more coolly.

And all Marsha said was, 'Gee, kid, that's swell.'

When Mr Finch said he would send the fly from Helmingham Hall to meet her train at Ipswich, seventy-five miles from London, she had been absurdly pleased. To be met! It sounded so grand. But now, after nearly six miles riding in an open two-wheeled carriage, she rather thought she would have preferred a motor. Already she had discovered that the good people of Suffolk were nowhere near as sophisticated as Londoners. For heaven's sakes! The driver spoke with such a strong accent, it was nearly a foreign language.

Very quickly they were in open countryside, bowling along beside ploughed fields and woodlands. Even the houses with their pastel coats of paint were few in number. Thatched roofs were in need of repair, dark barns sagged under the weight of collapsing red tile roofs. There were no sheep, no cows. She was sure there should be animals in the fields, grazing contentedly, but her companion told her with some amusement that there wasn't much for animals to eat when the ground was frozen solid. They had mostly been brought into shelter where they could be fed. She asked no more questions. She thought Suffolk was desolate, drained of people and exposed to arctic winds since the county, and Norfolk to the north, bulged into the North Sea.

They passed through the parish of Helmingham at a

trot. She saw a windmill, a general store, a school and a few cottages. Some of the inhabitants were peering curiously from their windows and she was tempted to wave to them, would have done so a week earlier, but now she was inclined to examine her every gesture and to wonder if this smile or that wave was the correct thing for a d'Avranche to do. This self-conscious behaviour was alien to her; she was evolving into another sort of person.

'The church,' said her driver.

'Oh, how picturesque!' It was ancient, grey and turreted with a few leafless trees for company, under which lay some lurching tombstones. She almost missed the red brick rectory as they trotted past.

They clip-clopped on for several minutes, skirting Helmingham parkland, then turned at a pair of very beautiful houses flanking the wrought-iron gates. Winged horses' heads topped the gate pillars, but Joyce gasped at the beauty of the twin two-storey lodges. Built of red brick, their walls were enlivened by darker bricks set in a diamond pattern, and on every gable there was a brick spire fashioned into a barley sugar twist or other design.

'Who lives in those beautiful houses?'

'Mr and Mrs Cook, he's head gardener, live in the one on the left and old Mr Trimble, the land agent, lives in the other.'

Joyce sucked in her breath, suddenly afraid. The twin lodges were grander than anything she and her mother had ever lived in. And there before her, down an arrow-straight drive, was Helmingham itself. It began to snow, huge flakes that swirled around in the air, landing in her hair, on her eyelashes and lips, obscuring her vision of Helmingham.

'Double avenue of oaks,' said the driver.

'Yes, yes.' She had no interest in so many leafless

trees. She had heard that some people could tell different trees in winter just by their shape, but wasn't sure she believed it. Meanwhile, she was having some difficulty recognizing Helmingham Hall because the only image she had of it – an old engraving – depicted it from a different angle. As they rode down the drive, the house seemed to sit on the horizon, huge and one dimensional, like the stage scenery for *The Merry Wives of Windsor*.

She hadn't noticed the deer. They startled her, dozens of them, by bounding across the drive, seeming to hang in the air, taking a perverse delight in waiting until the last possible moment to leap, as if their lives depended on crossing the road before, rather than after, the carriage had passed. Beautiful and graceful, they belonged to another era, the fairy tale time when ordinary everyday things didn't exist unless they had a part to play in the story, and each story had a moral.

She thought of troubadours and princes charming, of maidens in distress, of blazing logs and honey for tea. And all the time Helmingham was getting closer, becoming larger, until they were upon the moat, crossing sixty feet of black water on a narrow bridge.

'Biggest moated house in Suffolk,' said the driver proudly, as if it were his own.

'There are others? Do lots of houses in Suffolk have moats?'

'There's some, but we've got a moat round one of our gardens as well. I don't know of another that has a moat round the garden.'

The outer wall opened to swallow its visitors, depositing them in a large courtyard, where an old fire engine was neatly tucked out of the way. Having crossed the narrow bridge, she felt safe within a Tudor construction that would cherish its owners, protecting

27

them from poverty, loneliness and envy. Safe from real life, in fact.

She shivered with pleasure when told that the draw-bridges, which comprised part of the two sixty-foot bridges, were raised each night at dusk and not let down again until Mr Crow, the butler, came downstairs at half-past six. Safe! Never to be conquered by life again!

'Did Lord d'Avranche die here at Helmingham?'

He handed her down from the fly and began to unload her baggage. 'No, Miss, Lord d'Avranche died in his London home. He never lived here except for three months in the summer and maybe some shooting in winter, and of course over Christmas and New Year. He'd not lived here permanent since before the war.'

The handsome stone porch was directly before her, but a distinguished gentleman had emerged from a door to the right and was coming towards her. If she hadn't known better, she would have imagined him to be the owner of this beautiful mansion.

Not an inch less than six feet tall, he had silver hair and quite a few white hairs among the black of his moustache. She judged him to be about fifty, and decided that his Wellington-like beak of a nose actually suited him. He was the solicitor to the d'Avranche family, an employee, someone she need not fear. Nevertheless, she was awed by him and could not control her nervousness.

'Mr Finch?'

'Miss d'Avranche? Allow me to welcome you to Helmingham Hall.'

Was he looking her over? If so, it was probably because of her cloth coat with its moulting rabbit fur collar. Suddenly aware of the intense cold that had numbed her feet, she couldn't stop shivering.

Moving towards him too quickly, Joyce extended her hand, then withdrew it to remove her well-darned glove just as he extended his. Her embarrassment made her too loud when she spoke, and a moment's thought would have provided her with a less vulgar opening remark.

'Are you sure all of this is mine? Golly, I'm rich!'

'You are the *probable* heir to an enormous responsibility,' he said severely. 'Wealth is comparative. I'm afraid you will find that after your duties are discharged, there will be very little left to spend on frivolities.'

'Of course. I understand that.' She thought, he knows I'm poor and wants to put me in my place.

'Have you been to Helmingham before?'

She glared, detecting insults in every word he uttered. She drew herself up to the full five feet two and a half inches and raised her strong chin so that she could give the impression of looking down the straight d'Avranche nose at him. 'You must know I have not. Lord d'Avranche belonged to another branch of the family, the branch that always snubbed my mother and me. Nevertheless, I wrote to him when I heard about his son. In fact, I wrote to him each week while I was at Madame Puget's finishing school. I told him what I was studying and what I had seen in Paris. I told him I was grateful for the opportunity to go there, and about my friend, Miss Grissom. He never replied. When I heard his only child, Captain Cartwright d'Avranche, had died, I wrote a letter of condolence. I don't know why he acted as he did, but at least in leaving me this house, he has redressed the injustice done to us for so many years. He should have looked after my mother. As head of the family, that was his duty. I just wish she had lived to see me here.'

He sighed, visibly irritated by her. 'Miss d'Avranche, I am the family solicitor. I don't have opinions on such matters. I arranged for your year in Paris on his lordship's instructions. No explanation for his actions has

29

ever been given to me. It is my duty to warn you that it will be some months, perhaps years before the will is proved. Captain Cartwright was lost in the Amazon rain forest. At least, we presume so. His plane probably crashed in that vast expanse. It is unlikely that he stepped unhurt from the accident. There is even less likelihood that he could walk back to civilization. Yet neither plane nor body has been found. Proof of death is necessary before you can have a clear right to the property. Otherwise, we must wait two years to have him presumed dead, after which you would be declared the legal heir.' He smiled coldly. 'Now then, I want to complete the formalities, obtain your signature on some papers and explain to you about probate. I've arranged for a light luncheon to be served in the small dining-room. You will be able to take the three o'clock train back to London from Ipswich.'

'I'm not going back to London,' she whispered stricken. 'I have nowhere to go.'

'Your friend?'

'Miss Grissom? She has taken a boarder,' she lied.

'You can't stay here. Dear me, no. You have no right.' He paced the courtyard, scratched his head, tugged his tie. When he noticed her luggage, he turned to look at her, forcing a smile of sorts, reining in his annoyance. 'Until the will is proved, you cannot think of this property as yours. Besides, the entire house is under dust covers and no supplies have been bought in. It takes time and planning to get such a large establishment ready for the family.'

'I've nowhere else to go.'

Joyce had always found it difficult to glare and trade insults, to assert her rights and demand that she be given what she wanted. However, long ago she had discovered an element of steel in her personality. When she wanted something very, very much or when she had no alternative but to take a certain action, she simply dug in her heels and endured the storm that inevitably followed. Angry people, she had discovered, the blusterers who were accustomed to get their way, could not sustain their assault for long. After the storm had passed, after their anger and energy were spent, she was still there, still determined. And so it would be on this day.

Mr Finch raised his voice. 'This house is too large and isolated for comfort. With the exception of a few odd weeks, Lord d'Avranche spent just three months of the year here, in the summer.'

'When he held his family party to which my mother and I were not invited.'

He shook his head, then looked up as the snow increased in ferocity, swirling madly around the courtyard. 'Come inside. We can't discuss such an important matter on the doorstep. You cannot take possession until the will has been proved. Someone may contest it.'

'Who? Who is there to say that I have no right to this house? Cartwright d'Avranche was an only child and Cartwright is dead.'

'Cartwright was the only living child of his lordship, and he is only presumed dead. I cannot think who might contest the will or what other problems might arise, but it all takes time. Your cousin, Mr Rupert d'Avranche, was unhappy when told of your existence. He had expected to inherit, and would have done if the property passed down only through males. Nevertheless, in due course, he will be the next Lord d'Avranche.'

The hall was dark and she was immediately confused, unable to imagine where she was in this vast building. Stags' heads adorned the walls; on some of their antlers hats had been hung. Lord d'Avranche's entire style of life seemed to be displayed in those hats: homburgs, flat caps, fedoras, hard riding hats, even a tropical topi. His gum boots stood neatly beneath the hats. She felt his presence in this dark hall, as she had seen him in a recent *Country Life* magazine, a man in a wing collar glaring beneath shaggy eyebrows. Along with the portrait of his lordship, there had been photographs of his London home, but none of Helmingham.

'Have I inherited his house in Park Lane?'

Mr Finch smiled slightly. 'When everything is settled, that house will be turned over to a favourite charity of his lordship's.'

He turned to the right. She followed, now completely lost. 'The study,' he said, moving on. 'This is the small sitting-room, not much used. Beyond is the family dining-room where there is a nice fire. Ah, Crow. Miss d'Avranche, allow me to introduce you to the butler.'

She shook hands with a short, elderly man. Crow, Finch? Was she the victim of some subtle joke?

They moved on through the dining-room to the drawing-room with its ornate plaster ceiling. Another blazing fire filled the room with flickering light. No intimidating grandeur here, but elegance and comfort. This was a very large room in which even a shorthand-typist could relax. Huge windows showed her a fierce snow storm dashing against the panes, and huge flakes piling up against the glazing bars. The frenzied weather made the interior of this large room all the more inviting. She walked to the fireplace and held out her hands, then turned her back to the fire and smiled warmly at Mr Finch.

'I shall be very comfortable here, I think. Don't worry about my disposing of anything or doing what I have no right to do. I shall simply live here and take care of it all. That's better than leaving it empty, isn't it?'

He drew in his breath, finding her disturbing. 'The

Hall is not entirely empty. Mr and Mrs Crow live here, and they look after the Hall far better than you would be able to do. It would be irregular. I would not be performing my duty. I really can't allow it.'

'Dear Mr Finch, do consider my position. I am just an ignorant young woman who doesn't understand all this legal business. Believing all to be settled, I gave up my place at Miss Grissom's. I resigned from my post. I removed my small savings and spent some of the money on buying suitable clothes for the country. What am I to do now? Perhaps you think I am some harpy who will steal the silver.'

'No, no.'

'A dishonest person who would refuse to vacate this great house if someone comes along with a better claim?'

'There is no-one with a better claim.'

She felt his indecision, and thought she had done enough for the moment. Sitting down on the settee, she rubbed her hands, but otherwise remained very quiet. He would come to see that she posed no threat to anyone, and then he would agree to her request.

'Helmingham has not been modernized,' he said. 'The effluent empties into the moat, from which the drinking water is drawn. The roof leaks. There is no electricity. Have you ever lived in a house lit solely by candles and oil lamps?'

'Of course.' This was almost true. Joyce and her mother had never enjoyed electric light, but there had been gas lamps. In Thora d'Avranche's final years, they had rooms that were cold and damp. The pump and the lavatory had been in the back yard, and they had suffered great hardship. Only after moving to Marsha's flat had Joyce come to rely on electricity for her comfort.

Acknowledging defeat, Mr Finch retrieved his

briefcase and sat down beside her on the settee. A lamp was brought, and Joyce discovered exactly what she had inherited. It seemed that for the aristocracy nothing was as simple as it was for lesser folk. To begin with, she did not own Helmingham Hall. She held it in trust during her lifetime. She could not dispose of it as she chose. The trust had been set up sixteen generations earlier, and it travelled down the line of the eldest son of The Lord d'Avranche. In the present case, the last of the line had been Cartwright d'Avranche. He would eventually be presumed to have died without an heir. Therefore, the property was to go to a direct descendant, male or, if there were no such person, female, coming down the line of his lordship's next brother in line. Joyce's father had been the son of his lordship's brother, Ernest. She was her father's only child, therefore, she was the heir.

'And there isn't a man to inherit? It seems strange. I thought titles and houses went down the male line, always.'

Mr Finch shook his head. 'Not always. However the trust has been set up, that is the way it must continue. Some trusts are very eccentric, but the one governing Helmingham is quite straightforward. Lord d'Avranche had another brother, Mordecai, much younger than his lordship. His son is Rupert d'Avranche, of whom I have already spoken. Then there are innumerable males descended from his lordship's three sisters. I believe the three sisters produced eleven children, while the three brothers had, in the end, just three children among them. But so it often is.'

The trustees were two Scottish lords, Mr Finch told her. The Earl of MacClintock was at his winter home in Greece. The Marquis of Clanmair was at that time visiting members of his family in America.

Joyce, deep in thought, scarcely heard his words about the trustees. 'Excuse me, but his lordship must

34

have known all along that I was his heir. Why did he never tell me or my mother? For that matter, my mother must have known!'

'His lordship had no need even to consider that you might inherit until after the Great War when Captain Cartwright's health was uncertain and he seemed disinclined to marry. Lord d'Avranche had three sons. The original eldest son, Alastair, was one of twins. Alastair and Alexander were still at Oxford when, at the beginning of 1910, they went climbing on Ben Nevis. There was an accident and both were killed. Following this tragedy, I'm afraid Lady d'Avranche lost the will to live. She died in 1911. By that time your poor father had passed away.

'But to business. You will enjoy all the rents due to the estate, but no other money. There are four thousand and twenty-one acres, which once brought in a revenue of very nearly a pound an acre. Now they are worth no more than ten shillings the acre.'

'Two thousand pounds?'

'Of the four thousand acres, only four hundred are still being farmed. Several of the large farm houses are standing empty. The land lies unworked, and naturally no repairs are made on the buildings. One two-hundred acre farm together with a handsome seven-bedroom farm house has been leased to a Scottish farmer for no rent whatsoever over the next three years. Your land agent, Mr Dunmore, would be happy to make other such arrangements.'

'Oh, dear. What about the rents of the village? Surely, the estate owns the entire village.'

'Yes, and Lord d'Avranche owned other villages, not part of the entailed estate, but few can afford to pay the rent these days. Lord d'Avranche would never have been so heartless as to evict these people.'

'Then, how shall I live?'

He ignored the question. 'Your duties are many and onerous, Miss d'Avranche, and they are perhaps beyond the capabilities of someone not bred up to them. And you have a number of people to support. There are Mr Crow and his wife who is the house-keeper. They live in this house and make sure that it does not decay, that no-one steals the treasures here. Mrs Able comes from her cottage to cook when neces-sary. Two women come in to clean when the family is in residence. There are nine estate workers under the bailiff, Mr Trimble, a land agent who makes the annual evaluations, planning applications and attends to all bureaucratic matters. There are four gardeners, since Lord d'Avranche always insisted that the grounds should be maintained in the finest style. You are responsible for the stipend of the rector of Helmingham church. The Hall is in need of repair, lead is needed for the roof, but that is expensive. There are boundary walls and hedges to be attended to and woodland to be replanted. Many acres of woodland were felled during the war and none have been replanted.'

'We could replant and sell the wood!' cried Joyce, happy to think that there was some source of possible income.

Mr Finch gave her a withering look. 'There is no money in wood, never has been. Woodland is planted so that there is fuel for the fires and wood for your carpenters to make repairs. There are many buildings on this estate. Besides, managing woodland is a fifty year business.'

She was chastened. 'So how much will I have?'

'In the immediate future, I will make you a personal allowance. Eventually, I suppose it will be less than a thousand pounds a year.'

'Isn't there anything that can be sold?'

'What is sold cannot be retrieved. You must not think

36

of selling Helmingham's treasures, at least not until this property is well and truly yours.'

They were called to lunch which was served in the family dining-room, and in Mr Crow's presence restricted their conversation to minor matters.

'I gather,' said Joyce, when the butler left the room with the soup plates, 'that Lord d'Avranche sent me to finishing school in Paris when he thought there might be a remote chance that I would inherit.'

'You are crediting his lordship with too much concern about yourself. It may have been a simple gesture of generosity. His lordship and Captain Cartwright were reasonably friendly until after the captain returned from the war. A professional soldier with the Suffolk Regiment, he had been invalided out of the service at the end of hostilities, one of the last men in the regiment to be wounded. There were many things he might have done after leaving the Army, but he chose to travel the world on daredevil escapades. He broke a leg while skiing on dangerous terrain, was buried by a small avalanche and was lucky to survive. He was a racing driver for one season, again fortunate to walk whole from his demolished motor car. Finally, he learned to fly, at which point his father lost all hope of ever having a daughter-in-law. They quarrelled and had not spoken for eighteen months. His lordship didn't even know his son was in Brazil until he heard that Cartwright was missing, presumed to have perished with his aeroplane.'

After lunch, she was introduced to Mrs Crow and the cook, Mrs Able, who was quite old. They were polite but quiet, and she had no idea how to put them at their ease, nor how to dismiss them. There was an embarrassing hiatus until Mr Finch stepped in and with a few casual words released everyone from the awkward situation. Determined as she was to stay at Helmingham,

Joyce was beginning to dread the moment when she would be left in charge of these people.

It was half past three by the time Mr Finch took his leave. She saw him to the door, watched him wade across several inches of drifting snow, shivered as he cranked his car, then gratefully returned to the drawing-room where she huddled before the fire. She had come to dislike Mr Finch, but he had confounded her in the dying moments of their meeting by saying he would arrange an account for her with Harrods. She should send for their catalogue and order by post from it, since she seemed to have no plans to visit London. She had to admit this was very thoughtful, for he must know she was unprepared for country living.

Two oil lamps were brought into the drawing-room, but they scarcely dissipated the gloom. She would be sleeping alone in this great house, except for Mr and Mrs Crow. Yet they would be farther away than even Mr and Mrs Draper, in flat 2 in the mansion block, had been, and she had never even met the Drapers! The house might burn down before Joyce discovered where the servants slept. Helmingham was larger than most hotels.

The master bedroom to which she was shown after luncheon seemed inviting, large and slightly warmer than the rest of the house due to the fire which had been built an hour or so before. Joyce's bags had been unpacked and her clothes placed in drawers, giving her several minutes of frustration before she located them all. There had followed a chilly five minutes during which she had undressed, removed her step-ins and replaced them with woollen underwear, a knitted dress and a cardigan. Wool stockings completed her sensible outfit, but she was still cold.

Mr Crow had offered to take her out to the stables and coach house to introduce her to the rest of the staff.

He had indicated another bridge over the moat (with yet another drawbridge, of course) but it had all seemed a long way off in blizzard conditions. She pleaded a headache and promised to meet them all the next day. The size of her new home stunned her, temporarily destroying all pleasure in her good fortune.

Tomorrow, she would recover, would explore and make friends with those she employed. Later, much later, she might confront her future. What on earth was she going to do with the rest of her life? The thought of living walled up in a great house with none but servants for companions did not appeal to her. With Marsha she had enjoyed an interesting but unadventurous life with a few friends and many friendly acquaintances. There had been all the excitements of the big city, some of them free, there had been bustle and life, and interesting things to look at wherever one turned.

Now, here she was in the grand house about which her mother had talked so much, but about which she had revealed so little. Thora Jefferson had been born in 1880, and had come to work for Lady d'Avranche in 1900 as a dressmaker, having been brought up in an orphanage and apprenticed to a dressmaker at fourteen. Joyce could well imagine the joy of a young girl exposed to the grandeur that was Helmingham after a life spent in an East End orphanage. The young Thora had, at first, been given a room in the servants' quarters, but later had her own workman's cottage on the edge of woodland, which had been heaven to a woman unaccustomed to a home of her own.

Then in 1906, Thora had met Lord d'Avranche's nephew, Nicholas, and they had run off together, incurring Lord d'Avranche's undying hatred. Joyce had been born in 1907, and Nicholas had left Thora in 1909, travelling all the way to Australia, where he contracted dysentery and died. Men, her mother had said, were never to be trusted. They always let you down. Women were strong, put-upon and decent. Men were beasts.

Thinking about her mother brought tears to Joyce's eyes. How she would have loved to return to this house in triumph. She had missed the opportunity by such a short time.

The drawing-room door opened. Mrs Crow suddenly appeared in the room, startling Joyce. 'Old Betsy was scratching the door, ma'am. I thought I'd best open it and let her in.'

Old Betsy was a fat, ancient labrador who had sniffed Joyce's crotch in a most embarrassing way when first presented to her by Mr Finch. She thanked Mrs Crow, then directed Betsy to the hearth rug. The dog ignored instructions and heaved herself onto the sagging cushions of the sofa, resisting all attempts to dislodge her.

'Well, Betsy, how shall we entertain ourselves this afternoon?' she asked, moving to a chair.

Betsy lifted her head and looked sadly at Joyce, then ponderously removed herself from the settee and waddled to Joyce's chair. There was insufficient room for the two of them, but Betsy could not be persuaded of the fact. She scrambled up beside Joyce, turned around and settled herself down, her head on her new mistress's lap.

'You win,' said Joyce, and went to sit on the settee, which was better placed to capture the warmth of the fire. Betsy quickly followed and, after some manoeuvring, the two of them agreed on unequal shares of the space.

Absent-mindedly, Joyce pulled on one of Betsy's silky ears, which seemed to please the old dog. Nicholas d'Avranche's abandonment of his wife and daughter had haunted Joyce all her life. What had caused him to do such a thing? How could her mother have been so mistaken in a man?

At first, Thora had managed to hold on to the house by making attractive copies of the couture gowns shown in magazines. She had to visit clients in their homes for fittings and was consequently away a great deal. Joyce was left in the care of the daily for whom she developed a great love. However, when she was five years old, the house was sold and the daily maid tearfully departed. Mother and daughter moved to a modest flat in Shepherd's Bush. Thora took a job putting trimmings on hats; Joyce was enrolled in the local school where she was teased for her strange way of speaking and her excellent, if increasingly well-worn, clothes.

Over the years their situation deteriorated. Thora, at forty-two, was dismissed, forcing them to leave their flat for two rooms in an old house. A begging letter to Lord d'Avranche reaped a cheque for one hundred pounds and instructions not to trouble him again. Thora seemed to lose heart and never earned another penny until her death five years later.

Meanwhile, Joyce left school at fifteen and took a variety of unskilled jobs, until another letter arrived from Lord d'Avranche, together with a modest cheque. Joyce was to take a course in shorthand and typing.

The little family fared rather better once Joyce was trained. She was a quick student and found a position on completing her course. A year later, Thora, who had come unscathed through the great influenza epidemic of 1919, succumbed to it in 1927. By the time she died, their savings were gone, mostly on medical bills, and Joyce had been forced to sell their furniture.

Lord d'Avranche's letter sending her to Madame Puget's came at a desperately low moment in her life, but was not an unmixed blessing, for she discovered just how poor she and her mother had been. Their descent into extreme poverty had been gradual, almost unnoticed as each new trial took from them more and more of their small income. But in Paris there were the petty jibes and the giggles, the flaunting of sweaters of finer knit, stockings of glossier silk. Young women could be so cruel.

Like a great many women, Joyce was in the habit of tucking a leg under her when sitting casually, exposing the sole of one shoe. She hadn't been bothered that there was a hole in the leather until Miranda Copple from New York took the trouble to draw a circle around the hole. Then Sophie Bates from Leeds had torn up a piece of newspaper and handed it to her.

'Better stick this inside, Joyce dear, to keep the water out.' Then they had all laughed, as if Joyce's shoes were the funniest things they had ever seen.

A genuine leather handbag had been beyond her means, but the imitation leather on her only bag had cracked and could be peeled away from its cloth backing. During one vicious session of bitchiness, the girls had ruined the bag entirely. Marsha, as usual, had come to her aid, had scolded the girls for their thoughtlessness, had commiserated with Joyce and had finally given her one of her own old bags. Real leather and very attractive, but the others knew Joyce hadn't bought it.

A very pleasant supper was served to her in the dining-room at half past six. Later, Betsy was fetched for her evening trot around the ramparts before the Crows retired for the night. Together, Joyce and Betsy went early to bed where two hot water bottles had been placed between the sheets. She slept fitfully in the large, strange bed, but in the small hours she could not sleep at all. The bottles were cold, the sheets felt damp and her nightgown was insufficient protection against an exceptionally cold night. After curling into a ball for several minutes, she took a deep breath, threw back the covers and, tripping over unknown objects in the dark, located her cardigan which she managed to don over her gown. Deciding that she would never be able to bear removing the gown long enough to dress in the morning, she took her clothes with her into the bed. This clever wheeze meant that she would be able to shrug into warm things before leaving the covers.

Leaping back into bed, she discovered that Betsy had taken the opportunity to join her. The animal was warm and reassuring, so Joyce, no lover of dogs, allowed her to stay.

She decided it must be after seven when someone, presumably Mrs Crow, crept into the bedroom to light the fire. Joyce pretended to be asleep, and in fact soon did drift off, knowing that when she had to get out of bed, the room would be warm. Betsy, however, slid from beneath the covers and trotted out with the maid. Some time later, the curtains were drawn and a ewer of hot water was set on the washstand. The bearer introduced herself as Mary, who was one of the Hall's two cleaners. She had been summoned late the previous day and told to help Miss d'Avranche in any way she could. She asked if she might lay out Miss d'Avranche's clothes before the fire. Joyce, clutching her knitted dress beneath the covers, didn't know what to say. Apparently, the question was rhetorical. Mary fetched a complete set of underwear, selected a woollen skirt and blouse and a thick cardigan from one of the wardrobes and arranged them on a clothes horse.

It was another half an hour before her breakfast tray was delivered. Coffee, delicious hot rolls, home-made jam and fresh butter were supplied in abundance. Joyce, who never ate breakfast, didn't want Mrs Able to think her ungrateful, so she ate the lot.

When she came downstairs, Mr and Mrs Crow were ready to accompany her on a tour of the kitchens and linen cupboards. It took an hour, and by the time every cupboard and drawer had been inspected and discussed, her shyness was easing, as was their diffidence. She had not been expected to live in Helmingham so soon, they explained. They hoped she found everything to her liking, but really they would have liked a little more time to prepare. Joyce, always sensitive to the feelings of others, praised everything extravagantly and assured them that she was satisfied with all arrangements. Even so, she had to endure their praises for Cartwright, their grief at his death, the recollections of his favourite rooms, dishes, activities and friends. Joyce was left in no doubt that she was not the owner they had hoped for.

To emphasize her ignorance, Mr Crow fetched a book from the study and opened it to a description of Helmingham Hall. From this she discovered that the house, built round a courtyard, was about two hundred feet across its front range, but much deeper on each side, and that one range was two rooms deep and contained the formal rooms. She realized she had only been shown the everyday parts of the house.

Armed with this knowledge, she quickly found the gigantic hall, two floors high, the dining-room with its genuine Tudor table and sixteen chairs veiled in dust cloths. Tudor paintings by the half dozen were dimly visible by light that filtered through drawn blinds. A nightmare to heat, these rooms had probably never been used regularly.

Here was the grandeur she had been seeking, but in finding it she realized she could not live at Helmingham Hall. As soon as possible, she would close up the house and rent a modest flat in London. But what to do for friends? Marsha had not recovered from the shock of

44

seeing her impoverished friend become an heiress. Joyce had vaulted from poor working girl to fabulous heiress, richer – apparently – than the entire Grissom family. They had parted formally, each aware of the enormous gulf that had opened between them.

Chapter Two

Rosemary Dobson Cook put the kettle on the hob. She had been watching for Bill to come striding through the deer park to North Lodge for some fifteen minutes. From the kitchen window she could see the entire drive, all the way to the Hall and her neighbour's small garden. Old Mr Trimble, the bailiff, was out of doors gathering some wood from the stack by his front door, which was situated away from the road on the side that faced the Hall. Dressed as usual in breeches and gaiters, with a woollen scarf thrown round his neck, he had gathered an armful and was heading for his door when a short log slid from the top of the heap and fell to the icy ground. Mr Trimble bent to retrieve it, lost his balance, dropped his load and landed on his backside.

Rosemary turned towards her own door, intending to offer help, then changed her mind. He would prefer to believe that she hadn't seen him fall. Mr Trimble was extremely sensitive about his increasing frailty, and didn't like Rosemary or approve of her involvement in the Helmingham gardens. She had no right, he said, and he would not pay her for her efforts. Bill Cook was the head gardener. By setting herself up as an expert on roses, Rosemary was undermining his authority with the men, or so Mr Trimble said whenever the thought occurred to him.

The bailiff was becoming an embarrassing problem. She wondered how much longer he could continue in his position. A person would think she and Bill were newly married, that she hadn't lived in one of the twin lodges for the past eight years. This business about how she was damaging Bill was an old argument, resurrected recently when the land agent's mind began to fail him. Mr Trimble had raised objections to her rose-growing from the day he had first realized what she was up to. Lord d'Avranche had overruled him, however. His lordship had been interested in the breeding of roses in those days, had called her a sturdy girl who knew what she was doing.

Now Lord d'Avranche was gone, and the usurper might not take kindly to roses being bred on her property. Rosemary stepped back from the window so that the old man couldn't see that she was aware of his undignified struggles. He had been a tall man, straight and proud when she first arrived at Helmingham, but the death of his wife and the relentless curving of his spine with age had left him looking more pathetic than powerful.

She caught sight of her husband when he was about twenty yards away, coming across the park. Bill had seen Mr Trimble's difficulties and was soon jogging over the cattle grid to offer help. At forty, he was five years older than Rosemary. He was a stocky man of middle height with a round, cheerful face and an easy-going temperament. Generations of his family had worked on the estate, and the orphaned Bill had begun to help his uncle Esau when he was fourteen. Trained since boyhood to know the Helmingham soil, the Helmingham traditions and the Helmingham weather, he had developed into a very fine head gardener. Yet, it was the Great War that made it possible for him to hold the senior position. The war in the trenches had scythed fifty per cent of Helmingham gardeners, leaving the way for Bill.

Mr Trimble was helped inside with his wood. Bill would soon be coming through the door. He liked to get in an hour or two with the men before coming home for breakfast, but he was in a foul mood this morning.

Rosemary was nearly as tall as her husband. She was indeed a sturdy girl with wrist bones that stood up on her arms like marbles and feet that could take Bill's boots comfortably. Her fine, mousy hair was parted into three sections, the sides plaited and rolled into circular 'earphones' over each ear, the remainder being taken to the crown of her head and twisted into a bun. She made few other concessions to modern fashion, knowing herself to be sharp-nosed, thin-lipped and plain. Yet, when she smiled, a rare occurrence, her thin mouth stretched wide to reveal well-spaced, strong teeth.

She took two cups and saucers from the cupboard, a sturdy earthenware set for Bill, but a delicate, gold-trimmed cup and saucer with roses painted on the sides for herself. She always drank from this cup, always placed the George III knife and fork her grandmother had given her at her own plate, while Bill made do with the EPNS that had been given to them as a wedding present. She couldn't drink tea or coffee from a thick-rimmed cup and felt secure in the day that began with the knife and fork from her old life.

The plated bacon and eggs warming in the oven would provide the fuel for a cold day's work, and she would wipe her mouth with a damask napkin, while her husband would leave his folded and make do with the back of his hand. Bill teased her about her elegant ways, saying she was probably sorry to have married a common gardener when her father owned a thriving nursery in Essex. Rosemary didn't mind his rough ways. Refinement was not the spur that caused her to take so much trouble over small things. These little rituals were intended as constants in a life over which she felt she had no control. There was security in the

48

damask napkin, a certainty that each day another white cloth would be brought from the drawer to remind her of the girl who had married with such high hopes. The napkin was about the only thing she could depend upon, especially on this dangerous day.

She looked fondly at him. 'Take off your coat and sweater. You'll not get the benefit when you go out again.'

'I'm too old to change my ways,' he said, not referring to his coat, but to his new employer. 'I'll advertise as a head gardener. What do you say to Lancashire? I hear Lord Booper is short of a good man. Got a magnificent garden up there, they say.'

'I say I won't go to Lancashire. Essex, Suffolk or Norfolk. Maybe Hertfordshire. No further. You promised, Bill. I want to be able to see my family occasionally. Anyway, all this talk is a waste of time.'

He never pulled out his chair, always threw one leg over the seat before sitting down, then tucked his toes behind the front legs. The position pulled the cloth of his corduroy trousers tight over his thighs, giving a hint of powerful muscles. Bill was a strong man with unexpectedly graceful movements, and she loved him as much on this day as she had when they were married.

'There's no need to suppose she won't want you,' she said, putting the hot plate in front of him. 'Wait until you've met her. Give her a chance, can't you?'

He picked up the bacon in his fingers and bit off a piece. 'Thirteen degrees of frost we had last night, and this morning there's going to be a rapid thaw. Some plants are sure to go. I had to have them stoking up the boilers during the night. I sent Clifton home. He was up the better part of the night checking on the houses, making sure the heat stayed up. If she says anything, I'll tell her outright. Can't work the men till they drop, I'll say.'

'She won't know anything about Clifton. Bill, this isn't like you. Wait till she snarls before you bite her.'

'She's that woman's daughter, isn't she? I saw enough of *her* when I was a lad. The bitch. Led the old boy quite a dance.'

'That was years ago.' Nevertheless, Rosemary already hated the new occupant of Helmingham Hall. Miss Joyce d'Avranche had arrived the previous day, and everyone knew that she had refused to meet Mr Trimble and Bill and others who were important to her comfort and wealth.

'Is she pretty, do you suppose?' Always her first question about a woman she hadn't met.

'Bert Crow says she is. Shy like a mouse, he says, but I say she's probably biding her time like her mother did. Thora Jefferson was pretty and shy when she first came here. Oh, how sweetly she could talk! Little snake in the grass she turned out to be. His lordship sat down and cried like a baby, Crow says.'

He usually scoffed his food quickly, then sat back in the chair to linger over a second cup of coffee, discussing the plans for the day. Not on this important morning, however. He drank the last ounce of his first cup, made a face when he reached the undissolved sugar, and reached for his coat. Rosemary, feeling every bit as nervous as Bill, poured herself a second cup and sat on, thinking about the inevitable changes. If Captain Cartwright had lived they could all have carried on in their old ways, secure, sure of the future. But now . . .

Daisy, the fourteen-year-old girl who helped around the house before and after school, came into the kitchen to say that she had done the bedrooms, had changed the sheets on Mrs Cook's bed and was about to put them on to soak.

'Have some breakfast and then be off,' said Rosemary absent-mindedly. 'I must go out to the greenhouse to see what this cold weather has done to my roses overnight.'

She jammed an old felt hat on her head, then held it firmly against the wind by tying a woollen scarf over it and under her chin. Her woollen gloves had only half fingers so that she could feel her plants, sensing their needs through the tips of her fingers. They had been knitted by Daisy's mother, Betty, and were very useful. Rosemary had no time for such feminine pursuits as knitting. Roses filled her every waking moment, except when she was thinking about Bill. Other matters, those thoughts that could swamp her if she let them, were ruthlessly shut out. Rosemary loved Bill and was breeding roses. Nothing else mattered.

Her father, Harley Dobson, had five sons who had all joined him in the business, but little Rosie, his only daughter, had been his favourite. From an early age, Rosie had been in the fields and in the houses, helping her father. She had even spent a few days budding roses, work which was never done by women. You stood in the field all day, bent double as you made a t-shaped cut in the wild rose root stock (for roses were seldom grown on their own roots), slipped in a bud of the chosen variety and tied the two together with raffia. A good budder could bud a thousand roses in a day. Rosemary had managed a hundred and had a sore back for several days afterwards. But it had been worth it to win a few words of praise from her father.

Harley Dobson, Sons and Daughter, Satisfaction Relieves All Apprehension, had been growing roses for thirty-five years, and before the Great War had sold them by the thousand. Harley was a grower, not a breeder. New varieties came from abroad or from amateurs who happened to strike it lucky. But the breeder was usually a poor man, for his labour and skill gave him an advantage for only one year. After that, his competitors could strike cuttings from his roses to grow and sell without paying a penny to the breeder.

Breeding was for men with more time and money than sense. It could take five to seven years to breed a rose – if you were lucky. The great breeders had from twenty thousand to a hundred thousand roses in their fields at any given time. Who could afford to do that? Who had the patience? Not that he wouldn't be proud to grow any rose his daughter might happen to breed. His Rosemary knew her onions, he used to say, amused by his little joke.

She was good with a knife. Skilled men, those who could use a knife with precision and delicacy, were paid more than the others. Although Bill had three men under him, he hadn't her skill with the knife, and always turned to his wife for advice when a rose needed attention.

The long walk up to the rose house had her wishing for the warmth of the kitchen, for it was a raw day. The deer ignored her, as she ignored them. Rosemary couldn't see the purpose of keeping deer. They were bad for trees and didn't do much for the grass. People said they looked romantic. She couldn't see it. She was fond of venison, however, and Mr Trimble saw to it that they had venison whenever the deer were culled.

Her personal greenhouse was tucked away behind the stables, a fifty-year-old house that had seen better days. They had been planning to tear it down when the new ones were built, but she arrived at Helmingham in time to stop them. Bill had indulged her whim, and she hoped Lord d'Avranche had never regretted his tolerance.

She opened the door quickly, stepped in and shut it behind her, afraid of letting in the bitter cold. The heated air hit her in the face. To go from an outside temperature near freezing to fifty degrees could be a bit of a shock. Off came the hat and scarf to be plunged into her pockets. Off came the gloves.

Two types of roses were housed in the big old glasshouse: half was taken up with those plants from which she was breeding – delicate work requiring still air and freedom from damaging rain. After a rose had been pollinated, she'd put a paper bag over it to prevent any other pollen from reaching it.

There was a wall of brick and glass between the breeding section and the rest of the house where roses for cutting were grown to provide perfect blooms for the Hall from March onwards. Provided the heat was maintained and Rosemary was skilful in the disbudding, there would be a succession of perfect long-stemmed single blooms to take indoors. Grown in eight-inch pots, they were set outside during the summer months to make strong growth for the next season. With the pots imbedded in ashes, they could survive the entire winter out of doors if need be. However, that was not the way to bring roses into bloom early. Taking a few pots at a time and starting in October, she would bring them into the warmth of the house and prune them hard at the first sign of the buds breaking, and shortly afterwards there would be a crop of perfect blooms to cut, some with stems as long as ten inches. A few weeks later, other pots would be brought in, and so the process would go on, until the last pots bloomed in an unheated house, while the earliest pots were already out of doors for the summer.

Truth to tell, there was nothing to be done in the greenhouse. It was possible to bud a few roses under glass at this time of year, but she had completed that small task. Most budding took place out of doors. Mildew, the great enemy, had to be watched for and eradicated. Greenfly and whitefly could be a problem indoors. But today she had nothing to do but stand and dream of the great roses she would breed when the time was right.

In expectation of bad weather, she had ordered straw to be tucked among the branches of the rose bushes out of doors. Some of the more delicate or exposed plants had been tied up with sacking, yet she knew she would lose some during this unusually cold February. Tomorrow, she might make a tour of all the roses to see if the frost had lifted the soil around any of them. It was not her duty to check the condition of the pergolas. Bill would attend to that.

She turned left before reaching the moat. There was a strip of land between the moat that encircled the house and the one that surrounded the garden, which was reached not by a bridge but by an earth causeway, protected from rabbits by netting below the huge wrought iron gates. These formal gardens had been partly walled in the eighteenth century and the mellow red bricks were a wonderful foil for greenery and flowers, but it was said that the moated garden had existed in Saxon times, when it penned cattle instead of flowers and vegetables.

Helmingham was famous locally for its vegetable garden, the largest at any of the big houses. At this time of year, there was very little growing: cabbages, a few Brussels sprouts and a stand of cauliflowers, all miserable in the crusting of snow. The root vegetables had been clamped, safe from frost buried in a mound of soft earth. The soil had been dug and left rough for the frost to break up into clods. All beds at Helmingham were double dug, a back-breaking process that ensured the best growing conditions for almost every kind of plant.

In the height of summer, the herbaceous border was dazzling. On a frosty February day there was little to see, but what there was bore its coating of hoar frost dejectedly. And everything was tidy. Bill was a neat man with an encyclopedia of gardening in his head. He led his men like the best kind of general, from the front, never asking for work to be done that he couldn't do himself. Except for the roses. Rosemary clung to that. She came from a proud family, men and women who were major employers in the village of Harlow. People called her father 'sir' when they met him. He could never understand Bill's willingness to 'yes, my lord and no, my lord' his employer.

Rosemary, her father used to say, had her pick of wealthy men. It wasn't true, of course. There were perhaps some who would have proposed for the sake of her father's money. None who would have chosen her for her beauty and charm. Yet she and Bill had taken to each other the first time they met. He was a war veteran, one of the lucky ones to return whole, although he had been wounded in the side. He had come to the nursery to buy some roses for Helmingham. Within three months they were married. Father eventually wished them well before removing the 'and daughter' from all the nursery signs. Mother cried for the loss of the only other female in the house, and she had arrived at Helmingham at sunset. It was the grandest house she had ever seen. The lodge was very pretty, but not modernized like the Dobson house in Harlow. They didn't even have a proper bathroom or electric light. Father had been the first in the village to install . . . She paused by the box parterre. Someone was coming.

The new owner of Helmingham Hall, with Betsy waddling beside her, was wearing a grubby mackintosh that had once belonged to old Lord d'Avranche. The belt was buckled around her bottom and the hem dragged the ground. She had on the old man's rubber boots, making it impossible for her to do more than shuffle along. Rosemary saw a pretty face, pinched and pink from the cold, pale eyes and a mouth about which hovered a tentative smile.

'How do you do? I am Miss Joyce d'Avranche, the new owner of Helmingham Hall,' said Miss Joyce. 'You are . . . ?'

'I am Mrs Cook. My husband is the head gardener here. He has been hoping to meet you since yesterday.'

Miss Joyce looked uncertain. 'Oh, well I wasn't feeling . . . I'm sorry I didn't . . . Mr Crow said . . .' She stuck out a bare hand. 'It's nice to meet you.'

Rosemary thought some explanation was necessary. 'I was just looking at the roses. That is, there isn't much to see, but I am responsible for them. Not that my husband is not perfectly capable . . .' She sighed. 'My father is a rose grower in Essex. I know all about roses, you see.' It was a vulgar boast, unlike Rosemary, but necessary on this occasion. She had to impress the new owner of her right to tend the roses or risk losing her chance to breed seedlings at Miss d'Avranche's expense.

Joyce smiled slightly. 'That's very nice. Are you one of the four gardeners? I was told there are four gardeners. What I mean is, do I pay you?'

'Oh, no, you don't. I do it to help my husband, and to tell you the truth, because I love to do it. There's a small greenhouse where Lord d'Avranche encouraged me to force roses for cutting for the house and to breed others.'

Miss Joyce frowned, and Rosemary held her breath. 'It doesn't seem fair, my not paying you. However, Mr Finch controls the purse strings.'

'He knows the situation. Will you meet my husband now?' Rosemary indicated the direction in which they should walk, feeling more confident by the minute in this awkward social situation. Miss Joyce d'Avranche was gentle and charming. She would never find the courage to sack Bill. Nothing else mattered to Rosie.

'Yes, I would like to very much. That is, I look a mess. I mean, he won't care about that, I'm sure. I must buy some suitable clothes for . . . I mean, the house is so cold! Everything is cold and I haven't . . . I suppose I might as well meet everyone and get it over with. Oh, dear, I didn't mean that the way it sounds.' She laughed, and Rosie laughed with her.

Slowly, because of the too-big boots, Rosemary took Miss d'Avranche off to meet some of the men who worked on the estate. The new mistress of the Hall managed to comment on the wrong things, to criticize without seeming to know that she was criticizing, and just generally to offend everyone. Rosie winced several times, embarrassed for the young woman, yet beginning to feel quite protective towards her. Unlike most women, the more embarrassed she became, the prettier she was.

When she had returned to the Hall, shivering violently by this time, they all had a grand time tearing her to pieces behind her back. Mr Trimble was particularly scathing. He hated pretty young women at the best of times, assuming that they had neither brains nor character. He kept muttering in his shaky voice about flappers and bright young things and everything going to the dogs, until Rosemary was ready to scream. She thought the young girl was sweet and unpretentious, an inexperienced young person who probably had no idea of the drama played out twenty odd years before. And unlike those who were criticizing the young girl, Rosemary had not built up years of prejudice against her.

The days were lengthening, but the dark still came too soon for Rosemary's liking. There would be another heavy frost on this night. The day had been bright and clear once the fog lifted, and the sky was forecast to be clear during the night.

Rosemary had laid the table, put a freshly baked loaf on the breadboard with the knife beside it, taken the butter out of the larder to let it soften, and cut the fruit cake. Helmingham made its own cheese, and very good it was. Bill liked half a pound of it for his tea, together with a thick slice of Suffolk ham, and some of Rosie's home baked bread. It was all ready, daintily prepared and attractively laid. A few branches of flowering quince had been put into an earthenware jug and set in the middle of the table. Bill brought on a number of plants and flowers for the Hall in one of the glasshouses, although most of the time there was no-one to cut them for. Miss Joyce would have to have a vase of quince, but Rosemary got the first cut.

She slipped her coat over her shoulders and opened the door, shutting it quickly behind her to keep from cooling the house. No lights were visible from the big house, of course, but she could see the glow of the tilly lamp in Mr Trimble's kitchen. She should invite him over for a meal some time. She would be happy to do so, if only he could be pleasant for a few hours. The death of his wife had destroyed Mr Trimble, but in his presence her pity was always, sooner or later, drowned in irritation. The man was such a nag.

She moved around to the gate side of the house where no lights shone, feeling the scrunch of snow beneath her feet as the intense cold found its way into her very bones. The moon silhouetted the strong branches of the naked oak trees and glistened on the ground. Every breath seared her lungs, but she breathed deeply nevertheless as she lifted her head right back and studied the starry sky. The heavens were dusted with stars and she focused on one.

'Star light, star bright, first star I see tonight, I wish I may, I wish I might, I wish my wish come true tonight.' Her voice was no more than a hoarse whisper, reflecting her secret embarrassment at this childish ritual. Then, 'Fool!' she rasped. 'Fool, fool, fool!'

She heard the door open, the crispness of Bill's feet as he came in search of her. Hot tears, scalding her cold cheeks, were quickly wiped away. She was ready with a smile.

'What the devil are you doing out here? Do you want to catch your death? The kettle's boiling dry and I want my tea.' His harsh words were accompanied by a quick hug and a peck on the cheek. 'You've been crying again. And you're shivering. Rosie, what am I going to do with you?'

'Nothing to be done,' she sniffed, always undermined by his clumsy gentleness. 'Nothing to be done with your fool of a wife. Let's go indoors.'

'Arthur Trimble is coming over for tea. You don't mind, do you? He's feeling pretty poorly. You can set another place, and there's always plenty.'

'Yes, there's more than enough.' And Mr Trimble's presence would ensure that she had no time for gloomy thoughts. 'I'll get out the piccalilli and I've got a rhubarb pie I was saving for tomorrow night. But he'll have to eat in the kitchen. I'm not about to light a fire in the dining-room.'

He gave her a worried look, nuzzled her cheek, then led her back to the warm lodge. They didn't talk about it any more. There was nothing left to say.

Chapter Three

Joyce had lived at Helmingham for three whole days. As she held out her hands to the blazing fire, it seemed like a lifetime in purgatory. The moated fairy-tale palace that was to keep her safe from a cruel world had turned into a luxurious prison. Who was it who was locked in the tower until she spun straw into gold? Whoever, she was a lucky woman. Joyce was locked in, trapped by her lonely wealth. But what did she have to do to be freed? Would a prince come and kiss her into life? But that was a different fairy-tale. She felt more like the man in the iron mask, condemned for life.

Two days ago she had taken her courage in both hands and gone out in search of her outdoor staff and had met first of all the gardener's tall wife who turned out to be a positive woman with pride in her knowledge of roses. Big-boned and plain, she dressed her hair in a most unappealing style, and seemed not to care about her appearance. Mrs Cook demanded that one took her on her own terms. Of all the people she later met, Rosemary Cook was the one with whom Joyce felt most at ease.

As they strode along towards the greenhouse where her husband was working, Mrs Cook would suddenly break away to examine a bare rose bush that had a withered bloom or two still clinging to it. The snow had drifted wildly, exposing some plants, burying others. 'Frost lifts the soil,' she explained, going on to the next one. 'I must tour all the beds. Roses are Helmingham's speciality, you know. We've got . . . that is *you* have some of the oldest roses in cultivation: but there are new varieties, too, like that pillar to your left. It's called Albertine. Pale pink. What a scrambler, and scented, too! Wait until the summer. It's a sight for sore eyes. Just keeping the repeat flowering ones dead-headed is a full-time job. June through July, those are the months to give your garden parties. When your roses are pretty enough to break your heart.'

And Joyce thought, when *her* roses are pretty enough to break my heart. She walks around here like a woman in charge, like the owner. I am the ignorant visitor. Aloud, she said, 'I can hardly wait to see them. I love roses, although of course I know nothing about them.'

Having made, as she thought, a friend of Rosemary Cook, she was unprepared for the animosity of her husband, the head gardener. Wearing a large flat cap and a waistcoat with a huge watch chain under his overcoat, he looked like a shopkeeper, except for his muddy boots, half-finger gloves and the pruning knife in his hand. She would discover later that he walked everywhere with his pruning knife, even when there was no need to cut anything. Joyce had no male relatives, so she tended to view men with distrust, feeling awkward in their presence and full of suspicion about their motives. Bill Cook, lacking in guile, had left her in no doubt that he was ready to hand in his resignation if he was not satisfied with the performance of his new employer. She wondered how their roles had been so swiftly reversed. She had been the one eager to please; he had been the one to glare in disapproval.

Rather than standing in silent embarrassment, she had remarked quite casually that she understood his wife was the rose grower in the family and had the use of one of the greenhouses. For some reason, he had

taken this as an attack on him. How he had bristled!
How he had defended his wife's activities!

Mrs Cook had been the one to soothe ruffled
feathers, speaking gently in her deep voice. 'I'm sure
Miss Joyce doesn't mind, Bill, so long as there are
plenty of beautiful roses on the estate.'

'That's it exactly,' Joyce had cried. 'I'm delighted,
really I am.' Bill Cook had frowned fiercely, but no
further aggressive remarks had passed his lips.

Then, of course, she had to see the stables and meet
the elderly man who looked after the horses. He hoped
that she would be purchasing some horses, perhaps
some hunters. Did Miss Joyce like to hunt? No, she
said. She had never even witnessed people hunting on
horses, although she understood they chased foxes.
How his face had fallen! Another black mark for the
new chatelaine.

More agony was to come. Two of the most enormous
horses she had ever seen were led from their stables and
introduced to her as Suffolk Punches. Their pale coats
and hairy legs were very beautiful, and they seemed
docile enough, but their bulk and the way their hooves
echoed on the cobbles frightened her. No, she had said,
she could not possibly ride such big horses and didn't
intend to learn. Perhaps they should be sold.
Embarrassingly, it turned out that people didn't ride
Suffolk Punches. It seemed they were used for
ploughing. She had not recovered from this foolish
mistake when an old man in breeches and gaiters had
shuffled up to her.

This, she discovered, was Mr Trimble, her bailiff,
and his disapproval was even more obvious than had
been the gardener's and the stable hand's. He was
pleased to tell her that there was a motor car at
Helmingham, patently waiting for her to say that she
would certainly like to have the use of it, so that he

could say the car was broken and no-one on the estate knew how to fix it. It was nearly seven years old and probably beyond help.

'Well,' she had said, hoping to pass off the awkward moment with a joking remark. 'I suppose that means I can never leave the grounds.'

Mr Trimble said that was nonsense. Of course she could leave the grounds whenever she chose. The fly would take her to any of the nearby train stations. And needless to say she could buy a new motor car if that was what she wanted to do, and she could take on a chauffeur to drive it, as well. He personally would see to it. Or, if she didn't trust him, she could ask Mr Finch.

Joyce had not known how to answer. Well aware that Mr Finch might refuse to pay for a new motor until the property and its revenue were definitely hers, she tried to change the subject. 'There seem to be a great many deer.'

'Well, do you trust me or don't you?' had snapped Mr Trimble, leaving her with a terrible problem. Should she reply gently to an old man, or should she put down an impertinent employee? He seemed to have realized how rude he was; his chin was trembling.

'Of course I trust you, Mr Trimble. I'll have to see how the finances are. Now tell me about the deer. You have them very well trained. Even though the gates are open, they never wander onto the road or cross the bridge.'

'Well, of course they don't. There's a cattle grid, isn't there?' He wiped his mouth. 'You'll get used to our ways. You come from the city. You don't know about the country. Now, you should take advantage of the cold and go skating on the moat.'

'Oh, I don't think—'

'You must avoid the bridges. The ice doesn't freeze as hard under bridges, you know.'

She hadn't known it and wasn't sure she believed it. Why shouldn't ice freeze as hard under the bridges? He could stare at her as hard as he liked. She would not ask. Resisting all their attempts to get her on skates so that they could laugh at her clumsiness, she pressed to be shown the rest of the estate. The tour couldn't last for ever, she reckoned. It must be over some time.

She had been shown the dairy with its small herd. She had met the cow man, then the pig man with his pigs. She had been shown six different varieties of chicken, and had been assured that she would only ever eat her own hams, chicken, venison and lamb.

The shepherd talked of his flock, saying Helmingham folded fifty sheep, which she didn't understand at all, and to which information she merely nodded dumbly.

By the time she had done the rounds, she was frozen half to death and totally confused. Her silence was taken for disapproval.

'If there is anything not to your liking, please tell me,' Mr Trimble had said. 'No point in upsetting the others.'

They were alone now, as Mrs Cook had lingered to speak quietly with the shepherd. 'Mr Trimble, for heaven's sake please stop taking offence every minute. I know nothing about estates and livestock. I leave that all in your hands. My only comment is that I can see one of the bedrooms has had a terrible leak, because a tin hip bath is placed under the stain on the ceiling. No-one has even emptied the water from the bath, so I presume it happens all the time. Could not your men repair the roof?'

'We've tried, but some money must be spent. Large portions of the Hall require reroofing. And you must have seen that many of the terracotta tiles have fallen from the sides of the house. They're not bricks, you see, though they look like bricks. The Hall was not built with them, but clad later with half-inch thick tiles in the splendid fret pattern you see. But more must be made, because so many broke when they fell off the house. And some of the pinnacles are in poor shape. Do you see them? Decorative spires of bricks in fantastic shapes. I'm sure you saw that some of them have broken off entirely. That's skilled work and bound to be expensive. There are many repairs required on the house, but there is no money to do the work.'

'But the rents—'

'Not spent on this house by Lord d'Avranche. He preferred to use the money to maintain his London home. If you will spend your money on this house, I shall be pleased to put it in order.' There were tears standing in the old man's eyes. He seemed to get very worked up over the state of the house, perhaps because of his inability to maintain it properly. Joyce felt sorry for him.

'In due course I will, believe me. But the Will, you know. The house is not exactly mine until Captain Cartwright d'Avranche has been declared dead.'

'*He* would have got everything shipshape,' he muttered, and her pity evaporated.

Since that humiliating encounter on her first full day at Helmingham, she had not left the house. She had found a Marie Corelli novel and read it from cover to cover. She had scoured the cupboards and found some women's clothing thirty years out of date, a complete set of coronation robes and some very attractive paste jewellery to which she believed she had no right. She had wrapped up warmly and toured the rooms to take a good look at every painting throughout the house, hoping to recognize at least one. Unfortunately, none were by painters she had studied at Madame Puget's school.

As the hours passed, she had become desperate to

speak to someone and to hear words spoken to her. An opportunity arose when Mr Crow came to set the table for tea.

'When I gain control of my money, I'll buy some nice new furniture for the drawing room, Mr Crow.'

'Miss Joyce, the round table is a very find Georgian piece. That chair is Tudor as is the cabinet in the corner. All the furniture in the entire house is of the best from the past. I doubt if anyone makes furniture of this quality any more.'

So she had subsided into silence, too enervated even to cross the moat, too lazy to pen a letter to Marsha. If the lamps were not brought on time in the afternoon, she sat in darkness until they appeared. She made no special requests, eating lightly but consuming too much wine with dinner each night, hoping the alcohol would help her to sleep. It always did at first, but in the early hours when the house was still, she would open her eyes and stare into the darkness, and tears would fall as she pitied the girl who had inherited one of the grandest houses in England.

It was half past four on Friday afternoon. Mrs Crow came into the small sitting-room. 'Was your tea all right, Miss d'Avranche? Mrs Able would really like to know what you want to eat. You've hardly tasted your tea. Don't you like scones? She needn't send in any, you know. And the fruit cake?'

Joyce smiled listlessly. 'All delicious, but I'm not very hungry today. I do like Mrs Able's cooking. She is a very good cook. It must be boring to have to prepare all this food for just one woman.'

Mrs Crow stared hard at her as she sat by the fire next to the dog. 'I've come for Betsy, but why don't you wrap up well and take her for a walk? You need to get outside a bit. I'm sure the fresh air will be good for you. Now, the way it works is, there are little boards with names on them by the north footbridge. As you go out, you slide out the board with your name on it. Then when Mr Crow goes to raise the drawbridges, he checks to see everybody is inside who should be inside. You'll never get locked out that way.'

Joyce had intended to refuse to go out, but Mrs Crow was too positive for her in her present mood. She stood up and followed the housekeeper into the hall to collect a coat, scarf and hat. 'I'll keep to the path. No need to change my shoes, Mrs Crow.'

'Well, I don't know. That blessed dog is apt to run off from you. Mind you speak to her sharply. Let her know who's in charge.'

Joyce gave a hollow laugh. 'How could I possibly convince anyone that I am in charge?'

She and Betsy crossed the moat by the north bridge into the stillness that a carpet of snow always brought with it, immediately turning left to avoid the men who might be near the stables and coach house. At five o'clock, it was already dark. Stars twinkled palely, as if reflecting the glittering diamonds of snow crystals on the ground. The shadows were black and mysterious, but for the rest a huge moon cast a blue glow. Heading south, she made for the apple walk, but arrived first at one of the magnificent conifer trees which she had been told were cedars of Lebanon. They were several hundred years old and very beautiful as they spread their branches in flat layers. How wonderful that no branch seemed to be directly beneath the one above it. Their arrangement was almost a spiral, easily seen as snow lay lightly on each massive branch, like icing on a wedding cake. Fallen needles lay thickly underfoot, but the snow had not penetrated so the ground was spongy and dry.

With Betsy at her heels, she walked under the

branches, bending to avoid the lowest ones that swept the ground like a lady's ball gown, and stood with her back to the trunk, looking up. 'It reminds me of the vaulting in a cathedral,' she said, and Betsy gave a little yelp of pleasure at the sound of her mistress's voice, thrashing her tail against Joyce's legs in a frenzy of joy.

Joyce stood respectfully under the tree for several minutes, awed by a sense of its age and greatness, marvelling at its architecture, at its size. Incapable of appreciating the many beautiful objects indoors, she was for the first time aware of the splendour out of doors that was her inheritance.

'This tree is mine, Betsy. It has stood here for hundreds of years, owned by others in a long line and now belonging to me. I'll hand it on to my son and his son.' She sighed. 'If I ever have a son, that is.'

As a child, she used to think that the full moon would not shine the following month unless she made a point of appreciating it. Then she grew up and developed a cynicism in adolescence that had never left her. Better to be cynical than hurt. The London street lights dimmed the moon's brilliance, and in recent years she hadn't cared about anything that was not a part of her daily struggle for happiness.

Cupping her hands, she shouted to the sky. 'I don't appreciate you any more, moon! Will you carry on beaming?'

Distantly, Betsy yelped. Joyce whirled all round, calling the dog's name, but heard nothing further in reply. Scrambling in the darkness to get out from the cedar's shelter, she brushed against an overhead branch and brought down upon herself some of the snow that had lain on its branches. Powdery snow dusted her head and, when warm, slipped down the back of her neck. She made a hasty attempt to remove it before it trickled down her spine, but was largely unsuccessful. Unable to discover any tracks that would give her a clue to Betsy's direction, she spent the next twenty minutes dashing breathlessly among the apple trees, stumbling on uneven ground, crunching through the thin crust on the snow, into the orchard garden and then into the walled garden, careless where she stepped, aware in passing that all the gardeners would know in the morning exactly where she had been. And all the time she called out Betsy's name, until, very tired and out of breath, she reached the north bridge once more, intending to ask for help in the search. There stood Betsy on the drawbridge, wagging her tail, eager to go indoors so that she could shake off the wet snow and warm herself by the fire.

'Oh, Miss Joyce!' cried Bert Crow, coming to the door to take her coat. He slipped her name board back into its frame. 'You must be frozen. I was about to come looking for you.'

'Betsy ran away as Mrs Crow predicted. I've been looking for her for ages. I'm not cold, however, as I've worked up quite a glow in my exertions. Here, let me take off this cardigan. Oh, that was hot work looking for the wretched dog. Is this a cloth to dry her paws? I'll do it. Naughty Betsy.' The dog submitted to having her feet dried, then escaped Joyce's clutches to shake herself vigorously.

The lamps had been lit and the fire built up in her absence. Bert Crow immediately served her a sherry, urging her to rub some circulation back into her hands and feet. Joyce saw no need to change her stockings, believing that they would soon dry on her legs, although she did slip off her wet shoes to massage her feet until Mrs Crow came in with her slippers. The housekeeper took Joyce's shoes to the boot room so her husband could give them his expert attention.

Dinner, when it arrived, had never tasted so good,

and the butler suggested that she finish off the meal with a generous brandy and hot water. At ten o'clock, she trotted up to bed with a buzzing head and a happy glow that convinced her all her sorrows were behind her.

The wee hours of the night taught her differently. Awakened by a pounding head and an inability to get warm, she hugged the dog and prayed for the moment when Mary would come into the bedroom to light the fire.

Thursday passed in a haze. Everyone was extremely kind. They dosed her with home remedies and uttered helpful homilies. They looked in on her every hour and kept the room beautifully warm, but no amount of concern could remove the headache nor the pains in her joints. She thought of her mother's final illness and wondered if influenza would take her, too.

A grim Friday morning gave way to a sunny afternoon and the relentless drip of thawing snow. The headache was gone and she felt weak but on the mend, although Mrs Crow insisted that she stay in bed. Lunch, her first proper meal since falling ill, consisted of delicious soup and a wonderful custard, which she had not quite finished when Mrs Crow appeared in the doorway, bristling with disapproval to announce that Mrs Cook, the gardener's wife, was *insisting* on paying her a visit.

'Good heavens! Why, that's very kind. She must come up. Have I any more handkerchiefs? My nose is positively dripping.'

'You're scarcely well enough to have visitors, and Mrs Cook of all people,' scolded Mrs Crow. 'Excuse me, I'll fetch you a bed jacket that belonged to Lady d'Avranche. It will be clean and smelling of lavender if the moths haven't got to it.'

She was back in a moment with a pink knitted

garment smelling so strongly of lavender that even Joyce's blocked nose could detect it. By this time Joyce had discovered just how dizzying and exhausting it was to sit up. Gritting her teeth, she assured Mrs Crow that she was delighted to have a visitor.

Rosemary Cook came into the warm room breathing good health and contentment. Her gardening clothes had been cast aside in favour of a brown wool coat and a matching cloche hat that must have been difficult to put on over her braids. 'I brought you some branches of *Chaenomeles*. Flowering quince. Bill has a bush in one of the houses and always brings it into bloom early. Aren't they beautiful? Glowing orange is such a warming colour in the darkness of February. I've put them in one of the vases that is always kept for them. Here, by the window? Someone can take the vase down to your sitting-room when you're well enough to go downstairs.'

'That will be fine. Thank you very much, Mrs Cook ... may I call you Rosemary?' Joyce bit her lip, suddenly aware of the impropriety of the request. 'I won't if you don't want me to. I mean, whatever is proper.'

'I would be very pleased. Isn't the Hall beautiful? I've never seen more than the kitchen before. And you are looking better than I expected. Mrs Crow said you had a terrible dose of the influenza, but it couldn't be, or you wouldn't be looking better so soon. I was very worried, so I said to Bill, "I'm going up to Helmingham to see how Miss Joyce is and he said . . ."' She stopped and grinned ruefully. 'I'm running on, I'm afraid. The real reason I came is that I thought you might have misunderstood my husband's mood the other day. I came to apologize for anything he may have said to offend you.'

'Oh, no!' Joyce sat upright, then fell back as her head started to throb. 'Oh, no, I never thought . . . I certainly was not offended. I'm very ignorant about gardens. I'm afraid I made stupid comments and everyone lost patience with me. It will take time for me to learn about everything on the estate. There are so many beautiful treasures indoors, but I really love the gardens, that is, the grounds. All of them. I went out to walk the dog the other night—'

'Mrs Crow says you were soaked. Bert should have walked Betsy.'

'No, it was wonderful. I stood under one of those cedars and thought . . . I don't know what I thought, exactly. It was a very moving experience. Perhaps I didn't think anything. Perhaps it was a moment of pure emotion. I think I'm glad I came.'

'But you're not sure,' said Rosemary, laughing. 'I'm not surprised. This may seem a silly thing to say, but I never realized how huge Helmingham is. It's splendid, but awfully large for one young woman. And none of us has given you a very warm welcome.'

'No,' said Joyce, more to herself than to Rosemary. 'I have not been given the impression that the residents of Helmingham want me here. When you've gone, I don't expect I'll speak to another soul for a week.'

'But you must! Forgive me, but there are certain things that are expected of the lady of the house. There will be some entertaining. The rector will call, of course. He would have come to see you today, but heard you weren't well. Then there is the schoolmaster. And people will write to you from time to time asking to see some of the treasures of Helmingham.'

'The house is full of treasures, but I don't know what they are. At finishing school, we studied French art, but this house doesn't have a single painting by an artist that I have ever heard of!'

'I'm told there is a painting somewhere in the Hall by John Constable which is of the Helmingham dell, and it shows an oak tree that's still growing in the grounds.'

'We didn't study John Constable. Is he famous?'

'He was a Suffolk painter.'

Impulsively, Joyce threw back the covers. 'You know, I think I feel well enough to get up. I'll put on my dressing-gown over the bed jacket and we can go looking for the John Constable. I'd love to see it and I think I know where it is. There was this landscape painting in the drawing-room, but I don't care for landscapes, so I didn't look at it very carefully. I'm wearing bed socks, you see, and I'll keep them on so that my feet are really warm. Just hand me those slippers, will you?'

'You shouldn't get up. Mrs Crow will be very annoyed with me if you have a relapse.' Nevertheless, she set the slippers by the side of the bed.

'You seem amazingly frightened of Mrs Crow. I wouldn't have thought you were afraid of anyone.'

Rosemary laughed. 'Normally, I am not afraid of living people, only ghosts, and I'm not really afraid of Hilda Crow. If push comes to shove, I can stand toe to toe with her and battle it out. However, there's been enough trouble between her and Bert and Bill and me, so I try not to cause any more. Their only son used to be a gardener here and he had a knack for it. He really was very knowledgeable. But he and Bill just didn't hit it off. He never would do what he was told. A real law unto himself. One day last year they had a terrific row that almost came to blows and Henry quit. Well, there wasn't any work around here, so Henry took a job as head gardener to the owner of a manor house in Norfolk, not too far from Norwich. I believe it's quite pleasant, but nothing so grand as Helmingham. What's worse, as far as Hilda Crow is concerned, is that they don't get to see him very often. And he's found a lady friend. One day there will be grandchildren whom

Hilda will seldom see. So Bill is blamed for denying her the grandchildren. Silly but sad in a way.'

By this time they had reached the bottom of the stairs. They could hear voices. Joyce put a finger to her lips as they entered the linked rooms that formed the everyday part of the house.

'I think I know where that painting might be. Let's go directly into the drawing-room.'

They passed through the study, Joyce's small sitting-room and the small dining-room, then reached the large drawing-room with its huge windows framing views of the park, and Rosemary banged her shins on a heavy footstool as she admired the moulded plaster ceiling.

'Here it is,' said Joyce. 'Is it this funny tree in the fore-ground? I wonder how long ago it was painted.'

Together, they studied the painting and Rosemary described where the tree could be found.

'I say, it's awfully murky,' murmured Joyce. 'Are you sure this man is a great painter?'

'So I've been told,' said Rosemary. 'That wooden bridge isn't there any more. It's a stone one now. John Constable's brother was steward of the woodlands here. The pictures, there's more than one, were painted in the 1820s.'

'And the oak tree is still here?'

'Oh, some of the oaks are nine hundred years old.'

'I'm sorry to hear that,' said Joyce, laughing. 'I wish everything was new, like me. Then I wouldn't feel so out of place.'

They moved around the room, commenting on the paintings until they came to one of a small child in a blue satin and lace gown.

'Oh!' said Rosemary softly.

'Isn't it lovely?' cried Joyce. 'I really like this picture. There's a little brass plaque on this one. It says, "*Stuart Child*, Anthony Van Dyck". Such elaborate clothes for such a young child, and the apple in its hands looks enormous. I wonder whether it's a boy or girl. You can't tell.'

Rosemary nodded, her eyes on the painting. 'Little podgy hands. And the lace cap! Would a baby have a head shaped like that? And lace cuffs! My mother would have hated to have the six of us in lace cuffs.'

The room was very cold, as no fire had been lit in it since the previous Tuesday when Mr Finch had ordered the fire. Joyce now regularly sat in the small sitting-room, feeling more at ease in the cosy room.

'I beg your pardon, Rosemary, but I'm not feeling terribly well. I think I had better go back to bed.'

'Good lord, Mrs Crow will murder me. Here, let me give you a hand. You're looking very pale. But, I wanted to ask you, would you care to come to lunch on Sunday after church? If you're feeling well enough, that is. I hope you don't think I'm being too forward. The Crows generally go to her mother's on Sunday afternoon. She's very old . . . but of course, they won't go if you're unwell.'

They negotiated the hallway and stairs stealthily, as if on a mission to steal the silver. Joyce needed a minute with her head resting on the mound of pillows before she could give a proper reply.

'I would adore to come to lunch. I knew about the Crows having Sunday afternoons off and I was really dreading it, I can tell you.'

Mrs Crow was surprised that Joyce should consider going to the Cooks' home for lunch, but had to admit that she did want to see her eighty-six-year-old mother. She personally brought up a light supper that evening, and predicted another visitor on the Saturday. 'For the rector is sure to call on you when he hears you were well enough to see Rosemary Cook.'

*   *   *

On Saturday morning, Joyce, feeling much better, made a point of dressing carefully and arranging for a fire to be lit in the drawing-room. The rector called at ten o'clock, rather earlier than she had expected, but he soon explained why.

'I'm an old man, Miss d'Avranche, and prefer to be indoors as darkness falls, unless it's absolutely necessary to go out, of course. I would never shirk my duty.'

He was a short, well-spoken man in his late seventies or early eighties. Nearly bald, and with withered cheeks, he seemed even frailer than Mr Trimble. He lost no time in telling her that they were related. Second cousin once removed was his description. She asked if he had been the rector of Helmingham Church for long, and he said sixty years, so she revised his age upwards.

'Sixty years is but the blink of an eye in the history of Helmingham Church. It's known to have existed in the thirteenth century,' he said proudly.

'It must be a magnificent old church and I'm sure you're very proud of it. I look forward to seeing it on Sunday.'

'I'm older than almost all of my congregation, although Aaron Potts is nearly ninety. They are all your tenants, and you will come to love them as I do, I'm sure. You and I must work together, Miss d'Avranche. Mr Goodenough, the schoolmaster, will probably call on you next week. He is a new member of our community, been here just ten months, but we think very highly of him nevertheless. Especially since he started courting Clara Sparrow—'

'Another bird name!'

He smiled, revealing the absence of most of his teeth. 'A Suffolk tradition, you might say. Anyway, I christened Clara, her parents and her grandparents. They are an old Helmingham family. Clara's father is the village blacksmith, a worthy man. Her mother is a Butts. Her grandmother is a . . . but you won't want to hear all that today. You know, I'm sure that those in need of a warming meal will be arriving at the kitchen door shortly. Forty or fifty on a day like today, I imagine.'

'You mean poor people?' asked Joyce in horror. 'Coming to the kitchen door like beggars? I can't believe it!'

He frowned, mistrusting her tone of voice. 'You must know that there is much hardship in rural communities these days. Farming is so depressed that farm workers are being laid off. There being nothing else for them to do, they have no choice but to go without. And Helmingham's vegetable garden is famous. What would happen to all the vegetables and fruit otherwise?'

'What sort of food does Mrs Crow give them? Thin gruel? A nourishing broth? It's like in Dickens. I can't believe it's necessary in these times.'

'Very necessary, I assure you. These people are not indigent beggars. Not lazy, far from it. In this cold weather Mrs Able will have made rabbit stew, I imagine. I presume you have no objections.' He paused, looking thoughtful as if his conscience troubled him. 'We have become accustomed to making decisions that were perhaps not ours to make. What with Lord d'Avranche not being here. Perhaps we have let our hearts rule . . .' He met her eyes, staring rather defiantly. 'But we cannot allow some to starve while others cannot manage to consume what they have.'

'No, no, of course not. I have no objections. Rosemary, that is Mrs Cook, tells me rabbits are a great plague.'

'They are a plague, but they make a nourishing meal.' He rose to look out of the window. 'I see some people coming down the drive. Oh, there are the Fullaloves, all seven of them. Good, God-fearing people who have fallen on hard times. Shall we go into the kitchen?'

'I couldn't. I really couldn't. It's too embarrassing. They won't want to see me.'

'Oh, but they will. Otherwise, they will think you are too high and mighty for them. It's such a small thing that I don't hesitate to ask you to speak to them. They have nothing to be ashamed of after all. They don't refuse to work; there is no work for them.' When she still looked reluctant, he added more sternly, 'We all have our privileges, Miss d'Avranche, and we all have our duties. This is one of yours. I must warn you that there are many others. There is a price to be paid for living in luxury.'

She didn't argue further, but followed him meekly to the kitchen.

'I feel so guilty in having so much,' said Joyce fifteen minutes later when they were once more in the hallway. 'One woman in this great house, and all of them crowded into their hovels.'

'Not hovels, good sturdy cottages that were put up many years ago and built to last.'

'Then why are they in such poor repair? I was so embarrassed I wanted to sink. Why hasn't Mr Trimble seen to it?'

'He should have done, but, you see, what with Lord d'Avranche being elderly and very seldom in residence . . . if he and Captain Cartwright had not fallen out, perhaps the younger man would have exerted his influence. And he might not have trotted off all over the world in search of adventure.'

'And why did they fall out? Please tell me. They're both dead. What can be the harm in my knowing?'

'None. Cartwright, you must understand I knew him very well, could not settle after the war was over. He had been a professional soldier, but was invalided out of the service. Lord d'Avranche wanted him to find a wife and secure the inheritance. It wasn't that he had anything against you personally, but—'

'I have begun to suspect that he did.'

'Now that you are here, you must be strong enough to do whatever your position demands of you.'

'I don't feel strong.'

'Nevertheless, you must think of your tenants and see to it that all the cottages are properly repaired. Trimble is a decent man, but he has gone sadly downhill since the death of his wife.' He sighed. 'As I did following my wife's death forty years ago. Be firm with him. You have the upper hand.'

Once more in the drawing-room with its warm fire and its magnificent paintings, he persuaded her to accept the chairmanship of the summer fête committee, to invite the schoolmaster to discuss some of his pupils, to invite some of her neighbours for tea, to head the hospital committee in Stowmarket and to visit the sick parishioners with him the following Wednesday.

When he had gone, she sat down by the fire. 'I can't do it,' she said to Betsy. 'I can't visit those people. I can't entertain anyone or visit the rector's sick parishioners. I wasn't bred to it.' She put her head in her hands and wept quietly. Betsy, sensing distress or perhaps just vulnerability, leapt onto the settee and pushed her nose between Joyce's hands, forcing a pat on the head, offering a lick on Joyce's cheek. Her tail thumped on the cushions, but the old dog was unprepared for Joyce's sudden violent hug, and yelped her surprise.

Chapter Four

Joyce arrived on the Sunday carrying a bottle of claret that she said she had wrested from Bert Crow's unwilling fingers. 'But I said that I was very kindly being asked out to lunch and I could never drink all the wine in the cellar by myself, so he might as well let me have it.' She whirled about suddenly. 'What do you think of my new jumper and skirt? You know, I've never had good clothes before, but Mr Finch has kindly arranged for me to have an account at Harrods, and I bought all of these things from the catalogue.'

Bill muttered under his breath, rummaging through a cupboard drawer in search of a corkscrew.

'Oh, what a cheerful kitchen!' continued Joyce. 'So warm and cosy. Are we to eat in the dining-room? Do you normally eat in there on a Sunday? I wouldn't want to put you out.'

Rosie had no chance to answer, as Mr Trimble knocked briefly on the kitchen door before letting himself in as usual.

Rosie ushered them into the dining-room to hear extravagant praise of her table and its simple arrangement of forced daffodils and primulas. But suddenly Joyce lost interest in Rosie's home and began tackling Mr Trimble about a few pressing problems.

As she began dishing up the food, Rosie felt she had been touched by a whirlwind. It was exhilarating, a novelty after all the Sundays, marching back eight years, in which nothing whatsoever had happened.

Miss Joyce, so recently laid up, was in sparkling form.

She drank her share of the bottle. (Rosemary couldn't abide the taste.) She spoke of the friends she had left behind, of dear Marsha and the brothers Brant. She amused them with stories about Horace Brant who had once caused quite a stir in a Lyons Corner House when he ordered the special three-egg omelette which for one week only was being offered at the two-egg price. Horace had wanted the third egg in his hand to take home as he really only liked two-egg omelettes. 'And eventually the manager was called,' said Joyce as they all laughed, 'because Horace can be a devil when he gets going. He got the egg, too. Took it home to his brother.'

Rosemary's beef roast was succulent, her potatoes crusty on the outside and floury in the middle. The apple pie and custard had never been better. As she was far from a dedicated cook, this minor success boosted her mood. Since Miss Joyce d'Avranche was pretty and charming and lively, Rosie assumed that the men had enjoyed the afternoon as much as she had.

She was to find out differently the minute Joyce left the house and started back up the long drive.

Mr Trimble helped himself to the remains of the wine. 'I never thought I would see the day . . .' To which Bill shook his head and made a clucking noise. 'To think that such a young flibberty-gibbet should take Captain Cartwright's place,' continued Mr Trimble. 'She doesn't know how to behave, she's got no dignity. I do believe I would rather Rupert d'Avranche had inherited, and God knows he's a disaster. But at least he was brought up to know how things should be done. She's too free and easy.'

Bill nodded solemnly. 'The captain is probably turning in his grave, if he has a grave. I served him as batman from 1914 to 1919, and his father as a gardener before and after. How do you think I feel working for that flapper? It's diabolical.'

'Imagine how *I* felt,' said the bailiff. They were working each other up to a fever pitch. 'Being challenged about my work here, on a Sunday, in your presence, Bill.' Rosie's presence didn't seem to bother him.

'She'll be making crazy demands soon. Plant this here. Put that there.' Bill turned to his wife. 'Wait until she tells you to grub up all the roses, my dear.'

Rosemary had heard enough. 'Don't talk such utter rubbish. She is not going to make unreasonable demands. You've both seen her. She's sweet, gentle and very honest about how little she knows. It's not unreasonable of her, Mr Trimble, to ask for a dry home. And I'm sure you can get the money from Mr Finch to repair the estate houses if you really want to. Captain Cartwright would not have wanted his tenants to be uncomfortable.'

Mr Trimble turned red and tried without success to sputter out a reply.

'Captain Cartwright . . .' began Bill, then stopped because he knew perfectly well that the captain most certainly would have ensured that the tenants' property and the Hall were at least dry. He seemed very annoyed that she was in the right, took a deep breath and hit upon the perfect way to hurt her. 'I think you're altogether too friendly with that young woman. It's awkward. What about the indoor staff and other wives on the estate? She's playing favourites and you're making life difficult for me. I won't have it.'

Had they been alone, Rosemary would have had her say and forgotten about it, but Mr Trimble was sitting at her table nodding agreement with every word Bill uttered. She felt her heart pounding and the heat rising to her face as she tried to control her fury. 'I'll decide who to be friendly with, Bill Cook. I'm as good as she is. I'm not a servant. I'm not a labourer, turning up at the kitchen door for free soup. I'm the daughter of a very successful rose grower and I will not curtsey in the presence of my betters, nor flatten myself against the wall when they pass by. I like her and she likes me. I'll see her when I please.'

Now Bill's face took on a deep flush. 'I wondered how long it would be before you flung your rich father in my face. Well, let me tell you something. This is my house and you'll not invite her into it for lunch ever again.'

The soft voice of reason deep within her could not stop her from completing his humiliation. 'No, Bill, that's just the point, isn't it? It's not your house. It belongs to Miss Joyce d'Avranche, and it behooves you to keep on her best side.'

The weather remained cold during February, and very damaging to roses. The frosts which had begun on the tenth of February were still continuing, which was bad enough. But worse was the fact that the bright sun shone down each morning provoking a rapid thaw. South facing shoots were badly damaged, although overhanging foliage or shadowy walls protected some plants. There was little for Rosie to do, so she was quite pleased to teach Joyce how to drive the two-wheeled fly. Cora was harnessed to the old rig and the two went shopping in Stowmarket. Joyce drove all the way home without mishap.

Bill mentioned that Mr Goodenough, the school-master, found Miss Joyce young and poorly educated but willing to play the part of a great lady. He supposed some would say she was charming. Bill found that comment very amusing, but Rosie thought it boded ill for Miss Joyce's relationship with an important member of the community. The rector paid one of his frequent visits to the Lodge and expounded at length on his plans to teach his willing pupil how to fulfil her responsibilities.

During the next few days, Bill was sour but silent on the subject of rich ladies being friends with his wife, even when Rosie told him that she and Miss Joyce were going for the day to Ipswich, because his employer had decided that she didn't want to go to London until the summer.

Rosie put her husband's resentment out of her mind and enjoyed a much needed break from the routine at Helmingham. Like two young things, they visited every shop, had lunch in a splendid tearoom – at Miss Joyce's expense – and giggled over nothing at all as if neither had a care in the world.

On the way home, the younger woman's concentration slipped and she allowed the horse to take a wrong turning. They had trotted down a narrow lane for some time before Rosie, lost in thoughts of her new rose, realized what was happening. By this time, they had travelled about half a mile in the wrong direction. They were miles from home, and Rosie didn't recognize any landmarks.

It was necessary to turn round. Miss Joyce attempted this before Rosie had a chance to say that she had better be the one to execute this difficult manoeuvre. Inevitably, one of the fly's two wheels slid into the drainage ditch, so that they both had to get down to soothe the horse's shattered nerves and coax her into heaving the vehicle out of trouble. Her confidence thoroughly undermined, Joyce insisted that Rosie should drive the rest of the way home.

Rosie argued forcefully that Joyce must attempt the rest of the journey or she might lose her nerve for ever. At which admonition, Joyce suddenly burst into tears and said she couldn't go on. It was a minute or two before Rosie realized that she meant she couldn't go on *living*, not driving. She pulled the horse into a pathway before a farm gate and the two of them sat surrounded by ploughed fields that stretched to the wintry horizon.

Joyce pulled her coat closer around her neck and shivered. 'I should never have come to Helmingham. I thought it would be so wonderful, but . . . I've been lonely all my life, but never as much as now. There were always people I could talk to and go out with when I lived in London.'

'I say!' Rosie put her arm around Joyce's shoulders and gave her a little shake. 'I take offence at that. We've just been out for a very jolly day. You said yourself that you are kept busy each morning answering your mail or sorting the papers for the various committees you sit on. Good heavens, I should not have thought you had a moment in which to feel lonely.'

'You're a dear friend, Rosie, but you don't understand. What I mean is I'm not on an equal footing with anyone. Not even you, dear. Bill works for me and he doesn't like for us to be together. Do you think I haven't noticed how he acts around me? I have a feeling that everyone despises me because I'm not the person they think should be living at Helmingham Hall. Yet some of them want something from me, and all of them think life will be harder for them if they aren't especially nice to me. Horace Brant—'

'Oh, him!'

'Well, Horace says a lot of true things. He once said go to Oxford Street and watch how all the people bump into one another, brush past as they go their separate ways. Then, said Horace, notice how a policeman walking up Oxford Street never gets bumped by anyone, never brushes against anyone. People unconsciously part like waves to let him pass. It's the uniform, Horace said. We none of us want a brush with the law. But I'm not wearing a uniform. Unlike the

85

policeman, I can't go home and take off the clothes that say this is the woman who owns Helmingham Hall, this is the person who took Captain Cartwright's inheritance.'

'I'm sure I haven't noticed . . . that is, you mustn't pay any attention to Bill. I apologize if he has hurt your feelings. He's a rough man, you know.'

'I found out quite by chance that the land agent, Mr Dunmore, was at Helmingham the other day. I went out to meet him since he clearly didn't intend to call on me. I said the roof needs mending and some of the cupboard doors needed sanding down because they have warped, and that I would like to have several of the rooms redecorated, and that Mr Trimble seemed disinclined to do what I asked, so I was forced to ask him.

'He said – and I must tell you he was very cool – that there was no money for lead for the roof, but that the largest barn had to be repaired immediately if it was not to fall down, so that was what would be done next. And he said he was sure Mr Trimble would get round to my requests in due course.'

'That was . . .' began Rosie, not really knowing what to say. Approaching Mr Dunmore with complaints about the bailiff was bad form, especially in front of the estate workers. Rosie had heard all about it, because everyone had managed to be offended by the incident. Mr Dunmore was a highly educated man, a partner in Dunmore and Dunmore of Ipswich, estate agents. He was so grand that Bill had very little to do with him, being directly under Mr Trimble.

Rosie felt a degree of sympathy with the inexperienced mistress of the Hall, because Mr Trimble was an unpleasant man. Age and bereavement had served to turn the bailiff into a pathetic figure, but Rosie could remember him from her earliest days on the estate. Mr

Trimble was not above diverting a sack or two of wheat to be sold quietly for his own benefit. And no-one dared to approach the old lord to complain, although the bailiff was a hated man.

'And another thing,' said Joyce, 'Mary – you know, the cleaner with the wandering eye – well, Mary has been present whenever I needed her, ready to attend to my clothes and even to dress my hair before I went out to lunch with Sir David and Lady Notts. I never thought about it, I guess I should have wondered why a cleaner was being so helpful. Anyway, Mrs Crow tells me that she knew I needed a personal maid, so *she* hired Mary, who must now be called by her surname, Cutler, without a by-your-leave, then took on another cleaner, whom I haven't even seen. And I think, really, that if I had known I needed a personal maid, I would not have chosen Mary, I mean Cutler, but I can't sack her now because it would be too awful, and I don't know what to do. It's just ridiculous. I can't afford to repair my own roof, but I can take on a totally unnecessary personal maid.'

'I'm sure Mrs Crow meant well,' said Rosie sadly. 'Mary lives in the Hall now, which makes a bit more room at home. She has eleven brothers and sisters. She's fed from the estate, so that does not add to your costs. You have only to provide her with a couple of uniforms and pay her a few shillings a week. Her family are most grateful, I can assure you. A lady in your position would be expected to have a personal maid. On the other hand, lead is awfully expensive.'

'Try to put yourself in my place,' said Joyce, apparently sensing less than whole-hearted sympathy. 'I don't cook my own food. I don't decide who is to work for me. I don't control my own money. Sometimes, no-one bothers to ask me what I would like for dinner or how I want the furniture arranged. I daren't suggest

87

that something be taken out of one of the rooms, else Mr Crow will give me a little lecture on how precious the piece is or how Lord d'Avranche and his father and his father's father always wanted it to stand exactly where it is. I don't know what the estate revenue is nor how much money I have to spend.'

'You could—'

'I used to have a coin purse with my wages in it. I could budget. I had control of my life. And I had fun. Marsha and I used to go out somewhere almost every night, either with the gang or just the two of us. Nowadays, I sit alone reading all those big books on the shelves by lamplight. I'm learning about the furniture, about the paintings and the porcelain. I'm trying to learn about forestry and the management of five hundred deer, about vermin and sugar beet, but it's all very boring. I do wish I were dead.'

'No, no,' said Rosie in alarm. 'What you say is true, I'm sure. I don't envy you, I promise you. But what you must do is make friends with people who aren't in your pay. That's a problem around here, I admit. Although, if I may say so, you are rather more aware of your station than others are. It's new to you. What you must do is go to London for a week or two. There you could shop and go to the theatre and perhaps even see your London friends again.'

Joyce shook her head fiercely. 'I don't think they want to see me any more. Besides, I won't leave Helmingham. You may think me stupid, but I have the most awful feeling that if I leave, someone will take it away from me. I won't stay anywhere overnight. It's bad luck, you see.'

Rosie did see. Intensely superstitious herself, she could not criticize anyone else for wishing to avoid bad luck. 'Then, they must all visit you here. Why not write to them and invite them all? How many did you say?'

'We used to call ourselves the deadly eight. But I wouldn't know how to entertain staying guests.'

'Friday to Monday, it would be. There's plenty of space. Mrs Crow will see to the food and she and Bert will attend to all the arrangements.'

'I do long to see them. Do you really think they will want to come?'

Rosie was sure they would. Whether Helmingham and its inhabitants would be happy to have Joyce's friends was another matter. Rosie had heard enough about the great Horace Brant to make her determined to stay out of his way.

Joyce cheered up immensely after her little chat. How easy it is for the young, thought Rosie, if someone just wipes their tears away and offers them a treat, they're happy. If only all sorrows could be so easily mended!

March is the month when the rose grower gets busy, the month Rosemary always looked forward to. This year there was more to do than usual, for the bitter weather of February had taken its toll. It was still too early to see which of the roses would die. Every rose had to be trimmed back, beginning with the unruly older varieties of rose. Hybrid teas were the last to be pruned: work for April, not March.

This was her busiest month under glass. She syringed with plain water daily, but only the pots, floors and staging. Later, on bright days, she would spray the foliage as well. She had already fumigated against aphids, and planned to put some pieces of sulphur on the hot pipes as a precaution against mildew.

This first Monday in the month was the day on which Rosie had decided to begin the season, and the fact that a thick fog hugged the cold ground could not put her off. She was in the herb and knot east garden where a formal arrangement of box edging acted as a framework for the flowering plants. Two large beds each contained fifteen plants of Rosa Mundi, a rose which was first recorded in the sixteenth century. The flowers were semi-double, striped almost equally with a blush white and a deep pink. The shrub grew to about four feet and bloomed its heart out each summer for about four weeks. It was certainly a rose deserving of its place at Helmingham, but it had other associations which appealed to a woman of Rosemary's sensitivity.

Rosa Mundi was a sport of the deep pink *Rosa gallica officinalis*, a glorious plant which had undoubtedly been grown by the Greeks and the Romans. It was this link with the distant past, and the fact that the Gallicas were the ancestors of most of the later roses that charmed her. In this of all gardens, Rosa Mundi had to be given a special place.

The east garden presented a lesson in the history of the rose for those who cared to be taught. There were four beds, each edged with Lavender and each planted with certain types of roses. One held only Alba and species roses, another only Gallicas, Damasks and Bourbons. A third was glorious in summer with its nodding heads of Centifolia and Moss roses. Of course there had to be a bed for Chinas, Rugosas and Hybrid Perpetuals. Yes, a lesson in the history of the rose, but Rosemary, when asked, had not attempted to teach Joyce the differences between one type and another, preferring a simpler lesson.

'There are many ways to classify the rose,' she had said shortly after Joyce took up residence at Helmingham, 'but the difference that matters is the one that separates the repeat flowering varieties from those that have just one flush and don't bloom again, except occasionally in the autumn.'

She looked over at the Hall, now romantically

shrouded in heavy fog, and wondered what Joyce would be doing on this gloomy day. Risking Bill's anger, Rosemary had invited her for lunch on the following Sunday, for they had much to discuss. The invitations had been sent to London and eagerly accepted. Suddenly, Joyce had developed the mopes and wondered how she was going to entertain her guests for three days in the country, so far from civilized entertainments.

She stretched her arms, flexed her fingers and looked down at the equipment she had brought with her into the garden. There was work to do, and heavy work at that, but she preferred to struggle alone as she couldn't abide to be hemmed in by an unwilling helper. Bill and his men were in the west garden, working on the long herbaceous beds. Let them talk among themselves, receive their instructions from Bill and dream of dinnertime. She craved the solitude.

The planting of new bushes had to be finished this month, but there were other jobs as well. Today she would embark on one of her favourite chores: the pegging down of some types of rose. The shrub roses were large plants of sprawling habit that could grow to five feet high and deep. They produced some of the most beautiful blooms of all the roses, giving of their best for three or four weeks, then subsiding into a tangled mass of green leaves and murderous thorns. A few produced large, red hips, but mostly their glory was short-lived.

Rosemary thought of them as great ships of the rose world. Most were too large and unruly for the average man's suburban garden, which was why Father concentrated on growing hybrid teas with their well arranged petals and high centred-blooms.

The gardens of Helmingham Hall were the perfect home for the bigger roses, but even in these large beds, the roses needed to be trained and encouraged to give of their best.

There was a curious phenomenon in the rose world. A rose stem nearly four feet long might catch itself on other branches or fall to the ground or reach for the sky, but it would tend to bloom only at its tip. Left to itself over the years, it would decline and produce very few blooms for its size.

However, if one took a few of the long branches, arched them down and tied the tip to a peg in the ground, the stem would bloom all along its length, not just at the tip.

Pegging down, say, a ten-year-old rose was not easy. It was necessary to choose the right stem carefully, to ease it down without causing it to break and to tie it firmly to its newly driven peg. Long whippy rose stems had minds of their own and their thorns could be painful, but when a grand rose ship was properly rigged, it could sail on the June garden, so beautiful and abundant that it typified all that was bright and beautiful in the British garden.

Hard work for the gardener, then, but each year it had to be done all over again. Those branches that had been pegged the previous year had to be pruned hard back and new, lax stems chosen for the coming summer's display. Pegs had to be moved, the spaces between carefully calculated, the pegs driven home hard. Bill resented the time taken to peg down a couple of dozen roses each year, but the work gave Rosie great satisfaction even though it tired her out.

She worked steadily, moving methodically from one bed to another, noticing that the air was still and cold, with no chance of the fog lifting in the afternoon. At a quarter to one she wiped off her secateurs and placed them and the pegging down equipment in the shed, noticing as she did so that Bill made sure all the parts of the gardens under his control were neat and tidy. He was not the warmest of men towards those under him. His method of keeping standards high was to fine the men for the least infringement, but he had their respect for he was a brilliant gardener, one who was always learning his trade. There was no arrogance in Bill where his work was concerned, although he had this fault in abundance away from the gardens. He was a faithful husband and a gentle lover. She must do something to end their stupid quarrel.

Lunchtime passed in almost total silence. She told him that many of the roses had been pegged and that she would be finished by the end of the week. He asked, sarcastically and totally unnecessarily, if she could spare the time, what with her running off to Ipswich at the drop of a hat. Rosie answered him with silence.

Two strong-willed people could maintain a quarrel almost indefinitely, but the child who cleaned in their house was suffering from the poisonous atmosphere. Daisy was only fourteen years old, and her parents never ever exchanged a cross word. Bill, in his present mood, frightened her. She crept around the house and jumped whenever he spoke, which did nothing to improve his disposition.

By half-past three the fog was so thick that the men were taken indoors to work in the houses. Damp gloom settled on the Helmingham estate, separating it from the outside world, and its many buildings from each other.

That evening, Bill and Rosie sat in the warm kitchen at the scrubbed table with the lamp between them. Bill fiddled with the battery wireless, trying to find a clear signal. Rosie, as was her custom, sat with her breeding books, studying the parentage of her new variety, and the parents of its parents, back as far as records would go. Eventually, she closed her eyes, not to sleep but to dream, to conjure up the rose with its small, pale pink petals that would surely establish her as a rose breeder.

Normally, she would have told Bill about her hopes for the four-year-old roses that would come into bloom at Easter in the greenhouse, and in the open during June. But her superstitious nature combined with her resentment to encourage her to keep this news to herself, at least until she was sure she had a winner that wouldn't fade, was reasonably resistant to mildew, on which were abundant blooms with good strong necks. Her little seedling was a triumph, considering that she had a stock of just fifty varieties from which to breed.

She had achieved a near miracle and could hardly wait until their next visit to the Dobson nursery in Harlow. She would tell Father all about the rose, but she wouldn't tell Bill. That would teach him a lesson. When the time came, as was the privilege of the breeder, she would name the rose Felicia, because she had always wanted a girl. If God had blessed their union, and if they had produced a girl, her name would have been Felicia. With her eyes still closed, Rosie squeezed the lids tightly to prevent one single tear from escaping. Bill wouldn't be sympathetic this evening. He'd say something callous if the subject of babies were raised at this time. As usual, she would be silent.

At about half-past nine, they were aware of the unmistakable sound of a motorcycle. It seemed to stop outside the lodge, and Bill and Rosemary got up from the table. A motorcycle was unusual enough in these parts, and the Cooks never had visitors after dark.

When the doorbell rang, Bill said, 'I'll go. You stay here. It might be trouble.'

Unexpected callers invariably meant bad news. Rosemary walked to the fire for comfort and nervously

house. However, she hid her displeasure and said only that she would go straightaway to make up the guest's bed.

'This is very kind of you, Mrs Cook,' said Laurence. 'May I call you Rosemary? Cookie, you've got yourself a treasure.'

Bill gave a hollow laugh. 'That's what I tell myself sometimes.'

Laurence was shown the shed where he put away his motorbike, then directed to the guest room that was at the far end of the hall from Rosie and Bill's room. Even at this distance, however, they felt constrained, unaccustomed to having a house guest.

Bill was already in bed with his back to her when she climbed in and blew out the candle. He didn't speak, not even to say goodnight, and the silence lengthened. Rosie felt strung up, unable to find a comfortable position.

'I've never heard you called Cookie before,' she said at last.

'Everybody had a nickname in the trenches. Silly names, sometimes. It was a way of lightening the tension, I guess.'

'He was a junior officer. You were a serving man. I'm surprised you were so friendly.'

With a sigh of resignation, he rolled onto his back. Two or three inches separated them; she could feel his heat. 'Larry was not quite eighteen when he reported to Captain Cartwright. Not dry behind the ears, scared of the enemy, scared of how he would react under fire. One day a mortar exploded in the trenches. Smokey Salmon was blown to bits. Arms, legs . . . I shouldn't be telling you this. Larry was sort of paralyzed, couldn't move, couldn't take his eyes off what was left. We were under attack. He was a skinny chap at eighteen. I shoved him out of harm's way, and a minute or two later he got his nerve back.'

Bill's voice rose a few notes as he remembered old grievances. 'He was supposed to be a bloody officer! A leader of men! God help us, he was just out of school. They didn't give those young chaps any training, just sent them to the front to learn the ropes, if they weren't killed first. Larry always said I saved his life. I didn't, just kept him from making a bloody fool of himself, but I kind of looked out for him after that. Three months later, just days before the war was over, the captain really did . . . I couldn't wait to get home to Helmingham.

'Larry was in hospital for almost a year as was the captain. They got to know each other pretty well, never friends, you know, but sort of a man-to-man thing, and I think they probably shared a few confidences. I used to see Larry when I went to visit the captain.

'When Larry went home, he didn't get on with his old man, was at a bit of a loose end. We met in London a few times before he went off to university. I think older chaps who had been in the forces found it hard alongside the young ones, but he got his degree. By that time, we were married and I haven't seen him since. Oi! What are you doing?'

'My toes are cold.' In the darkness, she could pretend Bill was someone else, could explore his body, cover him with kisses, all the while thinking of Laurence. She had to touch *somebody*, had to relieve the ache within her. 'Are you still angry with me?'

'Not at this very moment,' he said huskily, and took her into his arms.

It turned out Laurence Ballard knew less about gardening than might any suburban stockbroker. Rosie was worried that his obvious ignorance would undermine Bill's authority. There were half a dozen men living nearby who had begged to be taken on, men with families, men who had lived in the neighbourhood all their lives. Bill had always said that there was no call to have more than four gardeners. There was bound to be talk in the village about Laurence. There would be resentment.

However, the explosion she expected never arrived. After a day or two, Rosie found out how he had handled the delicate situation. Larry Ballard, he told his men, had been in the army with him. The lad had fallen on hard times and needed a bit of work for a month or two. He was not being paid, Bill said, and would soon be gone. To her surprise, they all seemed to understand, all respected the act of kindness to a comrade in arms. If they did not greet Laurence Ballard with great warmth, they at least treated him fairly. As for Laurence, he showed no aptitude for the spade, was ham-fisted in the mending of fences and trellises, and was apt to put a careless foot on some burgeoning plant.

On the Friday morning after his arrival he discovered the yellow-bodied motor car in the coach house and fell on it with cries of glee. 'Crikey! A Rolls-Royce! These beauties will do eighty-five miles an hour, you know.' He touched it lovingly. 'Central gearshift and hand-brake. Six cylinders. It doesn't work, you say?'

'So I've been told,' said Rosie, who managed to be within hailing distance of Laurence most of the day. 'But there was never anyone here who knew about motors, and then Captain Cartwright lost interest. He left it here when he went flying.'

'It will work when I've finished with it.' He lifted the right side of the bonnet. 'Beautiful!' he breathed in the kind of ecstasy he would probably never feel for a woman, 'but someone has removed a few of her vital organs.'

At North Lodge they woke to heavy rain on Sunday morning and shivered on their way to church. One hour and a rambling sermon later, Rosie waved to Miss Joyce, miming that she would see her at one o'clock, then returned to the Lodge, all of them revelling in brilliant sunshine. Although it was damp underfoot, the sun felt warm on her back. The daffodils were still bowed with the weight of rainwater on their petals, but a green mist shrouded the willow trees. Spring would be glorious as always at Helmingham, but this year she would be less able to appreciate it, burdened as she was with a hideous yearning for an unobtainable man.

Today's roast was pork, an enormous joint that had barely fitted into the oven. The apple sauce she had bottled in the autumn was brought up from the cellar. There were to be four vegetables, earlies from beneath Bill's cloches. Rosie was a woman of quick decisions and deft movements. Yet, she had been unable to make up her mind what to serve for pudding, eventually making a bread pudding as well as a jam roly poly.

The dining-room had received special attention from Daisy and Rosemary during the week. The tan tiles on the small fireplace had been given a good going over. The windows had been cleaned and the nets rehung, since Rosie had no intention of being spied on by those passing on the road. Boughs of flowering plum stood stiffly in a brown earthenware vase on the sideboard, and a mixed bowl of roses was snuggling in a silver bowl that had been a wedding present from Uncle Charles and Aunt Edna. The best lace tablecloth covered the table, the cutlery had been polished, and old knives with their yellowing handles had been sharpened as insurance against tough meat. The table groaned with glassware, for Joyce had promised to bring two bottles each of white and red wine. Rosie thought, she's seen Laurence from a distance and wants to impress him.

She chewed her lip as she spooned fat over the roast potatoes. Every woman seemed to react in the same way towards Laurence. The contrast between the two men was cruel on Bill. What had the older man to commend him? Unlike Bill, Laurence Ballard used his table napkin properly, and he pulled out his chair before sitting down. He even waited politely to pull out Rosie's! She blushed every time he did so, but she had quickly come to expect this little courtesy.

On Friday, she and Miss Joyce had made yet another expedition to Ipswich where Rosie casually suggested that she really needed to have her hair cut into a more modern style. Plaits, she said as if she had only just thought of it, were a bore to do each morning. Miss Joyce was immediately enthusiastic for the change and suggested that the hair be marcelled to provide a few soft waves. This would have been more trouble and expense than Rosie could justify, however. She settled for a short bob inexpertly cut and a brutally straight fringe.

Bill had not noticed the change, but Laurence, ever the attentive gentleman, had immediately complimented her on the new style. Inevitably, a row had followed. Once the hairstyle was pointed out to him, Bill declared that it was ugly and made her look like mutton dressed as lamb. Rosie was extremely angry in response to his cutting words since she was not at all sure about the style either.

Her best brown wool skirt and the Fair Isle twinset, a little rouge on her cheeks and a touch on her lips was all the armour she had against a difficult lunch. For her pains Bill, angry and puzzled by his wife's strange moods, accused her of turning his Sunday upside down to impress the mistress of Helmingham Hall.

Tired of quarrelling, she said not to worry for there would be few invitations to dine at the Lodge in future, and went about her business.

Laurence entered the kitchen. 'Anything I can do to help?'

Rosie started to speak but was interrupted by a voice from behind her.

'Anybody home?'

Rosie and Laurence turned together, and together saw that their employer had changed after church into a fine wool frock of pale blue with a long patterned scarf wound around her neck and trailing down her back. She removed her rimless cloche, and her casual bob, brushed off her face and slightly waved, looked perfect.

Rosie said hello, and took the wicker basket with the wine in it, then turned back to the stove as if she could not leave it unattended for a moment.

'Miss d'Avranche,' Laurence said, holding out his hand. 'I am Laurence Ballard. I will be lending Bill a hand, if you don't object.'

'Whatever Bill thinks is best. Welcome to Helmingham. I hope you enjoy working here.'

'Thank you.' He picked up a bottle of wine and studied the label. 'Shall I open these bottles?' He raised his eyebrows. 'Hmm – 1920.'

Laurence wielded the corkscrew effectively without the sort of struggle Bill had. Their young guest was watching him carefully, probably surprised to find a guest of Rosie's who was so at home with a bottle of wine.

The heat of the moment combined with the warmth of the stove to give Rosie a very hot face. But what difference did it all make? she asked herself fiercely. She had Bill. She loved him and would spend the next forty or fifty years with him. Laurence, on the other hand, was a young man who had arrived out of the blue and would one day disappear the same way.

When they went into the dining-room, Laurence seemed to take charge of the seating by holding out a chair for Joyce. Rosie had been planning to sit next to the door to the kitchen, but apparently he wished to see the light fall on Joyce's face. Bill was urged to sit on Joyce's right, while Laurence placed himself opposite her. That left the seat by the fireplace, making it awkward for Rosie to rise between courses. She noticed that Laurence had a way of arranging matters to his own satisfaction. She also noticed that others, herself included, seemed happy to give in to him.

'I have mended your motor, Miss d'Avranche,' he said as Joyce began eating her soup.

'Thank you. What was wrong with it?'

He grinned. 'Some of the parts had wandered away.'

'Well, I'm very glad you have it running. Perhaps if Bill can spare you, you can drive me occasionally.'

'I'd be delighted!' cried Bill. He was being just a trifle too hearty and obliging, Rosie thought. Sometimes she had an overwhelming urge to kick him under the table.

She managed to serve the dinner without mishap, and even developed a taste for the fine red wine Joyce had brought. She drank more of it than she should and knew she would regret it later, and all the while she kept glancing at Bill to see if he were annoyed at the way their guests seemed so intrigued with one another. To her surprise, he was clearly enjoying himself as much as they were, and turned his head from one to the other as they engaged in a debate on the merits of Noel Coward's plays.

'Nothing ever happens in the first act,' said Laurence, 'and in the second there is always a quarrel. He's superficial. One of those smart people. All cocktails and cocaine.'

'That's most unfair,' said Joyce. 'He's witty and amusing. I've read all about him in *Good Housekeeping* magazine, and he's not a bit like you say. I suppose you would prefer a Galsworthy. That's your sort of play. Or Somerset Maugham. Not me. When I go to the theatre, I want to be amused.'

Laurence smiled slightly. 'Not Maugham, but R.C. Sherriff's *Journey's End*. That's my sort of play.'

'Oh, the war,' said Joyce. 'It is too sad. I saw it with my friend, Marsha, but it made me cry.'

Neither Rosie nor Bill had ever heard of Noel Coward, nor of this man Maugham, so why had Bill been so enthralled by the debate?

The answer came to her with a stab of pain. Bill was hoping that Joyce would take Laurence as a husband. Did he suppose his position would be protected then? Miss Joyce's choice of a husband was a matter of concern to them all, of course. A strong but unpleasant husband could affect their lives in a terrible way, for they were at the mercy of the owner of Helmingham. Bill had been so shocked when he heard of the presumed death of Captain Cartwright d'Avranche that she had been unable to get two consecutive words out of him for several hours.

When everyone had finished dessert, she jumped up from the table to wash the dishes. 'All of you go into the parlour. I'll bring in some coffee for you.'

Ignoring these instructions, the younger woman followed her into the kitchen, taking a spare pinny from a hook on the door and slipping it over her beautiful frock. 'You're not going to do all these dishes by yourself, Rosie. I know Daisy won't be back until late this afternoon. Besides, I haven't had a chance to talk to you.'

'What do you think of our lodger?' asked Rosie, pouring hot water from the kettle into the washing-up bowl.

'He looks like Ronald Coleman.'

'Who's he? Some London playwright?'

'An English actor who appears in Hollywood films. Of course, Ronald Coleman is older than Mr Ballard. How long do you think he'll stay?'

Rosie turned her head. 'How long do you want him to stay?'

Miss Joyce laughed, looking younger and prettier than ever. 'He's charming company. I haven't had such a stimulating conversation for absolutely ages.'

'Yes,' said Rosie softly. 'That's what I thought.'

On Monday morning, after Bill had gone to work, Rosie went to the rolltop desk in the parlour and began searching for the letter that had arrived the previous Friday. She had spent a wretched night, had lain awake for hours trying to understand her own emotions. The strange feeling she had for Laurence Ballard was tearing her apart. She couldn't control it, but she felt that if the strain continued for much longer she would go mad. She would, therefore, have to take matters into her own hands.

She found the letter with very little trouble, since Bill was as neat with his paperwork as with everything else he did. How to answer this particular letter had puzzled him, however. He had discussed it with Laurence when they both thought she was out of earshot. In the end, he had simply tucked it away, unable to face the question it posed.

Rosie, on the other hand, had no trouble in shaping a reply. She simply wrote:

Dear Mr Ballard, You have asked if your son has contacted my husband. In fact, he is living here at North Lodge and can be reached at this address. Unfortunately, we do not have a telephone. Yours sincerely, Mrs Rosemary Cook

Surely, once his father had located Laurence, he would drag him off to his home, and the Cook family could settle comfortably into the old routine.

Chapter Five

It had taken an exchange of letters to prevent Aaron Ballard from coming to Helmingham to confront his son, and another exchange to agree that they meet at a teashop in bustling Ipswich where no-one knew either of them.

Laurence had not approached Rosemary Cook about her actions, had not asked her why she wrote to his father. Bill had been furious, but Laurence assumed that she was simply tired of looking after him. He couldn't blame her and said so to Bill. Attempting to convey his gratitude for past hospitality, while obtaining for himself a little privacy in a few rooms over the stable, he had succeeded only in alienating both the Cooks.

He opened the tearoom door and gritted his teeth against the jangle of the overhead bell, looked over the head of the little woman who was trying to seat him, and waved to his father. Aaron Ballard was not a man for discreet corners. He had found a place in the centre of the room, had not one but two timid waitresses attending him, and greeted his son gruffly.

'There you are, Laurence. They have toasted teacakes or you could have a scone, but they look underdone to me. Are you going to have tea like a normal person, or must you indulge your taste for coffee?'

Laurence glanced round the room, found all the other customers engaged in studied inattention and grinned ruefully. This was not going to be a quiet, discreet discussion. He dreaded the day he would have to return to Ipswich for any reason, as he would probably be pointed out as the chap who had quarrelled with his father in Brambles tearoom. As insurance against future ructions, he smiled broadly at each member of staff in passing.

'Good to see you, Father.'

'Hummph.'

'It's been several months now. Is Mother well?'

'As well as can be expected under the circumstances. You might *occasionally* visit your home. She *is* your mother, after all. She *does* love you.'

Laurence sighed, feeling his chest beginning to tighten as it always did when he and Father decided to converse. Several replies were considered and rejected, before he said soothingly. 'I will do that very shortly, I promise you. And Gran?'

'Ha!'

'Is she well?'

'Ha!'

He noticed that the waitress was hovering three paces behind his chair and turned to address her. 'Are you going to take our order?'

'Mind your manners, young man.'

'Father . . .' He looked at the waitress, at her small, hunched frame, her pinched, hungry face, and remembered that in these depressing times East Anglia was particularly hard hit by the low farm prices and general lack of work. 'I will have a cup of your delicious coffee and one of your excellent teacakes, please.'

'No need to be sarcastic. Just give your order like a gentleman. I'll have a pot of tea for one and a scone. But you had better cut it open and toast it, because I'm sure they're all undercooked.'

Laurence gripped his hands together in his lap, wondering how many minutes they could be together before the shouting began. Then, to his dismay, Aaron

Ballard pulled his handkerchief from his pocket, lifted up his spectacles and wiped his eyes. He always felt as if his father was a stranger to him, yet there was no mistaking the relationship between the two. Both were a few inches short of six feet and of slender build. Both wore neat moustaches, but Aaron's was a salt and pepper colour, matching his hair, while Laurence had no grey hairs at all.

'I don't mean to quarrel with you, boy. Forgive me.'

As this was a new departure from old ways, Laurence was alarmed. Was Father terminally ill? Had some new disaster befallen the Ballard family? He snaked a hand across the cloth as if to pat his father's arm, but recollected himself in time. The Ballards were an undemonstrative family.

'A man,' began his father softly, 'is not supposed to feel affection for his mother-in-law.'

'But she's a grand old lady.'

'The best. Eighty-two. But she is desperately ill. You must visit her today. She hasn't much longer.'

'But—' began Laurence.

'Dammit, boy! That's the least you can do. She loves you! She's leaving you her estate. Hadleigh's not all that far from Helmingham. Even closer to Ipswich.'

Helmingham Hall was about six miles north of Ipswich and approximately the same distance to the east of Stowmarket. 'Hadleigh is a few miles due west of Ipswich, say seven miles from Helmingham,' he said. 'I will go to her later this afternoon or early evening.'

'Won't that wretched gardener even allow you the day off? What are you thinking of to work for such a man?'

'I need somewhere to work while I get my thoughts together. After I leave here I must collect—'

'It's Helmingham, isn't it? Crumbs from my lord's table. That's it, isn't it? I hear a young woman has inherited. What do you think those people can do for you? Chasing after . . .'

'One toasted teacake,' said the waitress, setting the plate before Laurence. 'One well-toasted scone. One tea, one coffee.' She departed smartly, and the men settled to preparing their food.

Laurence stirred two sugar cubes into his coffee and cut the teacake into manageable portions. The teashop was full, its customers mostly well-dressed women who could afford to spend a shilling on an unnecessary meal. The contented buzz of their conversation irritated him. But then, on this cold, windy spring day every sound tore at his nerves. The surprising thing was, he loved his father deeply, but he hated the feeling that he was seated across the table from a powder keg with a fuse lit. One never knew with Father . . .

Aaron Ballard lifted the lid of the teapot and stirred vigorously. 'What's she like?'

'Miss d'Avranche? Young, pretty, fraught. I think she's deeply unhappy, or perhaps she has a guilty secret. I can't get close enough to her to find out which.'

'That's it! I knew it! What do you want to get close to her for?'

'I just meant . . . Drink your tea, Father. I will not quarrel with you.'

The older man tasted his tea, winced, added more milk and another sugar cube. 'Does Helmingham have electricity laid on?'

Laurence smiled. His father had a lucrative business in Halstead, across the county line into Essex. Electrical turbines were his passion, as well as the source of his early income. 'There is no electricity at Helmingham. We live by candlelight.'

'That big place? Humph! The Ballards have had electricity since 1900. As for Chatsworth . . .'

Laurence took a sip of his coffee, safe for the moment

in Father's reminiscences. As a boy of eleven, Aaron Ballard had been apprenticed to the firm of Gilbert Gilkes and Gordon, makers of turbines. When in 1893, the Duke of Devonshire had three turbines installed to provide electricity for the great estate of Chatsworth, Aaron had been permitted to make one visit. His part in lighting up Chatsworth had been minimal, but the effect it had on him was far-reaching, for it provided his inspiration for a life making electricity, and eventually for a profitable business making the switches that turned on the power.

'You could do something for the industry,' said Father. 'You could suggest to that young woman that she should install turbines—'

'There's no water power. It's flat land. And I hardly think generators would make all that much difference. Anyway, no-one seems inclined to go to the expense. They are happy as they are.'

His father lifted half a scone to his mouth, and a small dribble of melted butter slithered onto his tie. 'They're as backward as fuzzie-wuzzies in Norfolk and Suffolk. Look at this tearoom. Gas lamps! Haven't joined the twentieth century. No gumption.' Unaware of the damage already done to his tie, Aaron picked up his napkin and tucked it under his chin before tackling the second half of the scone. 'I suppose you never will join the firm now. Not with your grandmother's estate to let you play the gentleman. Or isn't a hundred and fifty acres good enough for you now that you've sized up Helmingham?'

It turned out that Laurence was the powder keg with the lit fuse. 'I'm sorry I'm the only one of your sons to survive the war, Father. Believe me, I've wished myself dead often enough. I've prayed . . . No, I am not going to take over the business. You have three sons-in-law, all of them employed in the business, all of them ready to lay down their lives for you. Please leave me a modicum of peace.'

He spoke softly, but felt that every woman in the tearoom had heard his outburst. His father registered shock at first, then tears fogged his eyes. He tore off his wire framed spectacles and tossed them blindly onto the table, while reaching with his other hand for his handkerchief.

Laurence felt his face burning, and blinked away a few tears of his own, ashamed of his loss of control, yet curiously relieved to have said the words that had been eating into him for ten years.

'I've never wished you dead, boy. I love you. But you're precious to me and I would like to have you near. Just don't go chasing after some rich woman who wouldn't look at you twice. That's all I ask.'

They parted outside the tearoom, shaking hands solemnly, then suddenly embracing, patting one another on the back. It was over in seconds; their eyes didn't meet again.

Laurence turned and walked briskly back to the Westerfield train station where he had left the old-fashioned brake that had been uncovered in one of the barns. He had spent the morning cleaning it up, and should have spent half an hour getting to know the vagaries of a horse that did not wish to pull this old monster.

The party from London arrived promptly on the four o'clock train; three women and four men dressed in town clothes and acting as if they were on safari in lion territory. He approached them humbly and touched his cap. The party for Helmingham? This way, please.

Some blankets had been unearthed to cover their legs, but these smelled of damp and horse. There was much giggling among these seven young people, many jokes at the expense of passing strangers. They seemed to think that country people were incapable of understanding London English and that their driver was too stupid to take offence. It was the first amusing thing that had happened to Laurence all day.

Nothing stilled their smart chatter and complaints about the cold until he swung the brake between the two lodges and started the third of a mile drive towards Helmingham. It was growing dark on a day that had not seen much sun, the oak trees were still innocent of new leaves and the deer seemed content for once to stay away from the drive. Yet, the ancient house looked magnificent and intimidating as it loomed on the horizon, its spires pointing heavenward, its pennant flying in the chilling breeze. The women forgot to complain about the long drive from Ipswich in an open carriage. The men forgot to sneer.

'Bloody hell!' said one of the men. 'Our Joyce is going to be absolutely unbearable!'

Laurence succeeded in getting the brake across the moat and pulled to a stop before the door. Mr Crow opened the door and greeted them kindly, giving them a lesson in dignity and good manners. Laurence unloaded the baggage, tarried only long enough to see Joyce d'Avranche welcome her guests with a mixture of shyness and naïve pride. The last man to leave the brake gave him twopence.

Bill was waiting for him in front of the stables. 'Bill, old chap, my grandmother is dying. I must go tonight to see her.'

'Where's that?'

'Hadleigh.'

'S'truth man! Your motorbike is still in the shed.'

'Let me drive the Rolls. All I need is a gallon of petrol. I think I know where there is a can.'

'So do I, but will one gallon get you there and back?'

'Twenty-two miles to the gallon. I should be able to

do it, but don't expect me home until late. In order not to disturb you, I'll sleep in one of the empty stalls. It won't hurt me for one night. Alternatively, I may sleep at my grandmother's house and come back here at five o'clock or half past. Is that all right?'

'It's not my motor. We'll have to think up some story why you've taken it without Miss d'Avranche's permission. Besides, she might want to take her guests for a drive.'

'Not enough room for them all, thank God.'

From the moment she stepped out the door to greet her guests, Joyce knew the weekend was not going to be a success. There was the new gardener, Laurence Ballard, pretending to be humble but actually sneering at her guests. She would have been angry with him for his superior attitude, except that Horace Brant was making every effort to reinforce Laurence's prejudices about city types.

'Joyce, darling!' cried Marsha and pushed forward to give her an over-zealous hug. Joyce could feel her jaw slipping painfully to the left as Marsha planted a forceful kiss on her right cheek.

Over Marsha's shoulder, she saw the Brants looking around the courtyard with expressions of amazement. Bunny and Freddie Bishop were conferring quietly, while the lovers, Thelma and George, looked embarrassed and ill at ease.

Joyce could do no better than to follow Mr Crow's lead, and greet her guests with distant civility. She ushered them into the hall, accepted the gift of a bottle of gin which was accompanied by Horace's words: 'You will hardly need anything so humble as a bottle of gin in this place, but we couldn't afford anything else.'

'Thank you, Horace,' she said, and handed the bottle to Mr Crow.

'Does every grand house have a stag's head with hats on it?' asked Wilfred.

'I don't know.'

'What?' laughed Horace. 'Have you not been to any of the other grand houses in the area? Don't they fancy rubbing shoulders with a former typist?'

'Horace, you are dreadful,' said Marsha severely. 'Joyce, it is all beautiful. We do really feel terribly pleased for you.'

Mrs Crow appeared and offered to show the guests to their rooms. Thelma Goodison, svelte in a low-buttoned fur coat, hung back to whisper to Joyce. 'Have George and I got a room together?'

'Yes. Is that all right?'

Thelma giggled. 'Of course. I'll bet Mrs Crow was shocked.' With her T-bar shoes clattering on the bare wood, she tip-tapped up the stairs to join the others.

Joyce wrung her shaking hands. It was a mistake. The presence of her old friends at Helmingham pointed up the enormity of her change of fortune. They belonged to the old life, the skin she had sloughed off.

It took them twenty minutes to settle into their rooms. Eventually, she led them into the drawing-room with its Jacobean strapwork ceiling, its carved stone fireplace and oak panelled walls. A basket of logs stood by the blazing fire and, since it was a dark day, five lamps had been lit. Azaleas bloomed in a large pot by the fire. On the round table by the windows, a basket held a single spray of pale mauve orchids above a mass of strappy leaves. Huge brass candlesticks flanked the painting of an Elizabethan d'Avranche above the mantel. The chairs were arranged in a loose circle around the fire, their assorted fabrics each containing a warm red.

Mrs Able had sent in a most impressive afternoon tea which was laid out on the trolley. Joyce's guests entered the room, paused, gaped and then began to speak in whispers.

'It's beautiful,' said Bunny, a plump young woman with jet black hair and an almost imperceptible moustache. She looked across the room at her husband, Freddie, who was examining a Chinese pot. 'After this weekend, Freddie will never be satisfied with what we can afford.'

'Is that a *Holbein*?' asked Marsha, pointing to the painting above the fireplace.

'Yes. I must show you the John Constable. I had never heard of him, but I expect you have, Marsha. But first, won't you have some tea?'

These first few minutes set the tone for the rest of the day. They dined in the family dining-room, seated cosily around the small table, but although they directed questions at Joyce (largely about her possessions) they conversed with each other. Mr Crow had chosen the wines with care and kept all glasses topped up, so that no-one knew how much drink was actually being consumed.

The meal passed relatively smoothly. Bunny was not at all sure she wished to eat venison. Thelma insisted it was lamb. Horace told Joyce she should insist on tasting each wine before it was served, because that was the way it was done in all the best restaurants.

They had just been served the cheese course, and Mr Crow had retired to the kitchen, when the alcohol seemed to enter their bloodstreams all at the same time. The conversation became louder, the jokes crueller, and then Horace had a happy idea.

Taking a pat of ice-cold butter from the dish, he placed it on the napkin in his lap, then pulled the two sides taut. The butter trampolined upwards and stuck to the ceiling. Joyce stared at the pat in disbelief, but everyone else laughed delightedly. Soon all the butter was stuck to the ceiling, except the small amount on Joyce's plate.

'How could you?' cried Joyce. 'I wouldn't do such a thing in your home.'

'No, my dear,' purred Horace, 'but then we wouldn't have a houseful of servants to clean up the mess.' At that moment, the butter pats began to fall again, some on the diners, most on the table and the carpet. Joyce had no choice but to ring for Mr Crow and confess what her guests had been up to. Tears stood in her eyes as she spoke, but his cool demeanour and calm assurances made her want to kiss him.

They retired to the drawing-room where two bridge tables had been set up, but the men insisted on playing pontoon, as they consumed another half a bottle of brandy. Wilfred urged Joyce to wager one of her paintings, but she alone was quite sober, and spent the evening wearing such a tight fixed smile that her face ached.

It was half-past twelve and Marsha's head was throbbing. She had spent the most hideous seven hours of her life and fervently wished herself at home. This guest bedroom was near to Joyce's, but she had seen that it was much smaller. A double tester bed stood against a pale green wall opposite the small fireplace. A few logs had burned down to a powdery ash, while the ones more recently placed on the embers had not yet caught. The room was cold, and she longed for an electric fire.

Her thoughts were in a whirl. Helmingham was large and impressive, filled with the sort of treasures she had been studying in museums. She thought she would have killed for just one Holbein or Van Dyck, but could put her hand on her heart and say that in all honesty she would not want the responsibility of the estate, nor the isolation, nor the loneliness.

After tea that afternoon, they had all retired to their rooms. Bunny and Thelma had wanted to join Marsha for a chat, but she begged off on the grounds of tiredness. When she was sure they had returned to their part of the house, she had tiptoed across the hall to Joyce's bedroom for the sort of cosy gossip they used to enjoy.

Except that on this occasion, Marsha couldn't forget the difference in their circumstances. 'Oh, this is a lovely bedroom. I guess it's about the size of my flat. Is that Meissen china in the cupboards?'

There were matching built-in cupboards on either side of the fireplace, their doors left standing permanently open. The walls of the room were green, but the interiors of the cupboards were cream, providing an effective background for a selection of porcelain. Marsha remembered that the same simple device was used in the family dining-room with charming results.

Joyce picked up a cup and looked on the bottom, then showed it to Marsha. 'I can't tell. Can you?'

'Hmmm,' said Marsha. 'Crossed swords with a star between the hilts. I don't know exactly what the star means, but crossed swords are the mark of Meissen. It's beautiful. Don't you love it?' The cup had straight sides, a gold rim around the lip and a bouquet of flowers painted on the side. She ran her thumb over the decoration, thrilled to have something so beautiful in her hands. 'I'm ignorant about porcelain, but I know a little about paintings. I know a Holbein when I see one. You say the gardener's wife likes the Stuart child? Well, I don't like Van Dycks as much as Holbeins. I couldn't say why, but seeing one gives me a funny feeling in my stomach. Gee, Joyce, you are lucky.'

'I know.'

They sat in the pretty chintz chairs in front of Joyce's fire and were silent for a moment. 'But you never did care for works of art, did you, honey?'

Joyce's eyes narrowed. 'What are you saying? Maybe you think I shouldn't have nice things because I don't appreciate them.'

That was exactly what Marsha thought, although she denied it. 'I didn't mean that, but now you mention it—'

'Perhaps you think I should give them to you. Is that what you want? A painting or two?'

'What a thing to say, Joyce! What's gotten in to you?' But a seed of doubt had been sown. Marsha wondered if she had been hoping for *something* from this great treasure house. 'Of course I don't want anything of yours. I never took you out week after week and bought you things and paid more than half the bills, because I thought you might one day be filthy rich and able to give me a Holbein in return.'

Joyce pressed her hands to her flushed cheeks. 'All right, my dear friend, I will write you a cheque. Or—well, I can't write a cheque just yet, because I have no money. Nothing is really mine until Captain Cartwright d'Avranche is declared dead in two years' time.'

'You are a cat, Joyce. Boy, have you changed. You used to be a sweet, gentle person. I didn't want—'

'And I can't give you anything because nothing is mine to dispose of. I will, though, I promise you. As soon as these things are truly mine. I am well aware of the debt I owe you. I just didn't think you had been keeping accounts.'

'I wasn't! What would I do with a great painting? I couldn't hang it in my little flat. I probably couldn't afford the insurance. You say none of this is yours? You could lose it all if the great man turns up alive?'

'Try not to gloat, dear. You Americans are so materialistic. You do come out with some things, I must say.'

Marsha stood up. It was difficult to be both dignified

and angry while sitting down. 'My countrymen are not materialistic, and I cannot imagine what I've said to prompt your comment.'

'Dishwater blonde,' said Joyce.

'That was months ago! Anyway, I never called you a dishwater blonde! I only said that my friends and I used to call people with your colour hair dishwater blondes. I thought you had forgotten about it. What difference does it make now? You've let your wealth go to your head, haven't you? All I came in here to say was that when you get your hands on the money and the paintings, you should sell one and buy yourself a nice flat in London and move back to civilization. But I see I was wrong. You like living in a backwater, lording it over the peasants.'

Marsha put on her dressing-gown over her nightie and sat down by the fire. It was the afternoon's quarrel that led directly to her taking part in the butter episode, but she knew she had acted disgracefully. Mom and Dad would be horrified if they ever found she had helped to make grease spots on someone's ceiling.

It was true that people did crazy things these days. Women smoked in public and shortened their skirts. Young men sat on flagpoles, and people discussed the most amazing things in plays. But there were limits. Of them all, Marsha knew herself to be the only one with a proper aesthetic sense. She should cherish this house, not help to deface it.

She couldn't help wondering, however, if a person should be allowed to inherit beautiful things if they didn't appreciate them. Was that right? Was that justice? Her envy gnawed at her insides, making sleep unlikely. She closed her eyes and remembered the rooms she had seen. Now, what would she like Joyce to give her when the time came?

There was a noise outside the door, a giggle that belonged to Bunny, a waspish hiss that was unmistakably Horace. She got up to open the door and six people, some of them shrouded in eiderdowns, fell into her room with cries that they were cold.

'Ooh, you are lucky,' said Bunny, shouldering her way to the fireplace. 'Freddie and I have the coldest room in the house. Do you want to change?'

Marsha pulled the small settee from the foot of the bed over towards the fire. 'Certainly not. You two have each other. I'm on my own.'

'Let's all get into Marsha's bed,' said Wilfred. He put his hands together as if about to dive in. Horace showed everyone the neat leather case that held a silver flask and four small silver cups.

'Here you are chaps, something to keep the cold out.'

Marsha eyed him with loathing. 'You behaved very badly tonight, Horace Brant.'

'A little tomfoolery, that's all. You act as if I had committed a major crime. The butler deserves to be kept on his toes. What a dinner! Did you notice how he just came to each of us with a dish and waited for us to serve ourselves? If he had ever dined at a good restaurant in town he would have known better. And the food was very plain, wasn't it?'

'You're not exactly the perfect guest, Horace.' Thelma Goodison was sitting on the floor by the fire with her eiderdown drawn up to her neck.

As a clerk in an insurance company, she earned thirty shillings a week with which to support herself. There was no question of George living with her and sharing expenses. He had a wife somewhere who wouldn't divorce him. Her visit to Helmingham was reminding her of how much she was losing out by clinging to George. For the first time since their affair began, she felt a twinge of anger. It was all right for some people.

They had homes to go to if they wished. And she had heard that George's wife had a bit of money of her own.

Thelma poked the fire and a shower of sparks rose up the chimney, except for the one that landed on her eiderdown. Before anyone knew what was happening, the spark had burned a large hole in the down-filled cover, and if it hadn't been for George's quick thinking, might have set fire to the room.

'Roll on Monday morning,' said Marsha when all the excitement was over. 'I don't know about the rest of you, but I'm dog tired. I'm going to bed. You can all sleep on the floor or go back to your own rooms.'

Daringly, she slipped off her dressing-gown and crawled between the covers. Bunny announced her intention of doing the same. She turned back the sheets on the other side and with a small leap, joined Marsha. The springs had not known so much activity in years and promptly sagged nearly to the floor. Amid shouts of ribald laughter, the men pushed a pouffe on casters over to Marsha's side and, once she had got out of bed, slid it under the springs to give the bed some support.

Bunny said her back was probably broken, and got out of the bed.

Marsha said putting the pouffe under the mattress was hardly ideal, but she assured them she could get some sleep if only they would return to their own rooms. The fun was over, the joke had gone stale, and the party returned to their rooms, warning each other in loud whispers to be quiet as they walked down the corridor.

Eventually, all was quiet. Marsha turned down the lamp, strangely pleased that Joyce hadn't a decent guest bed, and went to sleep.

Joyce could not hear a word that was spoken in the bedroom next to her own. The old walls made eavesdropping impossible. Yet, Bunny's high-pitched giggle pierced the Tudor bricks and stabbed her heart. She knew that they were all in Marsha's room, and she knew also that they were talking about her. She reached down under the covers and dragged Betsy close. The tight embrace made Betsy whine, but she lay still, knowing what was required of her.

They came down to breakfast in a pack at half-past nine, and didn't hesitate to register their amazement when Joyce told them they were to have a ride in the Rolls Royce to the lodge where they would all have breakfast with the gardener's wife. Marsha asked why, but all Joyce could say was that it would be the start of a few surprises.

There were too many of them to fit properly into the motor car, so they piled in any way they could, with some of the women sitting on the men's laps, others standing on the running board. Laurence drove them to Rosemary's kitchen, where she and Daisy greeted them warmly. The big kitchen table had been laid with a checkered cloth. A whole Suffolk ham lay on a white ceramic stand. Yellow roses spewed from a blue jug and the smell of strong coffee fought a losing battle with the bacon sizzling on the grill. In spite of themselves, the guests were charmed.

'Welcome to the North Lodge,' said Rosemary. 'I await your orders. How will you have your eggs this morning? Scrambled, fried or omelette?'

While the others were thinking, Horace placed his order. 'I'll have a three-egg omelette. But, please, may I have one of the eggs to take home?'

Rosemary felt her cheeks go hot as the little party sniggered. Joyce looked desperate, but Rosemary would not answer the unspoken plea in her eyes. 'Of course, sir. Here you are.'

Grinning broadly, Horace held out his hand. Rosemary dug her thumbnail into the shell and one-handedly cracked the egg open. It slithered onto his palm, the yoke cradled there as the slimy white dripped between his fingers onto the quarry tiles.

Marsha's nervous giggle did little to hide her embarrassment. The others gaped, then burst into loud aggressive laughter, the moment made all the more enjoyable by Horace's stunned expression and Joyce's dismay.

'Your reputation has gone before you, sir,' said Rosemary quietly. She scooped the egg from his hand with a large spoon, then guided him to the pump where icy water splashed onto his hand. 'We wouldn't want you to think that we are as unsophisticated as those waitresses at the Corner House. Now then. Who's next? I promise all the eggs will be cooked from now on.'

Breakfast at the lodge turned out to be a very jolly affair. Horace recovered his sense of humour and even shook Rosemary's hand on the way out.

On the drive, awaiting their pleasure, were seven dogcarts hitched to donkeys. In each, was an estate worker. Joyce announced that they were all to have a chance to drive a donkey and cart along the quiet lanes of Suffolk, and that they would meet at the stables in one hour. There were cries of delight, and Joyce waved them off from the running board of the Rolls, as Laurence Ballard was in attendance to drive her back to the Hall.

'They are all city people,' she explained as Laurence drove swiftly up the drive. 'It has been difficult to find suitable entertainment for them.'

'Yes, ma'am.'

'I think sending them for a ride in the dog carts was a good idea, don't you? I know it takes several of the estate workers away from their duties, but it's hard to think of something to entertain city people.'

'Yes, ma'am.'

They crossed the moat and he pulled up before the door in the courtyard. 'Why did you come to Helmingham?'

'As you probably know, Bill and I were in the war together. My two older brothers were killed before I was old enough to join up. I feel that my father lost the wrong sons. I need a little time . . . we don't get along.'

'How very sad. What does your father do for a living?'

Laurence didn't answer immediately. 'He's an electrician. Very clever man.'

Joyce allowed him to open the door for her and stepped out carefully. 'You may stay at Helmingham as long as you like, but, really, you're wasted here. You ought to think of taking up a trade.'

He grinned, as if at some joke she didn't understand. 'Yes, ma'am. Shall I fetch you in an hour?'

'No thank you. I am no longer a city person, and I can perfectly well walk to the stables.'

By the time Joyce met her guests again, they had cheered up immensely. They went for a long walk in search of bluebells, then rode out in the brake for a lunch in the private room of a local inn, followed by a drive through some of the most beautiful villages in Britain. Afternoon tea was quickly over as everyone wanted a chance of a nap before dressing for dinner in the formal dining-room.

Marsha was stunning in a chiffon gown of palest pink with a handkerchief hem, but she soon returned to her room for a cardigan and thereafter looked eccentric but comfortable. The party was by now more accustomed to Joyce's grand property and so less intimidated by the chairs with four foot high backs, or the chimney, the mantel of which was over their heads. Seventeenth-century cabinets, displays of pikes and halberds, even the gloves of Queen Elizabeth failed to reduce them to the hushed reverence they had displayed the night before.

So unruly were they during supper that Joyce was afraid they would be rude to the only entertainers she could find in the neighbourhood: four Morris dancers who took their dancing very seriously. However, their performance met with general approval and brought requests for three encores. Later, the gramophone was wound up and everyone danced.

That night there was a frost, and the next morning was grim and very uninviting. Dense fog cloaked the park and gardens, marooning Helmingham in space. The party declared themselves too tired to attend church, but when Joyce returned after a long hour listening to the vicar, she was met by the small party dressed in hats and coats and with their cases standing next to them.

'Joyce, dear, I thought you knew we had to return to London today,' Marsha said rather aggressively. 'Some of us are working people, you know. Freddie must be back at Harrods. The shoe department can't do without him, and he did take off Friday afternoon, saying he was ill. And the insurance company wouldn't let Thelma and George have an extra day off. They had to pretend they were ill, too.'

'And I suppose your father insists on your presence at the store, does he?' asked Joyce sarcastically of the Brant brothers. She was sure they had all said they could stay until Monday morning, had made plans for their entertainment for the rest of the day. Mr and Mrs Crow and Mrs Able had lost their Sunday half day, for no reason as it turned out.

Her stubborn expression prompted Marsha to take

her by the arm and walk with her into the drawing-room. 'Now, listen, my old friend. We have had a simply marvellous time. We do thank you, but we've been with you long enough. Don't be cross. I shall come for a much longer visit, if you will invite me.'

'Of course. You are not all going because you're bored, are you, or because I have offended anyone?'

Marsha laughed. 'You know, at first I thought you had changed. But you haven't. You are the same dear sensitive Joyce that I've always known.' She smiled, making an enormous effort to regain the lost intimacy of the old days. 'I hope you won't take this the wrong way, but I must give you a word of advice, because my family has always had servants, and you haven't. That gardener's wife needs a severe talking to. She shouldn't have treated Horace the way she did. If you don't keep a tight grip on them, they will all take advantage of you. Besides, it's not dignified to be on such friendly terms with just one of your staff. Think how it looks.'

Joyce breathed in deeply, annoyed to have her own doubts so neatly put into words. 'She shouldn't have done it. She should have let Horace patronize her. She also forgot to curtsey. But I'll have you know, Marsha Grissom, that Rosemary is the daughter of a very wealthy and successful nurseryman. He's probably the greatest rose grower in the country. I wouldn't be surprised if her father isn't wealthier than yours. So I don't really think Horace should have been so smart with her. The wonderful thing about living in the country is that we all mix together much more than you do in town.'

'And the poor come to the back door with their begging bowls. I pretended not to see that. Aren't we the lady of the manor? I don't know about your gardener's wife. It's different in America.' Joyce recognized this last remark as the one always brought out when Marsha was unsure about something. It was a statement with which no-one could argue, the perfect silencer.

'I'm sure it is,' she said coolly. 'Trust me to know how to go on here. I tried very hard to entertain all of you. For my pains, you've stained my dining-room ceiling, attempted to embarrass my gardener's wife and now you are all leaving early. It's all over. You will none of you ever set foot here again, and I shall never, never come to London.'

They stood glaring at one another for several seconds, each regretting the depths to which their friendship had sunk. Marsha made the first attempt to retrieve the old relationship. 'You've been holding out on me, dear. You didn't tell me your chauffeur looks like Ronald Colman.'

Joyce recognized the teasing tone, the reference to Ronald Colman as an invitation from Marsha to recover the old closeness, her way of saying that she wanted their friendship to remain unchanged in spite of a few wounding words on both sides. But Joyce was too hurt by the behaviour of those she had believed she could trust, and her punishment was to deny Marsha this moment of intimacy. 'Ronald Colman! Who? Laurence Ballard? I must say I've never noticed it. Goodbye, Marsha. I hope you all have a very pleasant journey home.'

Chapter Six

Joyce had not enjoyed entertaining seven people in her home. The days had been anxious as she tried to please and tried to keep these young city dwellers entertained every moment. She was therefore hoping for a quiet period during which she could attempt to come to terms with her change of fortune. In the past, she had been very hard working, very organized, and inclined to accept whatever conditions life imposed on her. It seemed churlish to feel discontented now, yet sleep eluded her and sometimes as she was preparing for bed she realized that she had done nothing at all during the entire day. She was not to have the privacy she craved, however.

Rupert d'Avranche arrived on Wednesday at noon, having the previous day sent a telegram announcing his intended visit. He was not much older than herself, but immensely more confident. Of middling height, he had the regular features of many of the d'Avranches, wide blue eyes and a ready smile. His well-worn Norfolk jacket and comfortable but highly-polished brown shoes were in amusing contrast to Wilfred and Horace Brant's idea of country wear. He was at ease from the moment he crossed the threshold and effortlessly charmed Joyce with his first words.

'Well, cousin . . . Shall I call you cousin?' asked Rupert, handing her a bouquet of hothouse roses. 'Coals to Newcastle, I'm afraid, but I don't know you, so I could not think of a more acceptable gift.'

'Liquorice allsorts,' she said promptly, and he

laughed, promising to bring her pounds of allsorts the next time he came to Helmingham. This opening exchange set the tone for his three-day visit.

Rupert was twenty-five, only grandson of the youngest brother of Lord d'Avranche. He was 'something in the City', which he said he hated, and lived in London with his mother. He was not rude to the servants, spoke pleasantly to Rosemary and Bill when he chanced to meet them in the garden, exchanged views on forestry management with Mr Trimble and paid the cook extravagant compliments.

He had another sterling quality, for never once did he suggest that Joyce had no right to Helmingham, although he would one day be free to call himself Lord d'Avranche, and might have wished to have this fine house to support his title. He treated her as an equal, as a woman he found attractive and with whom he was at ease.

They dined that first night in the family dining-room, seated across from each other and conversing by candlelight. Joyce had banned lamps in favour of the softer light of candles and was pleased with the effect. A low bowl of fragrant pink roses almost overpowered the aroma of the dinner, but Rupert exclaimed with pleasure when Mr Crow offered him humble meatloaf.

'Dear Mrs Able! I shall have to give her a kiss. Do you mind if I give myself a very large helping, Joyce? I do adore meatloaf.'

'The entire household seems intent on pleasing you. Mrs Crow says she made up the rose bedroom for you because the bed is so awful in the main guest room. I wish someone had told me before I put my very best friend in it. You must have come here often when you were growing up and you must have behaved yourself.'

'Not always, I'm afraid. I was a tiresome little boy.' He smiled, looking off into the distance as he remembered. 'My father came for the shooting which my mother hated. In the evening the men were bad tempered and sleepy. A day's shooting with the sound of gunshot next to one's ear can give one a devilish headache, you know. When I was old enough, I went out with the men, but I'm a poor shot and prefer fishing. Then in the summer right up until last year, my uncle used to hold a family party. I'm surprised you were never invited. Your existence came as a terrible shock to me, I assure you. Uncle Oswald never mentioned you, so naturally, I thought—'

'Poor Rupert. That was unfair.'

'Strange, because you were his heir after Cartwright. I'm sure Cartwright must have known. How could he not? He was a strange chap, not one for idle chitchat. And after he and my uncle fell out, I scarcely saw him. He didn't come to the summer parties, you know. He was always off risking his neck somewhere.'

'There is a photograph of him on the desk in the study. He looks very handsome and forbidding.'

'He never seemed to care about Helmingham. I used to love those summer parties. However, I suggest you not revive them, at least not until you are confirmed as the heir. You will not be surprised to hear that there is much resentment.' He sipped his wine slowly, as if to indicate that this unpleasant subject would not be mentioned again. 'The garden always looked magnificent in early July. For all its formal parterres and clipped hedges, for all the beauty of the herbaceous border and the splendid vegetable garden, this is essentially a rose garden. She would not care to hear me say it, but it was a great rose garden even before Mrs Cook arrived in our midst. Uncle Oswald was not a pleasant man, but he was fond of your mother at one time.' He looked at her carefully, apparently hoping for a strong reaction to mention of her mother. 'I believe there was some antagonism towards her on the estate.'

'Pity that he let her starve after my father deserted us,' she replied tartly. 'Lord d'Avranche had a strange way of showing his regard.'

'Well, you know, they quarrelled after your mother married Nicholas. I don't remember him, of course.'

'I've never even seen a photograph of him. Isn't that sad?'

'Er, yes, I suppose it is. Poor Joyce. Crow! What have you brought us for dessert? Not my favourite Boodles Fool! Dear Mrs Able.'

As his visit was drawing to a close, Joyce felt herself strongly attracted to Rupert. He had told her many amusing stories about his eccentric mother and his six older sisters. 'Mama persevered in the boudoir until I was conceived, after which Father was barred from the bed,' he told her, going on to describe his favourite sister's appalling husband and her three naughty children. He was an amusing raconteur, and if she was inclined to take his outrageous stories with a pinch of salt, she was nevertheless entertained.

It was a pity that Rupert was the grandson of the wrong brother, a stroke of fate he didn't really deserve. She thought she might do him a favour and marry him and so live comfortably at Helmingham, raising little d'Avranches and making new friends, because Rupert would know how to get to know people. She was sure she would never be lonely if she married Rupert. He probably knew the occupants of every great house in the neighbourhood and wouldn't allow anyone to patronize her.

Rupert said he was going to Yorkshire for the weekend and so took his leave of Joyce on Friday morning. The Rolls was waiting in the courtyard with Laurence in the driver's seat to take him to Ipswich train station. Rupert met Joyce in the upstairs hallway. 'Dear Joyce, I hated to mention it earlier. Unpleasant subject, you know. Rather delicate. But you see, my dear, Uncle Oswald promised me some trinkets. I understand that I am not going to get the Hall. Dear me no. That can never be mine, but a few trinkets, you know, when the will is proved.'

'Oh, Rupert, I'm so glad he didn't forget you. I hope he left you something very beautiful. I suppose Mr Finch has it all down in the will.'

'Well, I believe it says something about "a few small objects as marked by me," meaning Uncle Oswald. There are little slips of paper stuck on the bottom of the *objets* he wished me to have. Shall I show you?'

Joyce was eager to learn what his lordship had left, so they went downstairs to the drawing-room where Joyce held her breath as he headed towards the paintings on the far wall. Rosemary would be sorry if the Stuart Child were to leave Helmingham.

Rupert lifted a small Holbein from the wall, looked fondly at the stiff painting of a Tudor woman, then held it up so that she could see the label stuck to the back of the painting.

'It's lovely, Rupert, and I am happy that it will be going to a good home. I'll have to find something else to put in its place.'

'And this small silver casket.' He picked it up, rubbing his thumbs over it with pleasure. 'See the label?'

'You shall have it the minute the will is proved.'

'Bless you, my *favourite* cousin.' He moved across to another painting. 'And this portrait of a boy with a dog, dated 1617. It's by a minor artist, but I always liked it. George Geldorp.'

'It's very large, Rupert. Don't take it off the wall. I believe you.'

'I'm afraid the bracket clock is mine.'

'It doesn't work, Cousin. It never tells the correct time. It's very fussy. All those fiddly brass bits and a brass Minerva on top. You are most welcome to it. We have too many erratic clocks. I don't know the correct time in six rooms!'

He smiled at her as he approached the large round library table that stood close to the window. 'Finally, just these two miniature silver soup tureens and covers. Nineteenth century, only, but they have the family crest on them and I've always admired them. That is why—'

'No!' cried Joyce, and Rupert, startled, dropped a tureen lid on the table, creating a small dent in the veneer. 'Those are mine!' she said. 'You could never have seen them, because they belonged to my father. He took everything else with him when he left us, but my mother said the tureens were in the attic and he forgot. They are all I have and I won't part with them.'

'You're mistaken,' he managed to say, although he was clearly unnerved. 'Do you see? My label is on the bottom of one of them.'

'Your label, indeed. You put all the labels on, didn't you? I wouldn't be surprised if Lord d'Avranche decided to leave you nothing, knowing you are a thief.' She rushed across the room to snatch up the small tureens, clutching them to her breast. 'You would steal from me the only things I have to remind me of my parents.'

'No, I—' Clearly at a loss as to how to extricate himself from a very awkward situation, he fell back on bluster and insult. 'If you had these all your life, your mother must have stolen them. I know all about the man who is supposed to be your father. Do you think some poor wretch like Cousin Nicholas enabled you to live here? It was your mother – a dressmaker – and her liaison with Uncle Oswald. A dressmaker, heaven help us! Come to your senses, Joyce, you're a d'Avranche all right, but on the wrong side of the blanket.'

She gasped, choked, coughed helplessly while he took a turn around the room, keeping his back turned to her. 'Get out!' she said when she could speak. 'I thought I could trust you. I thought I could relax with you, but I should have known better.'

He straightened his back and looked at her with desperate dignity. 'Those other things are mine, I swear it. Old Finchie will confirm it. Wait and see.'

'I hate you.'

'That is too bad, but as I believe our relationship to be an irregular one, I think I can survive without your friendship. If you are the true heir, I can't understand why no-one told me, why everyone, including Cartwright, allowed me to believe myself to be . . . My lawyers are working on the case right now. I should have inherited. I am the true heir. I shall see you in court, Miss Illegitimate.' He swept from the room, his face set in an expression of childish frustration.

She followed him into the hall where Crow was waiting. Rupert, still red with anger and embarrassment, nevertheless reached into his pocket to bring out a gift of money for Mrs Crow and Mrs Able. As the butler handed him his hat and coat, he too received a crumpled note and a kind word. It occurred to Joyce that her friends had given the servants nothing. At least, she comforted herself, embarrassed on their behalf, they weren't thieves.

Easter Sunday, and the gardens and greenhouses were strangely quiet. The holidays were early this year: April had scarcely begun. Rosemary and Bill had left early in the morning, for once missing the rector's Easter sermon in favour of travelling to visit her family's nursery in Harlow.

Laurence was still their house guest, a situation which he found increasingly unpleasant. For weeks he had begged for a pair of rooms in the stable. He also knew suitable accommodation was available elsewhere on the estate. He wanted to be away from the inexplicable emotional situation that poisoned the atmosphere in North Lodge.

Bill Cook was plainly anxious for Laurence to continue to sleep in the house and take his meals with them, while Rosemary followed his every move with her eyes, which made him extremely uncomfortable. He couldn't fathom her. Sometimes he thought she liked him quite well; at others he knew she loathed him.

Yet he could not leave the Helmingham estate. He had come for a purpose, had a task to perform. Since that purpose was both hostile and a secret he had shared with no-one, he tried not to confront the feeling of being comfortably at home on the estate. There was an agreeable sense of being in a club or a school; much bickering, much politicking, yet a sense of purpose and a feeling that everyone was working for the common good. At first he had stigmatized estate staff as clinging to an outmoded life because they were snobs to a man and woman.

Later a more charitable explanation occurred to him, confirmed by some casual comments of Bill's. Those who worked at Helmingham, particularly the indoor and gardening staff, did so because they had the chance to move among beautiful things, despite the fact that they could afford none of them. He thought it must be hard for them in some ways. No servant or estate worker could ever forget that these possessions were not theirs to arrange or dispose of as they pleased. Yet the trade-off appealed to them. Not for this lot the agitation for greater wages or increased rights. They had made a choice and were not particularly interested in upsetting the system.

As for the daily cleaners, who most definitely would have preferred to earn more money or to spend more time in their homes, the choices were starker. Cora Whitton expressed it most succinctly to him. If she had to come cleaning, she preferred a soft mistress in a beautiful home to a harsher one who inspected more carefully, worked her harder and had not such beautiful possessions to be dusted. Also, she added after a little hesitation, Mrs Crow was most sympathetic about left over food 'and things'. He liked them all and appreciated the brief respite which living at Helmingham was providing. He needed this peace and had actually begun to sleep a full seven hours a night. This was a blessing that had not been his for almost ten years.

Laurence had spent a difficult year after the war recovering from the wound in his left hip. There followed three joyless years at Loughborough studying engineering, because that was what his father thought he ought to do. He was too old for it, however. The young carefree students regarded him as too staid, too world-weary to enter into their high jinks. They spoke to him with respect, asked his advice, then went out together on drinking forays or weekend rambles, leaving him behind. The teaching staff also kept him at arm's length. He formed a liaison with a young lady in the town who provided him with welcome relief from more formal relationships. There were quarrels, periods of estrangement and emotional tugs from his mother and sisters, from his brothers-in-law, from his father.

After that, the days at the switch factory seemed to have passed in a dreary struggle to obtain orders, inspire a resentful workforce which was discovering its economic power, and avoid quarrels with his father. His mistake, he realized now, had been to accept a suite of rooms in the family home.

Each day had been much like the one before it until he saw a performance of Mr Sherriff's play about the Great War. Then, nightmarish memories, long suppressed, rose to haunt him. He had not slept peacefully since that time. Reminiscences about the war seemed to flood the bookshops, but only one, Robert Graves' book *Goodbye to All That*, sold in great numbers. It recounted the poet's own experiences of the war, expressing what many a serving man had endured but had been unable to put into words. Laurence, catapulted back to the time of his greatest terror, couldn't concentrate on his work and began to wonder where his life was leading. Home became intolerable, so he took himself off to Scotland, his excuse being that he wanted to attend Earl Haig's funeral, but actually to wander the moors in search of inner peace.

He had never forgotten the officer in charge, Captain Cartwright d'Avranche, but news of his disappearance in Brazil awakened powerful emotions that he could not quite understand. It was these memories that brought him to Helmingham. In vain did he tell himself that Helmingham was a place out of time, separated from the real world, an anachronism, a way of life that most ordinary people in Britain wanted swept away. He was happy here and he couldn't, at the moment, contemplate leaving to return to all the sorrows he had left behind in Halstead.

After church, where he noticed Joyce d'Avranche sitting alone, he had come home to a hot meal served up and put in the warming oven hours earlier by Rosemary. He sat in the kitchen in Bill's seat which faced the long drive, and bided his time until he saw the distant figure of the rector leaving Helmingham to take the shortcut across the park to the rectory. Laurence knew that Joyce was entertaining the rector for lunch, as Rosemary had expressed concern about her being alone. She had been relieved that neither the young girl nor the ailing old man was to be alone on this family day. It seemed that Miss Joyce and the octogenarian had more than their surname in common. Each had found something previously lacking in their lives.

Briefly, Laurence had been concerned that his plan would be upset by the demands of his parents to come to Halstead for dinner, but he put them off by saying he would spend the following day with them instead, thus stilling their noisy pleas. Also, he had feared that Mr Trimble would be moping within the confines of the Lodge's twin. But he, too, had taken himself off to friends. The way was clear.

Laurence combed his hair, slipped on his jacket, rubbed his shoe tops on the backs of his trousers and left the lodge to jog up the drive. It was getting late. There was not much time to accomplish his purpose before Bill and Rosemary returned.

Opening the door of Rosemary's greenhouse, he looked about eagerly. He needed an excuse to cross the threshold of Helmingham, and what better excuse than to say that Rosemary had ordered him to bring Miss Joyce some blooms for her sitting room. But what to cut?

It surprised him that there was so little left in the greenhouse, for he knew that the outdoor roses would not begin to bloom until June. Bush after bush was shorn of blooms, while the next flush was still in bud. Some had no buds at all and would probably be moved out of doors in their pots.

At last he came across several of the most beautiful and fragrant blooms he had ever seen. Not a man for flowers of any sort, he nevertheless appreciated the bright foliage, the shell-pink semi-double blooms and the overpowering scent. He removed the secateurs from his pocket and began cutting. It was the work of minutes to cut two dozen blooms. He left some of the buds in place when cutting to ensure a second flush, gathered the thorny stems in his hand and left the house, not forgetting to close the door carefully.

As he knew would be the case, Joyce herself opened the door when he had crossed the moat and rung the bell at the tradesman's entrance. A kind-hearted mistress, she had insisted that all the house staff have the day off. The rector would have been given a cold luncheon, Laurence thought, and being both notoriously forgetful and unwell would hardly have noticed what he ate.

'What is this?' asked Joyce when she saw the roses in Laurence's hand.

'Rosemary asked me to cut them for you, Miss Joyce, and I am ashamed to say that I forgot. You might have had them on your table for lunch.'

He thought she seemed eager, even desperate for company. 'Come in, come in. We must find a vase. How incredibly kind of Rosie. I can't believe she sent them to me. Oh, she is a love and she knows I have not been very . . . never mind. She certainly knows how to cheer me up.'

He followed her into the kitchen, looking around him, trying to notice everything, to store away mental photographs for future use. The kitchen was huge, brick-floored, its wooden surfaces scrubbed almost white.

'Here,' said Joyce, 'I believe I've found the vases. I see you cut some of the stems quite short.' She turned to him with a mischievous smile. 'Rosie will beat you.'

He responded to her teasing smile. She really was

deliciously pretty, but for the life of him he couldn't conceive why Rosie should beat him.

Joyce placed two crystal vases on the kitchen table, one tall and narrow and the other a low round bowl. 'When Bill delivers flowers to the Hall, he always arranges them.'

'Oh yes, ma'am. Then I must do the same,' he said heartily. They were playing a subtle game, he decided. He wanted any excuse to stay; she seemed desperate not to be alone. 'Shouldn't we put some water in the vases first?'

'It would be a good idea. I'll put in the water, then we'll take them into the room where they are to be displayed and you shall arrange them. Have you a pruning knife with you?'

'Secateurs. I have cut myself several times with a pruning knife, so Bill suggested that I use secateurs. Except that he won't allow me near a plant with them.'

He followed her from the kitchen and as he passed through each room, he felt the ghost of Cartwright d'Avranche at his shoulder. He remembered the Captain as he had seen him on that first dreadful day as enemy artillery maintained a constant, ear-splitting barrage – handsome, grim and distracted. Laurence wondered if Cartwright had been thinking about his family home, contrasting it with the mud of the trenches, remembering the peaceful rural sounds, the wind in the ancient trees. Much later, when they were both in hospital, Cartwright had talked at length about his home, but no words of his had prepared Laurence for the magnificence of the place. This was Cartwright's home! All other occupants were intruders, even the lovely Miss Joyce.

They reached the drawing-room and Laurence momentarily forgot all about his mission. The room had enormous windows with many small panes; there was an inviting window seat beneath the bay. The view was of the long drive, which meant that Joyce d'Avranche could see him coming from a great distance if he chose to reach her by the direct route.

A very large basket of logs sat on the hearth; a small fire warmed the room, although Betsy, the rather smelly Labrador, got the greatest share of the heat as she monopolized the hearth rug. He was aware of warm reds, opulence and comfort.

Joyce placed the tall vase in the middle of a large circular table and the low vase on a side table by the settee. Then she smiled at him wickedly and told him to begin.

It seemed a simple task. He chose the roses with the longest stems and began pushing them into the tall vase. One stem didn't go down into the water as it should, so he lifted it out again. As if chained together, all the other roses came with it and sprawled on the table. Beads of water were strewn across the highly polished surface. He removed his handkerchief and mopped up the water before putting the stems back in the vase. The last long-stemmed rose would still not go down, so he decided to cut its stem and use it in the other vase. As he removed it, all the roses once more left the vase and water splashed once again onto the table. He would have liked the relief of shouting a few military oaths.

Joyce laughed, a pleasant sound even though she was laughing at him. 'I can't believe that Rosemary trusted you with her precious roses. Aren't you supposed to remove the foliage that comes below the water line? And all of the thorns? They catch on each other, you know.'

He smiled at her with false warmth, sighed heavily and began to cut off the lower foliage and the thorns. He must continue to play the fool; she was amused. 'A slow business,' he said at last. She was still seated on the settee, still laughing at him.

'When Bill does it, he comes in with a cloth which he places over the table. Then with his trusty knife he slashes off all the thorns and all the foliage he doesn't want and the job is done in a minute. He wraps all the rubbish in the cloth and takes it away. Here, I'll help you. You seem to be at the end of your tether and I would hate to see a grown man cry.'

She stood close to him as, together, they stripped the stems. Joyce had learned a trick from Rosemary and snapped off the thorns quite expertly with her thumb. He thought she smelt deliciously of perfume, but it could be the roses. The heady scent of the flowers was transferred, at least in his thoughts, to the young woman.

'Well,' she said uncertainly, 'it's Easter and everybody is gone.'

'Yes, Miss Joyce. It must be rather lonely in the Hall when everyone is away. Nevertheless, I expect it's a wonderful feeling to know that all of this is yours.'

'I can't remember the moment when I ceased to think "All of this is mine", and began to think, "All of this is my responsibility". Haven't you a home to go to or has Bill made you hold the fort while he's away?'

'I volunteered. My family will be happy to see me tomorrow when my sisters and their husbands and children are visiting. We will be a merry bunch on Bank Holiday Monday.'

'How fortunate you are. I have no family at all. My friend Marsha speaks all the time about her father. Rosie positively dotes on hers. I suppose you have a wonderful father too.'

'I'm not sure I dote on him, however.'

'It must be wonderful to have relatives, even those one hates.'

'Miss Joyce! You are a member of a very large family. Mr Rupert d'Avranche has just visited you and—'

'Mr Rupert d'Avranche tried to claim that his lordship left him those little soup tureens. Do you see them? Well, they're mine. My father owned them. Rupert tried to steal them! Oh, dear! You mustn't tell anyone I said that. I've been indiscreet. But I'm sure I can trust you.'

Laurence looked away, too embarrassed to meet her eyes. 'I'm sorry to hear it. Surely, he didn't intend to steal from you. That is wicked and very short-sighted, if you ask me. How, exactly, did he intend to steal them? I beg your pardon. I should not have asked that.'

But she was eager to talk, to unburden herself. He suspected that even Rosemary had not been privy to this little secret, and adopted a most sympathetic expression as she walked over to the Holbein and lifted it from the wall. 'Here, do you see? There is a label that says "For Rupert". He said that everything marked in this way is to be his and that the will says something about a few small objects, so labelled, were to go to Rupert. Well, there are several things in this room. I should not have left him alone in here for a moment on that last night. Anyway, he went around the room showing me what was to be his. I did not object to anything, I promise you. It's little enough. Then he walked over to the soup tureens, and would you believe, there is a label on the bottom of one of them. Since I know that I brought those with me, and since I have nothing else, I knew that he was trying to steal not only my two pieces of silver, but also a Holbein and other things.'

Laurence studied the label on the Holbein and the one stuck, rather hastily it seemed to him, onto the silver soup tureen. 'He is a stupid man, undoubtedly, but perhaps not as wicked as you feared. These were done at different times, you know. The handwriting is different. The label on the tureen is definitely newer.'

She blushed to the roots of her hair. 'Oh, dear. So he is entitled to these other things. Well, he is still an evil person. My mother said all the d'Avranches were . . . but, I shouldn't say these things to you. It's just that I hate him for tricking me and I hate him for making me sound like a selfish shrew. And I had so enjoyed his visit. We are equals, or so I thought. He was someone with whom I thought I could relax. Now I've made a fool of myself and will have to apologize. I don't know if I have the courage to do it.'

Laurence listened in silence, his mind racing as he tried to sort out what to do or say to achieve his purpose. If he were very clever, he could get her to unburden herself, to tell him secrets no-one else had been told. But he must not appear to be too eager. 'Just be yourself,' he said finally. 'That's the best advice.'

'Myself!' she cried with surprising vehemence. He thought she was going to burst into tears. 'And who am I? That's what I want to know. Who am I that I should be?'

'As I understand it, you are the daughter of Mr Nicholas d'Avranche, who has died. Being the direct descendant of the Lord d'Avranche's first brother, and there being no-one else as Mr Rupert is only the son of Lord d'Avranche's youngest brother, you have a right to be the owner of Helmingham Hall. That is right, isn't it? So it was explained to me by Bill.'

She ran a hand through her hair, looking quite distraught. 'Apparently, I am the illegitimate daughter of Lord d'Avranche and therefore not entitled to this house at all! That's was Rupert said.' She recollected herself, suddenly distracted by her latest gaffe. 'You won't tell anyone, will you? Promise me, you won't mention this to Bill or Rosemary.'

'I give you my word.' His heart began thudding. He wanted to cry out, *Ah ha, foiled at last!* like the hero in one of the old melodramas, but he remained outwardly calm.

'Miss Joyce, this is a startling claim. Surely, Mr Finch . . .' He took a deep breath, attempting to control his excitement. 'Do you have your birth certificate? And were your mother's marriage lines with her personal papers?'

'Yes!' She was transformed. 'Oh, you have given me hope. I was in despair. I mean, Rupert's suggestions had horrible implications for my mother, who is not here to defend herself. I'm sure her reputation will be restored when I find the papers.'

As Joyce's hopes rose, all hope died within Laurence. She ran off in search of the documents. For some minutes he had been praying that Joyce had no right to all this grandeur, that she was an ordinary citizen like himself. If the papers proved her right to Helmingham, his self-imposed task was completed and with it his reason for staying at Helmingham. He realized with surprise that this mattered to him very much.

Minutes later, they were seated side by side studying the papers and calculating dates. Laurence saw straight away that Joyce was indeed the legitimate daughter of Nicholas d'Avranche. 'There, now you know that you are definitely Miss d'Avranche of Helmingham Hall. Mr Rupert cannot argue with the evidence. I suggest you demand an apology.'

'No. I just wish. Well, you know, except for Rosie I have no friends. Oh, I love the rector. He's like a grand-father to me. But that's different, isn't it? I call her Rosie; she calls me Miss Joyce. No-one calls me by my first name, except Reverend d'Avranche and Rupert and my friends in London. And they hate me now. Everybody is sort of—'

'Bowing and scraping?' He suggested.

'Yes. Not you. Never you, that's why I feel comfortable with you. And of course Rosie, but it's awkward because Bill doesn't like me.'

'Bill is concerned that your friendship for Rosie could be misinterpreted. It could cause jealousy. This is a very small community, based on yourself.'

'But I don't want it to be based on me. I feel most uncomfortable. You say it is based on me, but I have nothing useful to do.'

'Your committee work? I've driven you to several committee meetings, haven't I?'

'I sit there shaking in my shoes while all these people say things like: "If I may say, through the chair, I do not agree with Mrs So-and-So." And then they all start talking through the chair and the chair has nothing to say for herself and doesn't know when to call for order or how to maintain it. I dread the days on which I have a committee meeting. And another thing, while I'm having a good moan, I feel as if I'm wearing someone else's clothes. This is not my house, because if it were, people would treat me differently. They seem to be angry that Captain Cartwright is dead, but I can't help that. I didn't cause his death. This is supposed to be my furniture, but every time I suggest changing something around, Mr Crow tells me it's been in that exact spot since the Conquest and I daren't do anything.'

'You are allowing yourself to be bullied. This won't do. You know, there is probably an attic full of furniture. Why don't we go this minute and take a look? Have you a couple of torches? Then you can choose what you like and order your rooms to be rearranged.'

She clapped her hands together like a child. 'Oh, that would be great fun, but dare I do such a thing before the will is proved?'

He helped her to stand up by taking her elbow, then held on for a few seconds, looking into her eyes. 'You most certainly can. Nothing will be disposed of. And anyway, there is no chance now that your claim will be thrown out.'

It took them ten minutes to find the right stairs to the part of the attic where furniture was likely to be stored. Then Laurence had to run all the way downstairs when they discovered that the door was locked. He found Bert Crow's selection of keys, neatly labelled, and was out of breath by the time he returned to her. They spent a pleasant hour in the attic where Joyce rummaged among the old furniture, picking out pieces to be moved downstairs on Monday. He refrained from telling her that the objects she chose were less beautiful and far less valuable than those she intended to consign to the attics. Instead, he begged her to have everything that was precious and which she planned to store, removed to a part of the attic which was dry.

This was easier said than done, as there was evidence of leaks everywhere. 'I told Mr Trimble to fix the roof. He keeps saying that lead is expensive and that his men are needed elsewhere,' she said, moving an old brass-bound chest from directly beneath a hole in the roof. 'Look how the water has spoiled this top. I wonder what's in it.' When she lifted the lid, they saw that it was crammed full of yellowing papers and letters still in their envelopes. She closed the lid quickly. 'I must go through those papers when I have the time.'

Laurence, who reckoned he could persuade almost anyone to comply with his wishes if he put his mind to it, would have liked to read the contents of the chest. He admitted to himself that there was no way he could suggest such a thing, and would have to rely on an offer to share the contents.

'I'll carry the chest downstairs for you. Will you want to read them now?'

'No, I'll save that task for later. I'll take this vase

downstairs and see how it will look when filled with flowers. Perfect for daffodils, don't you think? I love to see yellow daffodils in blue containers.'

'I believe that's an old Chinese ginger jar.'

She gave him a hard, speculative look. 'How clever of you to know that. You're full of surprises, Laurence. How do you know about Chinese spice jars?'

It was time to leave; he was very afraid that his stay at Helmingham would come to an abrupt end if Bill discovered what he had been up to. Yet, how to gain entry again?

'Miss Joyce, this mantel clock is not working.'

'I know. Ugly old thing, isn't it? The clock man says it is a parliamentary clock and strikes the hours with Big Ben chimes, but he cannot get it to work, so Mr Crow brought it up here.'

'I can repair it.'

She frowned. 'I know you are clever at repairing motor cars, but—'

'I can do it. It will take me a week or two as I shall work in my spare time. But I promise you I can do it. Please let me try.'

'Well, all right then. You have been very helpful.'

Laurence left the Hall within minutes, struggling to carry the heavy clock without doing any further damage to it, and wondering where the devil he could keep it until it had been repaired. He decided he would keep it wrapped up in the Rolls until he could find the time to take it to a watchmaker he knew in Ipswich.

Dobson's nursery covered twenty acres which ran along the main road leading into Harlow, neatly placed for London and the flower markets. In the summer, the nursery sent thousands of cut blooms to Covent Garden, although their main business was the selling of bare root roses in season. At one time the enterprise had been called 'Dobson, Sons and Daughter', but Rosie's father had it changed as soon as she told him she planned to marry Bill and move away. The speed with which he had made the change had hurt her desperately.

Rosemary's five brothers, Thomas, Kyle, Aaron, Jacob and Frank, each had a section of the business to manage. Cut roses were Frank's responsibility and he seemed to have made a success of it over the past six years. Thomas, being the oldest, ran the nursery, while Kyle made frequent trips to America in search of new varieties and Aaron did the same on the Continent.

Wilhelm Kordes, a German, had opened a nursery in Surrey before the Great War, but when hostilities broke out he had been interned. Anti-German feeling was so strong during the war that Herr Kordes preferred to return to Germany on his release. The war had ended ten years earlier, when Aaron had been fifteen years old, the only one of Rosie's brothers who was younger than she was. He had no objections to dealing with the old enemy and was full of praise for the work Herr Kordes was doing. He often bought new roses from the German. Jacob was in charge of dispatch, ruling the packing house with a rod of iron.

Mr and Mrs Dobson occupied a large Victorian house that rambled this way and that. There were numerous trees but no flowers in the grounds, except for roses, including the rampant white *Rosa filipes* which nearly covered the house. When this once-flowering rose was in bloom, the house was a sight to behold, but the display lasted only for a few weeks. Several repeat flowering roses competed for space with *Rosa filipes* and climbed the red bricks. More tumbled over the walls. Mrs Dobson always claimed that the house was their greatest advertisement during its weeks of glory.

Rosemary's brothers all lived within a mile of the

nursery, an arrangement that sometimes led to friction among the wives. Bill said they were warming each other's backsides, and frequently said how pleased he was not to be living under his father-in-law's thumb, nor within quarrelling distance of the rest of the family.

Everyone else had arrived by the time Aaron had delivered Rosemary and Bill in his new motor car. All the brothers had automobiles, which caused Bill a certain amount of chagrin.

Mrs Dobson, a tall, broad woman with large teeth and coarse grey hair pulled into a bun, kissed her daughter warmly and put a peck on Bill's cheek, before giving way to Mr Dobson who caught his large daughter up in a bear hug and lifted her right off her feet. He was a giant of a man, broad-shouldered and red-faced from years spent in the open. After a handshake with Bill, they all went into the handsome drawing-room to catch up on the news. The talk was mostly of roses, which Bill found boring after a while. Rosemary's father usually made Bill an offer of a position, promising a motor car and help in purchasing a house. But this Easter Sunday was different.

The old man brought Rosemary a sherry and walked her to the far side of the large room. 'Have you seen our new catalogue? I've got a new slogan under the name. It was Aaron's idea – Every Plant a Specimen. What do you think?'

'I prefer the old slogan. I don't know that it makes too much sense.'

Harley Dobson bristled. 'Well, if you hadn't left us, you might have come up with something better. You deserted me, so I reckon I'll take advice where I can find it.'

'Dad,' she said wearily. 'Let's not go over old ground. It's been eight years and I'm still happy with Bill.'

He was silent for a moment, but never remained

angry for long. 'Wheatcroft's are pushing their Princess Elizabeth. Twenty-seven and six the dozen. Five bob for standards. We've budded some, but we won't be able to offer it until next year, of course. It's pretty gaudy. Orange yellow, splashed and edged with deep cerise. Not to everyone's taste,' said Mr Dobson. 'Easlea's are always introducing new varieties. We can't keep up. They've got a good bedder in Rupert Brooke, but what can we do? We can't produce enough to sell before next year, and by that time they will have several new ones for sale. Pemberton's are another one to watch. I like Iris Patricia Green. We can beat them on price if we can get the stocks.'

'You've always had strong competition, but you've always managed in the past.'

'Yes, I mustn't depress myself with all this talk of our rivals. Let's change the subject. What's this new owner like then? Does she treat you right?'

'She's delicious,' said Rosemary. 'We are quite good friends.'

Mr Dobson looked past Rosemary to call out to Bill. 'Are you happy with the new arrangement? The new owner, I mean. How do you like working for a young woman who probably doesn't know beans about gardening?'

'She lets me do as I please, I'm glad to say. I've taken on a new man. We're coming on a treat. It might as well be my own garden, for all the interference I get.'

Mr Dobson nodded solemnly, and the others were silent. 'Best stay where you are, my lad. Things are hard for nursery men these days. Aaron and his wife will be going to Germany next week. Upping stakes and moving there permanently. Going to work for Kordes. I don't know if that's a good idea, but—'

'Better than being unemployed,' said Aaron harshly. 'I can't continue to let you support me. There's not enough money coming in,' he explained to Rosie.

'I'm going to America,' said Kyle. 'Jackson and Perkins. There's nothing in Europe worth moving to. I'm sure of it. Aaron should go to Australia or New Zealand.'

Mrs Dobson cried: 'No!' and the family sat in silence for a moment.

Mr Dobson spoke heartily. 'But we're all together today and I'm determined it will be a celebration. Mother and I will be going to Germany in August and maybe to America in the winter. Why not? It's time we travelled. We've stayed at home too long. Eh, mother?' She nodded, tears in her eyes.

Rosemary knew Bill would be thinking about how he might well be without work if he had taken up her father's earlier suggestions. They really were better off, at least for the moment, living at Helmingham Hall. Working for one of the great families was as good a way of weathering bad times as any. She looked around at the strained faces of her family and felt an overpowering wave of love for them all. How she missed them. The distance between was not great, but no-one in the family cared for letter writing, and they met only a dozen times a year. Bill's hand came to rest on her shoulder. He gave her a little squeeze to let her know that he understood her shock and grief. He really was a splendid man. If only she could get through this long day without thinking about Laurence Ballard!

After a huge dinner which lasted for two hours, the family left the table to join the children who had eaten in the old nursery. Rosie whispered to her father that she would appreciate a stroll through the glasshouses with him. They managed to deter Frank from coming with them and headed for the largest of the houses.

'Well, my girl,' said Mr Dobson when they were

walking down the path between rows of the high-centred blooms that sold so well. 'How are you getting along with your hybridizing programme?'

'I've got three hundred seedlings in pots. Father, I think I have a winner! I haven't told Bill. I intend to wait until the outdoor plants bloom in June. The ones under glass look splendid. I've got them on briar root stock.'

'Well, what did you breed from? Tell me everything.'

'Perpetual flowering, cluster. China pink, shaded yellow. It's very fragrant. Rosette form. Its parents are Ophelia and Trier, and the foliage is very attractive.'

He laughed with pleasure and surprise. 'You're out to challenge the Reverend Pemberton, then? This will be a hybrid musk. Have you chosen a name?'

'Yes, but I'm not telling anyone. It would be bad luck.' She opened her handbag, then looked around as if checking for spies before pulling out a handkerchief. 'I've brought one for you to see. A little crushed, I'm afraid.' She opened the handkerchief and held out her hand for her father to inspect the flattened bloom.

'Looks a beauty. How about disease resistance?'

'Wonderful scent. Vigorous. Disease resistant, so far as I can tell at this stage. I'm on to a winner, Father. Perhaps this will revive the nursery's fortunes.'

'I'll be proud to sell it, I promise you. But there's just not the money about. Germany's in no better state than we are, but Aaron likes the Kordes family, and you never know, they may produce something of interest. What with my boy working for them, I stand a good chance of getting first whiff of it. Kyle will be better placed. Americans have plenty of money to spend. Wait and see, he'll be the saviour of us all. Trouble is, his wife doesn't want to go. Can't bear the thought of being so far from her mother. And Mrs Baker isn't in the best of health. We may take her with us when we go out there.'

'Mother seems desperately unhappy,' she said, and

he shrugged miserably. Through the glass, Rosemary could see Bill walking alone among the bare rose bushes. She thrust the rose back into her handbag and smiled at her father. 'Bill's a good man. Perhaps it all worked out for the best. You couldn't have kept him on in these hard times, and he would have lost his place at Helmingham.'

'You're married to a dashed *servant*, Rosie, and I hate that. But yes, he is a good man. If you're happy, that's all that matters. Try not to worry about your mother and me. The Great War was the hardest time for us. Fuel costs up, all the men off fighting. If it hadn't been for your strong back and young Aaron, we would not have made it. Thomas's oldest boy is doing some of the work you used to do, although he's not got your talent, and Kyle's oldest will be staying behind. We'll manage. I just sometimes feel we're too many souls in one lifeboat. If we're not careful, we'll sink.'

Chapter Seven

Marsha walked into the lounge of her small flat and flung her hat onto the settee. How she hated this room! Right up until the Friday morning before she visited Joyce, she had been very pleased with the effect she had achieved in her London flat. Now she was not so sure. Having seen real Tudor furniture, she regretted having purchased mock Tudor, especially for such a small space. What could she have been thinking of?

She blamed it on the influence of her old home in Kansas City. Overstuffed pieces, bought thirty years ago, had been comfortable, while the blazing mid-western sun was more often regarded as an enemy to be shut out than as a warming friend. Gloom and too much furniture were certainly faults in the old house, but her mother had added to the sense of clutter because she had a fondness for handiwork of all sorts. There were crocheted antimacassars, knitted rugs, framed cross-stitched mottos and Bible quotations as well as the latest hobby, pictures of flappers holding their skirts out, the entire scene rendered in coloured foil. Mom certainly enjoyed making all these things, but Marsha now decided that pleasure had nothing to do with it. One's home was where one displayed one's taste.

She had spent some months absorbing European culture, but none of it had dented her confidence in her own taste until she visited Joyce's Helmingham Hall. Since that time, she had been unable to settle, shunning the old gang as boorish and irritating – and poor.

and during her stay Joyce would be holding a small party. Marsha gave a Confederate Army rebel yell that would have brought a scolding from her mother, and waved her hat in the air. She was already beginning to feel like a bride.

Rosemary had waited all day for Laurence Ballard to return from a day spent with his family in Halstead. When on Monday morning she saw what had happened in the greenhouse to the six bushes of her precious, unnamed rose, her first thought was of thieves or vandals, of young boys bent on mischief or rival rose growers with more serious intent. Long before Laurence returned, however, she had visited Joyce and seen her precious babies, their beautiful pale pink heads crowding each other, rammed willy-nilly into vases. Laurence Ballard had kindly brought them to the Hall, she was told. He had been a naughty boy to cut the stems so short, but how sweet of Rosemary to have sent him!

Rosemary said nothing, gave nothing away. She had decided that no-one should know about the new rose and she would not change her mind at this troubled time. Father had been the first to know; Bill would be the second when she thought the time was right and when she thought he deserved to know. Until then, she would not share this secret with anyone. To do so would surely bring bad luck to the rose. In the meantime, her anger grew until it filled her head. She felt as if a real child had been violated. Common sense deserted her on this one subject, her fury fed by the secrecy she had imposed on the subject. If Bill knew about the rose, if he heard that a few blooms had been cut by other hands, he might persuade her into a more rational frame of mind, might tell her that no great crime had been committed. But Bill was being punished for his lack of sensitivity and for his close friendship with Laurence. And, it had to be said, she wanted to transfer a little of the pain she was suffering because her brothers were to travel abroad. Her family was being uprooted, forced by circumstances beyond their control to travel. She kept her agony over their departures to herself, but Bill's bovine good humour, coupled with the fact that his family still all lived within a ten minute walk, kept her from confiding in him.

It was growing dark when Laurence returned and, as luck would have it, Bill had gone next door to talk to Mr Trimble.

'How dare you?' she spat out as he came into the kitchen. Laurence stepped back in surprise.

'How dare I what, my dear?'

'Cut my roses, that's what! I had to spend half an hour tidying them up. Who gave you permission to practically destroy my dear . . . my precious . . .' She couldn't go on, had to stop to blow her nose.

Laurence approached, less mystified than he had been at first, but unable to understand the magnitude of his crime. He put an arm around her shoulders and felt her tremble.

'Forgive me, best of friends. I had no idea I was committing such a heinous crime. You see, I wanted to get into Helmingham and have a look round. I've never seen inside, you know. Well, I needed an excuse, so I took some of the roses. But I left plenty of buds for the next flush. Anyway, in a few weeks the outdoor roses will be coming into bloom, won't they? I do apologize. Can you forgive me?'

She broke away from him, red in the face and looking plainer than ever. 'See Helmingham, my eye.'

He shrugged. 'All right, I wanted to see Joyce and get to know her better.'

'*Joyce*?' she cried. 'You call her Joyce? You dirty devil. You lecherous, ungrateful sneak!'

'Steady, Rosemary. You're going too far. I do not have designs on the innocent Miss d'Avranche. She had no complaint about my visit. In fact, I think she enjoyed the company.'

'Worming your way in. I suppose that was something trumped up between you and Bill. He wants to control her, see to it that she never makes life unpleasant for him. He'd like to choose her husband for her, so that she doesn't end up with someone who will order him about.'

Laurence's apologetic air left him abruptly. 'You malign your husband and that I can't have. Bill and I have been through hell together. No outsider can understand what we share, nor would I care to tell them. I will not have him slandered, not even by his wife. I do most sincerely apologize for cutting a few roses, though for the life of me I can't understand your fury. You may think what you please about my feelings for Joyce d'Avranche. You wouldn't understand and I don't intend to enlighten you on that subject either. But Bill and I have not entered into any kind of conspiracy. He will not choose Joyce's – I beg your pardon, *Miss* Joyce's – husband, nor has he any need to fear a new employer. In future, he must mind his back against his wife, but I don't think he has another enemy on this earth. I will be moving to the stables this evening. I ask only that we keep this to ourselves. Don't let that good, decent man know what has passed between us.'

He left the room and Rosemary found her legs too weak to allow her to stand up. How had it happened? How had she come to say such dreadful things about the man she loved and admired, while the villain, Laurence, was able to move from her house with an air of injured innocence? How had she ever been so insane as to find him attractive? He was ugly, sly and undependable. In fact, she hated him.

A few minutes later, Bill found her, still seated at the kitchen table, clearly distressed. He was at once filled with sympathy and tenderness. Then Laurence entered the room carrying his suitcase to announce that he was moving immediately to the stables. Bill was stunned and tried without success to dissuade him. Laurence was adamant; Rosie was silent.

After he had gone, Bill turned to his wife. 'You've driven him out, haven't you? You never liked having him here.'

'I just want us to be on our own.'

'Why couldn't you discuss it with me first?' He slammed his cap down on the table and rubbed a calloused hand across his face. 'I was proud to have him here. I liked his company.'

'I'm sorry,' she murmured, 'but it's too late now, and anyway we're better on our own, Bill. Don't say any more.'

He snorted and paced the floor for a minute or two, then said he was going to the pub in the village with Trimble. Rosemary remained at the table, sunk in despair. How, she wondered, had she managed to end the day with both men thinking she was a spiteful witch when she knew she had right on her side?

Bill did not, after all, go to the pub with Mr Trimble. Stopping only to make his excuses to the bailiff, he went immediately to the stables where he found Laurence working half-heartedly by the light of a single candle, wiping the dust from the old furniture of a very uncomfortable flat above the stables.

'You can't stay in this bloody place, Laurence. There's a much better set of rooms by the coach house. You'd be more comfortable there for as long as you stay at Helmingham. The Lord only knows what you'll do for food. I'd better speak to Mrs Able.'

Laurence smiled grimly. 'I hadn't thought of that. Rosemary is very angry with me, Bill. I really ought to leave Helmingham, but I don't want to at the moment. In the meantime, these rooms will do perfectly well.'

Bill sat down on the metal-framed bed, struggling briefly with his loyalty to his wife. 'Rosie's broody, that's all. There's nothing wrong with her that a house full of kids wouldn't cure. Why did you come here? I can't help feeling you had a reason. Not that I don't welcome your presence. You have every right—'

'I have no right at all. I think I was slightly mad.'

'But you're a d'Avranche!'

Laurence snorted. 'Not really. Consider. One of my great-grandmothers was a d'Avranche. I had eight great-grandparents, but only one was a d'Avranche. I don't know anything about the others, nor have I ever cared. Yet I know that my great-grandmother on my mother's side was Emmaline d'Avranche, a cousin of the then Lord d'Avranche. She married Jacob Ballard, an Ipswich watchmaker, with whom she had fallen in love at seventeen. When Emmaline's only child, Hester, married a Hadleigh farmer, Emmaline felt that her daughter was going back to her d'Avranche roots, in spite of the fact that the farm had only a hundred and fifty acres. You wouldn't credit the things my Grandmother Hester would not do, the places she would not go, all because she had d'Avranche blood and had been taught to consider herself too good for most people. I loved her dearly, but she was a dreadful snob. She kept a scrapbook of every mention of the family that appeared in *The Times* or *Country Life*. I was brought up on stories of my drop of blue blood, but it doesn't amount to much and gives me no rights here.'

'Crikey,' said Bill, 'I thought the connection was closer.'

'Think back to my first day at the front when I met you and the Captain. I was gauche, stupid and scared out of my wits. Along came a senior officer, an older man, tall and broad-shouldered, a look of weariness in his eyes. Dark brown hair brushed back, a square jaw and straight, rather large nose. His teeth were even and white and his ears sat close to his skull. He was the handsomest man I had ever seen, a glamorous war hero, the man I would have liked to be. Someone told me his name was Captain d'Avranche. Like a first-class fool, I rushed up to him and said—I blush to think of it— "Captain d'Avranche! We are related!" To his eternal credit, he looked on me with kindly eyes and asked what our connection was. I started to tell him that my great-grandmother had been a cousin of the Lord d'Avranche of her day, and as I spoke a look of genuine amusement lit up his face. It had been a grim day, but I, by my stupidity, managed to make him laugh.

'"My kinsman!" he cried, laughing, and I was ready to sink with embarrassment.'

'It was a natural thing for you to do.'

Laurence laughed harshly. 'From that day forward, Captain d'Avranche always referred to me as his kinsman. You thought I was closely related in some way. I knew he was making fun of me, and what is more I knew I deserved it. Great families, particularly those who own great houses, are magnets for social climbers, time servers, confidence tricksters and awkward fools. I wish I had said nothing, believe me.'

'Yet you came here, Laurence. Why did you come, if you feel as you say you do?'

Laurence began removing his possessions from his open case, avoiding Bill's gaze. 'When we were in hospital all those long painful months, we were thrown together a great deal. The captain was in considerable pain. I think they gave him too much morphine, for his speech was slurred and he spoke of matters that were none of my business. I heard how his older brothers had died, how he became the heir to Helmingham and the title. And he spoke of a woman he had known in his youth, his father's mistress. Yes, it was Thora, Joyce's mother. He hated that woman with such intensity that I sometimes thought he would have a seizure while talking about her. Thora had made his mother's final years unbearable. In fact, he believed that the affair, together with the death of her sons, actually killed her. And the terrible thing about it was, Thora had eventually run off with the pathetic wretch who would have been Cartwright's heir, and they had a daughter. This daughter could not inherit the title, of course. That would be Rupert's, unless the captain produced an heir. But she could inherit Helmingham, due to the extraordinary workings of the trust, if anything happened to Cartwright. The thought tormented him. He said he had to get better, had to marry and provide an heir.'

Bill shook his head. 'The war took a lot out of him, but he had ten years in which to marry and cut her out. Why didn't he? Admittedly, he did have to return to spend another six months in hospital after you left, but he should have been able to get over that business in the following eight years. You know, it seemed to us here at Helmingham, and to his father, that Cartwright was doing his damnedest to get himself killed.'

'It's a mystery, and one which will never now be solved. I only know why I have not married. Each time I thought of doing so my family have been on me like a pack of hounds, urging me on, making plans, hemming me in. I couldn't stand it. I couldn't commit myself to a lifetime in one place with one woman. But then, I have no compelling reason to produce an heir.'

'You came to see what Joyce d'Avranche was like, didn't you?'

Laurence nodded. 'I did. I had some ridiculous idea that for Captain Cartwright's sake I might prove she had no right to the place. However, I am now convinced that she is the legitimate heir. Mr Finch would have made enquiries and satisfied himself on that score. Besides, I have seen her mother's marriage lines and her own birth certificate. Tell me, Bill, you have lived here all your life. Did you know this Thora?'

Bill snorted. 'Oh, I knew her all right. A hard-faced little woman who might have been pretty if she hadn't such a scheming look about her. Her daughter looks a lot like her, but without the cunning eyes. Everybody on the estate hated Thora, especially after his lordship gave her a cottage. One day I went along there and peeped into the window. She caught me and threatened to tell his lordship what I had been up to. It wasn't . . . I wasn't hoping to see her undressed or anything of that nature. I was only a nipper and I was curious about the woman who had everyone whispering. Anyway, she had me worried, I can tell you. She had a spiteful tongue. That night, I came back and threw a stone through one of her windows. Terrible thing to do and I've always been ashamed of it. The following day, we heard that she had run off with Mr Nicholas. It was years before I figured out that I hadn't anything to do with her going away.'

'And Nicholas? What was he like?'

'A pretty pathetic character. A horse fell on him when he was a boy, left him badly crippled up. I think it might have affected his brain, too. No-one would ever have married Nicholas if Thora hadn't. At least, someone might have if they had known how close he stood to inheriting everything.'

'Joyce is a decent person, Bill, a suitable owner of

Helmingham, even if she is not yet comfortable with her inheritance. I admire her. Consider this. She had a most unfortunate start in life. Neither parent was the sort we would choose for ourselves. Yet, here she is, an unpretentious young woman, always exquisitely groomed, unfailingly polite, determined to grow into her position.'

Bill jumped up from the bed. 'Exactly! Blood will out. Mr Nicholas might have been a capital chap, if he hadn't happened to fall under his horse. She's inherited the d'Avranche grit. Now listen. You're a d'Avranche, although you choose to play down the connection. All that young girl needs is a husband to show her how to go on.'

'And you think I am that person? So Rosemary is right. You want me to marry Joyce d'Avranche, because another husband might not be so friendly towards you. You worry unnecessarily. And I think Rosemary would never forgive me.'

Bill shoved his hands into his pockets, then walked to the window where he saw only the reflection of his own worried face and, dimly, the tawdry room. 'Pay no mind to Rosie. She knows about none of this. I didn't figure your being a d'Avranche was any of her business, at least not at the moment. This estate needs taking in hand, and Miss Joyce is not up to it. Trimble should be put out to grass. He was a contemporary of Lord d'Avranche. The Crows and Mrs Able are too old to do their work properly, and as for Mr Finch, I always suspected him of taking advantage of his lordship's old age. He wants watching, but can you imagine that young girl taking a tough line with him? You needn't think folks would imagine you married her for her money, either. Word is, his lordship, in a fit of pique, left all his money away from the estate, and gave none to young Rupert. If his son was dead, he didn't want anybody to be made happy by what was left. It all goes to various charities.'

Laurence frowned. 'I feel extremely sorry for the young lady and don't doubt that you are right in what you say. There is no money and Mr Finch is not being as careful as he should with what is left. Eventually, she will gain the confidence to retire those who should be retired, but that is her affair, not mine. I am not going to attempt to marry Joyce d'Avranche, so you can forget that. I thought I might open a garage, perhaps hire motor cars, maybe even offering a service to supply reliable drivers. I like motors, while I most definitely do not like electrical switches.'

'You could make her love you. You could do that and have a garage, too, I suppose.'

Laurence laughed at the idea. 'The husband for Joyce d'Avranche is that handsome young man, Rupert, the soon-to-be Lord d'Avranche. Could you not be happy working for him?'

'Oh, he's all right, but a bit of a loose cannon. He'll go along perfectly sensibly for ages, then do something stupid.'

When Laurence left Joyce on Easter Sunday, she experienced a piercing regret over having mentioned Rupert's accusations. What had possessed her to confide in a stranger? What, that is, except extreme loneliness? She had not wanted to tell Rosemary, fearing the loss of her friend's respect. As a result, Laurence Ballard, an unexpected visitor and one with a remarkably sympathetic air, had been the recipient of the most damaging confidence. She spent a full hour brooding about her indiscretion, before gritting her teeth and determining to get on with the duties of her position.

Finding herself owner of this vast building had

induced in her a strange lassitude, an inability to get on with things. She wandered the rooms, considered all the chores she ought to get on with, then wasted the remainder of the day trying to decide which one to begin. This inactivity worried her, yet she seemed incapable of breaking out of the habit of dithering. Usually she ended by discovering a compelling need to talk to Rosemary, and so walked down the long drive to the only friend she had. If Rosemary happened to be busy she walked over to the rectory. Sadly, the Reverend d'Avranche was seldom well these days. A wander around the estate, a shy word of greeting to the men, perhaps a trip into the village to take a present to a new mother or visit someone who was sick would complete the day. When others were sitting down with friends or family at the end of a busy day, Joyce was dining alone, preparing to read by lamplight or to listen to her battery-operated wireless.

She had always been methodical, a filer of papers, an organizer of facts, and sitting in the study was a large box temptingly filled with old papers and letters, most of them in their envelopes. She had recognized her mother's primitive scrawl and knew she must now sort through these old letters to discover Thora's past. This, at least, was a chore she might enjoy, one in which she could lose herself.

Although the bulk of the correspondence consisted of letters from her mother, there was other correspondence, mainly letters from Lord d'Avranche's sons to their parents, written while they were at Eton. She would read these later in an attempt to discover what sort of people they had been, since they were relatives. Joyce had never known uncles and aunts and cousins. Now, she felt it was vital to learn as much as she could about her family, so that she might begin to feel a part of it.

Primarily, however, she wished to read the correspondence from her mother to Lord d'Avranche. The fact that there were so many notes and letters told her that there must have been a liaison of some sort. Revulsion mixed with curiosity as she began assembling the folded notes, firstly those without dates on them, or stamps on the envelopes. These would be the earliest, the ones most difficult to put into chronological order. When she came across one that began, *My dearest darling, I can't tell you all that is in my hart after last night. What am I to do? She will be coming home tomorrow and I won't be able to see you for a while. Not like last night,* Joyce gasped, but she knew that this was probably the first letter written by her uneducated mother to her seducer, who had been at least thirty years her senior. She collected twenty more notes of the *when can we mete?* variety that told her nothing, except that Lord d'Avranche had considered them worth saving for over twenty years.

There were several brief notes of thanks for some small trinket, usually accompanied by complaints about the absence of something more substantial. On reading the first of these letters, Joyce was revolted, but she came to feel that Lord d'Avranche had truly been miserly. Thora's position on the estate must have been difficult, to say the least. Yet, Lord d'Avranche never gave her sums of money that would have given her independence. He probably wanted to keep her dependent upon him.

Finally, she came upon a longer letter which began formally with *My Lord* and went on to say that Thora didn't care a fig about his wife's feelings. When had Lady d'Avranche ever cared about her feelings? she would like to know.

From the tone of the letter, it was plain his lordship was tiring of her. Thora's limited command of the language prevented her from expressing her despair and panic at the impending end. There was even a plea to be allowed to stay on at the cottage, if she promised never to trouble Lord d'Avranche again.

Joyce felt frustrated at the absence of the other side of this correspondence. Reading only her mother's letters left her with the impression of an ignorant orphanage girl, forced to make her own way in the world without a parent or brother to advise and protect her. By the time she picked up the letter in which Thora announced that she had left Helmingham to marry Nicholas, Joyce was attempting to overcome her distaste for her mother's affair and come to some understanding of the circumstances that led to it.

In April of 1906, Thora wrote a letter filled with triumph and spite. Lord d'Avranche would be, she said, thrilled to discover that his mistress was now Mrs Nicholas d'Avranche, his lordship's niece by marriage. She had never been appreciated, had been badly treated by Lady d'Avranche, gossiped about by the estate staff, and would have been left to starve. But dear, kind Nick would look after her. She had married him 'legal' and would live 'proper' in London and have more 'brats' than his lordship ever imagined possible. He would be sorry he had spurned her. She hoped he roasted in hell.

All of this was very distressing for Thora's daughter to read almost a quarter of a century later, but worse was to come in the postscript.

By the way, that little snotty nose, Billy Cook, is a peeping Tom and I boxed his ears good for him. He threw a rock through my window last night. I hope somebody beats him.

So Bill knew about Thora's affair! He was bound to have told Rosemary and Laurence Ballard. In all probability, every person on the estate knew of her mother's past. And the rector! She suddenly remembered the dear old man who had given her such comfort and encouragement since she arrived at Helmingham.

Joyce wondered how she could face any of them. How wicked of Thora to have left her totally unprepared for her future. And there was, unfortunately, no doubt that Thora did know what was in store for Joyce. There were further letters.

In 1909, after Nicholas had left his little family, Thora was apparently told of his death. Her letter to Lord d'Avranche reeked of despair. Please, she begged him, please continue the allowance Nicholas had been sending her. There had been no word from his family. Had he left her nothing? Were she and little Joyce to starve?

Tucked into the envelope was a photograph of Joyce as a year-old baby. Joyce hugged the faded likeness to her breast and cried for all the lost happiness, the lost father, the lost family that might have been hers.

Thora sent her condolences when the d'Avranche twins drowned in 1910, and another letter of commiseration on the death of Lady d'Avranche, which must have struck the old lord as somewhat hypocritical. She begged to be taken back, to be given a chance to live quietly on the estate and bring up Joyce. Presumably, there was no reply. Shortly after this time, Thora sold the house and mother and child moved to Shepherd's Bush.

Joyce's clearest memories of her mother were after that move. She remembered a woman whose perpetually angry expression marred a once beautiful face. Thora d'Avranche had been eaten with hatred, her conversation concerned mostly with complaints about her treatment by almost everyone. She quarrelled with the newsagent, with the landlord, with the other tenants. The little family were isolated by Thora's feuds, and her only discussion of her work was of the ill treatment she had received at the hands of her customers. To Thora, the world was a cruel and unfair place, men were untrue, those with a halfpenny more in their pockets were to be envied and despised, because they could not have come by their good fortune honestly.

Joyce, as a young child, had been deeply confused. Thora hated those she called the nobs, yet told her daughter often that she was, herself, a nob. 'You're as good as them and don't you forget it.' What was a child to make of this? Now, filled with shame for the lewd behaviour of her mother, she could not help remembering all the injunctions not to kiss a boy, never to behave cheaply. Indeed not! Joyce had been so terrified of any boys she might happen to meet that she scarcely dared speak to them.

Her few happy memories of her mother were now spoiled for ever. Joyce began to consider her father. For years she had imagined that she hated him and had wondered how he could have abandoned his wife and child. Now, she thought she knew the reason; he had found out about Thora's affair with his uncle. Because of her mother's bad behaviour, Joyce had been denied the love of her father, a gentleman who would have helped to put her in her rightful place, who would have enabled her to assume the role of chatelaine of Helmingham with ease. She could not blame Nicholas for having despised her mother once he knew of her past, but what crime had Joyce committed? Why had her father chosen to punish her by going away?

Mr and Mrs Crow returned in the late afternoon. With a heavy heart, Joyce packed up all the letters, closed the chest and carried it with some effort up to her bedroom. There was to be no possibility that anyone else would read the contents.

*   *   *

Joyce had never ceased to feel a little afraid of the deer. They paid no attention to her when she walked in the park, but it seemed to her there might come the day when all the animals would rear up in anger at this imposter in their midst. For that reason, when visiting the rector, she always took Betsy as companion and guard dog. Not that Betsy was capable of guarding her from so much as a blue tit, but she felt better for the company.

Annie, the housekeeper who was nearly as old as her employer, opened the rectory door. 'Miss Joyce, do come in. His nibs needs a bit of company. Not feeling himself today. Down in the doldrums, I call it.'

'I will do what I can to cheer him up. Here are a dozen eggs. Perhaps a custard will make him feel a bit better.'

She found him in his comfortable sitting-room. He had a rug across his lap and an embroidered cap on his head. Annie had built such a large fire that Joyce was forced to remove her coat, hat and cardigan immediately. Yet the old man looked shrunken and cold as he smiled at her.

'Forgive me for not rising. I'm a trifle poorly this morning. How nice to see you. To what do I owe this mid-week visit?'

'I've come to invite you to a party. I received a letter from my friend, Marsha Grissom, and have sent a telegram inviting her to stay with me for a few weeks in May. I am planning to invite a few people in to meet her.'

'It is about time you did some entertaining. You must invite all those who have called on you in the past weeks. You still have their cards, I hope. Do make a point of inviting every one. They will then invite you to their homes and you will begin to have a proper social life.'

'Some of them were very stiff. I didn't know what to say to them, and they didn't seem to *want* to like me. I'm sure they think I'm an interloper. Must I invite them?'

'Certainly. They have sons and daughters. You will begin to see how it all works out. You must trust me on this. Oh, yes, you must invite all the members of the committees on which you sit.'

'I'm not keen to do that,' she said, 'because the people on my committees are not very pleasant. I'm considering resigning from them all.'

'Unthinkable!'

She laughed. 'No it's not. I think of it after every meeting. Must I invite them?'

He tried to answer, but a bout of coughing prevented an immediate response. Then, 'Who knows? An invitation to Helmingham Hall may help to remove some of the strain of your meetings. I most certainly will accept my invitation. How kind of you to ask. And you will accept Rupert's very pretty apology for his bad behaviour and invite him, too. And his youngest sister, Helen. No need to send an invitation to his mother, for she is always in the South of France at this time of year.' He closed his eyes for a minute and she wondered if he had fallen asleep.

'Yes, Rupert did write a sweet apology. What a strange man!' She had not told the rector about Rupert's accusations, only about his attempt to take her silver soup tureens. That Reverend d'Avranche knew all about Thora was beyond doubt. She wondered if she dared ask the old man about her father. Might she not live to regret it, if comments were made that she couldn't forgive?

'Mr and Mrs Finch, too,' said the vicar, suddenly opening his eyes. 'That will be in your best interests. He will have to approve the expenditure.'

'I never thought of that. Oh, I shall never get him to agree. I've only seen him once or twice since I moved to Helmingham. I wrote a letter to say that all the beds were uncomfortable. Do you know what he wrote back? He said of course they were. There were uncomfortable beds in the best houses in the land. I did manage to persuade him to pay for three new ones, though . . .'

She looked closely at the old man who was now soundly asleep. After waiting a few moments, she tiptoed from the room and went back to the Hall to do battle with both Mr and Mrs Crow concerning the removal of some furniture from the attics to the rooms downstairs. Husband and wife had been scandalized, and it had needed all her powers of quiet endurance to outlast the objections.

She had spent the Monday reflecting on the best response to difficulties about her mother's past. It was to be defiance. Perhaps the whole of Suffolk knew of her mother's affair. Never mind. She would carry on as the proud occupant of Helmingham and dare them all to snub her. Marsha's letter had arrived at just the right moment. What better reason to call her new acquaintances together than to introduce her dearest friend?

The Cook home was her next stop. Rosemary had visited her briefly on Easter Sunday evening, but she had not stayed long and seemed to be unwell.

Joyce knocked on the kitchen door, then let herself in. 'It's me! Anybody home?'

Rosemary was seated at the kitchen table. She looked up and smiled wanly, but she didn't rise. 'Good God, Rosie, you are ill,' said Joyce. 'What's the matter? Is there anything I can do?'

'Nothing at all. I was a week late! A whole week! I was sure that this time . . .' She shrugged. 'It has been like this ever since we married. Hopes dashed, month after month. I should stop caring, but I can't.'

'I'll put the kettle on. Can I get you anything? Some sherry, perhaps. Oh, Rosie, I had no idea. I thought perhaps you didn't care for children, but that was foolish of me.'

'I couldn't possibly drink sherry so early in the day. But sit down. I'm not an invalid. I'll make us a cup of tea and tell you all the news about my family.'

'No-one is ill, I hope,' said Joyce. 'You must go to them if they are.'

'No, it's the business. People just don't have the money to buy roses. I have so many brothers that the business can't support them. So Aaron and his wife are going to Germany. He's going to work for a rose grower named Kordes, although I believe business is as bad in Germany. And Kyle, he's going to America to work for Jackson and Perkins. So far away, I'm afraid I'll never see him again!'

'Oh, how sad. To have such a large family and then to see it broken up. That's terrible.' She watched Rosie measure tea into the hot pot. 'What is your mother like? Is she jolly? Does she breed roses, too?'

'My mum?' asked Rosie, smiling. 'Mum is just wonderful. No, she doesn't breed roses. She's an officer in the Women's Institute, a volunteer helper at the hospital and involved in everything that takes place at the church. She was always around for us children when we were young, and while Katie does the plain cooking, Mum cooks all the special dishes and desserts. Her pastries are works of art. She's being very brave about Aaron and Kyle. My parents will travel to Germany and America to see the boys when they can, of course.'

'You are fortunate to have such a fine family. I envy you, I really do.'

Rosie set the fine china cup before Joyce and an earthenware one on the table for herself. They drank for a moment in silence, then Rosie said, 'Bill and

Laurence are going to the British Legion this evening. I always hate it when Bill goes to a meeting.'

Joyce was puzzled. 'I know there's a fair amount of drinking, but . . .'

'Oh, it's not that. Have you ever thought how strange it is that our men went to France to kill people? I mean, women don't do that sort of thing. We don't know what it is to cause the death of someone. And, except for a few women who went to the front as nurses, we don't know what it's like to be fired upon. It's that experience that sets us apart from men. Bill and Laurence are very close, closer than Bill and me. They share terrible secrets. They stand up for each other. I might quarrel with both of them. They won't say a word against each other. I feel shut out, different, and a little guilty for being alive and in one piece. Bill has nightmares sometimes, but he won't tell me what they're about.'

'Well, the important thing is Bill came through it all.'

'Yes, of course.' Rosemary finished her tea. 'Will you have another cup? I'm a poor hostess this morning. When I'm feeling blue, I think how nearly I came to being an old maid.'

'Rosemary! What a thing to say!'

'So many men were killed. So many more women than men are left in England, and I was never pretty, never had any reason to believe that a man who had the whole country to choose from would pick me.'

'You're in the dumps, that's all. You must cheer up and not say such things. It's because of your not expecting, after all. But you mustn't give up hope. Now, I have some news. My friend, Marsha, is coming to stay with me for a couple of weeks.'

'Oh, that's very nice,' said Rosemary dully. 'I'm sure you will enjoy her company.'

'And I shall give a party for her. The vicar says it's

about time I did some entertaining. Will the roses be in bloom in May?'

'Only a few, and then only if we're lucky. Canary Bird, of course. One or two others towards the end of the month, weather permitting. The garden should look quite charming, especially if the sun is shining. There will be some bulbs. A few trees will be in bloom. I must tell Bill. He will be pleased that the May garden is going to be appreciated this year.'

Joyce didn't stay at the lodge for long. She sensed that Rosemary didn't care for Marsha and so refrained from talking about her American friend. She really wished only to talk to someone about her mother and Lord d'Avranche, but the subject was too delicate, too fraught with pitfalls. What if Rosemary were to admit that she knew all about the affair? What if she were to say something scathing about Thora? Joyce knew her mother had behaved badly, but she could not tolerate a word of criticism from anyone. The only thing to do was to keep her knowledge to herself and pretend to the world that she was happy.

As for Marsha, she must never find out the secret of Joyce's past!

Chapter Eight

At half-past six Bert Crow lowered the drawbridges and fifteen minutes later Laurence walked over from the stables to have his breakfast with the servants. He had a fair amount of free time as Joyce made few journeys during the week. His smart new uniform had been ordered from Harrods and fitted him reasonably well. He felt slightly uncomfortable accepting this seven guinea uniform with its double-breasted jacket and breeches. The peaked cap sat uneasily on his head, and he preferred to carry it whenever possible. She had kitted him out completely, even buying him a dustcoat and a pair of blue dungarees for those moments when he was tinkering with the car.

His position in the Helmingham kitchen was a delicate one. The Crows and Mrs Able could not place him socially and were uneasy in his presence. He was resented yet feared and, try though he might, he could not charm them into lowering their guard. He was too close to Joyce, on too familiar a footing for them to trust him. And he had overheard a conversation between Bill and Bert Crow that was all about Bill's stupidity in allowing his army mate such freedom of action.

One branch of Laurence's family had remained in the watchmaking and jewellery business. During the week after Easter, he had taken Joyce's clock to a cousin and received the unsurprising news that the clock man who called regularly at Helmingham was not satisfactorily skilled. Cousin Arnold soon had the clock working, but Laurence was left with the problem of what to do about his cousin's opinion. In the end, he told Bert what he had learned, and was not thanked for his initiative.

Without a word to Laurence, Bert replaced the clock, but when Joyce commented on its reappearance, he took the opportunity to express his opinion of interfering chauffeurs. Joyce mentioned it to Rosemary and Rosemary carried a complaint to Bill. In due course, Laurence was made aware of everyone's feelings on the subject and warned not to step on Bert Crow's toes again.

'Wait until you've married her, then take over the management of the house,' had been Bill's advice. 'You can retire everybody, except me, of course, and take on younger, better trained people when you have the position and the power.'

Laurence had not cared for this advice. Now that he knew what the butler thought of him, and Bert knew he knew, the simplest remark seemed to take on a life of its own. The Crows had a remarkable capacity for taking offence.

This afternoon, Laurence was to drive Miss Joyce to the train station in Ipswich to meet her friend, Miss Grissom, but the morning was his own. On the pretext of going off to buy petrol for the motor, he drove up to the farm of Commander Ranulph Higgs.

As he hoped, the commander was in the farmyard. Very much an active farmer, he was one of the few farmers to prosper in depressed times. His fields were impeccable, his workers apparently happy and his home in good order. He was one of the nearish neighbours who had called on Joyce d'Avranche. He was a cheerful man in his sixties with a pleasant wife who must have been comely in her youth, but who was now stringy and thin. The Higgs family lived about three miles from Helmingham Hall. They had called on Joyce one sunny March day and had been shown round the garden. A former naval man who had distinguished himself in the war, he already knew Bill and, when introduced to Laurence, had been most friendly. Any man who had served under Captain Cartwright deserved a few kind words from the commander.

'Well, young man,' he called when Laurence had brought the motor to a halt. 'What a surprise! What brings you to these parts?' Several of the men looked up from their work, but none offered a friendly greeting.

'Just a friendly visit, sir. I am out to buy some petrol for the Rolls.' The commander began walking back towards the farmhouse, and Laurence waited until he could speak without the others overhearing the conversation. 'I come on an errand for a friend. He's a farmer in a small way, sir. Just a hundred and fifty acres. He recently inherited it and has discovered that the land isn't being farmed at all. He is considering growing sugar beet, but knows nothing about the crop. I don't even know what a sugar beet looks like and was hoping you could show me one. I told him you are the finest farmer in Suffolk and that I would ask your advice.'

Commander Higgs laughed indulgently, no match for Laurence's charm. 'Let us hope your friend knows more about farming than you do. I can't show you a sugar beet in May. A sugar beet doesn't look like a beet. It's closely related to mangold, looks like a parsnip and has a tap root three feet long. Each beet weighs, if we're lucky, about a pound. It's harvested in the autumn when we take it to Ipswich to the sugar beet factory where it is miraculously turned into sugar for the table. We feed the tops to the cattle, and the wet pulp from the factory is returned for cattle food. Growing sugar beet improves the land and we've used it in the rotation to replace turnips, mangolds and swedes. It does well after cereals and potatoes. The following crop is usually a winter or spring cereal. You never want to grow it two years on the same land. Eel worm. In Germany and America they've got land that's beet sick from the eel worm.'

Laurence had whipped out a small notebook and was attempting to write down everything the older man said, but as it was totally unintelligible to him, he was finding it difficult.

'We always drill the seed early, so I can't show you that process in progress. We've got a seed drilling machine that drills four rows at a time. Now the next most important step is singling, that is cutting out the plants you don't want so that the ones you do want to grow on have enough space. The ideal is about thirty thousand plants per acre; spacing is important. And we start when plants are showing four secondary leaves.'

Laurence looked up from his notebook in surprise. 'But how do you take out the unwanted plants? Not by men in the field, surely, cutting out each unwanted seedling and leaving thirty thousand plants!'

'Indeed we do. How else? You can't get a machine to think. Labour is the big cost in beet production. Now I'm telling you what's desired. I don't suppose we get more than seventeen thousand plants to the acre in the end, due to bad singling or disease or other matters. At lifting time, I average eight and a half tons to the acre. I sow at ten-day intervals and harvest from late September to January, if the weather allows.'

'You harvest mechanically, I suppose.'

Commander Ranulph laughed. 'You motor men think in terms of machines, but farms are worked by men, too, you know. Yes, we have a harvester that runs between the rows and lifts the beets so that they can be pulled by hand, but if the weather is bad, a mechanical harvester cuts up the land too much. In any case, men have to lift the beets, knock them together to get off the soil and the crown has to be cut off with a knife.

Back-breaking work at the best of times, cruelly hard on a raw day.'

Laurence had stopped writing, his mind turning to mechanical solutions. 'The wage bill must indeed be one of the greatest costs in beet growing.'

'Oh, it is! Since the passing of the Agricultural Wages Act in 1924, wages are set by a board. We pay seven pence halfpenny an hour, ninepence overtime. They work a fifty hour week. We get some itinerant workers, but I must tell you that sugar beet has put shoes on the children of many a poor man. The crop needs men. Sugar beet factories need men. The building of those factories has helped unemployment. Not so many people going hungry these days. Still too many, of course.'

'But if someone were to invent machines . . .' began Laurence, his mind filled with visions of ploughs and wheels.

'Tell your friend if he wants to come round here when singling starts, or lifting, I shall be happy to show him around. There are problems with the crop besides eel worm. It's not quite so simple as I have made out, but only a farmer like myself would be interested in going farther into it.'

'And as a farmer, may I be very presumptuous and ask what sort of profit one might make per acre?'

Commander Higgs threw back his head and laughed heartily. 'Young man, tell your friend that I'm the best farmer hereabouts, but I lose, over all, a pound or two per acre per year. That's the honest answer to your question.'

'But, then why do you farm at all?'

'Well, because I have always farmed. I can afford to make a small loss on each acre, and I don't want to get out of farming, because I am convinced that the situation will change eventually. Besides, it is my duty to

188

farm my land. What would these men do if every farmer packed it in?'

It was a cold clear afternoon when Marsha saw Joyce at the station. She told her porter to take her luggage to the chauffeur whom she could see several paces behind Joyce, and rushed into her friend's arms. Joyce looked pretty and extremely happy to see her, and Marsha realized how much she had missed her.

'I've brought you some marmalade, but now I think of it you probably have it made and won't need what I have. And I've brought you a couple of scarves. It's the latest thing. A chiffon scarf tied to your handbag and allowed to trail, and of course at the neck. *Très chic*. You look marvellous. Country life suits you. Don't you ever come up to town? Heavens, I think I would go mad. Isn't it cold? I thought May would be warmer than this. Are you really having a party just for me? You are kind.'

'Let's get into the car,' said Joyce when Marsha paused for breath. 'I have a rug to keep us warm. I'm so glad to see you. It's still too early to see the garden at its best, but the cowslips are blooming on the banks of the moat, and there are still some daffodils. There's the cherry blossom, of course . . .'

Marsha wasn't paying attention to this description of the grounds. The chauffeur had her undivided attention. In a certain light, wearing a particular expression, he did look very much like Ronald Coleman. Marsha wasn't fooled. She knew Joyce employed him for that very reason. Marsha would watch carefully for signs of intimacy. Of course, Joyce would have to marry someone appropriate, but Marsha wouldn't be a bit surprised if Joyce wasn't having a flirtation with this handsome young man. She gave him a warm smile as he helped her into the motor car.

Arriving at the twin lodges of Helmingham for the second time, she looked down the long drive at the grand house very carefully, at the avenue of oaks, not yet in leaf, at the deer grazing happily, admiring the way the house sat on the horizon. So vast a house for one small shorthand typist! Marsha swallowed her envy and stretched her face into a smile.

'Gee, Joyce, I always thought my daddy was rich, but we never had anything like this. I mean, you have to cross the moat and walk for *miles* to get to your own garden. There was an old trellis outside my window that was just bowed down with honeysuckle in the summer. The scent of that honeysuckle used to come into my bedroom of a hot afternoon and just send me to sleep. My mother has some snowball bushes in front of the house, and it's just a hop, skip and a jump to the vegetable patch. But you won't be able to smell a flower unless someone brings it inside and I'll bet you daren't pick so much as a pea without your gardener's permission.'

'Helmingham is considered to have one of the finest gardens in the county!' said Joyce.

'Yes, but it isn't exactly yours, is it? I mean—'

'It is exactly mine,' said Joyce firmly. 'There is a new bed in the main guest room, so I'm sure you will be comfortable.'

Marsha said of course she would, and as soon as she was unpacked she would just come right over to Joyce's room and give her the scarves she had picked for her friend.

Laurence drove the car into the garage, flung his hat onto the seat and began to unbutton his jacket. The Rolls had splashed through innumerable puddles still on the roadside after the previous night's rain, and he welcomed the need for elbow grease as he began to polish up the body. Miss Grissom always made his hackles rise.

Bill and Mr Trimble soon joined him. 'What do you think of Miss Grissom?' asked Bill. 'Rosie has taken against her, says she's pushy and loud.'

'I agree with Rosie. Also she takes delight in putting Miss Joyce down. An unpleasant woman, eaten with jealousy. After the party Miss Joyce is giving in her honour, I expect she will be unbearable.'

'Husband hunting,' said Mr Trimble wisely. 'That's what it's all about.'

'I wouldn't doubt it . . .' began Laurence, but stopped speaking when he saw that they were being joined by two men who had driven their wagon into the yard. He thought he recognized them as farm labourers of Commander Higgs.

'Good afternoon. Have you a message for me?'

'From the Guv'nor? No, we want a word with you, Ballard,' said the elder man. Laurence thought they must be brothers. Both were short, gaunt men with hardly any teeth. Their hands were calloused and dirty and their backs were slightly bent. He put them in their late twenties – his own age. There the similarity ended. His own well-tailored uniform was in telling contrast to the collection of old clothes the men wore.

'I am happy to have a word with you. How can I help?'

'By not putting ideas into our governor's head,' replied the shorter one.

'Me? Putting ideas into the commander's head? What nonsense. I visited him this morning to ask a few questions about sugar beet, that's all.'

'Saying machines should do the work of men. You want us to starve, don't you? Where's your solidarity? And you a working man, like the rest of us. I can keep my family on thirty shillings a week and old Higgs can well afford to pay me. So why are you trying to talk him into more machines? Don't you like human beings?'

From the corner of his eye, Laurence could see that this conversation had Bill and Mr Trimble dumbfounded. He placed a hand on the shoulder of each of his visitors and smiled warmly. 'Believe me, I never thought my suggestions would be taken as an attempt to replace you. My point, you see, is that with machines, the commander could farm more land, thus using more men and growing more crops.'

'He already farms every last inch of it. He can't do more.'

'The farm next door is lying vacant. He could rent that,' pointed out Laurence, but the men were not interested. They continued to complain for several minutes, reminded him that farm workers were now unionized and warned him not to stir up trouble. He promised solemnly to do as they demanded.

'What the devil was that all about?' cried Bill when the men had gone. 'Why didn't you tell them to get lost?'

'Because I really don't want them to lose their jobs. I was interested in what they had to say. I want to find out as much as I can about running a farm. I've inherited a hundred and fifty acres in Hadleigh from my grandmother, and the land is just lying there.'

'Hire a farm manager,' said Bill dryly. 'You'll never be a farmer.'

'Don't farm at all,' said Mr Trimble. 'Every year since the war, two hundred thousand acres of farmland has gone out of production. If it carries on at this rate, there won't be so much as a grain of wheat grown in this country. The farmer is caught between the low prices he can get for his produce and the high wages he's now required to pay his labourers. Farmland is down to ten pounds the acre, but I doubt you'd be able to sell your farm at the present time.'

'I don't want to sell it, although I have to admit the house is in a terrible state.'

'What are you doing working here if you own property?' asked Trimble. He had been suspicious of Laurence from the moment he arrived and now eyed the younger man coolly.

'I must find some way of earning a living eventually. My savings are running out. I'm not a charge on the estate, Mr Trimble. I give my services free, you know.'

'Hmmph. No man works for nothing. What's your game? Fancy the heiress, do you?'

Laurence faced the old man angrily. 'I resent that.'

'Oh, well, I'm an old man and you should not be so cheeky. I meant no harm, now back off. I'm tired. I think I'll go home and rest. I apologize, if you think I should.'

Bill stayed on, giving his old friend a worried look. 'I thought you were going into the garage business. Now you talk of farming. I know those men. They'll be talking about you in the pub tonight. Have you gone off the idea of owning a garage?'

'Not at all. I am the new owner of a garage in Halstead. It's doing fairly well, but I think I'll sell it. My father helped me to purchase it and . . . well, that was perhaps a mistake.'

'You'll live on your estate in Hadleigh? What will you do for money? Did your grandmother leave you enough? What's the matter with you, Laurence? I can't make you out. You keep chopping and changing. You might as well stay here until you know exactly what you are going to do with yourself.'

Laurence picked up a chamois and began polishing the offside wing fiercely. 'I'm sure you're right, my old friend. I'm not up to much, am I? I also opened a garage in Hadleigh. Now I am stretched too thinly. What must you think of me?'

Bill, never a demonstrative man, walked over and patted Laurence on the back. He said nothing, believing that another reminder about marrying Joyce would be a serious mistake. He recognized the pangs of love when he saw them. Laurence would simply have to work out for himself what he wanted. As for himself, Bill couldn't understand the difficulty. To marry or not to marry an heiress and live happily ever after? Laurence was mad for sure.

The days passed more pleasantly than either Joyce or Marsha had thought they would, as each of them refrained from the sort of bickering that had often marked their friendship. Laurence was constantly on duty to drive them to Ipswich or Stowmarket or even Lowestoft. They made one journey to Cambridge, but it rained most of the day.

Meanwhile, preparations for the party went ahead. The invitations had been sent out well before Marsha arrived, and everyone had already replied. There would be sixty guests, and Joyce was beginning to panic.

She had written a list of the refreshments she wanted and handed it to Mrs Able. Chicken patties, anchovy eggs and salmon mayonnaise, together with plenty of sandwiches, was her menu. For dessert, she thought an assortment of cakes, some fruit salad and a few ices would be sufficient.

The following day, Mrs Able presented her with 'a few suggestions'. Eggs in aspic, sausage rolls, lobster cutlets, vol-au-vents of veal, together with *bouchées à la reine* and bridge rolls spread with gentlemen's relish was her proposal. To follow, she suggested royal trifles, individual charlotte russes, caramel and ginger creams, rhum babas and jellies *à la Suisse.*

'There is nothing here that I suggested!' exclaimed Joyce.

'Well, I've put down all the ices you wanted,' protested Mrs Able. 'I can do this affair for five shillings a head, and Bert says claret cup, cider cup and lemonade are what's to be drunk.'

Joyce took a deep breath, calculating silently that the party would cost in excess of fifteen pounds, and tried not to imagine what Mr Finch would think of such extravagance.

'Miss Joyce,' began Mrs Able slowly, as if talking to a backward child, 'you must have a decent spread or tongues will wag for ever.'

There was no answer to this, so she agreed to her cook's suggestions. She certainly didn't want tongues to wag. She just hoped that she would be allowed to choose the frock she would wear without suggestions from her maid or Marsha. Occasionally, Joyce felt that her life was not her own, and longed to take some outrageous action for which she had not asked prior permission from the servants or the villagers.

It was important to Rosie and Bill that the garden should look absolutely perfect for her guests, who, they assured her, would expect to view at least the formal gardens if the weather permitted. It was too early for roses and the lavender that edged some of the beds. Most of the trees were just acquiring their summer foliage, although the cherries and the apples were a pleasant sight. The daffodils had not yet gone over, and almost half of the tulips were in bloom. The plants in the herbaceous border were neat clumps, giving no hint of the extravagant blossom to come when there would be no earth showing and delphiniums, lupins and achilleas would crowd the back of the border and lady's mantle and dainty dianthus would spread onto the grass path at the front.

In Elizabethan times the walled garden had been divided into eight vegetable beds, and Bill never considered changing the arrangement. Vegetables grew like soldiers in neat lines, well hidden behind climbing roses which Rosie carefully trained on wires. One of the most amusing features of the walled garden was the arched tunnels over some of the paths on which Bill grew gourds or sweet peas or runner beans. On the day of the party there would be nothing to see but the bare metal arches. The greenhouses, by contrast, would be well furnished and therefore opened for inspection by Joyce's guests.

As Joyce had feared, May the eighth dawned grey and cold with a strong north-easterly wind whipping spring blossom to the ground and ruffling the water in the moat. Rosie and Bill and his men spread out across the gardens to strengthen ties and pick up fallen twigs.

Joyce had lived at Helmingham for just under three months, but she had already learned to dress warmly even on important occasions. She put on a new frock of fine Jersey wool in a bluey-green colour that suited her very well. Geometrical pin tucks in a series of diamonds decorated the hip line, a style requiring the narrowest of hips, especially as the pencil-thin belt sat directly on the hip bone. The long warm sleeves were full, and also decorated with pin tucks in a diamond pattern. She left her room and had not yet reached the staircase when Marsha joined her.

'Well!' said Marsha, standing back to take a good look. 'Don't you look smart! Are you sure that colour suits you?'

'It's all I have to wear.'

Marsha frowned. 'I've put on the wrong dress. It's a Callot. Do you like it?'

Joyce smiled. 'It's absolutely beautiful, but I don't think white is ideal today, and such short sleeves! You'll freeze. Have you something else?'

'Of course. I wouldn't come here with just one frock, although I can't afford anything as expensive as yours.' She turned and trotted back to her room, as Joyce congratulated herself on having at last bought a frock that Marsha envied.

Fifteen minutes later, Marsha entered the great hall wearing a grey-green frock with huge matching loops of satin appliquéd to the front. The neck was high and the sleeves were long. She looked charming, but worried.

'Our colours clash.'

'Oh, Marsha, don't be silly. We won't be standing close together all day. You must not worry.'

'What time is it?' Marsha looked at her wristwatch. 'I can change. No-one will be here right on time.' She took off like a marathon runner, complaining about the distance between the great hall and her bedroom.

Joyce walked over to the huge fire and looked up at the painting of a d'Avranche mother and swaddled baby that hung above the fireplace. 'Sir Anthony Van Dyck,' she said. 'Fifteen ninety-nine to sixteen forty-one.' Then she smiled. She had been studying the paintings in the house, recording the artists with a description and approximate date. She had then read all she could find about every painter as a means of coming to terms with them. To own such great works of art was less terrifying if one knew all about the painter.

She smoothed her frock over her hips with a little sigh of self-satisfaction. Marsha was such a self-confident young woman that Joyce usually felt inadequate in her presence. However, Marsha did not always display the best of taste in her clothes. Not that the two frocks she had worn briefly were not in good taste. In fact, they were exquisite. They simply did not suit Marsha or the occasion. Joyce did hope her friend's day would not be spoiled by her misjudgement.

The door opened. Marsha rushed in, breathless but happy. 'They're on their way. I heard voices.' She made a quick twirl. 'Do you like it?'

'Beautiful,' said Joyce sincerely, but with a sinking heart. Marsha was wearing a yellow frock of heavy crêpe de Chine. It had a V neck, intricate seaming and a huge self bow tied over the left hip. The colour complemented Marsha's rich brown hair and made her complexion glow.

Mr and Mrs Finch were announced. Marsha became animated, a carefree young woman who knew she looked her very best. The Finches were clearly charmed, and Joyce felt herself shrink.

Rupert and his sister arrived shortly afterwards. He sauntered towards Joyce with his hand extended, a cheeky smile brightening his handsome face. He really was shameless, but she felt herself warming to him. Not so his sister who extended a limp hand while glaring angrily. Her lips moved. She may have said something civil, but she may not have. Joyce couldn't hear the words, but Cousin Helen's expression spoke of undying hatred.

'This is my friend, Miss Grissom.'

'So pleased to meet you,' said Marsha, shaking hands heartily. 'May I call you Lord d'Avranche?'

'It's too soon.' He was grinning, already enchanted by Marsha's vivacity.

'Well, then I shall think of you as my lord, while I'll call you Cousin Rupert. You are Joyce's cousin, aren't you?'

Joyce and Rupert laughed and Helen glared before moving away. The American glowed with vitality and health. Nothing was going to spoil this day for Marsha.

The trickle of guests became a flood. The level of

noise rose steadily as Joyce continued to shake hands, trying to remember if each guest was someone she had met before and if so, where. Above the noise, she imagined she could hear Marsha's raucous laugh. She could certainly see the yellow frock as her friend moved among the throng, stopping here and there like a butterfly collecting nectar. Joyce consulted her watch. Twenty minutes had passed. Another few hours to go. She stopped Mr Crow who was carrying a tray of claret cup, and helped herself to a glass. It was time to summon the guests and lead them into the garden.

'I must get a coat!' cried Marsha, and Rupert, who seemed to have attached himself to her, agreed that she would be chilly out of doors. 'I am forever getting lost at Helmingham. If I'm not back in fifteen minutes, send out a search party.'

'Shall I come with you to show you the way?' asked Rupert, and Joyce, who was standing nearby, waited with some amusement for the answer. Marsha had been finding her way around the great house without difficulty for the past week.

'Would you?' asked Marsha, sweetly. 'You are so kind to go to so much trouble just for me.'

The guests were leaving the great hall and collecting warm clothing for what Joyce had promised them would be a quick tour of the walled garden only. She looked for the rector and found him leaning against the back of one of the dark oak dining chairs. 'You must sit down! What are you thinking of? Surely, you were not planning to go into the garden.'

'I would like to be able to tour it, but perhaps another day if you will invite me. There is a strong wind blowing and I cannot fight against it. My weakening heart is causing congestion of the lungs, apparently. But a word with you, Joyce, my dear. Beware of the schoolmaster. I am convinced Mr Goodenough is a

Bolshevik. But don't stop to talk to me now. Go and join your guests.'

He seemed to be tiring rapidly, and this was no time to discuss the schoolmaster's politics. She helped him to take a seat, then hurried away to join the others. Leaving by the great door, she crossed the cobbled courtyard and the bridge, turned right and began walking towards the walled garden which was also moated. At the causeway she was joined by Marsha and Rupert.

'You see, Cousin Rupert, it is as I was saying. Joyce has to walk for *miles* to reach her own garden. Now, at home, I have a honeysuckle . . .'

Joyce turned to look back at the house, standing imposingly against a backdrop of racing black clouds. Yellow wallflowers clung like jewels to the wall that protected the house against the moat. At the entrance to the walled garden, two huge, but shallow stone urns sat proudly on their plinths, as yet with no plants frothing from the top. The low hedges were neatly trimmed. This outer garden was a tidy picture of bare stems and raw earth.

Long, straight herbaceous borders ran the length of the garden, as well as across, and in the squares created would be the vegetables. Straw protected the strawberry plants, promising a feast later on. There was nothing much else to see, but in the summer roses, fantrained on wires with mathematical exactness would provide a backing for the borders and screening for the vegetables. Huge arched tunnels of black wrought-iron would be covered during the heat of the summer, providing shaded walks. But, for the moment, there was little to see. Many of the guests knew the grounds far better than Joyce did. They walked down the garden and through the gate at the far end to the orchard garden. It began to rain heavily and the wind rose in the north-east. Joyce heard Marsha squeal and turned to see her friend huddling under Rupert's umbrella. His sister, Helen, was sheltering, with less noise, under an umbrella held by Mr Hapgood Finch.

An umbrella appeared over her own head, and she turned round to smile at the gaunt face of Mr Goodenough who smiled back stiffly.

'You should have brought an umbrella with you, Miss Joyce.'

'Yes, I should. I'm surprised you are willing to shelter me. I understand you are a Bolshevik.'

He did not laugh, as she had expected, but smiled sadly. 'You have been talking to the rector.'

'He's an old man and not terribly well. I thought you would find it funny. I didn't mean to offend you.'

He reached the gate, opened it and allowed her to pass through. 'I assure you, being called a Bolshevik does not offend me. If taking an interest in the rights of the working man is Bolshevism, then I shall be happy to be so named. Yet, I promise you, I am no threat to you or to the rector. I suppose this is the wrong time to ask a favour of you, but may I have an appointment with you when your guest has returned to the more exciting pleasures of London?'

'You may have an appointment with me at ten o'clock tomorrow morning. Now, perhaps you will offer your umbrella to Mrs Finch. She seems to have been abandoned. Mr Finch is deep in conversation with Mr Trimble. I presume you do consider Mr Finch to be a working man.'

'Mr Finch is one of the enemy,' he said, ready to take part in the joke. Then he added more seriously, 'And no friend of yours.'

'But,' she said, striving for a light note, 'he can't be the enemy of the working man as well as the enemy of the aristocracy.'

'Do you call yourself aristocracy, Miss Joyce? I had thought you knew yourself better.'

He left her before she could say another word, which was probably fortunate, for she had no answer to his rudeness and needed time to think up a suitably barbed reply. Tomorrow she would put him down once and for all, as the rector had been urging her to do. The problem was, putting people down was not something of which Joyce had much experience.

The shrubbery walk which led back towards the hall on the outside of the walled garden provided a little protection from the wind, as well as a charming view of the spring border which sheltered on the outside of the old brick wall. The narrow garden moat came between the shrubbery and the border, forcing the visitor to take a more distant view of the bright red tulips now in bloom and the tall brown stems of the peonies which would bloom a month or so later.

'Miss d'Avranche, may I have a word with you?'

Joyce turned to see a plump little woman with black-rimmed spectacles looking up at her anxiously. Many of the guests were very elegantly dressed, especially the men, but this lady was not among them. Her woollen frock was undoubtedly pre-war and showing signs of wear. Lisle stockings and lace-up shoes protected her feet, but a long cardigan was all that protected her from the weather. Her cheeks were extremely rosy, and she didn't seem to mind the rain.

'I'm sorry,' said Joyce, trying to remember the woman's name and where they had met.

'Mrs Hupple, on the hospital committee. I live in Stowmarket.'

'Yes, I'm afraid I was dreaming. Of course I know who you are.'

'Are we going to the herb and knot garden?'

'I thought we might go in. It's raining heavily.'

'I don't mind a little rain, I assure you.' Mrs Hupple strode on, not to be put off. Joyce hurried to catch her up, noticing that others also seemed determined to visit the formal herb and knot garden. They crossed the main drive and walked the length of the moat before turning left. This smaller garden was reached just before the second moat bridge, and as the grassy bank was above the garden, it was possible to get the full effect of its charm by looking down on it.

'Miss d'Avranche, I wonder if you would host a garden fête here this summer to raise funds for the National Orphanages. I thought you might be willing in view of the fact that your own mother was . . .'

She didn't finish the sentence, but ended with an embarrassed smile. Why did she have to mention Thora? wondered Joyce. It would have been sufficient to ask to have the event on the grounds. Due to her careful choice of words, Joyce could now be in no doubt that everyone knew who Thora was and what her history had been. One could live one's entire life in London and never be known at all. She was continually surprised by how much complete strangers in a Suffolk village knew of her past life.

'As my mother was an orphan, I will be happy to allow a fête to take place here. What is the date?'

'June the tenth. Thank you very much. We all appreciate it, and I promise you there will be very little for you to do except to declare the fête open.'

Eventually, even the keenest of garden lovers had read every label, commented on every rose and marvelled at the intricately trimmed hedging. They trooped indoors, bringing their mud with them. The gleaming stone floor of the great hall was soon dimmed. The buffet had been laid out on long white-clothed tables at the far end. Several of the estate workers were wearing their indoor clothes to hold trays of glasses or to clear the tables of used plates.

Joyce saw Laurence smiling at her as he clutched a tray. His handsome presence was a friendly oasis in a sea of potential enemies. She approached him. 'You look very smart in your indoor clothes. I hope you are enjoying this experience.'

'No,' he said. 'I hate it, but not so much as you do.'

'Yes, I do hate it and they all despise me. I can feel it.'

'Miss Joyce, this is cider cup. Please take a glass. Mr Crow is looking at us with a face like thunder. You must circulate.'

'I can't. They all patronize me.'

'Miss Grissom is moving among your guests as if she were the hostess.'

'She's very confident, and her parents had a more conventional courtship than mine did, and she hasn't inherited Helmingham, and they would prefer her to me if she had. I can't speak to any more of these sneering people.'

He spoke sternly, turning his back to Crow so that the butler could not see his expression, or Joyce's. 'The sneers are in your imagination, and no-one is patronizing you. Yellow doesn't suit her. She's not as pretty as you are and she is far too pushy. Please take control of your party.'

She laughed nervously, grateful for his encouragement. 'How nice it would be just to sit around the kitchen table at the Lodge, talking to Rosie and you and Bill!'

'I am inclined to agree. I know you would be happier, but here is your duty and you must do it. If only you could be made to see that they will respond to your confidence and pleasure in their company. Try to smile. Show that cheeky friend of yours that you are the grand lady, not she. There is Commander Higgs and his wife who is looking a little out of things. He even had time to speak to me this afternoon. He will not snub you. Go on!'

Joyce finished the small glass of cider cup, put the glass on the tray and walked away, buoyed by Laurence's support. She had reason to be especially grateful to him, since the Higgses were clearly pleased to have her attention. She introduced them to a couple from Stowmarket who were tireless workers for the hospital, before excusing herself to talk to the rector.

Several hours later two tired women sank gratefully into the big easy chairs in Joyce's handsome drawing-room, slipped off their shoes and prepared to relive the day.

'I heard you squealing in the rain,' said Joyce. 'Anyone would think they don't have weather in Kansas City.'

Marsha laughed. 'Rain, snow, drought, temperatures in the hundreds or twenty degrees below freezing. Even the occasional tornado. I've seen them all. However, men like to think that women are too delicate for anything but the sunniest, warmest summer day. Your cousin Rupert is very handsome, Joyce. Are you sure you don't want to marry him?'

'I detest him.'

'Then I really think I shall marry him. He's going to be Lord d'Avranche. We'd have the same surname. Wouldn't that be a scream? I told him my father has a thousand-acre ranch. After that, he clung to me like ivy.'

'You're outrageous,' said Joyce, not sure how she felt about having Marsha as a cousin.

'Rupert wants to take me riding tomorrow. He's staying with some friends nearby. Do you mind?'

'Not at all. I have an appointment with the school-master at ten. We'll meet for luncheon at one o'clock. I've nothing planned for the day.'

'Oh, do invite Cousin Rupert to lunch. Please! You know, I had this silly idea that people like Rupert were different. All these aristocrats being not like you and me. But it isn't true. We're just the same. Just people, wherever we come from.'

'I would disagree.'

'You're being difficult, Joyce. Why, I actually met a lady who had met my mother at a party in Kansas City! It's a small world.'

'But it's not my world. Marsha, dear, I'm dreadfully tired. If you don't mind I'll just go up to my room and lie down.'

Her bedroom was peaceful, its pale green and cream decor providing a soothing retreat. She threw back the cover and lay down, drawing the spread over her. Even the rain beating on her window failed to spoil the solitude. She closed her eyes and reviewed the party. It had been a nightmare. She knew she was at her best in the company of just a few people. Sixty guests, some of whom were her enemies, or enemies in the past of her mother, were unnerving. Mr Finch had introduced his wife, who, Joyce was certain, held her in contempt. Women seemed to view her warily, speaking in stilted voices until an old friend or acquaintance came along, when they turned with relief to talk of shared interests.

Marsha's outgoing personality, her assumption that everyone would like her had helped to diminish Joyce's own confidence. *I will not allow her to take over my position*, she thought, in a flash of spirit. *I will fight her and I do not want her to be Rupert's wife!* Then she admitted this was an unworthy thought. Her mind's eye conjured up Laurence, a man better looking, better mannered and far more intelligent than any of her guests. Her only friend at the party. How strange that friendship had come from the chauffeur who was acting as a waiter. She smiled at the thought of him and fell asleep.

The schoolmaster was on time to the minute. 'Good morning, Mr Goodenough. How nice to see you.' She might have held the meeting in any one of several rooms, but had chosen the drawing-room to give herself the edge. She had felt somewhat overwhelmed when she first saw it. Might not Mr Goodenough feel the same?

He did indeed seem ill at ease as soon as he entered the room. 'Please allow me to apologize for my rudeness yesterday. I have been unable to sleep. I didn't mean to be impertinent.'

Taken by surprise, she tried to think exactly what he had said that was so offensive. Oh, yes. 'Well, Mr Goodenough, I was surprised by your attitude.'

'I do most humbly . . . that is, I don't know what came over me.' He hung his head and picked at a hangnail on his thumb.

Enlightenment came suddenly. 'You must not worry. I've no intention of sacking you.'

His head came up. He gave an uncertain smile. He was not sorry for having spoken after all. He was simply bitterly regretting having put his livelihood at risk.

'Actually, I have come upon a pleasant mission, Miss Joyce. I was hoping that you would have a small party at the end of the school year for the children and their parents. An afternoon of ice cream and jelly, of sack races and balloons. Would the twentieth of July be acceptable to you?'

She knew it was. There were no engagements in her diary, except the one for the garden fête, written in only the day before. 'Will you excuse me while I consult my diary?'

The diary was nearby, in the study, but she took her time, taking advantage of a few moments to herself to readjust her attitude to the schoolmaster. Reverend d'Avranche was clearly wrong, and she had been wrong to trust the judgement of an old man in such poor health. Mr Goodenough was a fiery young man, someone who spoke his mind, but he would surely never have asked the lady of Helmingham Hall to hold a party for the schoolchildren if he were the revolutionary that the rector imagined he was. Admittedly, it was probably the custom for the party to take place at Helmingham Hall, but a man who hated what Joyce represented would have found a way to change this custom. Thanks to the rector's warning, she had put up her guard against someone who meant no incivility at all. Feeling certain now that she was in the company of a friend, she returned to the drawing-room with a broad smile.

'The day is free and I'm looking forward to it very much. We must give this some thought and make it a special day for the children. Perhaps we could have a meeting or two to plan out events.'

They spent a pleasant hour discussing the party, and Joyce felt able to relax in the young man's company. As the meeting became less formal, she saw that Mr Goodenough looked uncomfortable. When Mr Crow entered with coffee on a tray, the young schoolmaster jumped to his feet, attempted to help position the tray. His every gesture served to remind her that she paid his salary, and that he was unlikely to forget the difference in their positions.

With a sigh, she said coolly, 'Will you have a piece of fruitcake, Mr Goodenough?'

Chapter Nine

Joyce stood up and wandered around the drawing-room, touching an object here and there, running her hand over polished wood, slapping a cushion into shape. The change of furniture had not been a success, so she had called the men back to take into the attics those pieces which had been so recently brought downstairs. The rooms were once again as she had seen them on her arrival a few short months ago. And she still did not feel that this was her home, these possessions hers to love and dispose of as she saw fit.

Each day she toured the rooms, believing that she had no right to live in so large a house if she didn't at least visit every part of it regularly. She tried to do the same in the gardens and grounds, but soon discovered that there was very little time for anything else if she made her rounds with any sort of thoroughness.

Some of the changes wrought in her life were very easy to get used to. For instance, she no longer regarded it as an intrusion of her privacy when Cutler sorted her clothes, washing and pressing those in need of it. Cutler quite often chose and laid out something for her to wear in the morning, and Joyce was soon content to have her do so.

Nor did she miss the cooking and cleaning. If she were honest with herself, she had to admit that Marsha had done most of the cooking, and the cleaning lady did all of the cleaning on one morning a week. Joyce's only duty had been to tidy up. This she still did, and at Helmingham Hall it was even more necessary than in

London. An item carelessly laid down and later needed was a sore trial. She once spent half an hour in search of her wristwatch which she had taken off to wind and set, then laid down absentmindedly when Mr Crow approached to ask a question.

She had taken to carrying a small wastepaper basket around with her, into which she put stray items. As she went around the house, she replaced whatever had been out of place, while taking up whatever was still away from its proper home. Later, she would pick up those things which were supposed to be upstairs and leave the wastepaper basket at the foot of the stairs. On going to bed or upstairs to change, she would take the basket with her. Until one day, Mr Crow, thinking he was being helpful, took the basket upstairs and Cutler redistributed the contents as she saw fit. The one and only time Joyce was ever cross with the servants was over their attempts to help her tidy. They couldn't understand the depth of her feelings; she marvelled at their energy. They never seemed to consider saving themselves a journey. In her first days at Helmingham, she calculated every step, preferring not to read the new novel, if it was not to hand when she wanted it. She was also willing to be cold if her cardigan was half a house away.

She had agreed to meet Marsha and Rupert in the stableyard at one, and so thought she had better start walking. The most direct route was across the foot-bridge and along the gravel path to the area containing the coach house, stables, greenhouses and other outbuildings. Both the stable block and the coach house were fine buildings, cleaner and more comfortable than many a home. She particularly liked the coach house with its arched doors and high ceiling. In the heat of summer it would probably be a cool haven, but on this cold May day she knew she would be struck by the dampness and gloomy echoes.

Joyce hated horses and mistrusted people who rode them, convinced that they changed their nature once in the saddle. Rupert and Marsha arrived less than a minute after she reached the yard, laughing and full of themselves as they towered over her. Their lathered horses seemed to pose a threat, so she backed towards the coach house, where Laurence was dimly visible doing something to the Rolls by the light of a lantern.

'Joyce, you really must learn to ride. You must set up your stables and be a part of the riding community here,' said Marsha, turning her horse round to show off. 'Commander Higgs lent us these mounts and they really are wonderful. Wouldn't you like to own an animal like this?'

'No, I wouldn't. I don't see the need.'

'Cousin Joyce, you must make an effort to fit in. This is a rural community. Everyone rides,' added Rupert.

'I don't care. Do get down, you two. I'm afraid I'm going to be trampled any minute.'

Rupert and Marsha laughed at this absurd idea, and Rupert rode right up close to her, amused by her obvious fear.

'Miss Joyce,' said a voice behind her, and Joyce turned to see Laurence frowning as he wiped the grease from his hands, 'Miss Joyce is going to learn to drive the Rolls. Motor cars are the vehicles of the future. Why should she depend on single horsepower?'

Joyce smiled at him. He always came to her rescue, even if it were necessary to talk nonsense in order to save her from embarrassment.

Marsha was unimpressed. 'Joyce, you can't! Driving is so masculine. Ladies prefer to be driven. My family have had motor cars for ever, but my mother doesn't drive. You would do better to learn to handle a horse before taking on anything so mechanical.'

'Miss Joyce will drive. She will make motoring fashionable for ladies.'

'Yes,' added Joyce. 'That is exactly what I plan to do, although I don't care whether I set a fashion or not.'

Marsha woke each morning with a sense of excitement. She was having fun! No-one could persuade her that she was not. She was determined to fall in love with Rupert d'Avranche, to share Joyce's family and live almost as well as Joyce did. She *would* fall in love with him. It was only a matter of time and putting her mind to it. After all, he was very handsome, close to her own age and about to become Lord d'Avranche. She must learn to love him because she had always said she would never marry for worldly reasons.

Rupert had one quality that attracted her to him; he had told her about his unhappy childhood. A distant and disapproving father had sent him away to school at six. His mother was cold, his sisters jealous of his place as the heir. When he stopped making foolish jokes and swaggering about, she could like him very well. And when he sat quietly with her and told her of his past unhappiness, Marsha felt a very genuine love, although it was more in the nature of a maternal desire to kiss the wounded soul and make him better.

Joyce was watching the rapidly deepening affair with tight lips and patent disapproval. This attitude spurred Marsha on to flirt with Rupert even more daringly. Her old friend no longer needed her to protect her from rude people or to introduce her to new friends. Joyce had acquired a degree of self confidence that made Marsha grind her teeth because an essential ingredient of their friendship had been Marsha's belief that Joyce depended upon her.

Joyce had found a new friend; the gardener's wife of all people. Marsha simply couldn't understand this friendship, since Rosemary Cook made her feel quite uncomfortable. She felt she was being judged. How dare a servant pass judgement on Marsha Grissom! Such a plain, quiet woman too.

Joyce had invited a few people to Helmingham for dinner. They were all young, all were mad on riding, all were people whom Marsha had met through the commander's son, Hector. Marsha called them the new gang and urged Joyce to show a bit of enthusiasm when in their company.

'My daddy used to say, "Gentlemen like women who are enthusiastic. It's unattractive in a woman to be list-less. Come on, Marsha," he used to tell me. "Look lively and interested in what a man has to say."'

'Did he tell the men to look interested in what you have to say?'

'No, of course not,' laughed Marsha. 'He always told me not to say too much. However, he knew that was a lost cause. I can't stay silent. However . . .' She patted her hair into place. 'I will say that his advice was very good. He used to say that men don't like girls who show their tempers. And always to dress as if I'm going to meet the man of my dreams in the next ten minutes. Daddy likes women to be well groomed, and my mother always looks just so. Daddy said you only need to meet one man, but how can you know which one it will be? So you should be nice to all of them. I think he's right, too, because marriage is every girl's dream, don't you think? I mean, what else is there? You wouldn't have wanted to be a shorthand typist all your life, would you? I mean there's nothing wrong with it, of course, but marriage would have saved you from the drudgery if Lord d'Avranche hadn't. But I do show enthusiasm whenever I am in the company of the op-posite sex and most men seem to like me. Don't you think so?'

'Oh, you are a great favourite with the men,' said Joyce with just a hint of sarcasm.

Marsha looked at her old friend appraisingly. 'You know, you've developed quite a nasty streak. It comes from having all this opulence, I expect. Don't think I didn't notice the tone of voice. I noticed it all right. You think I'm a hopeless flirt. Well, let me tell you something, Joyce, *my lady*, d'Avranche. I'll put myself out to get a husband, and we'll make a home and have lots of children. You, on the other hand, will end up a lonely old maid in this great barn of a house. You can't marry the chauffeur, you know, even if he is the only man to take an interest in you. Rupert says he can't fathom you. He says you're a lot like your mother, and that you would do well to behave differently. He's noticed how you moon about the chauffeur. What's his name? Laurence. I didn't mention it first, I promise you. But it is obvious to everyone.'

'It's only a house, Marsha,' replied Joyce, coolly. 'You really must try not to be so jealous.'

They parted shortly afterwards and Joyce went for a walk in the gardens for an hour, while Marsha was left with the uncomfortable feeling that she might truly be jealous. She examined her emotions carefully, before finally pronouncing herself innocent. Joyce had spoiled their friendship, she decided. Joyce was the one who had changed.

Marsha thought she would die laughing that night when Joyce tried to be animated at the dinner party. Why, she had no idea how to go about it! Marsha sparkled that evening, her happiness tinged with regret and a degree of panic that she would be leaving the comfort of Helmingham the following day.

Rupert and all the new gang promised to get in touch in London. They would have some grand times. Only Joyce spoiled it all by flatly refusing to leave

Helmingham and come to London for some fun. What was the matter with the girl? Did she think Helmingham Hall would disappear if she turned her back?

The next morning they said goodbye at the front door as Joyce had some sort of appointment. Marsha suspected that her friend was only trying to make herself seem important, for who would want to have a meeting with Joyce?

She settled into the back seat of the Rolls and for several miles pretended that the motor was hers, that the chauffeur was hers to command and that she was going to her own grand establishment.

Studying the back of Laurence's head with its crisp brown hair under the jaunty cap, she felt an irresistible urge to protect Joyce from the consequences of her poor judgement. Leaning forward, she tapped him on the shoulder, and Laurence duly pulled over into a farm lane before turning round to see what she wanted.

'You are very fond of Miss Joyce, aren't you?'

'Yes, Miss Grissom, I am. I would lay down my life for her.'

He was looking at Marsha with narrowed suspicious eyes, which unsettled her. 'She is a trusting woman. I, on the other hand, know exactly what you are up to.'

'I beg your pardon!'

Marsha flinched. This chauffeur had a very impertinent manner. She was almost afraid of him. 'You think that by making Miss Joyce fall in love with you, you can become the owner of Helmingham Hall. But you will be foiled. She will see through your plot and eventually marry – if she marries at all – a suitable person with his own fortune.'

Now his face was red and Marsha wished she had not spoken. It crossed her mind that he might murder her and throw her body into the bushes, and she would never see London again. But no, he was going to destroy her with words, which was worse.

'Joyce d'Avranche is a very fine woman who deserves to have better friends around her than people like you. I want nothing from her, most especially not her house. You, on the other hand, are using her to settle yourself in life. For shame, Miss Grissom, to accuse me of your own bad behaviour. I will not overstep the mark if you will agree never to come here again.'

Marsha sat back in the seat, breathing hard and wishing the ground would open up and swallow her whole. Why had she interfered? She didn't care who Joyce married, must have been off her head to have mentioned it. Worst of all, she had no idea how to bring this uncomfortable interview to an end.

'I cannot make that promise. I love my friend. Now please drive me to the station.'

But he didn't turn back to the wheel or show any sign of being prepared to drive off. 'I am tempted to make you a few promises. I will not try to worm my way into Miss Joyce's affections, and I promise you most solemnly that I have no desire to live at Helmingham. I promise, also, to tell Miss Joyce of your warning.'

'No! That is, I should not have spoken. I'm sorry. I guess I misunderstood the situation. It's just that you are very sassy, and I thought the last thing Miss Joyce needs is a sassy chauffeur.'

He grimaced. 'I don't know what she needs, except that I don't think she needs either of us.'

At last, he turned round and drove off. They travelled in silence and when he had helped her from the motor and handed over her luggage to a porter, he tipped his hat in a deferential way. She knew he was mocking her, but she simply turned her thoughts to Rupert, who would one day be Baron d'Avranche, and to the new clothes she would need for the summer.

$\star \qquad \star \qquad \star$

A series of warm days and bright sunshine had brought the garden out in all its late spring glory. Already Bill was worrying about drought. East Anglia was the driest part of the country, and although the Helmingham land was mostly a heavy clay and not the treacherous sand or thin chalk that characterized much of the region, dry weather, nevertheless, played havoc with the estate crops, as well as shrivelling the garden.

Rosie was out of doors in her own patch of garden. The roses that climbed against the lodge received less attention than those of the Hall, but she had time this morning to make sure they were tied in properly. Already the fat buds were swelling on Mme Alfred Carrière, a splendid old rose of the noisette type. Its large flowers were always blush pink when they opened, but they faded to pure white. The scent was strong, reaching her at night as she lay in bed. She had climbed ten feet up a ladder on the road side of the lodge when she realized she had left her raffia indoors on the kitchen table. Descending the ladder, she rounded the corner of the lodge in time to see Joyce cycling down the long drive with Betsy panting by her side. The bicycle had a basket attached to the front, and in the basket was a large box. Joyce seemed to be in imminent danger of losing her balance, her box or, possibly, her exhausted wheezing dog.

'Here, let me help you!' she called, running forward. 'I think Betsy is too old for such an energetic work out.'

'I know. I shouldn't have brought her. Oh, Rosie, I wanted to deliver this myself, but that was possibly a mistake. Take the box so that I can put the bike on the ground. Have you a bowl of water for Betsy? I'll walk back with her, I promise you.' Joyce saw that the box was in safe hands, laid her bicycle on the lawn and looked with some alarm at Betsy's lolling tongue.

The box was quite heavy. 'What have we here? Shall I take it indoors?'

'Yes, please. It's for you.'

Rosie was soon unwrapping a dozen tea cups, saucers and plates onto her kitchen table. There was wrapping paper everywhere and just enough confusion; Joyce was filling the kettle and putting it on to boil, to enable Rosie to collect her thoughts.

'It's Doulton,' Joyce said, excitedly. 'Sprays of pink roses with a gilt edge. Do you like the design? I know you always give me the best cup when I visit you, so now you can drink from a fine cup, too.'

'You are so sweet.' Rosie lifted one cup and turned it round and round in her rough hands. 'But where did you buy them?'

'Mail order from Harrods. It's a very good service. It doesn't take any time at all. They send what you order by rail and then Laurence picks it up. He doesn't know what's in the box, of course. I didn't tell him.'

'I don't know what to say, except thank you.' Rosie could hardly add that she preferred to drink from the good china cup because it had been a gift from her grandfather, or that she already possessed a complete tea service in Crown Derby that she had put at the back of a cupboard in the dining-room and never ever used because it came from Aunt Edna whom she hated. All possessions carried an extra dimension for Rosie. They were the extensions of the people who gave them. The new tea service would be loved as a present from Joyce, but carry embarrassing overtones because Joyce clearly thought she was too poor to have a decent set of her own.

'Well, we must make some tea and drink a toast in the new cups. I'll wash two now and get the rest seen to later. Bill will be surprised!'

'It's to cheer you up,' said Joyce shyly. 'You know.'

Rosie made the tea and set the pot on the table. She took her time pouring milk into a jug and set it down with the sugar bowl before answering. By this time Joyce was looking very worried, probably afraid that she had offended.

'I do thank you for your concern, Miss Joyce. You caught me at an awkward moment the other day. I was feeling low, else I would never have mentioned it. You must understand . . .' She jumped up and moved towards the cupboard. 'I baked a ginger cake yesterday. Will you have a piece?'

'Yes, thank you.' Poor Joyce looked very embarrassed, now convinced that she had erred in some way.

Rosie cut the cake. 'I have come to terms with it, I promise you. Bill and I are very happy together. We are happy to be living at Helmingham. Of course, there is much sadness in my family as my brothers have left the country, but otherwise . . .' She took a bite of her cake, aware that she had not reassured her young friend. 'I'm going to let you into a secret. One that even Bill doesn't know.'

'Don't tell me if you don't want to. I don't mean to pry.'

Rosie smiled. 'This secret is very precious. It is the reason why I won't be mourning my childlessness. I have . . . I have given birth to a new rose!'

Joyce was still looking puzzled. 'You have bred a rose?'

'Yes! It's the most beautiful thing. A very vigorous shrub. I daresay it will reach four or five feet high and spread even further. The flowers are apricot pink, but they fade to a sort of silvery pink. Oh, it's glorious, and I shall give it the name I would have given a daughter. I can't tell you what that name is, because it would be bad luck, but this rose is my baby and there will be others. Come on, let's go up to the field behind the greenhouse where I'm raising some specimens.'

Joyce was full of enthusiasm, pleased to have been taken into Rosie's confidence, but still apparently puzzled. 'And you haven't told Bill about it?'

'It's a long story. I think we had better leave Betsy. She looks very tired, poor old thing.'

Joyce began walking her cycle across the park. Rosie was relieved when, halfway to the stables, the dog decided to go with them. 'So Miss Grissom has returned to London! Do you miss her?'

'In a way. We don't . . . we aren't so close anymore. Cycling is fun. Do you have a bike, Rosie? Could we go cycling some time? Laurence is going to teach me to drive the Rolls. He insists. But I'm a little nervous.'

'I do have a bicycle and I would greatly enjoy riding with you when I have the time. This is a rose grower's busiest time, you know. I plan to enter a number of shows and must prepare my blooms. Everything is entered in your name, of course. Perhaps you will come to one of the shows.'

'That would be wonderful. Will you be entering your secret rose?'

'Oh, no. When I'm sure I have a good rose, I will register it with the National Rose Society. After that I will exhibit it.' They walked on in silence. Joyce seemed distracted this morning, and Rosie put this down to the departure of her friend. She hated lazy, noisy people like Marsha Grissom, and always called her the Yankee Doodle when talking to Laurence or Bill. 'I don't wish to pry, but I hope you and Miss Grissom didn't quarrel.'

Joyce looked round. 'Oh, is it so obvious? She is dead set on getting Rupert to marry her. I don't mind that, I promise you, but she said the most dreadful things to me. She said I was going to be an old maid. She said the only man who shows any interest in me is the chauffeur.'

'She is a very cruel lady. She takes too much on herself, and I can't imagine Mr Rupert will be in her clutches for long.'

'Since I never had a father, Rosie, I feel that I may have missed out on the good advice a father can give. Did your father advise you about how to find a husband? How to behave in the company of men?'

'My father told me that one must always be vigilant. That mildew is frequently due to soft growth and you should not feed roses too much nitrogenous fertilizer, that red spider mite in the greenhouse is due to dry air. He told me that a delicate touch and vigilance are vital if one wants to breed roses. I don't remember his ever mentioning men or how to behave in their company. Did Miss Grissom receive some good advice on the subject from her father? If she did, I think she has failed to heed it. She is an appalling flirt.'

But Joyce would not allow her friend to be criticized. Rosie, who had never enjoyed a close female friendship before, discovered that she was jealous of Joyce's affection for Marsha Grissom, while still jealous of Laurence's attraction to Joyce. She was mortified to realize just what an unworthy person she was and thought she had no character at all. Her depression grew, even as she reassured Joyce that she would most certainly not be a spinster, and that Laurence clearly admired her, but no, he had never spoken of it to Rosie. She was quite exhausted by the time they reached the rose bed, her emotions were in turmoil, yet she knew the younger woman was looking to her for moral support in the absence of any sort of family.

'Well, here we are. That's it. My baby. None of the buds are showing any colour yet. Just wait a few weeks.'

'I think I recognize your new rose from the description. You grew several bushes in the greenhouse, didn't you?'

'Yes.'

'And Laurence cut all the blooms.'

'Yes, but I—'

'I remember it well. It was Easter, and the next day he moved out of your house and into the stable block. I always wondered why he left so suddenly.'

'Miss Joyce, I was annoyed that he had taken the roses without permission, but I didn't tell him that he had cut my most precious rose. It was time he moved into premises of his own. I understand he is very happy, by the way, and gets splendid meals cooked for him by Mrs Able.'

'How awful for you. You must have been devastated. I know you, Rosie. You take your work very seriously.'

'Roses are my life. I was born to raise roses. I shan't mind about not having a family, please believe me.'

'And I shan't mind about never marrying. I'm going to make Helmingham Hall my life's work. I will know everything about it. I will possess it by knowledge. I will know every member of the family, past and present. I will own them because I will know everything about them.' She looked hard at Rosie, then said, 'I've got over the shock of finding out about my mother's love affair, I assure you. I will only say in her defence that she was so young and Lord d'Avranche was so old.'

'Well, it is best that you should know. People can be cruel, so you must learn to ignore the snubs. You are Miss d'Avranche of Helmingham Hall, that's all that matters. Have you told Miss Grissom?'

'Certainly not! She must never find out. She wouldn't understand at all. You see, I realize that my parentage sort of rules me out of a good marriage. I've learned to accept that. I shall be Miss d'Avranche of Helmingham Hall, the eccentric spinster who does good work and whom everybody likes very well, but no-one loves.'

Rosie didn't know what to say to this. She busied herself with the roses, turning up leaves and looking for signs of greenfly.

'I shall have to give these plants a nicotine spray soon.'

'I found a picture of my father, taken when he was about twenty. He wasn't very handsome. In fact, he looked rather peculiar.'

'He fell off his horse as a child and was rolled on.'

'Yes, I know. How dreadful! He must have suffered terribly.' Joyce was silent for a moment. 'Perhaps that's why I'm so afraid of horses.'

This fitted in with Rosie's way of thinking. It seemed to her perfectly reasonable that a man could pass on his fear of horses to his daughter. 'He was a decent man who suffered all his life from the broken bones he sustained at ten years old. You would have liked him, I believe. Bill saw him a few times, and everyone spoke well of him.'

'Thank you for telling me, Rosie, but please don't say anything about my mother. Please, I couldn't bear it. She had such a hard upbringing. She was just an ignorant young woman, but Lord d'Avranche was an educated man. I believe he took advantage of her and I don't want to hear otherwise.' She started to walk towards the Hall, but turned. 'I think your rose is exquisite, and I won't tell a soul about it. You are a very dear friend, Rosie.'

Betsy trotted after Joyce as Rosie stood staring blindly at the horizon for several minutes. The friendship of Joyce d'Avranche was the one bright spot in a bleak existence. She wasn't old enough to be Joyce's mother, but felt strong maternal stirrings in the girl's presence.

Rosie felt that her life was in turmoil and couldn't understand the conflicting, intrusive emotions that prevented her from enjoying the tranquillity that had once been hers. No longer did she scan the night sky for a star to wish upon. It was a small denial, but her improper feelings towards Laurence had to be punished in some way. Sometimes she wondered if she were going mad. She would comb her short hair, now growing out most unattractively, and wonder what Laurence thought of it. She would plan the Sunday menu, hoping that Laurence would like it, although he seldom came to dinner. Occasionally, she actually forgot she was married to Bill, and began to think of herself as a young woman embarking on life. She cried for no reason, and had a difficult time preventing Bill from seeing her in tears, for he always acted with such monumental patience and understanding that she wanted to hit him.

With long angry strides, she entered one of the storerooms and fetched twine, secateurs and a pair of steps. From the storeroom it was a short distance to the east rose garden. She stared down at it from the raised grass walk, taking little pleasure in the vision before her. The beds containing the Rosa Mundis were edged in catmint, not yet showing to effect, while the four outer beds were surrounded by lavender which would perfume the air, competing with the roses. Among the roses, but still mere clumps in late May, were pink and white foxgloves, blue and white Canterbury bells, yellow flowered lady's mantle, purple violas and hardy geraniums, both pink and blue. In high summer, there would be scarcely an inch of ground showing which reduced the need for weeding, but made it more difficult for Rosie to do any deadheading.

In the centre of the garden was a brick circle within a square within a circle, the sort of mystical pattern that Rosie loved. She loved the golden thyme with which the surrounding bed was planted, but most of all she loved the large statue of Flora that towered over the garden from the centre of the brick pattern, the perfect name for a little girl, if she were not to be named Felicia.

The pegged branches needed some attention following the previous day's violent winds. She bent to attend to a Centifolia, tugging the long whippy stem into position, pulling down hard to secure it. Suddenly, the branch gave way. She released it and saw that it hung limply, broken three feet above the ground. Rosie straightened, anger paralyzing her ribcage. In all her life she had never been so clumsy. To have applied such force that a sturdy stem broke was inconceivable. The pattern of pegged branches was spoiled, the rose would not look right to her critical eye, no matter how profusely the rest of the bush bloomed. Worst of all, Bill would see it. He would know that she had lost her touch.

She was filled with dread. This was an omen of bad luck. Something terrible was about to happen. And since her family was already splitting up, since she already knew that she would never have a child, and since obscene thoughts of Laurence already tormented her, there was only one more thing to dread. She was about to lose Bill! Only later did she wonder if it could be the rose that was under threat.

It was half-past seven in the morning when Joyce walked into the kitchen where all the staff had gathered. The laughter was relaxed; everyone seemed to be talking at once, even though they were all busy with some task.

'Excuse me.' The laughter died. The smiles faded and they turned to listen with respectful faces. 'I won't take much of your time. I've brought my note pad and I want to take down exactly what each of you do. You know, what your duties are.'

'I was only in the kitchen to fetch some scouring powder,' said Annie, the cleaner, and Lucille who had been taken on to replace Cutler as a cleaner, began to cry.

'No, no. I'm not criticizing. I just want to know what your duties are.'

Mr Crow broke the ensuing silence. 'One of my tasks is to manage the staff, Miss d'Avranche.'

Joyce knew she was being reprimanded. 'That's fine, Mr Crow. I'll put that down. Now then, what are your other duties?'

'Well now, I have responsibility for all the wine. I'm supposed to write down in my book each bottle that's drunk, so that I can reorder. That is, *if* I know a bottle has been taken.'

Joyce was writing rapidly in shorthand. 'I see. In future, I must not take a bottle of wine without first getting your permission.'

'Not permission! No, no, not permission. Just if I know, that's all. Just if you ask me to go down to the cellars for you. The stairs are steep, you see. The cellars weren't built when the house was built. Only in the old queen's time. Victoria, that is, not Elizabeth. And being as this house is surrounded by a moat, the cellars flood in wet weather. It's best if I get the wine. I can pick out what's proper for you.'

'Thank you, Mr Crow. And what else is your responsibility?'

'The silver.' His voice was growing icy. She knew he was losing face among the women of the household. 'The table. Setting the table. Serving. I trust you have no complaints about the serving.'

'I have no complaints about anything, Mr Crow. This is my house and I think I have a right to know what each person on the estate does.'

'I'm getting old,' cried Mrs Able. 'Sunday's lunch

wasn't up to what I normally do, but the meat was tough and that's not my fault. The gravy was—'

'Do you wish to retire?'

'No! What would I do all day? No, Miss Joyce. You can't make me . . . the old lord wouldn't have—'

'It's all right, Mrs Able.' Joyce could feel the wall of truculence they were erecting against her. 'I just asked. I'm perfectly happy with your cooking.'

She wished she had never decided to question the staff, but as the interviews went on, she became convinced that she had a right to know what each person did. And each woman in her own way did her best to obstruct the inquiry or register a subtle protest. Mrs Crow gave the least information she possibly could, speaking in clipped tones.

Annie said she was not a cleaner, she was the senior housemaid, which brought a snort of derision from Mrs Crow. Annie gave her duties in great detail, starting with, 'I fetch the dusters from the cupboard . . .'

Cutler clearly felt that she did not work very hard, and Joyce supposed it was an easy job being her personal maid. Joyce always picked up her clothes after herself and put away whatever she had removed from a cupboard or drawer. She knew this was not always the case with women who employed personal maids.

She was in the kitchen for just fifteen minutes, but felt quite exhausted when she left it. The staff probably felt exhausted as well, but that couldn't be helped. They needn't think that she would allow them to rule her life. She was the owner. She would be in charge.

Not until several hours later did she venture onto the grounds to stop anyone who crossed her path, asking what they did on the estate and writing it down in shorthand. None of the outdoor employees was caught by surprise. They had been warned by Mr Crow. And Mr Trimble tracked her down, his lined face white with anger as he told her that he should have been consulted. He could tell her what each of his men did. It was not right that she had asked the men directly. Was she trying to undermine his authority? Did she not know how estates were run?

No, she said, she didn't know how estates were run, which was precisely why she had decided to find out. If she paid the men's wages, was she not also entitled to speak to them?

He didn't reply but stormed off. Joyce's knees were shaking, but she shouted after him, 'You may send me a written report about your duties and those of your men. I shall expect it next Monday.'

Mr Trimble stumbled, stopped for a moment, then carried on without reply. 'I've made a mess of this,' Joyce murmured to herself. Then she headed towards the coach house where she felt reasonably sure Laurence would not be so difficult.

'Good morning, Laurence. May I ask you some questions?'

'Like those you have been asking everybody on the estate? Oh, dear, I don't work very hard, Miss. I'm afraid I'm a lazy devil.' He was laughing, so she felt she could permit herself a weak smile.

'Please don't be difficult, Laurence, and please don't tell me I've made a muddle of everything because I already know it.'

'You've sown the seeds of rebellion. There hasn't been so much excitement in years.'

'I've come to the conclusion that I would have to sack every single person and take on new staff if I wanted to be truly in charge of my estate. They are all against me. I've asked Mr Trimble a dozen times to repair the ceiling in two of the first floor rooms. The plaster is coming down and you can see that the laths are not in very good condition. He never says no, he just tells me there are ever so many other things for the men to do first.'

Laurence leaned against the Rolls and folded his arms. 'You need only replace your bailiff.'

'To encourage the others?'

'You require a man who knows that you are the mistress of Helmingham, who will obey your wishes while seeing to it that the workers do what is necessary. Mr Trimble is old and cantankerous and no friend of yours.'

'But he's been here for ever. How could I possibly get rid of him? Everyone would think I was beastly, and I want to be liked.'

'Miss Joyce, it is not possible to be fully in charge of a large operation and to be liked by everyone. But I must not interfere. My duties are to keep this motor in tip-top condition. Sometimes I go to the train station in Ipswich to collect parcels. Occasionally I am placed upon my motorbike to deliver a message to a tenant. When I first arrived, they put me to helping with the hedge laying. Very interesting work, I must say. Unfortunately, I hated it, possibly because everyone else was so much quicker and more skilful.' He laughed at the memory. 'I've seen hedges all my life but never thought about them. Never examined them. It's fascinating. I hope I never have to do it again. After we had removed the dead wood and the elder and brambles and the rotten stumps, we had to select pleachers. I didn't know what they were.'

'I still don't.'

'They're long stems that are going to be woven into the hedge. You make a cut about three or four inches from the ground and you cut almost three-quarters of the way through it. Then you take this long stem and you weave it along. If you haven't cut enough the thing won't bend. If you cut too much, it snaps off. My partner wouldn't let me cut them at all. It was jolly hard work, but a good team can go along at a great rate. Did you know that Old Man's Beard will smother a hedge? You have to pick out every bit of it. I always thought it was rather attractive, but no, out it must go.'

'A lot of birds and little animals live in hedgerows. Didn't you disturb them all when you were cutting and bending down the branches?'

'Apparently not. Only crows, pigeons and magpies nest in neglected hedges, but all sorts of birds, hundreds of wild flowers and I don't know how many little animals will make their home in a well-laid hedgerow. It was knowledge that was gained at the expense of the skin on my fingers, but thankfully you can only do the work when the hedgerow is dormant. I shall make a point of being busy when autumn comes.'

'It's not a chauffeur's work.'

'Teaching my employer to drive the Rolls is a chauffeur's work. I could give you the first lesson right now. In fact, we could go somewhere far from the estate. It would be a good idea, I think.'

'So that they can all plot against me?'

'They will learn to respect you. If you are knowledgeable, if you know everything each of them should be doing, you will gain control. Knowledge, they say, is power.'

'I shall probably smash up the motor.'

'I won't let you. Trust me.'

He spoke so intensely that she felt the heat come to her cheeks, not knowing why he should have this effect on her. 'I do trust you, and I think I would like to get away from Helmingham for several hours. Can we manage that?'

'I'll send a message to the house to say that you will not be having lunch today. Think how they will rejoice.'

Chapter Ten

June came in with a flourish, a day that touched eighty degrees and had the gardening staff rushing to water flagging plants in the greenhouses. The red, black and white tiles of the old houses glistened with water as Bill ordered the floors to be kept damp. What with no rain having fallen in April and very little in May, the roses had suffered along with other plants. Nights were still cold, and there had been night frosts until very late in the season. Scarcely a rose was in bloom on the first day of the month. So far it had been a difficult year.

Rosie could only hope for better days to come as the rose season arrived. The rugosas, a few of the species and hybrid teas against walls might be expected to bloom during the early days, but the great display would begin towards the end of the month. She smiled in anticipation as she searched each plant for greenfly, mildew or blackspot. Throughout the month she would be disbudding, removing the side buds as soon as possible, leaving two buds, then taking out one later. This was necessary if good sized blooms were to be obtained on hybrid teas, although of course she never touched those intended to bloom in trusses. In a week or two, she would apply liquid manure and, later still, a sprinkling of lime. Those greenhouse pots which she had held indoors because of the cold weather, she now plunged out of doors in ashes for the summer.

The weather which had tormented them all year was not finished yet, for the next day it rained. A north-east wind chilled the bones and the temperature sank during the small hours of the night. Delicate bedding plants suffered wind damage, and some showed signs of shock. Rosie, tight-lipped, visited her rose nursery beds and checked each bud for damage. There wasn't any, but this fact didn't lessen her sense of dread.

Joyce had been taking driving lessons for several days with great success. As she told Laurence, driving a motor car was far easier than managing the fly because of her inborn fear of horses. 'Motoring holds no fears for me. I feel quite at home behind the wheel.' She didn't mention that operating the brake and gear levers made her hand ache, or that steering the fast car required more strength than she could readily call upon. She had taken to exercising with two heavy statues in her hands to strengthen her upper arms.

'Yes, Miss Joyce,' he had said after one hair-raising encounter with a motor car at a crossroads. 'But it is as well to slow down, if not stop, when you approach a crossroads. If the banks are high, you might not see another motor approaching.'

There were problems with the gear shift and the brake, as both were positioned on the driver's left, next to the passenger. This was a perfectly practical arrangement, in case of emergencies when the passenger was teaching the person behind the wheel how to drive. However, it was generally conceded that this arrangement was too American for British tastes. Newer Rolls-Royces had the levers on the driver's right. Gradually, as Joyce learned which lever was which and how not to strip the gears, he relaxed in the seat beside her. There were four forward gears which gave the twenty horsepower engine a smooth start.

The lessons that struck terror into him were soon over. Joyce was a natural driver, which was just as well since the motor had not been designed for genteel trips around the neighbourhood. Captain Cartwright had reputedly driven it at close to the limit along Suffolk by-ways, but as with everything he did, had soon tired of driving his fast car.

Yesterday when the weather was hot and sunny, they had planned their first long distance drive. They were to travel thirty-five miles to a small town called Halstead in north Essex. There, they would have a light luncheon at the Bull Inn before returning to Helmingham. Laurence was now regretting his enthusiasm of the previous day, not simply because of the change in the weather.

He had recently, on impulse, purchased another garage with a petrol pump on the High Street of Halstead, about a mile from his parents' home. He told himself he had suggested this long outing with Halstead as its destination solely because he wanted to give her a nice day away from Helmingham. But less than half an hour before they were due to start, he admitted that there was another motive. He was hoping his father would see them. He was surprised by the urge, but it was true, he wanted to show Joyce off to the old man. Strange to say, the chance that his father would be somewhere near the garage in time to see them sail past had influenced his choice of destination.

And what better place to eat and have a refreshing drink than at the Bull Inn? The sober answer now came to him with stunning clarity: anywhere that he was unlikely to be recognized. He had been less than honest with Joyce about his past. She might feel he had misled her into thinking that he was both homeless and poor. His father, should they happen to meet, or any of the locals at the inn, would soon put her right. He was not yet prepared to tell her the truth, but for her to hear it from someone else was infinitely worse.

She came outside promptly when he rang the front door bell, leading him to think she had been waiting in the hall. Wearing a Mackintosh with a rainproof hat pulled low over her forehead, she was dressed for the bad weather, thus removing his only excuse for calling off the trip.

'Oh, Laurence, I'm so excited. Now, you must drive until we are well away from Helmingham. I don't want anyone to know that I am going out with you for such a long journey. Here, I'll sit in the back until the time comes for me to drive. You know, it's a good thing I am going out today. Sometimes I think I'm too wrapped up in everything that happens at Helmingham.' She climbed into the back seat and he took his place at the wheel. The canvas top of the car had been brought over the seats, and this gave protection from the rain, but not from the breeze created by speed. There were no complaints from Joyce, in fact she didn't speak.

Five miles from Helmingham, he pulled onto a disused farm track so that Joyce could take her place in the driver's seat. Laurence sat beside her and they started up smoothly.

'Is owning such a large estate becoming a bore?' he asked hopefully.

'No, of course not. It's just that my attempts to exercise some control over my property seem to come to nothing. Everyone thwarts me.'

He smiled, remembering a few frustrating moments of his own. 'Helmingham is a large estate, but we are a small community. I have not, since leaving the army, experienced such interest in everything I do. It must be much worse for you.'

She sighed. 'Yes. You know, I am a private person and I don't want to be on display. My friend Marsha says I should entertain more often and have large parties so that I will be invited back to other people's homes. But I don't care for that sort of thing. I don't want to be scrutinized every moment. I prefer to be in the company of just a few friends at a time.'

'Just Rosie and Bill and me,' he teased.

'Exactly. We have some jolly times, don't we?'

He was silent for a moment. 'We used to. Nowadays, Rosie is very strange. Is there something worrying her?'

'No,' said Joyce firmly.

'I mean something besides the fact that she can't seem to have children.'

'You know about that? Oh, Laurence, there truly are no secrets at Helmingham. What else do you know?'

He glanced at her. 'Nothing, I swear it. Is there something I should know?'

'Of course not.'

He leaned back in his seat, almost relaxed enough to enjoy the scenery. 'I understand the rector is so ill he may well be dead by next month.'

'What?' Joyce, in her agitation, allowed the motor to hit the high bank. There was the pop and fizz of a burst tyre, and Laurence muttered something incomprehensible under his breath. 'Oh, I'm so sorry. But . . . I can't believe it. Are you sure? What makes you say such a thing? Oh, Laurence, will it be so much trouble to change the tyre?'

'No, but drive on until the road widens. I can't do it here.'

'What are you saying about the rector? He isn't dying. He can't die. I need him.'

'He's a very old man, Miss Joyce. Some say he is approaching ninety. And he is extremely ill. Can't you see it in his face? He's suffering.'

She drove on erratically for a hundred yards with tears staining her cheeks. 'He mustn't die. What will I do without him? I love him dearly.'

He climbed from the motor and heaved the spare tyre

from its resting place. 'I apologize for being so brutal. I had not realized that you were so close to him. But, Miss Joyce, it is your duty to choose another rector soon. You can't leave the parishioners without a minister.'

'I suppose I must write to someone. The bishop? And ask him to send a new man.'

'That is not the way it's done, I believe. You must advertise the post in the *Church Times*, interview a few candidates, and when you've made your choice, you have to write to the bishop with your decision.'

She smiled weakly. 'There is no-one less qualified than I am for such a task. I don't suppose I even know what qualities are necessary.'

Laurence had not intended to travel through Hadleigh, where his grandmother's estate was lying empty and uncared for, but dared not travel all the way to Halstead with a punctured spare tyre, so he guided her down the High Street of the small town to Station Road where he owned the single pump garage.

A wooden structure with double doors was where the repairs were carried out. At right angles to it a larger wooden building had a tiled roof and a very large treble window overlooking the road and, of course, the pump. Metal advertisement signs cluttered every available space on both buildings, with Mobiloil or Pratts written in large letters. A small sign had been erected on a crossbar, held up by two two-by-fours. It read 'Ballard Practical Motor and General Engineers'. The sign was new. Everything else needed painting. Laurence had fully intended to make the place more presentable when he bought it, but funds were low.

Len, hardly overworked, came out from the garage to greet his employer enthusiastically. His hands worked fruitlessly to clean themselves of oil, on an oily rag. 'I've sold six gallons today, Mr Ballard, and twenty yesterday! Best two days we've had. A Pierce Arrow yesterday, would you believe. And an Alfa Romeo today.'

'Well done. I need you to repair the spare tyre, Len, as we've had a puncture.'

Len touched his cap and smiled at Joyce, clearly intrigued to see her behind the wheel. He lifted the spare from its position on the running board in front of the passenger door and wheeled it away.

There was no-one abroad in this wicked weather, except an elderly woman in a mackintosh that reached her ankles, a chiffon scarf anchoring her straw hat, and a torn umbrella that could hardly protect its owner from the elements. Mrs Harper, who knew everyone in Hadleigh and what they were doing, approached the garage. Laurence walked over to head her off, having no intention of introducing this busybody to Joyce.

'Filthy weather,' she called. 'Haven't seen you around here for some time. Thought you would have come to stay by now.' Her umbrella partially shielded her face, but he could see that her eyes were on Joyce who was standing beside the motor car massaging her left hand.

'Isn't that Miss d'Avranche of Helmingham?'

'Mrs Harper, how on earth do you know that?'

She smiled, ignoring the rain that dripped down her back from the torn umbrella. 'She was pointed out to me one day in Stowmarket. She was with a very lively American. My friend said, "That's the young heiress who inherited Helmingham Hall, and isn't it a shame the rightful heir died?" She seems quite attractive.' Her inquisitive eyes searched Laurence's face for some revealing emotion.

'She is a splendid lady. Ah, Len has fixed the tyre. Well, we must be off, Mrs Harper.' Joyce gracefully climbed behind the wheel. He heard Mrs Harper gasp as he added, 'I have taught Miss d'Avranche to drive.'

'Isn't that rather a fast thing to—'

But he was already leaping into his position on the passenger side as Joyce fired the motor, and the noise of the engine muffled whatever else the old lady said.

'So you own this garage, Laurence,' Joyce said when they were safely onto the Sudbury Road. 'You must be a wealthy man.'

'Hardly. I bought the business for twenty pounds from an acquaintance who had an opportunity to emigrate to Australia. Petrol sells for just over a shilling a gallon. Len doesn't do enough business to pay his wages.'

'You would be wise to continue to work for me.'

'For a time, Miss Joyce, but one day I really must make my way in the world.'

She frowned. 'There is nothing wrong with working on the Helmingham estate. Bill seems happy enough.'

But Laurence was not happy. He was falling in love with Miss Joyce d'Avranche, and he did not wish to spend his life as her poodle, a kept man. The logical thing to do would be to take up residence in Hadleigh and maintain his grandmother's property, but although she had left him a little money as well as the house and farm, there was not enough to fund an idle life. He had quickly learned the truth about owning a farming estate in 1929. If Commander Higgs considered himself successful while losing a pound a year per acre, how was Laurence to make a go of it? He couldn't even rent out his land, he discovered. At ten shillings the acre per annum there were no takers. He hadn't the capital to start up farming on his own behalf, to buy seed and equipment, to pay for the labour until the first crops were in. Everywhere skilled farmers were going bankrupt, leaving farm-houses empty and land untended. This in turn created terrible poverty in the countryside as there was no work for the men.

His father, totally unsympathetic to his dreams of living like a country gentleman, had given him a stark choice: take his rightful place at the factory which would one day be his (ownership to be shared with his sisters) or marry Joyce d'Avranche. Father saw nothing at all wrong in his marrying Joyce for her supposed wealth and magnificent home.

Laurence, liking neither alternative, planned to make his fortune by owning a chain of garages. He loved automobiles, had a sensitive touch where their engines were concerned and knew that the combustion engine would one day almost replace horsepower. So much for the dream. He could not bring himself to leave Helmingham, because he knew he would never see Joyce again. Yet he could not afford to employ good labour to run his business for him. His father had bought the Halstead garage in partnership with Laurence, saying that the lad could pay back the cost from his profits. Although this garage thrived, neither of them was happy, Mr Ballard because he had been praying for failure to lure Laurence back to the factory, and Laurence because the profits were not sufficient to cover his losses in Hadleigh and provide him with enough to live on.

Sudbury, a few miles from Hadleigh, was another pretty Suffolk market town with a broad High Street, a famous native son, Thomas Gainsborough, and an abundance of old buildings painted in delightful pastel colours. Joyce whizzed through it, easily avoiding what little traffic there was, and progressing smoothly towards Halstead which was seven miles further on.

At first, the Sudbury Road led fairly gently down towards Halstead High Street, but when they passed St Andrews church, the road curved to expose the full drop of the High Street. The hills beyond were visible, emphasizing the swiftness with which the land fell.

'Oh, no!' cried Joyce, and Laurence put a steadying hand on the wheel.

'I know it looks steep. It's about four hundred yards to the Bull at the bottom and the gradient is about one in fifteen. The Rolls will take this easily, but you must change down to first.'

The High Street was very wide, the market was in full swing and the road seemed to be teeming with wagons and motor cars. Driving courtesy was at a minimum. Drivers were determined to put their motor cars, buses and wagons wherever it was most convenient, and no-one made any concessions to the lady driver, although several lost their concentration as they stared at her.

'Change down, Joyce! Put your foot on the clutch and change down.'

'I can't! The gear lever is so hard!' She took her right hand off the wheel in order to squeeze the lever with both hands. The motor veered slightly towards the war memorial. Laurence grabbed the wheel, wincing as Joyce screeched through the gears to first.

'Pull over to the garage you can see on your right. See the pump? Pull over there. Joyce. *Pull over!*'

She gripped the wheel, wiggling it nervously. 'I can't get over. Look, that man is blocking my way. And the big wagon. Why are they so rude? Oh, let me drive on, Laurence. I'll find somewhere else to stop.'

Laurence looked at the petrol station and garage he had bought with his father. It was cheek by jowl with other High Street shops. Owners of vehicles who wished to use the services of the garage had to make a carefully executed turn in order to get into the building, and a dangerous one to get out. Those who merely wanted petrol could not get off the road at all. The pump had been installed at the roadside. The premises were too small, and they would presently have to move to a better site. But this was not the thought uppermost in Laurence's mind. He was more interested in the activities of two men who were in the process of erecting a very large sign consisting of two-foot-tall cutout letters which read, Ballard's Garage. It obstructed a couple of first floor windows.

Worse was to come. He could see his father standing by the petrol pump waving his arms. 'Get her to drive in here!' called the old man loudly, then stepped out into the road and imperiously waved all other vehicles out of the way. For a split second, Laurence thought his employer was going to run over his father. Joyce, caught by surprise and afraid of hitting this madman in the middle of the road, turned towards the curb and hit it with some force. The front nearside tyre burst.

'Miss d'Avranche of Helmingham?' said his father, then drily to Laurence, 'I think you got away with only one burst tyre.' Trotting over to the driver's side of the Rolls, he opened the door. 'Step down and rest. Pretty terrifying to drive on the High Street, eh? We're a go-ahead town. Essex, you know. Not like you slow tops in Suffolk. No electricity, indeed. Electricity is the future, I can tell you. I'm wired up at home. My good lady would turn up her nose at a house without electricity.'

Laurence swallowed hard. The dreaded moment had arrived. His father would tell her about his factory, would boast about his wealth like the naïve self-made man he was, and would refer to Laurence as 'his heir'.

But already his vitality and patent love of the human race had enchanted Joyce. 'How do you know who I am? You're quite right. We do not have electricity. Do you know Helmingham? Have you ever worked there?'

Mr Ballard was not wearing his wing collar and sober suit, but was on this day playing the garage attendant in breeches, gaiters and flat hat. 'No, but I've helped to put in the turbine at Chatsworth. You're not as grand as Chatsworth.' This was not a question, but a statement.

Joyce laughed at his bluntness, not at all offended. 'Oh, if you have worked at Chatsworth then you're too grand for me. I wish we had electricity at Helmingham, but I can't afford to have my own generating plant, and there is certainly no other way.'

'Pity. You're not living in the twentieth century. Hmm, d'Avranche. Yes, I can see the resemblance. The nose. A lot alike.' He glanced over at Laurence who had just succeeded in removing the tyre. 'He's my boy, you know. My son.'

'Laurence?' She caught Laurence's eye, grinning broadly. 'Then this is another one of his garages.'

'Well, you might call it that. I bought this one and—'

'You are a good father.'

'Well,' said Mr Ballard, touched, 'I don't know about that.' He pointed upward. 'Just putting a sign up as a surprise to the boy. He's my only son. Lost two in the war, you know.'

'No, I didn't.' She looked at Laurence again, this time with greater sympathy.

A customer wished to have his motor filled with petrol, but the Rolls and a small admiring crowd were blocking the way. Laurence released the brake and pushed it a few feet down the hill, ran back, urged the customer into the right position and began pumping petrol into the Morris Minor, since Dickie was busy repairing the tyre. All the while, Laurence felt as if his ears were growing towards his father and Joyce as he strained to hear what was said.

'I had other plans for him, but he's got this bee in his bonnet to own a chain of garages. I told him, you haven't done your homework. Most folks only license their motors for half a year, because what's the point of licensing it when the weather's bad? If they're not on the road, then they don't need repairs or petrol. So how's he going to make money? You've got to know your market, I said. Got to understand the pounds, shillings and pence. He's taken a long time settling. Well, the war and all. We just thank God he came back. His mother couldn't have taken more grief, poor thing. The war changed her almost as much as it changed Laurence.' He looked fondly at his son, and Joyce looked as well. 'He do look smart in his uniform, not that I like to see him in it. Made for better things, he is. More like a bit of a joke, him working as a chauffeur. But it's good experience, that's what I told his mother, but she don't like it. It won't do him any harm for a while, him having a break from more serious things.'

'I see nothing wrong with his staying at Helmingham,' Joyce's smile was becoming a bit strained, but she still looked at his father as if the old man were some sort of matinée idol.

Mr Ballard's eyes suddenly lit up, clearly surprising Joyce by his sudden apparent about-face. 'Aye, that's what I said to him. Your future lies at Helmingham, my boy, I said. It was meant. Destiny, sort of.'

'Oh, God,' said Laurence under his breath, and the customer said, 'I beg your pardon?'

Joyce was looking puzzled, as well she might. Dickie returned, rolling the wheel ahead of him. 'New inner tube,' he said, never one to waste words, and quickly began to replace the tyre on the Rolls.

'Five shillings,' said Laurence, holding out his hand to the customer.

'Well, I'll try to persuade him to stay,' said Joyce, hesitantly.

At any moment, she and his father would connect, and each would understand what the other was talking about. He handed the two half crowns to Dickie and took Joyce by the arm, guiding her swiftly to the passenger seat. 'Dad, will you stand back?'

'Well, if you must be going. We were just having a good old chinwag. Nice to meet you, Miss d'Avranche. I look forward to getting to know you better.'

The engine fired, Laurence released the brake and pulled out just ahead of a farm cart, which drew a few curses from the driver. He waved an apology, knowing that another minute's wait could bring down his house of cards, and drove at a dangerous speed down the long High Street. Joyce put her hand over her mouth in fright, but she said nothing until they had pulled into the yard of the Bull.

'You drove too fast. You scared me half to death. I'm not driving on the return journey. I could never make it up the hill and my nerves are shot, as well as my hand and shoulders. Good heavens, Laurence. That was dangerous!'

'Yes, well . . . Do you drink beer?'

'Occasionally. Why?'

'I shall buy you a glass of beer. The steak and kidney pudding is excellent and always available on market day. I'll try to get us a private room.'

'That won't be necessary. I'm not some precious fairy-tale princess. We can sit in the saloon bar with everybody else. You know, I feel as if I've known your father for ever. I think he is delicious.'

'Strange, I have never seen him in that light.' But Laurence was extremely pleased by her reaction. Everyone seemed to like the old man. Laurence often wondered why.

The Bull, always busy on market days, was crowded to overflowing. He pushed his way to the bar, afraid that someone would speak to Joyce before he could get her safely tucked away.

'Two halves,' he said to Cora, the barmaid. 'Have you a private room?'

'Not today, Laurence. Miss d'Avranche will have to eat with the common folk. Are you having the steak and kidney?'

He groaned. News tended to travel fast in Halstead, but some onlooker would have had to run down the High Street in order to broadcast Joyce's name before their arrival. Surely something of a record.

While speeding down the hill, he had been determined to tell Joyce of his true position during lunch. He would explain about the switch factory and even tell her about the d'Avranche blood and the inheritance of a nice little property in Hadleigh. Honesty was the best policy, he assured himself. However, once they were seated at a small table in the Bull, he changed his mind. The room was noisy and other customers were seated or standing too close by. Several men sent over pints of beer for them, which Laurence was obliged to drink because Joyce felt one glass of beer was her limit. Most of the locals stood at a slight distance from them, gawping and grinning. The occasion was wrong and, anyway, he had lost his nerve.

Joyce, on the other hand, had a wonderful time, enjoying the lively atmosphere and the smiling drinkers. There was a sparkle in her eyes as she chatted amusingly about her days in Paris. So relaxed was their lunch that he even told her of his one visit to Paris during the war, and about the deaths of his brothers. He had never discussed this with anyone, not even Bill, and he found it surprisingly cathartic. On the way back up the hill, she waved to his father who waved back enthusiastically.

The return journey, with Laurence behind the wheel, was uneventful. Joyce was able to look about her without having to concentrate on her driving and was totally relaxed. He had too much to think about to be totally at ease, but he thought he would remember this day with pleasure for the rest of his life.

'Laurence, your business must thrive, because tyres get punctures all the time. Don't you get paid for fixing them?'

'Yes, but not every journey has two punctures. We were unfortunate.'

'I was inept. But I had such a lovely time. I do feel in control of the car most of the time, but I would never dare drive out alone. It's heavy work and my arms get tired. I wouldn't know what to do if I punctured a tyre when I was miles from one of your garages.'

'I don't want you to drive alone. Only with me. For driving yourself, you really need a more suitable vehicle. Will you allow me to purchase something for you?'

'I can't afford another motor. What would Mr Finch say to such extravagance? If I am never to drive without you, then you will have to stay at Helmingham for ever.'

There were long periods when neither spoke, but neither was straining to find something to talk about. The miles whizzed by and all too soon the Helmingham land was in view.

Joyce saw the church ahead and decided to see the ailing old man. 'Stop at the rectory, please, Laurence. If the rector is as poorly as you say he is, I must visit him, and afterwards I will walk home. I had a wonderful time. Thank you for taking me on such a long journey. Your nerves must have been shredded. Nevertheless, we must go somewhere again. I promise to have only one puncture.'

He smiled warmly. 'Yes, but next time we must go somewhere totally different, without steep roads for you to negotiate. Perhaps to the seaside.'

She watched him drive away and gave a sigh of deepest pleasure. It had been a wonderful day in which she had been able to relax in the company of ordinary people. Laurence's father had the same warm personality as his son, the same hint of Ronald Coleman in his features. She did like both of them enormously. How happy she was!

She walked up the gravel driveway of the rectory, but was spared the necessity of knocking as Reverend d'Avranche opened the door himself.

'Good afternoon! You are looking very well today.'

'Come in, Joyce. I don't know why you think I look well. I should be in my bed from all the worry. You are creating a scandal, my dear, and it is my duty to warn you.'

The happiness of the day evaporated with his words. She stepped into the hall with bowed head, feeling like a schoolgirl summoned to the headmistress's study.

'I don't know what I've done.'

'Gone off with the chauffeur. You were seen driving!'

'He is my chauffeur. I pay his wages. The Rolls is mine. If I want to drive it I don't see why I shouldn't. Surely, I can do what I wish with my possessions and my employees.'

He was tiring very quickly. His hands shook as he attempted to pull a shawl around his shoulders. She supposed he had seen her arrive and in the heat of his anger had found the strength to reach the front door. 'You are Miss d'Avranche of Helmingham Hall and a great deal is expected of you. You must maintain the dignity of the family, especially as your own mother led a less than exemplary life. You must understand that.'

Blind fury engulfed her, snatching her breath away. Just the same, she gently took his arm and led him slowly back into the sitting-room, helping him to sit down in his favourite chair before speaking.

'Are you going to tell me that no aristocrat ever misbehaves, that no noble lord has been known to do something you would deplore? I am an adult, sir, with views of my own on how to behave. I am not my mother and I will not be held responsible for her actions before I was born.'

'Fine words, Joyce.' He winced and put a hand to his chest. 'But you will live in Helmingham for the rest of your life. Whether you live there alone or with the companionship of a husband and family depends entirely upon you. I understand you address the gardener as Bill! And have made a friend on first name terms of his wife. These are your servants, and others on the estate resent it. You will make trouble for the Cooks as well as for yourself. Find more suitable companions. That very nice young lady from America soon fitted into local society. She would help you to make new friends. Why, you should take part in the season. Attend the parties as others in your position do.'

'But the eccentric Miss d'Avranche does not wish to be a part of the season. I'm sorry I have displeased you, but I can't help it. I'll leave you now as I can see I have tired you considerably.'

A shaky, blue-veined hand snaked out to snatch up a scrap of paper. He held it out to her. 'I have drafted an advertisement to be put into the *Church Times*. It is for a new rector for this church. I cannot go on, Joyce. The choice is yours, of course, but I do hope you will employ a man who can exert some . . . who can guide you along the right path.'

Walking home, she read the advertisement carefully, scanning the copy for the choice of words which would ensure that only her potential enemies applied for the position. She was determined not to take onto the estate another critic. He must be young and outward-looking. Above all, he must be prepared to believe that her life was hers to live as she chose.

Several deer skittered away from her, but she hardly

noticed and certainly felt no fear of them. To live as she chose. How stupid of her to think that she could do such a thing. In her imagination, the years ahead looked very bleak. She must not enjoy the company of Rosie or Bill, must not drive out for the day with Laurence who had already told her that he would one day leave Helmingham. What did the future hold but isolation? The rector's praise of Marsha was particularly galling. Marsha had become friends with Rupert and Hector Higgs with the greatest ease, saying she took people as she found them. If she felt comfortable with someone, she didn't care what class they were. All very well, but Joyce had been brought up by a woman who both feared and kowtowed to the Ruperts and naval commanders of England. She could not forget the attitudes she had learned as a child, could not make the leap from a position of inferiority and envy to embrace the very people who had despised her mother.

And was it necessary? This was 1929. Women were showing their knees and smoking cigarettes, dining in public with male escorts. They were holding important jobs and winning seats in Parliament. Women had the vote. Joyce lifted her chin, responding to her own internal exhortation to battle. She would not be defeated. She would make friends wherever she chose, and with luck she would marry the man of her choice. She bit her thumbnail nervously. If he would have her.

The day of the garden fête was beautiful if not particularly warm. The volunteers set up trestle tables in the orchard garden which was behind the walled garden. This entailed a very long walk for Mr Crow to bring cups and saucers, tea plates and knives. Laurence was soon involved, because Mr Crow never hesitated to call on others for help. Visitors came in their hundreds to buy cakes and scones, to play tombola and to throw sponges at the schoolmaster who had nobly poked his head through a board for the purpose.

Joyce took small parties on a guided tour of the walled garden and the herb and knot garden, then demanded 'pennies for the guide'. She collected three pounds this way, and everyone told her what a charming tour she had given them. In fact, for a woman who was reserved and rather shy, she put on a lively performance, surprising herself with her abandon.

The fête raised a hundred pounds, thanks to the generosity of one or two well-to-do people who slipped five pound notes into the collecting boxes. Joyce thought she had found her role in life at last. Miss d'Avranche of Helmingham received profuse thanks from the ladies of the committee who told her she had been absolutely splendid and so amusing on her tour of the formal gardens.

The gardeners spent the following day collecting a hessian sackful of rubbish from among the plants, replacing divots, cutting off broken branches of the herbaceous plants and skimming the moats for wrappers and other flotsam.

Meanwhile, Joyce dealt with a flood of requests. Would she open her gardens for the Red Cross, for the hospital, outings for the housebound? She would. Dates were fixed for seven more garden events. She wrote to committees and made a note of the days the garden would be required to look its best. She needn't have worried that Bill would find this all an unnecessary way to give him extra work. Bill believed that gardens were to be visited, to be appreciated and shared with as many people as possible. He was convinced that the extra work on the two days before the garden party and for the two days afterwards to repair damage were well spent.

Chapter Eleven

Rosie woke at half-past five, threw back the covers and searched in the gloom for her slippers. Bill groaned, not yet awake; she would let him sleep for another half an hour. On this morning of the twenty-ninth of June the day was forecast to be fine and warm. Not too hot, she hoped, for then the roses would open too much, dip their heads and refuse to sparkle for the judges.

She made herself a cup of tea and buttered one of yesterday's scones, but she was too excited to eat. The National Rose Society was holding its Great Summer Show on the grounds of the Royal Hospital, Chelsea. Everyone would be there, including Rosie's family who always entered the competitions as well as putting on a great trade display. She had been to the show many times with Dad, had helped to stage his entries, to set up his trade stand, but today for the first time she was entering in her own right.

By the time she returned to the bedroom to dress, Bill was awake. 'Excited?' He rubbed his chin. 'I suppose you will expect me to have a shave today.'

'I will.' She leaned across the bed to kiss his stubbly cheek. 'Wish me luck, Bill. And say a little prayer for Miss Joyce. Without her permission, we wouldn't be going to London on a Friday and a Saturday. I'm so pleased we will be staying overnight. Do you know anything about the Cora Hotel?'

'Only that it's off Russell Square and a stone's throw from the Russell Hotel.'

'Perfect. With Miss Joyce staying so close to us, we'll be able to get together in the evening.'

Bill shook his head. 'Why don't you protect yourself from getting hurt? She won't want to be with us when she can so easily contact her London friends.'

'Well, anyway . . .' Rosie sighed. It was true, but she kept forgetting that the pretty little owner of Helmingham might have some life away from Suffolk. She wanted Joyce to herself, always close by to share the good moments and the bad. Miss Joyce was her only female friend, and she had never known before what joy it was to spend time in the company of one's own sex. Of course she couldn't explain this to Bill. Her relationship with Miss Joyce was yet another secret she was forced to keep from him.

A straw hat and a cotton print dress with a long cardigan were her choice for this important occasion. She felt quite smart until she reached the stableyard and saw the pretty younger woman talking to Laurence. Effortlessly chic, Joyce was wearing a turquoise chiffon silk print over a darker slip. Her little hat cast a shadow over her eyes, giving her a remote glamour.

'Of course she won't want to be with me this evening,' muttered Rosie to herself as she entered the stableyard. 'What was I thinking of?'

'Oh, Rosie, it's so exciting! I want to help you get ready. What can I do?'

Rosie wanted to be alone when she cut the blooms, so she directed the two young people to the display boxes, suggesting that they find some way of fitting them into the Rolls. Then, taking her secateurs from the greenhouse, she went into the rose cutting beds and looked about for suitable blooms.

She had already cut the hybrid teas. They had been chosen with care the evening before – Etoile de Hollande, Betty Uprichard, Shot Silk and Dainty Bess, as well as many others. She had picked blooms that were about to open and tied them closed with white soft worsted. They were deep in cold water and would soon be packed for the journey.

Her task at the moment was to cut a selection of decorative roses, the ones which were naturally small-bloomed or which bloomed in trusses. She cut sprays of Francesca and Kathleen, Penelope and Cornelia, all beautiful names, all hybrid musks bred by the Reverend Pemberton. With her arms full, she hurried back to the motor which was standing in the stableyard.

'Rosie, this box is awfully big, and this one, too. There won't be room for all your roses,' called Joyce.

She was standing beside the show boxes, one for twenty-four blooms, one for twelve. The National Rose Society laid down the size and shape of these boxes; there was no question of deviating. 'All blooms,' ran the regulation, '(except where directed to be shown in vases or otherwise) shall be staged in boxes of the regulation size, viz. 4 inches high in front and 18 inches wide, and for 24 blooms, 3 feet, 6 inches long; for 12 blooms, 2 feet long.' The lidded boxes were cumbersome, but they held long tubes into which water and single blooms were placed for maximum display effect. 'In all cases, in which three blooms of each variety are required to be shown in boxes the three blooms shall be arranged in the stand triangularly.' The larger box had cost her nearly four pounds and the smaller had been one pound twelve and sixpence. Together with the rose baskets and other equipment, this rose show had been very expensive.

Rosie, to be sure of having enough blooms of each type in good condition, had cut eighteen of each hybrid tea. Decorative roses needed a background and Rosie was planning to take stout card on which she would drape black cloth. This had already been stowed in the motor together with the shorter of the two boxes and vases and the overnight cases for Bill and Rosie, Laurence and Joyce. The three foot six box simply would not fit.

'We should have hired a van!' cried Rosie. 'Or I'll send them by rail if we can just get everything to the station!' She clutched the sprays tightly to her breast in a murderous embrace, realized what she was doing and took a deep breath as she relaxed. 'I must get these into boxes. Oh, how are we to get everything in?'

'I won't go,' said Joyce. 'I'll get someone to take me to the station in the fly, then I'll meet you at the show-ground.'

As Bill had just joined them, he added his voice to Joyce's. 'I'll go by train as well. There will be plenty of room for the two of you in the motor.'

But Rosie could not contemplate such a thing. Perhaps she and Bill and the roses should travel by train, or no, she didn't know what to do.

There was silence for a moment. Everyone knew how close Rosie was to tears. It was left to Bill to break the silence. 'This is bloody nonsense. I beg your pardon, Miss Joyce, but it is. We have decided to travel to London in the Rolls, and we will do so. Laurence, that box can be lashed to the side. The box of moss goes on the floor in the front seat. Rosie, get into the barn and pack up your roses. We will all carry a box on our laps. I'll get the scissors, the brush and the paper knife, oh, and the rose wires. Now, go!'

Rosie looked at him with gratitude, nodded and raced for the barn where the hybrid teas were awaiting her attention.

The two-hour journey to London was actually incident free. Traffic was less than Laurence had feared, nor did he get lost as Rosie had thought he would. They arrived at the showground and found a place to park among all the early arrivals. Nevertheless, Rosie was exhausted, her muscles screaming from such a long journey with a precious box of wet-stemmed roses on her lap. Joyce looked tired and Bill was grimly silent as he began to unload. Only Laurence seemed unmoved by the strain that Rosie's nerves were putting on them. He cheerfully removed the box of hybrid teas from her grasp and headed for the huge marquee.

The damp floral smell of the marquee, its muted light and the sounds of old friends calling to Rosie were distilled into a heady perfume. How she remembered every rose show they had all taken part in when she had lived at home! How she had missed the excitement!

She found the space allotted to her and spotted her father coming towards her at almost the same moment. Mr Dobson leaned down to give her a kiss on the cheek and to be introduced to Joyce. 'Big day for you, my dear. Have you got some good specimens? Then you'd best set about getting your display ready. You've not too much time.'

Joyce and Laurence knew that they must leave immediately and were soon on their way. Bill stayed only long enough to ensure that everything was to hand. He squeezed her shoulder in silent encouragement before he, too, left the marquee.

She opened up her box of moss and began fitting the velvety green chunks around the rose tubes to make a vivid 'lawn' against which the blooms would show to effect. Then she began removing the soft ties around each bloom, checking for weak heads and damaged foliage, and placing the roses in the tubes, avoiding clashing colours, working according to the plan she had drawn out the night before. As each rose was untied, she studied it carefully to see if it needed a little dressing. With thumb and forefinger slightly pinching just behind the petals, she blew gently on the centre of the rose. If it opened as desired, well and good. Otherwise, she gingerly prised the petals back, starting with the outer ones and working inwards with the help of the handle of her little bone paper knife or the large camel-hair brush. Her hands shook so fiercely that she ruined the first three blooms she attempted to dress.

A quick glance to her right told her that old Mr Perkins was watching her nervous movements with undisguised glee. To her left, Mr Crane, a man no more than five feet tall, with black wire-framed glasses and thin lips, well known for his sly faking on occasion, was keeping his head down. Determined not to show her rising panic, she took up the next bloom with deliberation and set about conquering her nerves. Finally, a rose wire was shaped into a loop into which the flower sat, forced to lift its face up to the judges, whether it wanted to or not.

It took her twenty minutes to arrange three dozen hybrid tea blooms, but eventually she was ready to set up the display for her decorative roses. As she had no hopes in this class, the work went well. Afterwards, there was time to tour the marquee and take a look at the competition. There was also time for her father to visit her exhibits, where he made a few shrewd suggestions and offered copious praise. Mr Crane had a particularly good selection this year, he told her. Mr Crane was the competition to beat.

At last, she was forced to leave the tent so that judging could take place. She quickly found her mother and brothers, greeting Aaron with particular pleasure.

'Well, how are you finding life in Germany?' she asked, giving him a quick hug.

'I've come home. Mr Kordes doesn't need me to worry about. Things are looking grim for Germany. Foreign investors have begun removing their money from the country, and Herr Kordes fears the worst. I'm better off helping Dad.'

'At least we have him with us,' said Mrs Dobson, looking at Aaron proudly. 'If only we could get Kyle to come back.'

'Leave him where he is,' growled Mr Dobson. 'He's making good money. They're rich in America. The whole country is booming. Not like here.'

Bill joined them to say that Joyce and Laurence would come back from lunch and join them in time to see who had won the prizes. In the meantime, the family all went off to a large inn close to the showground where other rosarians had already gathered to down a few pints, eat sandwiches and talk of roses. Rosie drank in the atmosphere, so fondly remembered from her younger days, but she limited herself to one half pint of beer. She wanted to be clear-headed for the prize giving, and the strain of recent hours was throbbing in her temples.

She returned to the showground with her arm tucked into Bill's. His quiet strength and warm understanding never failed to rally her, no matter how deeply she was sunk into depression. But even in moments of great stress, as now, her feelings for her husband could be undermined by the sight of Laurence. He was standing by the entrance to the marquee. He had changed his clothes, not content to appear as the breeches-clad chauffeur. His Norfolk jacket was similar to many others, yet his seemed to be better cut, more recently pressed. He and Joyce made the perfect pair, like models for a Saville Row advertisement.

With an effort, she turned her head and looked into Bill's weather-beaten face. 'How many prizes have you won for vegetables over the years?'

'I don't remember exactly.'

She laughed. 'Yes you do. One hundred and forty,

and we still have every certificate. And here I am about to faint with nerves in the hope that I will win one prize.'

'There's nothing like winning the first one, believe me. The rest all get muddled up in your mind, but you remember the first. I say, Laurence, aren't you the dandy?'

Laurence waved. 'Dressed for the prize-giving. Good luck, Rosie.'

They walked down the aisles, and the first thing that registered in Rosie's mind was the card in front of Mr Crane's exhibit which said First Prize.

Her own entry had won Second Prize. 'Well done,' said Laurence beside her.

'Too bad,' said her husband, who understood.

Joyce put an arm around her waist and squeezed. 'You've really done very well for your first time out.'

Father approached, looking grim. 'We won six prizes, four firsts and two seconds, but this is the only one I care about, Rosie. Bad luck. Miss d'Avranche, may I have a word with you?'

He led Joyce a few feet away, but Rosie could hear every word he said. 'Mr Crane, who thinks he's won First Prize, wired in some foliage from another rose to go with his Shot Silk. He should be disqualified for cheating.' He waited. 'Someone should register a protest.'

Joyce said nothing for a few seconds, then. 'You mean me? You mean I should register a protest?'

'Well, the entry is in your name. Miss d'Avranche, Helmingham Hall. That man over there is Mr Courtney Page, the hon. sec. Go up to him and tell him of your suspicions.'

Rosie knew that such a move would test Joyce's nerve, but the young girl resolutely headed for three men at the far end of the tent where the prizes had been assembled.

They all saw her gain the attention of Mr Page, saw him look in their direction, saw the three of them approaching. They walked past Rosie's exhibit, although Joyce, her face bright red, went no further. The three men carried on, spoke to Mr Crane, lifted the roses from some of his tubes, among them the Shot Silk specimens. Now Rosie could see that the foliage was attached by fine wires and that it was not Shot Silk foliage which had perhaps broken off at the last minute. The card saying First Prize was taken up. Mr Page, with a curt nod to Joyce, laid it by Rosie's exhibit. He picked up the Second Prize and consulted his list.

Mr Crane, a bank manager in his middle fifties, looked stunned. He and his dowdy wife turned and left the tent, probably planning – if their minds were working at all – to return after others had left to remove his entry. Their embarrassment was profound, their downfall complete. Rosie didn't feel much better. Why had she not stopped Joyce from complaining? Why had she allowed this gentle young woman to risk humiliation? For, there had been every chance that Father was mistaken. What then, for all of them?

She turned her back on her father, but heard Laurence speak to him. 'Not very sporting perhaps.'

'Not very sporting of Miss d'Avranche,' said Father curtly. 'Rosie made no complaint.'

'And if you had been mistaken?'

'Miss d'Avranche is ignorant of rose matters. No-one would have blamed her.' He chuckled. 'Except Mr Crane, of course. But the man has done it before. He deserved to be brought down a peg. Rosie got a Specially Commended for her decorative roses, by the way. Shows she's a real Dobson.'

When the prizes were being announced and the cups handed out, Joyce insisted that Rosie come up to the prize table with her. She accepted the trophy graciously, but handed it immediately to Rosie.

Later, she said to Bill, 'So this is the prize I will always remember. I do hope not. I'm happier with my Specially Commended for the decorative roses.'

'What I will remember,' said Bill grimly, 'is that your father once again imposed himself on our lives. I saw that Crane had the wrong foliage with his Shot Silk. Do you think I know nothing about roses? I saw it and was planning to discuss with you what should be done. It was your decision, not your old man's.'

'No, that is, I didn't hear what he said to Joyce or I would have . . .' She fell silent, unable to complete the lie.

Mr Dobson invited Joyce and Laurence to join the family in a grand celebration. What with brothers, wives and older children, as well as some of the staff at the nursery, they made a party of thirty. Mr Dobson had hired a room at the Russell Hotel and engaged a three-piece band.

The food was excellent, the alcohol plentiful. All Rosie's brothers were capable of drinking heavily and with abandon, knowing that their heads were strong and that they would be back at work in the early hours of the next day. Bill, not averse to a few jars, as he called it, invariably stayed morosely sober when with her family. Laurence, too, seemed to disapprove of their rowdy behaviour. Joyce, however, was at her most charming. Rosie noticed that Joyce always relaxed in the company of ordinary people.

Bill stood up to ask Jacob's wife to dance. He was systematically working his way through the sisters-in-law with his usual good manners. Laurence invited Mrs Dobson onto the floor, and Father came to sit beside Rosie.

His tie was loosened, his collar wilted. He smiled as he wiped the sweat from his face. 'I'm proud of you, my dear. First Prize and you deserved it. Not that your husband would have spoken up for you like I did. He wouldn't have done it. He's too busy bowing and scraping to his betters. I wish I hadn't let you marry him.'

'Dad, please—'

'Why did you go away from me, baby? We were always close, weren't we? You and me? You always loved me more than your ma, didn't you?'

'Dad—'

'Dobson, Sons and Daughter. Ah, those were the days. None of them can hold a candle to you. And here you are calling some young flapper *Miss* Joyce. Oh, she's nice enough, I don't say she isn't. But she's not your better. Why, she looks up to you. I can see it. Tell your old dad you still love him best. Tell me, sweetheart.'

She leaned back from his beery breath, from the glassy, drunken look in his eyes which always repulsed her. 'Next to my Bill I love you best. I guess Mum and I were never close.'

'Not like you and me,' he muttered, now slurring his words.

The dance ended. Bill turned, saw her in close conversation with her father, and frowned fiercely. Mr Dobson, drunk as he was, knew that he must return to his own chair at the far end of the table.

She had won a coveted first prize for her hybrid teas, yet she felt only sadness. When she had been younger, living at home and working every day on the nursery, she had revelled in her father's love, knowing herself to be the favourite. Only after she married did she realize that his love was not healthy. Perversely, every time Bill reminded her of it, she defended her father, finding herself torn between two men and unable to confide completely in either of them.

The visit to London was a welcome break from routine, a time that grew more glorious in her imagination as the days passed. Her first prize brought her compliments from all who knew her, and Joyce, ever the loyal friend, revelled in her success.

They had been back at Helmingham for three days when Rosie gathered up her gloves and pruning knife and headed for the strip of ground which had been set aside for her breeding work and for growing cutting roses. She walked across the park, crossing in front of the Hall to take a look at the herb and knot garden where her special pegged-down roses were now making a breathtaking display. Each old rose stood five feet tall and almost as much through, and many were covered entirely in blossom. This was a result of her rigorous training and attention to the pegging. The extra work involved made the garden splendid.

No rosarian would dream of planting anything but roses in a bed. However, Bill was not a rosarian, nor would he be governed by what he considered to be short-sighted rules. There was neat box edging to the herbs, and controlled edgings of lavender and catmint around the roses. Foxgloves raised their white spikes among the rosy prima-donnas, and a mound of yellow thyme surrounded the statue of Flora. Tall clipped yew trees gave the garden a secret feel. Rosie loved it best of all, partly because the men were so often working on the vegetable beds in the walled garden, leaving the herb and knot garden to silence and profound peace. This space was hers, although sometimes Joyce would join her. They would sit on one of the stone benches and gossip away precious minutes, largely out of sight of the staff. However, she didn't linger this morning, being anxious to see how her seedlings were progressing out of doors.

The stables hid the rose ground from view until the moment when she rounded the building. Then she saw Bill standing among the roses, looking about him with a frown.

'Anything want doing?' she called, but she felt a terrible sense of dread.

'I've just come over to see how your crosses are progressing. This one looks exceptional. The one with the palest pink trusses of single blooms. When were you planning to tell the world about it? Or, I suppose your father already knows.'

'I was going to tell you. In fact, I just came up here today to see if it really is good enough to be propagated. You don't mind if my father has a few dozen bushes to bud from, do you? The nursery badly needs a new rose. We . . . that is, they haven't had a decent introduction in three years. And what with Aaron coming back . . .'

'Thank you for your trust. I know where I come in your affections. After your dear father and brothers, but well ahead of your poor mother.'

'Bill!'

'Have you given it a name?'

'No.' How could she court further disaster by admitting that she planned to name it after the daughter they couldn't have? 'No, of course not. It's too soon to choose a name.'

Bill looked into her eyes with such steady concentration that she eventually had to look away. 'Humph,' he said and walked away.

Chapter Twelve

The tall windows had been opened and the high ceiling insulated the interior on the hottest of days, but it was only cool in the echoing darkness when there were no people present. Today, the church was full. Laurence thought that virtually every person in Helmingham was present, all of them having dressed with unusual care: summer prints and straw bonnets, best suits and polished shoes. Amid the discomfort of starched collars and tight corsets and the amplified coughs and wheezes of a solemn congregation, the Reverend d'Avranche was being laid to rest, and they all wanted to pay their respects. Laurence, ever conscious of his position as an outsider, refused to sit up closer to the altar beside Rosie and Bill. He had hardly known the old man, so he sat at the very back and studied the restless congregation.

By twisting his body and peering between butcher Orcast and his wife, he had a very good view of the service, although he could not see the chief mourner, the only person who genuinely grieved for the old man – Joyce d'Avranche.

The new rector, the Reverend Catchpole, was in his early forties, a stocky bachelor with a thick mane of hair greying at the temples, who checked his image in every shiny surface he passed, a man whose smile displayed perfect teeth and cold eyes. His deep voice rolled out in church, giving each syllable ponderous weight, confusing simple souls into thinking they were hearing something worthwhile, curling itself around the consciences of the congregation, making every man squirm, every woman swoon.

Laurence hated the man on sight, certain that he was a hypocrite and a sneak, sure that he had his eyes on Joyce and Helmingham Hall. It pained him that Joyce, having her pick of half a dozen men, should have chosen this pouter pigeon of the Cloth. His smooth-talking ways had completely fooled her, and the old rector had been too far gone to raise objections by the time Catchpole had wormed his way into Joyce's regard.

Laurence stood and sang or knelt in prayer or sat silent as the service progressed, but he was scarcely aware of what he was doing, so busy was he concentrating on his anger and, yes, he had to admit it, his jealousy. For Jonathan Catchpole had lost no time in letting it be known that he had a considerable private income. Amy Crockford, who cleaned for him, assured everyone that the rectory was filled with the most magnificent artefacts. Anyone could see that she had fallen in love with him, though no-one commented, so universal was his effect on the women of the congregation. There would be no gossip about Reverend Catchpole being a fortune hunter, should he happen to persuade Joyce to the altar. Helmingham society, which might well howl in derision if Laurence married her, would coo with pleasure if Catchpole did.

Laurence had asked Joyce why she chose this man, and she said she had done so as an antidote to Mr Goodenough. 'But what has the schoolmaster ever done to deserve a Catchpole in his life?'

'You don't understand, Laurence,' she had said, being very much the lady of the manor. 'Mr Goodenough gave me a little lecture on socialist thinking and kindly pointed out that I was no higher class than he was, but that I enjoyed a higher status and greater wealth through no efforts of my own.'

'And have you so quickly forgotten the truth that you can't bear to hear it spoken?'

They had been headed for Woodbridge, luxuriating in the sort of English summer day that was not at all common. Rain had freshened the air, but the sun shone brightly, and there was not the hint of a breeze.

'Yes, of course, I know the truth when I hear it. I also know that I must not let Mr Goodenough get the better of me. I am his employer and I will not have him sneering at me whenever he chooses. I am indebted to Reverend Catchpole for his sensitivity. He does not think we should be looking for a new schoolmaster, but he does believe that I must maintain my position.'

'The man makes my flesh crawl.'

'Shame on you for saying that. He has worked hard and made a successful career for himself. He deserves credit for that.'

'He was born with a silver spoon in his mouth!'

There was silence for a second or two, then Joyce said lightly, 'There's nothing wrong with being born with a silver spoon in one's mouth. Some of the best people have come into the world that way.'

He had laughed and changed the subject, after which the outing was happier and more relaxed than any he had ever known. He had been wondering ever since if she felt the same way.

She had desperately needed to unburden herself about the problems at the Hall, which was apparently a terrible drain. Not that she expressed herself in those words. Her complaints were of a particular nature.

One day as she had been trying to close the curtains in the Great Hall to protect some paintings from the light, the entire pair of curtains had come down. They were some twelve feet long and had been hanging for so many years that the huge curtain rail had also come away from its moorings.

Joyce had missed serious injury by inches, and then had had trouble escaping from yards and yards of dusty rotting material. It was impossible to rely on anyone coming to help her as her voice would not carry beyond the Great Hall.

'And the curtains were in shreds,' she said. 'I sent a telegram to Mr Finch, saying that I must really have new curtains. He arrived within hours to tell me personally that I could not afford new curtains.

'To make matters worse, I couldn't get Mr Trimble to allow his men to rehang the smelly old things. After two weeks, I caught him in the workshop with several of his men and I told him just what I thought of him. I even wrote to the land agent. Two days later, the rail was put back up and the curtains rehung. Then the cleaners complained about the dust.'

Laurence had heard about the row, of course. Mr Trimble had vowed revenge. 'You must put Mr Trimble out to grass as soon as you are able to do so.'

She continued as if he hadn't spoken, 'We have six very beautiful Sheraton chairs. I have been spending my evenings making new tapestry seat covers for them. It's taken me hours to complete just one. I'm only half through the second. Mr Trimble says there is no-one who can re-upholster the chairs and put on the new cover.'

'That may be true.'

'Well, so I thought, but Mr Finch wrote to me to say the workshop always recovered drop-in chair seats, and that he certainly will not release funds for them to be sent to an outside upholsterer. I don't know who is telling the truth.'

'Perhaps . . .' he began, then sighed. 'No, there is nothing you can do about all this bickering until the will has been proved. Until that time, you have no power.'

'They'll have me in my grave before then.'

The service was over. Reverend d'Avranche's body was about to be laid to rest in the churchyard. Reverend Catchpole passed down the aisle, smirking to left and right. Laurence decided he must do something desperate. He had made up his mind that he would not become the Helmingham lap-dog, but he certainly had no intention of allowing any other man that privilege. He stood next to Bill at the graveside, bowed his head as the body was lowered into the grave, then replaced his hat and strode away.

Rosie put a bowl of hard-boiled eggs into the huge wicker hamper on top of the bread she had baked the night before, the thick slices of ham, the rhubarb pie and the three bottles of wine. The chocolate cake, being somewhat delicate, was the last to go in except for the red and white checked tablecloth and four matching napkins. They were to be away from Helmingham for the best part of Sunday, but they would not starve.

'How big is this estate of Laurence's?' she asked Bill.

'Bigger than the rectory, he says. You could bring up ten kids, house three or four servants indoors and still have room for visiting relatives. There's a couple of cottages and some rooms over the stables and a hundred and fifty acres, none in cultivation. I understand it's in pretty poor condition.'

'If he's got all that,' she wondered, 'why is he wasting his time working as a chauffeur here at Helmingham?'

Bill laughed. 'Trying to make up his mind about Miss Joyce. Laurence thinks if Miss Joyce sees Boscomb House she'll think it's so wonderful that she'll say something like, "Oh, I wish I lived here instead of at big old

Helmingham." Then he'll say, "It so happens that I own Boscomb House and I would like you to be my wife and live here with me."'

'He's surely not that stupid.'

'No, but he is that much in love. I do understand his unwillingness to be thought to be a fortune hunter. He once asked me if I could imagine the sort of comments everyone would make if the chauffeur was to marry Miss Joyce. I told him, no worse than they're already making. But he said that's exactly why he wants to take her away. She doesn't deserve to be the subject of continual gossip, her every move commented upon and probably criticized.'

'It's very sad,' said Rosie. 'He's wasting his life in daydreaming. She is not going to leave Helmingham. She loves the house, and who shall blame her? What woman would willingly give up so much for a man?'

'You gave up a great deal,' he said quietly, 'and so your father reminds me whenever we meet.'

'I gave up nothing I wanted. I'm better off here.'

There was silence between them for a moment, then Bill said heartily, 'Give him time. He'll come to his senses. He'll either settle for being laughed at behind his back, or he'll move away and find some other girl. Let's humour him today, play it the way he wants us to. Remember, she's to be told that Boscomb House is looking for a manager and he is considering taking the post.'

'Fat lot he knows about running an estate.'

'Yes,' said Bill, 'I thought that was pretty funny, but Miss Joyce won't know the difference.'

The Rolls made slow progress down the long drive and pulled to a halt at the lodge. The four of them had long since stopped trying to hide the fact that they went about together. As Rosie joined Joyce in the back seat, Bill and Laurence positioned the picnic on the floor behind the driver, then climbed into the front seat.

'We're off!' said Joyce, 'and no-one will tell me where we're going. It must be some distance because we have brought a picnic. But what is our destination?'

'It's a mystery tour,' said Laurence. 'You must be patient.'

Rosie stretched out her legs, determined to enjoy this trip in the luxurious motor car, as she had not enjoyed the long haul to London. How strange it all is, she thought. Without fully appreciating what they were doing, Joyce and Laurence had turned Helmingham Hall and the village upside down. It had long been understood that if you were not family or guests you did not walk or ride up the long drive. There was another entrance to Helmingham further along, and all staff came and went that way. All staff, that was, except for Laurence, who seemed not to understand. He used the long drive to the front of the house as much as Miss Joyce did.

Laurence willingly rang the tradesmen's bell when he wished to speak to Joyce, but Rosie thought he did so only because it was convenient. If he ever decided he wanted to summon her to either of the doors in the courtyard he would do so.

And Miss Joyce regularly muddied the invisible line that separated staff from family. She spoke to whom she chose, made friends where it suited her and either ignored the black looks she received or was ignorant of them. No wonder the schoolmaster frequently annoyed her with his insolence. He was confused, poor man.

Bill was apparently even more confused. He had always ruled the under gardeners with a rod of iron. Every tool must be cleaned and put in its place before the men could go home at night. They must arrive on time, disappear if they saw Lord d'Avranche, and never, ever walk onto those parts of the grounds where they could be directly seen from the windows of the reception rooms. They crept around in the early hours to do what was necessary before the old lord rose, then worked the rest of the day away from his chance gaze. Any man failing to observe the rules could be fined.

Laurence, needless to say, cared nothing for such rules. And Bill allowed him to get away with previously unheard of insubordination. What were the men to think? Rosie had looked for signs of deteriorating standards in the maintenance of the grounds, but could find none. Perhaps the world was entering a new era as the third decade of the century approached. She wasn't sure she approved, except that her friendship with Joyce was precious to her.

Rosie was putting her trust in Reverend Catchpole who seemed to have some influence over Joyce's behaviour. She sighed at the thought of him, and rubbed her temples. One morning not long ago, she had awakened to discover that her infatuation with Laurence was over, having faded during the night like a bad dream. Her relief at her return to sanity didn't last long, however. For Rosie quickly developed the same sort of feelings for the new rector. A much more satisfactory object of her secret affections, he would take her hand and speak to her as if no other woman existed. In his company, she felt important and pretty. She felt wanted. The excitement of her secret longing had at first buoyed her up with absurd daydreams, but soon she came to realize that this otherwise inexplicable interest in men was a sign of madness. She tried to convince herself that her barren state was a blessing, for what child deserves an insane mother? Yet the longing and torment continued.

Bill mistrusted Reverend Catchpole, of course, but then Bill was a poor judge of character. Or so her father had always said. But today, as they motored through the lush countryside, Rosie tried to put these thoughts to one side.

The small town of Hadleigh enjoyed a long High Street and an ancient red brick guildhall that stood facing the great church. Its houses were a jumble of different roof heights and colours of plaster, its streets far from busy. They drove through without catching sight of another motor car, and turned up a narrow farm road which they followed for a mile or two.

Mellow brick pillars with stone pineapple finials marked the entrance to Boscomb House, but the florid design of the wrought iron gates needed to have the rust removed. The gravel drive, twisting and overhung with ancient yews and dying hollies, was pockmarked with clumps of weeds. A short ride through over-hanging trees brought them to a very substantial red brick house of three storeys. Its symmetry was pleasing and its white portico was in harmony with a Georgian house, but it was obviously in a very sorry condition. As for the grounds . . .

'The ivy is growing through the window frames, Laurence!' said Bill. 'Something will have to be done about that. And, good grief, the grounds will take years to recover!'

'Whose house is this?' asked Joyce. 'Why are we here?'

'It is owned by an eccentric old lady,' answered Laurence, and Rosie looked away, unwilling to be a part of this lie. 'She lives in London, but she wants me to bring the grounds into order. I suppose I will be put in charge of repairing the house, as well.'

'It's no wonder she doesn't want to live here,' said Joyce, and Rosie smiled. Deception did not pay, since one could end up hearing a few very unwelcome home truths.

Laurence urged them all down the gravel path to the

back of the house where the grounds had been formally set out long ago. A double avenue of yew trees, crying out for a formal trim, marched down the garden to a low round stone pond which was choked with weeds. A pergola in the distance was groaning with unpruned roses, while weeds grew up from the flagstones to meet them. There were some excellent trees nearby, all in need of the saw. Innumerable farm buildings all had red tiled roofs, but they sagged in different directions, old and infirm.

Naturally, the property had its walled garden where vegetables could be grown free from the depredations of rabbits. However, someone had long ago left the green wooden door ajar. When they entered, rabbits scurried in every direction.

'Someone will have to get rid of the rabbits, Laurence,' said Joyce. 'We kill six thousand a year at Helmingham, and still they come, defying everyone's efforts.'

'The rabbits will be attended to. Would anyone care to have a look inside the house? I have the key.'

They were all curious, so they waited by the back door, while Laurence struggled with the rusty lock, then stepped into domestic quarters that had seen no improvements in fifty years. The sink was carved from a block of wood, a pump handle was not far away. Bricks laid on bare earth made an uneven walking surface, and the old cooking range was covered in rust since there had been no-one to black it for some time.

Every reception room was of a good size and would have been light and airy if ivy had not grown to obscure the windows. A smell of soot hung in the air, and huge pieces of furniture lay eerily shrouded in white dust sheets. Everywhere cried out for a coat of paint, for new wallpaper, for mop and polish. Yet, it must have been a very handsome residence at one time. Rosie could not imagine herself living in this house, for it was twice the size of her father's. Nevertheless, she thought any woman would be extremely fortunate to own it. Anyone, that is, except a woman who already lived in one of the great mansions of England.

'Good Lord, Laurence!' Joyce cried. 'I hope you are not deceiving me. You don't own Buscomb, do you? How could you possibly take on such a task if you don't have to? You would be well advised to continue working at Helmingham. This estate will break your heart. Not that I don't envy anyone with such a small house to put to rights. I could do it in a trice after my experiences with Helmingham. I do hope the mysterious old lady you spoke of intends to spend a little money on some improvements.'

Laurence's face was a picture of pain and disappointment. Bill positioned himself behind the younger man's back in order to wink at Rosie. Joyce was not usually so cruel in her judgements. Rosie knew that she was critical today in order to put Laurence off leaving Helmingham. He didn't understand her motive and was very hurt, but it was not the business of the gardener's wife to explain one to the other. They must sort out their own misunderstandings. She turned at the top of the stairs, holding tightly to the rickety bannister in order not to trip on the torn carpet runner and shut her ears to the crisp, pained exchanges between Joyce and Laurence.

They ate their picnic in the garden. Laurence found some old teak garden furniture, a little twisted and bleached grey by years in the sun, yet perfectly comfortable, which made it unnecessary for them to sit on the ground.

A couple of bottles of Joyce's excellent wine lightened the mood. Laurence cheered up, devoting himself to entertaining Joyce, while Bill and Rosie luxuriated in unaccustomed inactivity. Rosie closed her eyes and drifted into a light sleep, but she was brought to the edge of consciousness by Joyce's voice describing the roses on the pergola to Laurence.

'Now, I know this one. It's Albertine. Rosie taught me how to recognize it. Lovely, isn't it? I'm learning all about roses. And this one that's not climbing up the pergola is a rugosa. See the bright green leaves? Rugosas look like that. What's its name, Rosie?'

Rosie peered. 'Max Graf, probably, and that's Bloomfield Abundance by your foot, Laurence. I'm sure Miss Joyce would have been able to tell you.'

'And this one?' called Joyce over her shoulder as they moved along a mixed border.

'That's a potentilla,' said Bill, before Rosie could answer.

'That's a potentilla rose,' said Joyce importantly, and Rosie and Bill burst out laughing.

'That's a potentilla, full stop,' said Bill. 'A different plant altogether. Although, come to think of it, it is a member of the rose family.'

Laurence bent to pick one of the single yellow flowers from the low shrub. 'You're confusing us, Bill. If it's not a rose, how does it happen to be a member of the rose family?'

'The whole of the plant kingdom has been classified by this Swedish bloke called Linnaeus. Plants start in big groups and get more and more particular, so everything has its place, like in a public library. It goes like this. Let me see, the whole thing is the *plant kingdom*, then there's the *division* which is—'

'Angiosperms,' said Rosie, afraid that Bill had forgotten. 'That's flowering plants.'

'Then the *class*,' cut in Bill. 'Dicotyledons, that's the seed in two halves.'

'Then the *order*,' said Rosie, smiling at Bill. 'That's *Rosales*.'

Botanical classification was something Rosie had known very little about when she married Bill. He was not an educated man, but happening upon a textbook on botany, he had taken in what he could. On her first day at Helmingham, when he was showing her the gardens, he had set out to impress by explaining that many years ago, some Swedish chap named Linnaeus had come up with a classification for all sorts of things, including plants, henceforth known as the Linnaean classification. She had been impressed, too. Some women liked a handsome man, some a rich one. Rosie's priorities had always been elsewhere. When Bill had laid out his knowledge for her appreciation, it was as a rich man might present his lady love with a string of pearls. And she had taken the gift with the same delight some might find in precious jewels.

'Now, your *Rosales* is divided into *Rosacea*, *Saxifragacea and Leguminosea*, the last one is the peas, you know. And—' he put a finger on Rosie's lips to stop her from telling, 'under *Rosacea* we have the *genus Rosa* and then the *species* and *cultivars*.'

Joyce and Laurence applauded and shouted bravo. 'Very well done, you two,' said Laurence. 'Now, how does this little potentilla come into it all?'

Bill looked confounded, and Rosie, for the life of her, could not think where the plant fitted into the scheme of things. When she returned home, she could look it up, could give them an answer. But that, she knew, was not the point. She didn't want Bill to look foolish.

'Well, its *family* is *rosacea*, and it's a cinquefoil, anyway,' Bill said, and this seemed to be sufficient. 'Oh, I know. How could I have forgotten? Its *genus* is *potentilla*!' cried Bill, suddenly, but the young people had already lost interest.

Joyce and Laurence turned away to continue their discussion about the mixed border. Bill reached into his pocket and pulled out his pruning knife, testing its edge with his thumb.

Rosie laughed. 'You never brought that with you.'

'I'm never without it and just as well, too, because I can't stand to see such a mess of a garden. It's a crime to see trees allowed to get in this state. Look at those chestnuts, crowding out that cedar. It makes me feel sick to my stomach and—'

'And what family is the cedar?' she asked, giving him a saucy look.

'I can see I'm going to have to sort you out first.' He took her face in both hands and kissed her on the lips. 'There. That should keep you quiet for a while, Miss sauce box.'

The colour flooded Rosie's face. She felt a queer mixture of pride and love, and embarrassment. Had they seen? Did they know how much she was loved? And, God forbid, had they any idea of the indecent, disloyal thoughts that had plagued her in recent months? Briefly, the gloom that had enshrouded her for so many weeks lifted, allowing her to acknowledge that she could never love a man who knew nothing about gardening, who didn't carry a pruning knife in his pocket, who could bear to look at an overgrown garden and do nothing.

'I suppose we could at least tidy up the Albertine. It's liable to take over the garden.' She examined the last few coppery-pink blooms. Albertine bloomed just once a year, giving a magnificent show for a few weeks, then looking untidy for most of the year. 'Look at the mildew. I wouldn't plant one at Helmingham. Here, be careful, it's very prickly. Cut out this bit. I don't suppose you've got any twine in one of your pockets.'

He reached into his waistcoat pocket and pulled out some raffia. 'Of course I have. Did you think I'd come out of the house naked?'

They worked together for half an hour, pleased that Joyce and Laurence were exploring the farming acres, so that they could get on with their chosen task unhindered. Bill, frustrated, announced that no workman could do a good job without the right tools. He managed to force open the old barn door and discovered a garden fork with bent tines, and in doing so disturbed a feral cat who chased away some pigeons. Dark clouds filled the sky, giving them momentary relief from the summer sun, and Rosie paused in her work to look at Bill.

'Are young lovers always selfish?'

'I wouldn't be surprised. Are you talking about them two? Are they any more selfish than anyone else?'

'They do what they please,' she said. 'You know the entire estate, the entire village is in an uproar about the way she's made friends with us, the way she looks at Laurence as if she could eat him. It's not right. Everybody has his place and those two are making trouble. It will catch up with us all.'

'You're the one. You didn't want to give up your friendship with Miss Joyce, no matter what. I warned you.'

'I know. I hope you won't suffer for it. But she has no-one else. I can't turn my back on her. Oh, Bill, what's to become of us all?'

'I don't know. Laurence is going through hell. Maybe you don't think so, but I know him. He loves her, but he knows he'd be the butt of some pretty foul jokes if he was to marry her.'

She sighed. 'Young people just consider their own appetites these days. They don't think of the consequences.'

'Not like they did in our day,' he teased. 'What will become of the next generation?'

He had been digging out weeds, but now he pushed the fork under an old peony and lifted it with a considerable ball of soil clinging to its roots.

'What are you doing, Bill? We don't live here. This isn't our garden. Let whoever is going to work here dig over these beds.'

'I'm taking this peony home. No-one in this place will miss it, and I've not seen its like. Peonies cross-fertilize without any help from breeders. This is a new variety, I tell you. Look at that shade of pink and tell me if you've ever seen anything like it.' He picked up a few browning petals from the ground. Most peonies had long since flowered, but this variety had just gone over. 'And there seems to be frilly petals in the centre. I'm having it. I saw some sacking in the barn. I'll wrap it up in that. See if you can find a watering can. Laurence won't mind if I take it.'

'I don't suppose he will, though he should. He doesn't seem to care about anything.'

As Rosie seemed disinclined to move, Bill went back into the barn for the sacking and a watering can, and was soon busy tying up the soil ball. 'I have to tell you, he's had a terrible time since the war. He lost his two older brothers, and I believe his mother lost one nephew and two others were badly wounded. Then there's the uncle who was gassed and hasn't been right in all these years. His parents fell on Laurence when he came home. He must do this. He mustn't do that. They were so afraid of losing him that they wrapped him up in swaddling cloths, treated him like a child. He tried to go along with it, feeling sorry for them, but last year he couldn't take it anymore. He took off without a word of warning and went to Scotland for Earl Haig's funeral and it was like he was putting the entire war to rest. His

279

family went hairless. Where had he gone? What was he doing in Scotland? He must come home immediately. There was a big bust up, and he hasn't settled since, but he was working things out for himself, before he fell in love with Miss Whatsit.'

'Maybe he doesn't really love her. Maybe he's still confused.'

Bill set the peony onto the grass, picked up the fork and began trawling through the bed, looking for other prizes. 'He'll not tell her this place is his. He'll sulk because she insulted it. But what could he have expected? It's much smaller than Helmingham and in a worse state. Though in fairness, it's better than anything she will ever have known.'

Rosie sighed. 'The two of them may not be happy, although they look happy enough to me. But it's been fun for us, hasn't it? Coming here. We should go out more often, Bill.'

'Look, Crambe! Goes perfect at the back of the border. Look at the size of those leaves. Good contrast with its flowers. Always reminds me of gypsophila. What do we want to go out for? Isn't Helmingham the nicest place you've ever seen?'

Laurence rubbed the towel over his freshly washed hair and began to comb it into place, grimacing at himself in the small, mildewed mirror. He was reminded of the perfectly good shaving mirror in his grandmother's house, and of how Joyce had sneered at the old place. The past few days had not been the most pleasant in his life. Everything was wrong and he knew his escape from the reality of life outside Helmingham couldn't last.

The day had been hot and he had found himself roped in to help the men dredge the horse pond. They had taken out a cartload of blanket weed and other plants that were choking the pond, then somehow he found himself the butt of some rather vicious teasing. Inevitably, he ended up in the stagnant pond. It was all good natured on the surface. They were laughing when they threw him in, but they left him in no doubt that his presence at Helmingham was resented. He could not blame the men; he had no business to be staying, for he was not prepared to play the humble servant. He went more or less where he pleased and spoke to everyone.

Buttoning up his clean shirt, he looked out the window and felt that he could not stay indoors any longer. The hot day was giving way to a warm and humid evening. To the west, the sky had a rosy glow. The groom's son had brought him his supper five minutes ago: cold roast beef, Helmingham cheese, pickles and four thick slices of generously buttered bread. No more than ten years old, the blond child had repeated parrot-fashion the message from the kitchen. Mr Crow thought he might appreciate eating in his own rooms this evening. Never slow to take a hint, Laurence knew that soon life on the estate would be untenable. Within three minutes, he had eaten everything and drunk the pint of beer that came with his food.

Later, or perhaps the next day, he would return the used dishes, but the small room was oppressing him. He felt his way down the dark staircase and emerged onto the cobbles of the stableyard. The smell of horse was heavy in the air. He headed towards the Hall as if drawn by a magnet. The drawbridges were up, the house throwing long shadows over the grounds.

Walking past the herb and knot garden, he turned to his right and crossed the front of the house, then let himself through the gate to the main garden and headed north with the house on his right. A burst of late sunlight turned the many windows to gold and he stopped to appreciate the sight. Helmingham was magnificent. A Tudor jewel that had been lived in by the same family for about five hundred years. It was also suffering from generations of neglect. It needed to have vast sums of money spent on its fabric, on its decoration, on its furnishings. Millstones didn't come much bigger than the old Hall.

There was movement on the ramparts: Joyce was there, safely contained, encircled by her moat. He waved.

'I'm the king of the castle,' she called.

He laughed. 'Rapunzel, Rapunzel, let down your hair.'

She shook her head, running her fingers through her short bob. 'No luck, I'm afraid.'

'Boys and girls come out to play . . .' he sang. 'The moon is shining as bright as day.'

'Shall I?'

'Please.'

She pointed to the south front of the house where the main drawbridge was situated, then began walking rapidly towards it. He followed at a trot, having by far the greater distance to travel.

The old mechanism creaked, but he was on the bridge to help push the drawbridge into place and to take her hand when she had walked across it.

'Do you feel like a fairy-tale princess when the drawbridges go up?'

She laughed. 'No, I feel like the king of the castle. No-one can harm me. I can do as I please.'

'So long as you stay within your castle walls. You have very little freedom outside them.'

'I know. It's a strange life and I am not accustomed to it yet. Mr Crow would be furious if he knew I had let down the drawbridge.'

'You are the owner, Miss Joyce. You should remind him of that fact from time to time.'

'I would like to find a way of reminding them all.

There is something in their manner. I can't put my finger on it, but they all do just as they please. They are very polite to me, of course, no outward signs of rebellion.'

'Perhaps not, but there is resentment in the air.' He rubbed his thumb across the top of her hand, and she looked up at him quizzically, alerted to his feelings by the intimacy of the gesture.

'Where shall we go, your majesty?'

'Since Bill took one of the peonies from the garden at Boscomb House, I thought we might go over to the peony border and see where he's planted it.'

'I know approximately where it is. He told Rosie it's a new variety.'

'Then he should not have dug it up. Have you noticed how rapacious gardeners are? People who would not dream of stealing something of real value will help themselves to a plant.'

They walked to the causeway which led over the smaller moat, but instead of going on to enter the walled garden, they walked around the outside to the spring border which hugged the south side of the wall for warmth. Here clumps of irises alternated with peonies. Having reached the part of the garden where the peonies were planted, neither Joyce nor Laurence carried on with the search.

'I understand they ducked you in the horse pond.'

He shrugged. 'News travels fast, I must say. Yes, I was clearly the object of their good humour right from the moment I arrived to help.'

'It must have been frightening.'

He shook his head. He had taken her hand and pulled it through the crook of his arm, forcing her close to him. He could smell her perfume, although the fading light blurred her features. 'Boys' stuff, you know. However, I did not fail to grasp their meaning. You and I are not particularly welcome at Helmingham.'

She stiffened. 'Perhaps not. I, however, have my position to strengthen me. As chauffeur, you are vulnerable. Laurence, Mr Trimble must retire soon. If you were to be the bailiff . . .'

'What have I done to make you suppose I could handle such a position?'

'Well, nothing,' she laughed, 'but it would be better than your going to that dreadful old house in Hadleigh. You would have to start from scratch there. You'd be much better off here.'

'I think you would be much better off at Boscomb House. At least you wouldn't be watched every minute, your smallest action commented upon and criticized. You would have some privacy there.' He was talking nonsense, her slight smile told him.

'Are you going to take the position at Boscomb?'

'Well, there is nothing to be done at the moment. I might live in a cottage on the estate, I suppose. But my dream is to expand my motor business. The combustion engine points the way to the future, you know. It has been my dream to become something important in the motor business.'

'I used to have dreams,' she said. 'Then Lord d'Avranche died. Now I have no dreams, because I have had given to me more than I could ever have wished for. I don't go to bed and dream about being rich one day. It's a funny feeling to have your wildest wish granted.'

'Did you ever wish you owned Helmingham?'

'No,' she said sadly. 'I only wished that I might be invited to visit.'

'No dreams at all?' he pressed. 'No dreams of a lover, a husband or children?'

'No, just worried thoughts about wishing I had

enough money to order new curtains. But then I would have to choose the fabric, find the curtain maker, get the work done. It's not a daydream if you have to think about getting your wish fulfilled. These are the sort of wishes that keep me awake.'

They had reached the orchard garden and, searching for a means of changing the subject, he said, 'Oh, look at that old cedar of Lebanon. Have you ever noticed the arrangement of the branches? It always reminds me of the vaulting of a cathedral.'

'You too? Oh, that's exactly what I always think.' She broke away from him and ran towards the tree, staring upwards while turning round slowly until she was dizzy. He watched her with intense pleasure, but from a distance. She was wearing some sort of blue knitted frock that clung to her boyish figure so tightly that he could see the bony protuberances of her hip bones. Her short glossy hair suited her. Her face, so youthful and sweet, was saved from insipidity by straight, no-nonsense eyebrows. But he was remembering her features rather than seeing them; it was too dark to make them out as she stood in the shadow of the old tree. He thought he remembered hearing something about these cedars having a tendency to drop a branch without warning, and should have called her away to safety. Instead, he moved forward just as she headed for the massive trunk and turned to lean against it, looking skywards.

'It will be a new moon tonight. I always go out on the ramparts and look at the moon, but this place is better. I will be able to see it through the branches of the tree.'

He didn't look up, but approached her and put a hand to rest on the trunk on either side of her head. She lowered her chin to meet his eyes, and for several long seconds they said nothing. Then, to his surprise, she lifted her hand and caressed his cheek. 'Oh, Laurence!'

He bent his head to kiss her upturned face and felt her mouth open slightly, her arms encircle his neck. He pulled her towards him and they settled against one another awkwardly, each learning the other's contours, finding the most comfortable position as they kissed. And the kiss lasted for perhaps half a minute.

He breathed deeply, savouring the beauty of the moment and the intensity of his emotions. She had not hesitated, had not flinched from his touch and her receptiveness fired him beyond enduring, beyond reason, beyond caution. Frantically, he kissed every inch of her face and still she smiled. He fondled one breast, and although she was startled at first that too was permitted. He slipped his hands down to press her buttocks closer and she gave a little sigh, answering his kisses, caressing his face until his head was spinning. She loved him, and she must know that he loved her deeply. There were no barriers between them, no taboos, no shyness.

As their kissing became more frenzied, it occurred to him that she trusted him completely. A young woman with no experience of men and no-one to protect her interests could not be possessed like some girl on the streets. As his need increased and he felt his control slipping, so he knew he must call a halt before it was too late.

On the other hand, he could propose marriage to her there and then. It was a desperate plan, born of euphoria. Strike while the iron is hot, his heart told him. He felt sure that at this moment she would agree. Then, whatever followed would not be so despicable. Yet, his cooler self reminded him that marriage between them would require some careful working out, some compromises. She must be made to see that he would not take Helmingham when he took her. And thoughts of Helmingham and remembered comments about his beloved Boscomb House acted like a cold douche. He lifted his head, broke the fevered contact with her lips, straightened his body and smiled into her startled eyes.

'This won't do,' he whispered, wishing he could see her expression. 'I must get you back to the Hall where you will be safe, surrounded by your very own moat.'

'Laurence, I don't want to be safe.' When he didn't answer, unwilling to trust his voice, she sagged against the tree. 'Yes, all right. I'm sorry. Of course. Yes, I'm sure . . .'

They returned in silence, walking quickly but carefully in the growing darkness. The ground was uneven, but he didn't dare to offer his hand for fear that physical contact would destroy his resolve. He watched her cross the drawbridge, waited while she cranked it up after her, and only then looked up to catch a faint hint of movement in a window above. Bert Crow? He couldn't tell, and was frankly too upset to care. He had mismanaged the moment, but at least she could be in no doubt that he loved her. Tomorrow, in the cool light of day, he would speak to her calmly and tell her what he planned.

Joyce, bewildered and shaking, went indoors and straight up to bed. Her experience of men was minimal, her attitudes formed by her mother's warnings. Laurence, she therefore concluded, had used her for his selfish pleasure. He didn't love her; he despised her for being cheap. Her mother had warned her endlessly about the evil ways of men, frightening the child into feeling afraid of every man she met. She had grown up with Thora's words imbedded in her mind, words that popped into her head every time a man smiled at her. *She must not make herself cheap. She must save herself for marriage. Men would take advantage.* When she had discovered the truth about her mother, she had felt betrayed. It had all been lies, taught to her by an arch hypocrite. However, this harsh judgement had not lasted for long. Joyce decided that, having been led into indecent ways by the wicked Lord d'Avranche, Thora had wanted to spare her daughter similar humiliation. Laurence, meanwhile, must have concluded that she was as easy to seduce as her mother had been. She spent a wakeful night in torment, convinced that she had lost Laurence's love by her readiness to kiss him.

She was writing down the names of all the paintings in the drawing-room, prior to recording them in the contents book, when Mr Crow, his face the perfect picture of contempt, ushered in Laurence.

'Laurence wants a word with you, Miss Joyce.'

She didn't bother to disguise her pleasure. Now, he would make it all right. He would say he loved her. He would propose marriage. She would accept and they would live happily ever after.

He approached, and when Mr Crow had closed the door, took Joyce into his arms and kissed her warmly.

'You know I love you,' he said.

To say yes seemed arrogant and knowing, so she just smiled.

'And I want to marry you.'

'Oh, Laurence! And I—'

'Just a minute.' He held up his hand for silence. 'I want to marry you, not Helmingham.'

'Well, dear, we sort of go together. What would happen if—'

'No.' Again he interrupted. She was beginning to be just a little annoyed. 'I cannot be thought to have married you for your money, your house or your position. If you marry me, you will be Mrs Laurence Ballard and take your chances. We will live where I can afford for us to live, spend what money I have and forget about Helmingham. No-one wants you here anyway.'

'Just a minute. I inherited this house. I'm not giving it up. If I want to marry you that is my business and no-one will criticize my decision.'

'Oh, Joyce, wake up. The whole village is seething with gossip. After your mother and Lord—'

'Don't you dare to bring my mother into this!' She glared at him, amazed by the strength of her anger when a few seconds earlier she had been filled with love.

Laurence ran a hand through his hair, took a turn round the library table and came to a halt in front of her. 'I may not have expressed myself very well.'

'That's putting it mildly. However, I understand you perfectly. You want me to give up the only thing the d'Avranche family has ever given me. You don't think I'm good enough to live in a grand house. Why should I give up anything to starve with you? Where would we live? Above the stables? That would be a pretty picture. Helmingham would lie empty while its rightful owner slept with the chauffeur above the stables. Don't be absurd, Laurence. You must take me as I am or not at all.'

'We wouldn't starve, you ninny. Actually, although you didn't . . . I'm not what . . . oh, to hell with it. You wouldn't understand. Greed colours your entire life.'

He turned to walk from the room. 'You're a cad, Laurence Ballard!' she cried.

'But not a gigolo,' he retorted, and she vowed to look up the word in the dictionary as soon as her breathing returned to normal.

Before then, she gave way to a bout of tears and despair. The quarrel had been so swift and fierce, so quickly concluded. He had not played fair by walking out before she had her say. She wished she had known what he was going to suggest. In that case, she could have put her side of it less heatedly, could have gently persuaded him that he was talking nonsense, that those capable of making trouble would soon be brought round, and awkward behaviour from others could soon be stepped on by Laurence if he were firm.

But the more she thought about those brief seconds when her happiness was left in ruins, the angrier she became. How dare Laurence lay down such conditions? Who did he think he was? She was Miss d'Avranche of Helmingham and she would not be treated in such a high-handed manner. She would never leave Helmingham! It was hers, intended to be passed on to her son. Had Laurence thought of that? He had just deprived his son of a magnificent inheritance. Anger sustained her for several minutes, but it was not in her nature to continue to be angry. She needed support for her views, reassurance and comfort. She needed Rosemary Cook.

When she was sufficiently calm to be able to speak to the servants without outward signs of distress, she announced that she would be visiting Rosie where she could be reached if needed.

Chapter Thirteen

Reverend Catchpole had never come to call before. She knew he had made a number of visits in the village and had heard all about his fondness for fruitcake and how every woman was competing to make the best one. Yet Rosie had not expected him to call at the Lodge, at least not so soon. Her fruitcake was ready, however.

'Will you have another piece of cake, Reverend?' She took his cup and emptied the slops, before pouring another cup of strong tea. Reverend Catchpole liked strong tea.

'I believe I will. I'm partial to fruitcake and yours is the best I've tasted.' His voice dropped to little more than a whisper. 'You know, Mrs Cook,' he leaned forward slightly, smiling his wise smile, 'there is a good deal of gossip hereabouts concerning your friendship with Miss d'Avranche. How typical of her generous spirit to appreciate kindness wherever she finds it. She must have been very lonely and confused in those first months at the Hall. She must have welcomed your attention.'

'Miss Joyce and I just seem to get along.'

'Yes, of course. But now . . .' He left the words to hang in the air while he drank his tea and broke off a piece of fruitcake to pop into his mouth. She watched, and the waiting was painful, because she knew what was coming: a blow, like the sting of the schoolmaster's ruler on a cringing palm, a punishment.

'Now, Mrs Cook, you must set her free. You must let her get on with the business of being Miss d'Avranche of Helmingham Hall. The truth is, she doesn't need your *friendship* any more. She needs your service, and that of Mr Cook, especially. She must learn to distance herself from those who serve her, because otherwise there is the matter of playing favourites. I'm sure you agree.'

'Yes,' she whispered, head bent. She didn't agree at all. She believed that Miss Joyce needed her very much, but the rector's position in Helmingham society meant that there could be no argument.

'And as for that young ne'er-do-well, Ballard. Well, I must see what I can do to protect the young lady from his impertinent attentions. He has caused enough trouble here and must move on, no doubt to ruffle feathers and try for a rich wife elsewhere.'

Rosie could have defended Laurence. She could have told him about Boscomb House, about Laurence's well-to-do family, his garages and his reluctance to live at Helmingham Hall. Yet, she was silent, intimidated by Mr Catchpole's fine ways, his handsome appearance and by his certainty about everything.

When he was convinced that he had made his point, he said a brief prayer with her, then stood up to take her hand and smile deeply into her eyes. On this occasion, she was immune to his charm, knowing that he had manipulated her to his own ends. He wanted Miss Joyce for himself, she thought angrily, so he had to make sure Rosie was no longer able to influence the vulnerable young woman.

As luck would have it, Joyce herself turned up on the doorstep fifteen minutes later.

'Laurence and I have quarrelled!' she cried. 'He asked me to marry him, but I must give up Helmingham. What were we supposed to do, live over the stable? He's the most thoughtless beast in the world. He could have come to live at the Hall. Everybody would soon have got used to the idea. I hate him.'

'It would never have worked,' said Rosie dully. 'Consider yourself well out of it. Let him go.'

'But—'

'This was all a mad daydream. You must look to people of your own sort. What can you be thinking of to choose Laurence and Bill and me for your only friends? Your Miss Grissom knows you must cleave to your own class. She makes friends wherever she goes.'

Joyce sat down on a kitchen chair. 'Oh, Rosie, how can you speak to me this way?'

'Your friendship with Laurence is causing trouble. The whole village is turned upside down. The rector has been making comments. Your mother caused enough of a storm here. You must behave especially carefully.'

'But surely what I do and who I marry is my own business. It's not as if I've done anything lewd. I own Helmingham, the Hall and most of the village. I pay the Reverend Catchpole's stipend. I don't have to ask permission.'

Rosie folded her arms and looked out of the window. 'You may own everything in sight, but you'd be in a right pickle without us. We do your work, make your home lovely for you. If everybody is upset because you play favourites and want to make sheep's eyes at the chauffeur, then you'd better pay some heed to what your tenants and estate workers think. I'm sorry, Miss Joyce, but that is the truth. Somebody had to tell you.'

'Yes, indeed,' said Joyce, rising from the table. 'I am grateful for your frankness. I believed you were my friend, but that was foolish, wasn't it? The lovely day out we all spent, the trip to London, and all the meals we've shared. How foolish of me to suppose I could depend upon you. I should have known better. I suppose, if my mother had been an heiress and my

293

father had been Lord d'Avranche, whatever I chose to do would have been all right.'

'I expect so. I'm sorry you think I have let you down, but I have had the error of my ways pointed out to me.'

'It's because of my mother, isn't it? Everyone is against me because of the affair my mother had all those years ago.'

'Well, don't blame me,' said Rosie bitterly. 'I didn't make her do all those things.'

Joyce left the house without saying goodbye. Rosie, sickened by her own cruelty, watched Joyce walk up the drive, then tackled the dishes as if she were doing battle with them, before fetching her hat and striding angrily through the grounds to her rose growing area. It had not rained for several weeks and the drought was providing her new rose with a severe test. She found the rose she had secretly named Felicia blooming merrily, with great trusses of small pink buds opening to palest pink. The growth was lax, but bright green and healthy looking. It would take well to being pegged down when the bush was three years old. She thought about exactly where she would plant a few of them in the herb and knot garden. Perhaps one or two in the other garden where some of the roses were past their best. And she must write to her father to fetch a few bushes for bud wood. It would be satisfying to know that she was helping to keep the nursery from failing.

On her way back to the lodge, Bill joined her. 'If it's something I've done, please tell me and I'll apologize.'

She turned to look at him, shaken out of her gloomy thoughts. 'What are you talking about?'

'You're in a fine old temper. I can tell by the way you're walking. So what is it?'

'Reverend Catchpole called.'

'That must have been nice for you,' he said with heavy sarcasm. 'You like him, don't you?'

'Not any more. Oh, Bill, he as much as told me not to be friendly with Miss Joyce any more.'

'That pompous dandy has no business telling my wife what to do.'

She laid a restraining hand on his arm, afraid he would do something foolish. 'He's right, in a way, so don't go making trouble for yourself by complaining. He's going to get rid of Laurence, you wait and see.'

Bill laughed. 'He's too late there. Laurence packed his bags and left not half an hour ago.'

Rosie nodded. 'I'm sure I know why he's going. He asked Miss Joyce to marry him provided she was willing to give up the Hall. She said no.'

'Look, my dear,' said Bill with a heavy sigh. 'Perhaps the rector is right. We are all in a turmoil. It's not done you and me any good, all this being friendly. She's got to make a proper life for herself. And Laurence needs a good kick up the backside. He must make something of himself, like we have had to do.'

She nodded, coming round to his point of view. 'But she's not at all happy, poor thing.'

'She's a rich woman living in a damned great house, having all of us running around and touching our caps to her. She can't expect to be happy as well.'

That made her laugh harshly. 'Anybody would think she wasn't human. Oh, you are hard, Bill Cook. Sometimes you take my breath away.' She clutched his arm. 'I'll bet your ancestors supported Cromwell, didn't they?'

He had to laugh at himself. 'Just about everybody in these parts did. But I'm no Bolshevik. It's just, well, we've got our own troubles and our own lives. Them two lovers have had us in a tizzy, but no longer.'

The Reverend Catchpole had not wasted his smooth charm on Laurence. 'You there, young man!' he had called, seeing Laurence in the stableyard. 'I think we all know what you are up to. So just pack your bags and get off this estate.'

Laurence, in the act of removing his chauffeur's jacket, paused to glare at the rector. 'And exactly what does that mean?'

'Fortune hunting. Don't deny it. You've set your sights on the supreme prize. I've come to tell you that your gamble has failed.'

'I haven't—'

'Don't bother to deny it. I have just come from Mrs Cook. We have had a serious discussion, and I think I know what you had in mind. Now, kindly collect your possessions, and only your possessions, and leave Helmingham. You may try your wiles elsewhere.'

Laurence, who had, as it happened, already packed his bags, smiled slightly. 'What, sir, and leave the field to you? I pity Miss Joyce, I really do. She deserves better than a pompous ass. Fancy living at Helmingham, do you? I assure you I never did.'

He turned away, removed his jacket and began to unbutton his breeches, before turning to bestow a mischievous grin. 'Shall I change here, or may I return to my luxurious quarters to put on my own clothes?'

The rector, stunned to meet such mocking defiance, took a few steps backward. 'Take care, young man, you're due for a thrashing.' Apparently, he had no intention of administering this thrashing himself, for he turned on his heel and walked away very quickly.

'God help her,' said Laurence to himself. He knew he had made a dog's dinner of his proposal, and in so doing, risked losing Joyce for ever. Until a moment or two ago, he had thought he would go away and give Joyce a chance to forgive his clumsiness. Given time to clear his thoughts, he was sure he could present his case more persuasively. It really was a mystery how two people who loved one another could descend into a desperate quarrel so quickly.

Perhaps she didn't love him! The more he thought about it, the more certain he was that this was the truth. There was nothing for it but to move to Boscomb House and try to pick up the pieces of his life. He would set about putting his property to rights as he should have done months ago. Then, he must make some money, although he had no idea how to go about it.

Of course, he could return to Halstead and his father's switch factory. He could beg for a small part of the company and work out his days there, but he was determined to do no such thing. Something would come up or someone would arrive on his doorstep with a plan or an offer of money. He must not tie himself to his father. That was the most important thing.

He gave his quarters above the stables a quick search, decided he had left nothing behind and closed the door. He would not miss these two dark rooms, but outside, he glanced at the Rolls with affection. The Hall, glowing in the hot summer sunshine, he regarded as his enemy. He didn't spare even a second trying to memorize its sturdy Tudor lines, its ornate chimneys and twisting spires, for Helmingham Hall was his rival for Joyce's love.

He put down his bag in the stableyard, then walked over to the walled garden in search of Bill.

'I'm leaving,' he said, when Bill had seen him from a distance and come to join him. 'Please say goodbye to Rosie for me. You've been very kind, but I cannot stay longer. Joyce has chosen the Hall.'

'You're a fool, Laurence. You should not have forced her to make such a choice.'

'There is no other solution. Can you not just imagine the wagging tongues? Miss Joyce d'Avranche marries the chauffeur, who hopes for a generous allowance. I cannot continue here, and Joyce has enough on her plate. All I ask is that you don't let her marry Catchpole.'

Bill shook his friend's hand solemnly. 'If you had told everyone that you are a member of the family—'

'Who would believe me now? The truth is, I made a terrible mess of everything. I deserve my unhappiness. Joyce deserves—'

'Loneliness?'

'It's her choice, Bill.'

'You may be sure that I don't want her to marry the rector. She made a bad mistake taking him on. See how much she needs your wise counsel?'

'She needs Rosie. I must be going. I will keep in touch, however.'

'You must come to supper occasionally. Don't forget,' said Bill. 'But now you must excuse me. We're trying to keep the vegetables and the herbaceous border from dying in this weather, and it's quite a job getting water to the plants. I must be going.'

Laurence had recently moved his motorbike to the coach house, and now tied his case over the back wheel. It was a pleasant day, so he welcomed the short ride in the sun, reminding himself that for centuries artists had revelled in the special Suffolk light.

Boscomb seemed to have sunk a further foot or two into the dry land. The kitchen was even less inviting than it had been when Joyce visited it with him. His grandmother had left him four hundred pounds; he thought it would take most of this money to put the house to rights. The grounds would take years to get into shape. Perhaps Bill and Rosie would give him some advice. He walked through the rooms, remembering visits to his grandmother, hearing the childish voices of his dead brothers.

He had been a boy, still, when news of his brothers' deaths at Ypres had reached them. The grief of the entire family had been so intense that he could not, after all these years, dwell on it. From that moment, his parents and grandmother had prayed for a swift end to the war before it would be necessary for Laurence to go into the army. Their prayers had not been answered, and no amount of patriotic speeches helped them to accept his departure.

Was it wise to live at Boscomb? he wondered briefly. Was it the best thing he could do to stir up old memories, especially since he had spent the past ten years trying to lay the ghosts? He removed the dust sheet from his grandmother's favourite chair and sat down. As the seat cushion sagged beneath him and his back sank into the upholstery, there arose around him the tender spirit of the old lady whose favourite he had been. Yes, it was right to live in Boscomb, to be surrounded by the happier family memories, to know that in this place he had been loved. That love was in the air, in the very walls, and he could have shared it with Joyce who had known so little love.

But there was nothing to eat. He rode into Hadleigh for a pint and some bread and cheese, and purchased a few necessary supplies. Waving to the three customers at his garage, he thought how different was his treatment in Hadleigh where he had been known since he was a baby, and the wary attitude of the Helmingham folk.

The next morning, he went into the town and quickly found two young women willing to help him clean up his house. By the end of the week the house was beginning to look habitable.

Leaving the women to their chores one morning, he visited his petrol station and arrived in time to be held up by a funeral. As the sad procession passed with a pair of black horses pulling the hearse, he had a brilliant idea.

The following day, he rode to Halstead where he went immediately to the bank. His proposition was a simple one. He intended to purchase several motor cars and two hearses, one for Hadleigh and one for Halstead. He would employ a small team of driver mechanics. He also intended to approach Courtaulds factory and silk mill, and other businesses in the town with a view to signing them up for a servicing contract. He would save them all a great deal of money by undertaking to maintain their vehicles.

Mr Woolerton had a simple reply. He would lend Laurence a thousand pounds provided his father acted as guarantor. There was nothing for it but to travel to his parents' home and ask for this favour. Before Laurence arrived, he knew what the reply would be.

'You went to the bank?' cried Mr Ballard. 'You went cap in hand to the bank without even asking me for the money? How could you? I will lend you what you need, and without charging you interest. How much do you want? Wait a moment while I get my cheque book.'

'A thousand pounds, Father.'

'What? You want a thousand pounds? That's nonsense. You don't want to get yourself so deeply in debt. What can you be thinking of? Don't do it, Laurence. Learn a little about business before going into debt. I can't lay my hands on so much. What interest is the bank planning to charge? You're mistaken, I know it. I'm not saying that you haven't got a very good plan there. You're clever, but then I always said you were clever. But must you start with a splash? I suppose you feel you have to earn some money quickly to impress that young lady. It stands to reason that someone living in Helmingham would turn up her nose at a small business. You ought to explain it to her, make her see that it's sensible to . . . Oh, I don't know. You'll be the death of me one of these days. And your mother! Why don't you ever come home for a meal? Can you stay tonight? Sleep in your old room just for tonight. I'll go over and have a word with the bank. The cheek of it, asking my son for a guarantor. Doesn't Woolerton know you were born in this town? Fought for your country?'

Laurence was quickly exhausted by so much enthusiasm and affection, too tired to resist the invitation to spend the night in Halstead. What he had supposed would be a dinner with his parents ended by being a family reunion. Twenty people sat down in the dining-room, all talking at once, all offering advice.

He went to bed with their voices ringing in his ears. They were too much for him *en masse* and had to be taken in small doses. Their affection, concern and interest in his activities warmed his heart, however, for his heart was in sore need of mending. His last thoughts were of Joyce, alone and without the support a family could give, without the advice of anyone but Rosie Cook and the smooth Mr Catchpole. Many would consider her a very fortunate heiress. He knew better.

For several days after he left Helmingham, Joyce was sure that Laurence would return. He would smile at her in his sweet way and apologize for his hasty words. And Rosie would regret her unfriendly attitude. She could not believe that two staunch friends could desert her on the same day.

By the time the rector called and made it plain that he had been responsible for Laurence's departure and Rosie's coolness, she was past hoping for a small miracle. Mr Catchpole had a hypnotic voice, the grey hairs of maturity and a conviction that everything he thought right was beyond argument. It was easy, in her present listless state, to let him dictate to her.

It was time to put away childish ways, he told her, time to shoulder the burdens of her great estate and the centuries' long tradition of the d'Avranches. He proposed holding a small dinner party for some of the 'better sort' in the neighbourhood.

Joyce said she would be happy to attend.

The hard-working committees of several worthy causes had approached him, wondering if they could hold late summer events in the grounds of Helmingham. Mr Catchpole was certain that Joyce would agree, though it was short notice.

Joyce fetched her diary and pencilled in the dates he gave her.

Mr Catchpole wondered if Joyce could make herself available on the following day to visit several people in the village who had not seen her of late.

She agreed, thinking that this must be what it was like to have a father. *Do as I say and I will buy you a new dolly. Disobey me and I will send you to your room.* She felt as if she were looking at him from a great distance, as if her own voice was coming from even further away. But she agreed to everything, hoping in the depth of her being to please him. Yet, she knew in her heart that she was past needing a substitute father and should be making decisions without the rector's prompting.

Only in the matter of Betsy did she dig in her heels. She was well aware, she said, that Betsy should not be allowed into the drawing-room, nor allowed to sit on the furniture. However, she would continue to take the dog everywhere with her, since Mr Catchpole had cruelly warned off her only other friends.

Mr Catchpole was too experienced to press her when she defied him on unimportant issues, so he merely smiled indulgently, saying half under his breath, 'You are so young, my dear.'

★   ★   ★

The following two weeks were extremely busy and tiring, so there was very little time for brooding. Although she didn't actually enjoy the two dinner parties given by the rector, she managed to get through them with dignity. Everyone was very kind. Others maintained the thrust of the conversation, leaving her with little more to do than make suitable replies. They complimented her garden, lamented the crisis in agriculture, complained about servants.

The Hall was her refuge and unending source of comfort and study. There was no list of the old books that lined the wall of the library, so she decided to make one, taking the opportunity to look at and dust each one. She had recorded the titles of two hundred and fifty-seven when a newspaper clipping fell out of the two hundred and fifty-eighth. It was a brief news item about the death of her father which had taken place not in Australia, as she had always imagined, but in Austria. He had stepped in front of a motor car. Lord d'Avranche, who had been with him, had told the reporter that poor Mr Nicholas d'Avranche had sustained severe injuries in a riding accident in his childhood. This had left him less agile than other men of his age. Mr Nicholas d'Avranche had simply been too slow in getting out of the way. 'He stepped into the road before I could stop him, poor chap,' his lordship had been quoted as saying.

Joyce crumpled the delicate paper in her hand and threw it immediately into the waste paper basket, only to change her mind and retrieve it, trying to smooth the wrinkles. The last piece of the puzzle had fallen into place. She must not turn away from its implications.

All her life, Joyce had been in the habit of inventing tender scenes between her father and herself. She held long conversations with him, telling him of her favourite teacher, her first undisclosed love, her hopes for her future. Always on these occasions, her father had answered with wisdom and compassion. Her conversations with an imagined father were her hidden strength, her secret weapon against a world in which everyone, it seemed, was armoured with a complete and loving family. Now she knew that she had been depending on a lie.

Not only had her mother been too ignorant to distinguish between Australia and Austria, her father had been too ill to look after his own safety. Only later did it occur to her that Thora had taken this man to bed in order to have revenge on her lover. Thora had been an orphan, never knowing her 'pedigree', as she was fond of saying. Joyce realized that she, too, was an orphan, not truly knowing who her parents were. But whereas Thora would have been happy to have some small tangible evidence of her ancestors' existence, Joyce had Helmingham. In future, the Hall was to be both mother and father to her. And she would be a dutiful daughter.

A new-found strength enabled her to stand back from the stressful scenes of her committee meetings, and to see that her role was to give each passionate member a chance to air opposing views, and to lead them all to a compromise decision. Understanding her purpose at the many meetings made it easier for her to handle entrenched attitudes and large egos with a measure of calm. She still found them exhausting and rather frightening, but she could see that all the committee members were according her growing respect.

The rector called daily on the smallest of pretexts and once arrived with a book in his hand which he said she had shown an interest in reading. She couldn't recall the book at all, but invited him to take tea with her in the small private garden which was bounded by tall conifers, and which held a charming, well-appointed summer house. This was a very secluded spot and Mr Catchpole marvelled at length that he had not known of its existence.

'You have so many fine facilities at the Hall,' he said, after suggesting that she should have another piece of cake because she was really rather too thin. 'But no game keeper and no horses.'

'I don't hunt, I don't shoot, I don't even like horses.'

'But I do,' he said, then seeing her startled expression, added. 'which is why I have bought several hunters. And I'm a pretty fair shot, I can tell you.'

'You're welcome to shoot rabbits.'

He struggled for a suitable response and ended by saying weakly, 'Thank you. But I have come on a happy mission! May I suggest, Miss d'Avranche, that we give that splendid motor of yours an outing?'

'But who will drive?'

'Oh, Commander Higgs is a splendid driver and has been dropping hints this past fortnight. He wants to take the splendid Rolls-Royce for a spin. Would you care for it? We could make it a day-long journey somewhere.'

'What fun,' she said coolly. 'We could go to . . . Halstead. I would like to choose some silks from the mill and I'm sure Mrs Higgs would like that, too.'

'Halstead. I don't believe I know it, but I expect Commander Higgs will. Shall we say next Friday?'

Unlike her previous visit to Halstead, Joyce sat in the back seat and revelled in the wind in her hair. It was the eighth of September and, incredibly, the temperature was in the eighties. No rain had fallen for weeks. The countryside was burnt to an unattractive yellow and the sun blazed down on their heads relentlessly.

Ranulph Higgs was, in truth, a superb driver, managing the great car with ease. They arrived in Halstead without incident. Joyce suggested that it might be necessary to fill up the motor with petrol before the return journey and pointed out Laurence's garage. Generally, she was not the sort of person who sought to manipulate others, but she had to congratulate herself on this day's work, for Laurence was standing by the pump talking to his father as they drove up.

'Fill up the tank,' said the commander to the attendant.

'My word!' exclaimed Catchpole as he recognized Laurence.

'Excuse me.' Joyce climbed out of the motor car and approached Mr Ballard with her hand extended. 'How are you, sir?'

'Could be better,' he said sadly.

'How are *you*?' asked Laurence softly.

She waved a hand in the direction of her companions. 'As you see.'

Mr Ballard was holding fiercely to the other hand. 'Miss d'Avranche, my son is a fool. He's told me everything, and I've told him he's a fool. Two young people—'

'Dad, be quiet.'

Joyce smiled at Mr Ballard. For one brief moment, she loved his father more than she loved Laurence. Then the old pain returned. 'It seems as if it can't be helped.' She looked into Laurence's face, memorizing his features, drinking in his beauty, until her eyes filled with tears and she couldn't see him any longer.

'Who was that buffoon with your former chauffeur?' asked the rector.

'He's not a buffoon. He's Laurence's father and a respected tradesman, I imagine.'

'How unfortunate that we should meet . . .' began Mrs Higgs. 'Ranulph, isn't there a splendid inn in Great Yeldham?'

Her three companions felt constrained and the atmosphere was, for a while, very tense. But Joyce felt strangely light-headed and soon relieved the others of any sense of embarrassment. No-one could be blamed for assuming that she had met an old love and discovered that he didn't matter to her anymore.

Her light-hearted air on the journey to Halstead, and the fact that she spoke scarcely at all to Laurence when they met, probably led to Reverend Catchpole's profound misunderstanding of her feelings, and his subsequent stupidity. For he chose the very next day to propose marriage.

'We have had such pleasant times together, my dear Miss d'Avranche, that I feel emboldened to ask for your hand in marriage. It is unfortunate that you have no male relative to whom—'

'No.'

'I beg your pardon?'

'I said no, Mr Catchpole.'

His mouth worked, searching for something to say that would save his embarrassment. 'Not even "No thank you?"'

'No, I will not marry you and I am astonished that you should have asked.'

He left soon after, and she saw considerably less of him in the next few weeks.

It rained for the first time in six weeks on September the twenty-ninth. Joyce took Betsy for a walk in it, but the dog could not rejoice. She waddled beside her mistress, tongue lolling until they came within sight of Rosie's rose field. Joyce had planned to use the ending of the drought as the opening in an overture of friendship.

However, she noticed from a distance of a hundred

yards that Rosie was with her father. They were digging up rose bushes, busy in their work and talking rapidly. There was a sense of their both working for a common cause. She couldn't bring herself to interrupt such an intense moment between father and daughter.

The rain had been heavy, but didn't last long. The following day there were few signs of the recent downpour, except that the lawns were slightly greener. Yet the fine weather couldn't last. Soon autumn would be upon them, and while each season had its charms, she could not look forward to the dark winter. The late September sunshine was warm on her back, although not nearly as hot as it had been earlier in the month. She held her papers – diary, notebook and correspondence – in the crook of her arm and wondered where would be the best place to work, finally deciding on the secret garden with its large summer house which was her favourite.

Mr Crow hurried ahead to open the summer house and fetch a couple of comfortable wicker chairs and a small table. He settled her in a shady spot and promised to bring her a jug of lemonade at eleven o'clock.

For several minutes, she went through her correspondence, laying those that required an answer on one side. Soon, she would need a secretary to help her with the letters. Another young woman in the house could be pleasant company for her.

She put down her pen and looked at the fading roses. Some, she knew, would carry on blooming until December, most would not. October was nearly upon her. The months since February had flown. Official Summer Time would end on October the third. Then darkness would fall too early, leaving her long evenings indoors alone with only her embroidery for company.

However, she did not wish to dwell on that. She had come far and achieved much since last February.

During the summer, the grounds had been opened for fifteen events. There would be other parties during the next few months, culminating in the Christmas party she proposed to make an annual event for all the children. She had been secretly planning it for several weeks.

Mr Goodenough had become very subdued since the arrival of the rector and no longer made challenging remarks to her. In fact, he went so far as to apologize for any possible past rudeness and assured her that he loved his post as schoolmaster in Helmingham.

Joyce played the rector against the schoolmaster, in spite of the fact that they needed to work together. They both depended upon her for their income and, cruelly, she was discovering that the exercise of power could be an agreeable substitute for happiness.

In the same way, keeping busy could be an acceptable substitute for loneliness. She spoke to so many people during the course of each day, discussing this, planning that, greeting guests to the grounds and exchanging pleasantries – the same pleasantries a hundred times over – that she could fool herself into thinking she was glad of evening solitude.

Occasionally her determination left her, and idle thoughts crept in. *I must tell Laurence about the lady who breeds pigs.* Or *I wish Laurence could see that woman's absurd frock* or, *If only Rosie could see this garden, which is not nearly so fine as Helmingham.* Then she would shake her head in annoyance, think, 'I don't need anyone. I was always alone and I always will be.' And she would remember the absurdity of her mother confusing Australia with Austria, able almost, but not quite, to laugh about it.

Then she would think of the man who had fathered her, wondering what exactly he was doing in Austria and why he happened to be there with Lord d'Avranche. She hoped he had not suffered too much during his short life, and that he had found some happiness. He had certainly been a pawn in her mother's schemes. But both of them were complete strangers to her. They were her parents, but she did not know them at all, had no idea how they had thought or felt, how they had suffered. Her inability to think of them as her real mother and father haunted her.

In her blackest moods, she actually wondered if she would not have been better off had she never inherited Helmingham. But this she always rejected. Life in the country had opened to her so many pleasures that she invariably felt a prickling of fear when she considered how diminished her life would have been had Cartwright lived to claim his inheritance.

What if it had not happened? The quiet shorthand typist would never have given a thought to such creatures as deer. On her arrival, she had been enchanted by the deer, but had not known that the Helmingham Park housed red and fallow, or that the stags shed their horns in the spring. This was an alarming sight for a city girl, and had caused her to run to Mr Trimble in alarm. In June, the fawns were born, beautiful and apparently vulnerable, yet soon on their feet and following their mothers. Now she was looking forward to the October rut when the stags would groan, thrash bushes and fray the bark on any trees left unprotected.

Farming would have remained a mystery to her. She had followed the progress of the farm crops and was still awaiting the lifting of the sugar beet in the autumn. She regularly drank the milk and ate the butter and cheese from her own dairy. She dined on her own lamb and pork, enjoyed a morning rasher, tucked into fresh eggs. The vegetables that Bill grew were considered the finest anywhere around. Food had taken on a new importance. She now cared very much how that food was produced and how it tasted.

The church calendar also dictated her activities from week to week. Life in London had only limited conditions: winter and summer, cold and hot, wet and dry. At Helmingham, each day had its own importance. When the leaves fell, she would be able to identify half a dozen deciduous trees by their shape alone, an ability she had once thought impossible.

It was the same indoors. Careful study enabled her to identify all the furniture, all the paintings and prints, all the china. She had recently dined at a fine home outside Stowmarket and had been able to discuss Van Dyck's paintings for several minutes without revealing how new such knowledge was.

Only Mr Trimble defied the new Joyce. She wanted an extensive scheme of replanting in the woodland, since so many trees had been felled during the Great War. The bailiff would not even discuss the matter with her. Mr Trimble found a thousand ways to put off this task, to plead lack of money, shortage of labour, the folly of planting her choice of trees. He was as hard to pin down as a bead of mercury, an old man who shamelessly traded on his age, her youth, Mr Finch's orders, the weather. But she would get the better of him. Time was on her side. When she felt more confident, she would retire him to one of the cottages. She would appoint her own man who would never consider defying her. She was content. She had almost everything she wanted in this world, and no-one had *everything*. She was indeed the Queen of the Castle.

Her sense of contentment as she sat in the summer house was short-lived. Five minutes later, when Rosie walked into the garden, Joyce felt anger welling inside her. Why had she been forced to make all the sacrifices? No-one was forgiving or accommodating. Joyce was being moulded by Helmingham, its residents and staff.

'Good morning, Rosemary. How are you? Come and sit down.'

Rosie hesitated, looked around briefly then sank into the second of two chairs provided by Mr Crow.

'I must not disturb you. I didn't know you were here.'

Joyce smiled. 'I'm not a monster. I remember when we used to meet quite often in a most casual way. I miss those moments.'

'But everything is easier for you now. People are settled, getting used to having you here. It is better. You have a position.'

'Hmmm. I have a position all right. All the minor decisions are mine. If I say I will wear the green woollen frock with the fur around the hem on the hottest day of summer, Cutler will lay out the clothes without a murmur. But just let me say that I love the chauffeur, and Cutler and all the rest of you would rise up to stop me.'

'It's not quite like—'

'If I demand that you and Bill cut every rose in the grounds and bring them indoors for one grand event, you might be heartsick, but you would do it. Let me ask the two of you to speak to me as if I am still a good friend and wait for the fireworks.'

'Miss Joyce, that's not fair! The rector called on me. I do see that you must begin to make friends among suitable people.'

Joyce pinched the bridge of her nose. She was being unkind as well as unfair. With an effort, she smiled. 'It's not your fault. Please tell me, now while no-one is around, how are you? Any luck? How is your secret rose?'

'I used to go out of doors on clear nights and wish on a star, but that was stupid and I haven't done it for ages. I shall be childless, I know that now. I have almost come to terms with it. My roses, on the other hand, progress mightily. My special one is to be grown by my father at the nursery. He will make some money with it, I'm glad to say. I haven't told anyone its name yet, but it will be called Felicia. That's the name I would have given my baby. You see, I can talk about it now. I'm over the worst disappointment. Before today, I have not told a soul. Felicia. Do you like the name?'

'It's beautiful. I hope it one day becomes the most famous rose in the world.'

Rosie saw Mr Crow approaching and leapt up from her chair.

'Miss Joyce. A telegram has arrived for you.'

He eyed Rosie coolly, then turned to leave the garden.

'Just a minute,' called Joyce. 'It is from Miss Grissom and she wishes me to come to London at once. Tell Cutler I will come indoors shortly to choose what I want to pack.'

'Bad news?' asked Rosie.

'I don't know for sure. She begs me to come immediately. It sounds rather ominous, don't you think?'

Chapter Fourteen

With difficulty, Marsha settled into her upper berth on the Golden Arrow train, sighed heavily and tried to compose herself for sleep. Tomorrow morning she would arrive in Paris, and she did want to be fresh. Overnight the train would travel to the docks at Dover to be loaded onto a ferry and transported to Calais. The passengers need not move from their cabins all the way from London to Paris. Bliss, theoretically.

However, after half an hour afloat on a choppy sea it occurred to Marsha that if the ship sank, she would never be able to get out of the train, much less the ferry. They would all sink with the weight of the carriages. Sleep, therefore, eluded her, giving her the opportunity to review the past few months.

Rupert was a darling. He had taken her everywhere, doing the season, as he called it. She had met heaps of people whose names never registered, had been given the chance to decide if she really did want to live for ever in England. And she did. It was ever so much fun, and if one occasionally saw a sadder England, one where men loitered on the streets or begged a few coppers, she had only to remind herself that there were such people in America. Rupert said there was an agricultural crisis and that there was no work in the towns and cities, but he always reminded her that many were too lazy or drunk to work. This comforting thought kept her from exercising her well-known gift for coming to the aid of those in need of help.

She had spent an absolute fortune on clothes and

wondered what her daddy would say if he could see her daring new bathing costume. She had spent weekends in some splendid homes and been treated with the utmost friendliness. England's cool summers, so different from the baking heat of Kansas, were very much to her liking, and she felt that one day soon she would be on an equal footing with Joyce. Rupert – she just knew it – was going to propose. Why else would he want to take her to Paris?

'Darling, you look fresh as a daisy,' said Rupert when they met for breakfast. 'Rotten crossing. I hardly slept a wink.'

She straightened her shoulders. 'You'll find I'm an intrepid traveller. I think I will just have orange juice and coffee this morning. It was a rough crossing, wasn't it? Now, do tell me. Who are we to stay with in Paris?'

'The Flemyngs. Good address. The Avenue Montaigne. I was at school with Jason. You'll love Sylvia. She's a good sport and almost as good a rider as you are. They'll provide us with mounts, of course. Have you ridden in the Bois de Boulogne?'

'No, we weren't given the opportunity to ride when I was at finishing school. It was a terrible place. I shan't tell you the name of it, because you'll only think less of me.'

'Never,' he said, giving her a long passionate look. Marsha hoped he wouldn't propose over breakfast. She wanted something much more romantic.

The Flemyngs were every bit as charming as Rupert had promised. Old friends of Cartwright's, they spoke of the late captain with great affection which annoyed Rupert.

'I've lived my entire life in that damned chap's shadow,' he later told her. 'It was always, look what Cartwright has done, and Cartwright is so brave, stroke, clever, stroke, decent. You've no idea what a trial it was. And now he's gone and got himself killed in Brazil which is even more romantic than anything he did before.'

'Poor you,' said Marsha, 'was he really horrible?'

Rupert shook his head sadly. 'I can't say he was. Handsomest man you ever saw. Six feet tall and straight as a ramrod. Every woman fell in love with him and every man wanted to be just like him. Shame really. The war did for him. Couldn't settle afterwards. We all said he did all those daredevil things to try to get himself killed.'

Rupert's honesty worked powerfully on Marsha. Sometimes he postured and acted the snobbish gentleman, but when he stopped play-acting he could be very pleasant. She did like him. He wasn't boring, and it was unkind of her to think he was on occasion. She did like him, yes she did. And it would be absolutely wonderful to be Lady d'Avranche. She and Joyce would be cousins. And she really *did* like Rupert whose irritating little ways she would grow accustomed to.

On the Saturday evening following their arrival, the Flemyngs were invited to a very grand party at the Elysée Palace, and there was no question of getting invitations for Rupert and Marsha. They said they didn't mind at all, that they would make their own entertainment.

Rupert took her to the Folies Bergère. Marsha had the most wonderful time, and afterwards they dined at Les Deux Magots. She had never had so much fun in all her life. She was happy and convinced that soon Rupert would pop the question. They drank two whole bottles of champagne, and the question Rupert popped was an invitation to a little hotel he knew that rented rooms by the hour.

Marsha heard herself agree. First a night of passion, she told herself, then the inevitable proposal. Rupert could not be so ungentlemanly as to fail her. Rupert was a man of honour.

The hotel was just a few blocks from the elegance and excitement of the Champs Elysée, but yet a world away. An unimposing door opened directly onto the pavement which led to a reception area under a glass roof.

A well-dressed gentleman was just leaving. '*A bientôt*,' sang the gaudy woman who shook hands with him. He dropped his chin and hurried out the door.

'Rupert, don't you think—'

But Rupert had quickly paid the concierge and been told to mount the stairs to room six. A maid passed them coming down the stairs with an armful of used sheets.

'Rupert, this is a brothel!'

'Not entirely. Come on, darling. You know I love you and we'll soon be in our own little love nest. Don't worry. We won't meet anyone we know.'

The stairs were small and creaked loudly, but Marsha's difficulty in mounting them had more to do with champagne, as she was extremely dizzy. The room was very small and sparsely furnished, with a bed, a wash basin and bidet and a pair of French windows leading on to a minuscule balcony. Rupert did not test the light switch, saying they could manage in the dark.

Marsha opened the French windows, and her hand came away from the frame bearing several flakes of paint and a great deal of dirt. Below was the glass ceiling of the reception area which covered the entire well of the hotel, now glowing with light. Rupert came up behind her and put his arms around her waist, pressing her close to him. He had already removed his trousers, shoes and tie.

Fright cleared her head of alcohol with great speed. What was she doing here? She must have been mad! Grasping his fingers, she tried to prise them off her.

'Darling,' he murmured into the bun of artificial hair at the nape of her neck. 'Come to bed, little sweetheart.'

'No. I've changed my mind. Rupert, I don't want to do this. Take me back to the Flemyngs' house. This is madness. I'm not that sort of girl, Rupert. Please.'

Rupert made no reply, just quite revolting snuffling noises as he nuzzled her neck. 'Damned thing,' he said after a minute of nearly silent struggle. She felt him rip the remaining pins from her bun and toss the false hair aside.

She twisted round, which turned out to be exactly what he wanted. They wrestled for several seconds, and Marsha realized that in a battle of strength she would always lose. To save her virtue, she must outwit him, not such a difficult task, surely, as Rupert had drunk a great deal.

'All right, my darling,' she whispered, 'but please don't tear my frock. It's my very best and it's only chiffon. Get into bed and I will take it off.'

'No, I'll take it off.'

'What, clumsy old you? Get into bed.'

She watched as he turned and climbed into the narrow bed, just five feet from the window. Swiftly, she stepped out onto the narrow balcony, climbed over the wrought iron railing and hung out over the atrium.

'What are you doing?' he asked in considerable surprise.

'I don't want to make love to you, Rupert. I am a decent woman. You should never have asked it of me. I know you got me drunk just so you could have your way, but I will die first. Leave this room at once or I will fling myself onto the glass below. Think of the scandal.'

Not surprisingly, he did not stay in the bed to hear all of this speech, but leapt to the window and grabbed one wrist. 'Get back in here, you little idiot. What can you be thinking of?'

'My honour.'

'I didn't force you, you know. Oh, all right, all right, I'm going. You'll let me put on my trousers, I suppose.'

The French doors of the room next door opened wide. An enormous man with a wobbly belly stepped out to enquire in French what was going on. He was stark naked. Marsha looked away, trying to see inside her own little room where Rupert seemed to be getting dressed and grumbling in a low voice. It was too dark to make out what exactly he was doing, but then the door opened and she saw him silhouetted against the hall light. He shut the door. She began to climb back into the room. The Frenchman stopped berating her in terms she didn't understand at all and went back to his companion. She stayed in the dark bedroom just long enough to make sure her clothes were properly arranged and that she still had her handbag, then opened the door, looked both ways and headed for the stairs.

Halfway down she encountered the maid coming up with her arms full of clean sheets. Rupert was hovering in the lobby and pounced out at her.

'I've called a taxi and will take you back to the Avenue Montaigne as soon as it arrives.'

'Thank you,' she said, in truth very grateful not to be alone at one o'clock in the morning.

'Well,' he said with heavy sarcasm, 'this has been fun. We must do it again some time. You have turned out to be an absolute peach. I swear Cousin Joyce would never have treated me this way.'

'Joyce would not have come in the first place. But you should marry her, Rupert. That way you could have the title and Helmingham.'

'But I fancied you,' he said quietly.

Tears blinded her. It was absolutely vital to work

herself into a rage of injured innocence. Otherwise, she might have to face up to her part in the débâcle. 'Oh, you needn't fancy me any longer. My father has got some hare-brained idea in his head that the American stock market is over-heating. He has sold all his shares and put the money in the bank, or something. So you see, I'm not as rich as you had hoped.'

'By jove! You don't say? Must know something. The old boy seems to be pretty shrewd.'

'Is that all you can say?' she cried. 'You are an un-principled brute.'

'Yes, well you're better off without me.'

The next morning, Marsha made her excuses and returned to England alone. The light of day found her filled with shame and unable to find a shred of comfort in any part of the affair. She even wondered if it would not have been less embarrassing to allow Rupert to have his way. But, she knew she could never marry him. He was not the proper husband for her, not the Mr Right she was always dreaming of.

Her first act on arriving in London was to send Joyce a cable asking her to come to town. Joyce was always the first person Marsha thought of in times of crisis.

Laurence's days were so busy that he seldom had a moment to sit down and think. He had signed up a number of firms on a maintenance contract, had taken on a total of twenty men and was attempting to train them all in the art of motor mechanics. In the evening, he wrote up his accounts, promising himself to employ a bookkeeper in the very near future. He calculated that he would be earning six pounds a week by the end of the year, a nice income, the prospect of which brought unstinting praise from his father.

He also tried to sell off the farmland surrounding Boscomb House, but found that he couldn't have given it away. Land was down to four pounds the acre, yet there were no buyers. Farmworkers were leaving their homes and walking to Ipswich or even London in search of work. Occasionally they left behind their families, consigning them to the mercy of the community when they went looking.

Laurence's nights were not, of course, busy and this was the time when gloomy thoughts kept him awake. Eventually, he realized that he had been behaving childishly. There was no reason on earth why he should not marry Joyce and live at Helmingham. His business interests would be his answer to those who said he had married her for her money. Why, he might one day be a very rich man if the business continued to expand! And he would announce that he was related to the d'Avranches, which should stop some of the more contemptible gossip.

Awaking one morning at the beginning of October with these happy thoughts, he decided to visit Helmingham Hall immediately after paying a call on Mr Finch. He put on his best clothes and entered the lawyer's premises without an appointment.

Mr Finch was reading *Country Life*, seated in a red leather armchair in his office. He was smoking a cigarette and there was a cup of coffee on the table by his side. There were no papers on his desk or any other indications of ongoing business. Laurence felt a surge of anger.

'It's not necessary to work very hard when one has control of Helmingham Hall, is it, Mr Finch?'

'What? You? What are you doing here?'

'I have come to enquire of the financial position of the estate. You see, I have become concerned that Miss d'Avranche has no friend to look after her interests. She is entirely in your hands.' He stood smiling as Finch collected his thoughts.

'The rector threw you off the premises. I know because he told me so himself.'

'He is mistaken. I went of my own accord. I repeat, I want to know how the estate is financed, what monies are owed to it and how well you pay yourself.'

'By what right do you ask these questions?'

'I suspect you may be committing some irregularities.'

'There are no irregularities here, except that I should never have allowed Miss d'Avranche to move into Helmingham before the Captain is officially declared dead.' He sneered. 'I suppose you are planning to insinuate yourself into the lady's affections. Therefore, let me set your mind straight on a few important matters.'

Laurence looked around him, then settled for the other leather chair opposite the lawyer. 'I would be obliged. Let us deal together sensibly, Mr Finch. I cannot get rid of you. You cannot get rid of me. We will have to learn to get along. You have kept Miss d'Avranche on a ridiculously tight financial rein. She is an heiress and should be able to spend a few pounds without your permission.'

'Ah,' said Finch, 'now we come down to it. You think you will be marrying a fortune. Let me disabuse you of that idea. Perhaps you will marry Miss d'Avranche after all. I don't know. What I do know is that the two of you would not live at Helmingham for long.'

'Miss d'Avranche has no intention of leaving Helmingham. She loves the old house.'

'Let me explain. In order for you to understand, I must start at the beginning of the century, before the Great War. There was an extraordinary mood among the landed aristocracy to sell their land. I believe it was all the fault of Herbrand, the eleventh Duke of Bedford who was a Whig. He thought the power of his own class should be diminished. He began selling off vast tracks of the Russell inheritance. Others followed his lead. In the years before the war, eight hundred thousand acres of farmland were sold off. Prices were good – twenty-five pounds the acre. Much of the non-entailed land owned by Lord d'Avranche was sold, most of it in other counties, rather than Suffolk. The money was reinvested, some of it in Russian bonds, much more in America. The mood, you see, was for living economically. For instance, since shooting could be rented, there was no need to own hunting lodges and Scottish estates.'

'I thought the great families believed that their power and wealth depended upon landowning.'

Mr Finch shrugged. 'Well, attitudes were changing. I believe it was the Marquis of Northampton who said that landowning on a large scale was felt to be a monopoly and was unpopular. It has been estimated that half the farmland of Britain was up for sale and by the end of 1921 a quarter of it was sold, most of it to tenant farmers.'

'I don't see what this has to do with the Helmingham estate. The land is entailed, isn't it? It can't be sold.'

'You'll see where I'm headed in a moment. Let's consider the budget of 1919. Parliament in its wisdom introduced a new method of assessing death duties. It is based on the freehold vacant possession market price of land, and not on its calculated rent roll. Death duties were, at a stroke, doubled. Many landlords panicked, although they need not have done. It was still possible to transfer a fortune from living father to son. Lord d'Avranche did this on my advice. And, as I have already said, land sold before 1921 fetched a good price. After that . . .'

'But the rents,' persisted Laurence. 'The entailed estate must have an income from rents.'

'The houses in the village, those which Miss d'Avranche can expect to bring in an income, are all small, their occupants are poor and sometimes have no work at all. Many cannot pay any rent, but at least they keep the houses warm. You've no idea how quickly a dwelling falls into decay when it is left unoccupied. The properties are becoming a burden, however, as they must be maintained by the estate. Do you not realize that there are some estate properties in the country totalling seven hundred acres that are empty, their houses and farm buildings falling down?'

'So there is nothing.'

'Britain has to import ninety per cent of its wood. Much of the wood this country did produce was cut down during the war. A great planting scheme must be put in hand.'

'Joyce wanted to plant, but Trimble—'

Mr Finch smiled wryly. 'Who would pay for the fencing, the planting and the maintenance? No, after the war the Forestry Commission came into being to replenish stocks of wood. They began to buy up or lease thousands of acres, mostly in Scotland and Wales, but I was fortunate in persuading them to take out a nine hundred and ninety-nine year lease on three hundred entailed acres of Helmingham land at two shillings and sixpence the acre.'

Laurence stood up, making a few mental calculations. 'But that's just thirty-seven pounds fifty a year! Ten years from now that may not seem such a bargain. Joyce should be getting something like ten shillings to the acre, not two and six.'

'It's better than nothing. Many of the great families are doing it, have done it. My advice was sound. It's off Miss d'Avranche's hands. Anyway, it doesn't matter.'

'Is there nothing that could be sold?'

'I have no doubt that the two of you will strip the old

place of its treasures. You will be able to live hand-somely on the proceeds.'

'The National Trust?'

'They won't have it.'

'Some shares. Captain Cartwright is dead. Every-thing must come to Joyce.'

'No. Lord d'Avranche hated to leave anything to the daughter of his former mistress, but could not prevent her from having Helmingham. He had already trans-ferred everything possible to Cartwright, the rest is donated to charity. Cartwright's will continues the plan. Some money will go to Rupert to support the title. The rest is to be put into a charitable trust.'

'So because of his lordship's spite the house will fall into decay.'

'Probably. He didn't care. Imagine being forced to give your most prized possession to your greatest enemy. It broke his heart and he was determined to do all in his power to ensure that she received no money.'

'And what did the captain think of this scheme?'

'He saw it as preventing a scheming woman from realizing her dream from the grave. He should have married in his twenties, of course. I told him so myself on one occasion, but he was not the sort of man to take advice from his solicitor. We didn't really see eye to eye.'

'How is it that all the wages are being paid?'

Hapgood Finch closed his eyes briefly, as if at some remembered pain. 'I felt it best to have the house lived in during the two years necessary to prove the captain was dead. I confess I did hope that somehow . . . So I myself have been paying the wages and giving Miss d'Avranche a small allowance out of the estate of Captain Cartwright. I will sort it out eventually. And it is an irregularity, I admit, though not the sort you had in mind. Ironic, isn't it? The captain did not love

Helmingham as Miss d'Avranche does, yet had he lived the estate would have been saved. He certainly had enough money to run it. Now, all is lost.'

'And when the will is proved, all the estate staff will be sacked?'

'Precisely,' smirked the lawyer. 'Your dear friends, the Cooks, will be unemployed and homeless. Although, they will be better off than most, as I'm sure Rosemary Cook's father will take them in. Now will you excuse me? My telephone is ringing.'

Laurence left the office, shaking his head, wondering what the future held for himself and Joyce. He should have come earlier to speak to Mr Finch. He should have done a thousand things, but he had been too puffed up with pride. Poor Joyce. He heard Finch shouting into the telephone.

'What? London calling? I can't hear. What's that you said? *Who*?'

Laurence went immediately to Helmingham, but Mr Crow informed him coolly that Joyce had travelled to London to visit her friend the previous day and would be gone for a week. Disappointed, he went in search of Bill and by careful management of the conversation, was successful in getting himself invited to stay overnight the day before Joyce was due to return. He didn't tell Bill the purpose of his visit, but his old friend smiled broadly, having guessed the reason.

If it had not been for the pressed rose, its petals crisp and brown and so fragile that a gentle breeze would have destroyed it, he would probably have lived out his few remaining days in an alcoholic daze in a village in northern Brazil.

But there it was early one morning, lying in the dusty road, dropped perhaps by some fat old woman who had saved it for fifty years in memory of a lost lover. Or perhaps it had been plucked from the funeral wreath of a loved one. Certainly it could not have deeply moving memories attached to it, for otherwise it would not have been dropped in the road for donkeys to trample over. He bent to pick it up. It must have been red at one time. The base of the petals, protected from the ravages of the sun and pressure put upon them, had kept a hint of their original glory. He held the flattened disk in both hands, carried it to a nearby doorstep and sat down to weep.

Some events in a person's life never lose their emotive connections, and the faded rose called to mind one of the most bitter incidents in a life of sorrow, brought about by another faded rose. Cartwright was eleven years old. His father had just settled Thora Jefferson in a cottage close to the hundred-acre Beam's Wood on the estate, which was some distance from the Hall and largely sheltered by trees. Thora was twenty, but she seemed to belong to another generation entirely, more cynical and sophisticated, having all the allure of the scarlet woman.

He had left the Hall at first light and, on the pretence of going fishing, had made his way to this isolated house. His father, he knew, never spent the entire night with Thora, but invariably returned to the Hall in the late evening. It was safe, therefore, to knock on the door at seven o'clock in the morning, to confront the voluptuous woman who made his mother cry each evening at nine o'clock.

'Yes, what do you want, Cartwright?' Thora had said, standing in the doorway in a Japanese kimono. 'Does your father know you're here? Or perhaps your mother sent you.'

'My father does not know I am here, Miss Jefferson, nor did my mother send me. I have come to plead with you to go away. You are breaking my mother's heart.'

'No-one thinks of my heart, do they? No-one cares what I've gone through since I was a baby. Certainly not you, brought up in cotton wool. I'll not be pushed out, so you can go on your way, young man, or I'll tell your dad on you.'

From his jacket pocket, Cartwright had removed a tissue-paper parcel which he unwrapped gingerly. 'Look at this. My father keeps it in his Bible and I have borrowed it to make you think. It's a rose from my mother's wedding bouquet. Do you think he would have kept it all these years if she meant nothing to him? Please go away and leave them in peace.'

'He hates her! He loves me! I make him happy in a way she never could. You'd better get used to me, young snotty nose, because I'm going to be around a long time. He loves me.'

Thora's face had gone very red, and he knew she was going to do something dreadful. He cringed, expecting a blow, but she had a crueller idea in mind. She snatched the rose and crushed it fiercely, then opened her hand and allowed the brown dust to drop on her doorstep. Only the stem was left, and this she dropped onto the ground as well, where she stamped on it.

Horrified, afraid that his father would thrash him for having taken the rose, and certain that whatever Thora chose to tell him would be believed, he had stood rooted to the ground as she slammed the door behind her.

At this moment, far away in Brazil and nearly thirty years later, Cartwright experienced heart-piercing pain all over again. The shock of it all had never left him. Surprisingly, his father had not noticed or ever commented on the missing rose. Cartwright had gone weeping to his mother's dressing-room and confessed all. Together they had cried, and of course he had been forgiven. Years later, this gentle woman drowned herself and Cartwright knew where the blame lay.

After the war, the years passed in misery and pain, and he couldn't bring himself to choose a bride. He could not understand the workings of his own mind, nor could he control the resentment he had harboured against his father for twenty-nine years. He had lived on the edge of danger, seeking it out, defying the gods to destroy him, stoking his courage with Scotch whisky. His last escapade had been to fly over the Amazon river.

His ill-considered visit to Brazil was driven by the fact that the Brazilians had declared war on Germany in 1917, an act that Cartwright had always thought was jolly decent, considering the distance from the fighting. They had sent part of their fleet to the war zone, as well as a medical mission and a few pilots. Having met one of these fliers, Cartwright had developed a romantic vision of the country, always intending to visit it one day.

He had brought his Buhl monoplane by stages to the northern coastal town of Macapa, having stopped at Greenland, New York and Cuba. There, not knowing what else to do, he had drunk himself into a stupor night after night, and when that palled, had climbed into his plane one beautiful morning while still scarcely able to focus his eyes. He had set the rising sun at his back and flown west in search of the greatest river in the world.

When he located what he presumed to be the Amazon, he had flown south until he ran out of petrol, crash landing on the river in a desperate attempt to avoid breaking up his craft among the trees. He would have drowned had it not been for some Brazilian Indians. The plane sank, together with all his possessions except those he carried around his neck in a waterproof pouch.

There followed a month or so about which he knew very little. He was taken to the Indian village and nursed through a fearful fever that left him praying for death.

Eventually, these primitive people who might have killed him, instead helped him on his way with a guide who spoke no English. He discovered to his cost that he had not been following the Amazon, but the Araguaia. Consequently, he fetched up not at Macapa where he was known, but at Belem where he was not. There followed months of illness, drink and self-pity.

Finding the rose put a halt to most of that. Cartwright rediscovered the will to live and the determination to prevent Thora's daughter from inheriting Helmingham. He had been living hand to mouth, begging what he could, working at menial tasks when his health permitted. Now, he set about cleaning himself up and getting passage on a ship to England. The return journey was made in the most appalling conditions, and took him fully three months on no less than seven ships.

When he finally reached the front door of his house on Park Lane, he was a shadow of his former self, bearded and emaciated. He found the house shut up and knew that his father must have died. Having not enough change to take a taxi, he walked to his club, then had difficulty convincing the porter that he was who he said he was. It seemed he had been considered dead since the previous February. Cartwright, now fighting for control of his incandescent rage, placed a telephone call to his solicitor. When the conversation ended, Mr Finch was in imminent danger of losing his most lucrative client, but promised to take the next train to London with the keys to d'Avranche House.

Chapter Fifteen

Joyce hailed a taxi when she reached the Ipswich railway station. She had just spent the most wonderful week in London with Marsha. Old friends were the best friends, she decided. Whereas Rosie, Bill and Laurence had let her down, Marsha was a shoulder to cry on. She had sympathized totally with Joyce about Laurence's refusal to live at the Hall.

'Silly man,' had said Marsha. 'Even if he does look like Ronald Coleman. Don't you give up that wonderful house for anyone. It's yours and it's time you had a bit of good luck. Now let me tell you about my adventures.'

She had given a detailed account of her friendship with Rupert and its ludicrous, but comparatively happy ending. Having had a few days to think about it, Marsha had chosen to tell the story as farce, and Joyce had laughed appreciatively at each new twist and each carefully rehearsed humorous phase, even though she knew the episode had not been funny at the time. What a wonderful friend Marsha was. They had agreed that she should visit Helmingham in two weeks' time, and she was to stay for a whole month.

Joyce had not felt so cheerful for several months. Mr Finch had allowed her fifty pounds, which was more money than she had ever felt free to spend in her entire life. So abandoned had been her spending on a new winter wardrobe that she had to buy a trunk in which to take the frocks, suits, sweaters, coats and hats back to Helmingham.

The taxi turned between the gateposts for the slow

drive up to the Hall. Joyce sucked in her breath with intense joy at the sight of it. How beautiful it was, and not so terribly large after all. She really didn't think she could manage with even one main room fewer, and she was determined to have several of the bedrooms renovated. A rose chintz in the principal guest room and sitting-room, she decided, with a new rug in shades of pink. Before that, she must get the roof fixed and the wallpaper replaced.

Some years earlier, the rain had come pouring in, making great dark streaks down the walls and leaving ugly patches on the ceiling. Joyce had told Mr Trimble several times in the sternest voice that she wanted the men to repair the Hall. Damp had lifted some of the moulding on the main staircase. These pieces needed to be collected and glued back in place. Then there were the loose floorboards. The whole house squeaked and squealed. She supposed she might have to wait until the Hall was officially hers in little more than a year, and even then she might need to force Mr Trimble to retire before she could get the Hall into prime condition.

The trouble was she didn't know how much money she would have when that moment arrived. Mr Finch had rebuffed all her attempts to find out just how rich she would be. Of course, anyone could see that the revenue from the estate was diminishing week by week. Some of her poorer tenants simply could not pay, nor would she allow them to be evicted. Something would come up, she would say, life could surely not continue to be so bad for country people.

She smiled at the memory of herself of last February, too shy to greet those who came to the door for food. Since that time which seemed so long ago, those who were hungry had begun to seem like friends. She had soon made a point of being present when they queued for food, offering a sympathetic word, chatting with the children. Later still, her growing understanding of country people enabled her to see that they were ashamed of their inability to earn enough for food and resentful of all that she seemed to possess. In order not to witness their embarrassment, she stayed away from the kitchen, and so earned a reputation for not caring. She had learned that her every action was of intense interest to the small community. Her most casual exchanges with old Miss Collins might be repeated to her weeks later by some other villager. Or the blacksmith might hint to her that Mr Platt had been offended by a simple comment. Her words and actions were mulled over and, as often as not, misinterpreted. Being the object of so much intense speculation continued to annoy her, but she was beginning to accept it.

Her frustration lay in being unable to make a real difference to the lives of those who needed help. There simply was no work. She could not employ them all. Everywhere she looked there was so much despair.

Frankly, it had been a relief to stay in London briefly, to mix with others who had enough to eat, who were intent on having a good time. She had been happy to forget for a while, but it was just a brief respite. She was so glad to be home.

Mr Crow greeted her at the door with more warmth than she had ever detected before, and set about removing her trunk and other parcels to the bedroom for Cutler to unpack.

Joyce removed her alpaca coat and hung it on a peg, then flicked her cloche onto the deer horns, among the other hats. The doorbell clanged, making her jump. Mr Crow was upstairs, but she was standing just a few feet from the door, so she opened it.

Bill had just entered the kitchen to have his dinner. Laurence had come to Helmingham after a trip to Stowmarket for some household supplies, and Rosie was about to serve the food when they all saw Joyce's taxi start up the long drive.

'Eat your dinner first, Laurence,' said Rosie, reasonably enough. 'Give Miss Joyce a chance to unpack.'

'You start without me, Rosie. I could not enjoy your wonderful cooking until I've spoken to her. These past few days have been a torment. I'll just trot up to the Hall.'

When Joyce opened the door, it was to see Laurence's smiling face. He put out a hand and pulled her into the courtyard. 'Come outside so that I can speak to you privately.'

She closed the door behind her. 'You must have followed me up the drive. I've only just this minute arrived home.'

'I've been waiting a week to tell you that I was wrong and you were right. If you will have me, I'll be happy to move to the Hall.'

'Oh, Laurence! I knew you would come round to my way of thinking if I just waited.' She flung her arms around his neck and placed a kiss on his cheek. 'You won't be sorry, I promise you. We can be so happy here. You'll come to love it as I do.'

'Fortunately, my business is thriving. I have a number of contracts for motor maintenance and I expect I'll be able to earn about three hundred pounds a year. That may not seem much to the mistress of Helmingham, but I'm afraid we will need the money, for you are unlikely to inherit enough to maintain the place. However, together we will try to keep up the Hall. I love you. How could I have been so stupid as to refuse to live here? There will be enough work for the two of us, I promise you.'

'Yes, I'm afraid Mr Finch is going to be very difficult to deal with. He won't give me any money.'

'There isn't going to be much money. I've been to speak to him. He predicts that you won't be able to maintain the Hall for long.'

'Never.'

He put his arms around her tightly. 'There is so much to tell you. We'll work it all out, you'll see. We will do our best, won't we?'

He kissed her lingeringly. 'Now, let us not waste any more time. We must tell Rosie and Bill our good news.'

'What, right this minute? Do you really think they will want to hear? Oh, Laurence, I have missed Rosie so much, but I'm the mistress of Helmingham and she is the gardener's wife. I can't make a special friend of her, and now that we are to be married, you will have to give up your close friendship with Bill.'

'I have no intention of doing any such thing. If we pursue our lives as we choose, and do it with style and conviction, people will come to accept us as we are. Many things are going to change in the next year or so, and—'

'Do you think so? That would be wonderful. I am so tired of trying to get Mr Trimble to do as I want him to. Come inside. I must tell you all the work that needs doing. You must learn all about the house, and then when I get the money we will know how to spend it efficiently.'

She was tugging on his hand, but he hung back a little. 'Must we? Right now? I would much rather talk about us and our future together. I want you to meet all my family. We must go to Halstead. I've not told you everything about myself—'

Joyce was not listening, being preoccupied by

something past his shoulder. He turned round and saw a motor car making its way towards them. It had almost reached the bridge, and it was a splendid vehicle.

'Have you ordered a new motor car?'

'No, nor am I expecting guests.'

The motor crept silkily to a halt in front of them. The chauffeur nipped from the driver's seat to open the passenger door with a flourish. A large, tired-looking man struggled to alight.

'Captain Cartwright!' cried Laurence, and Joyce gasped in disbelief. 'How . . . how good to see you. We thought you were lost in Brazil.'

The big man smiled slightly, his eyes flicking in her direction. 'Laurence, my kinsman! What are you doing here? Come to protect my interests?'

'Well . . .' Laurence glanced at Joyce. She could not move. Her face felt frozen in horror. 'That was my original thought, but—'

'No!' she said.

'Is this . . .?' asked Captain Cartwright coldly.

'Oh, yes, forgive my rudeness. Miss Joyce d'Avranche, Captain, that is, Lord d'Avranche. Miss Joyce has done a splendid job of—'

'You can't come in,' Joyce heard herself say. Cartwright d'Avranche was a hideous man, bearing only a slight resemblance to his photograph. How could people have thought he was handsome? She hated him. 'You are not going to throw me out.'

'Joyce!' cried Laurence. 'The captain has no intention of evicting you immediately.'

'Yes, I have,' said Cartwright. 'That is precisely why I have come. Do you think I would let Thora's daughter live in my house?'

'How dare you criticize my mother? She was seduced by an old roué, your father! She hardly knew what she was doing.'

'She knew what she was doing, all right. She was born knowing what she was doing.'

'She was not!'

'Pack up your belongings, Joyce, and be off these premises within one hour. Now, where is Crow?'

Laurence seemed to be hopping from one to the other, anxious to stop the two, but unable to find the right words. 'Oh, Captain, please! Don't worry, Joyce. This can all be done in a dignified way.' He would have taken her hand, but she shrank away from him. 'This is the way all families behave at times, I assure you.'

'No they don't,' shouted Cartwright. 'How dare you interfere? This has nothing to do with you.'

'I am, after all, a d'Avranche, sir.'

'Well, your opinion counts for nothing with me. Crow! Where the devil are you?'

Mr Crow appeared. 'My Lord, thank God you are safe.'

Joyce had expected nothing less. Mrs Crow, the maids and Mrs Able would be along any second, bowing and scraping. She was not prepared for the appearance of Betsy, however. The old dog showed renewed vigour as she bounded out of the doorway, yelping with delight as she raked Cartwright's legs with her front paws, nearly oversetting him.

He bent to fondle her head. 'Well, hello, old girl. Down! Where are your manners? I'm glad to see you too, but you know better than to jump up on me.'

Joyce wanted to cry and felt she was entitled to do so, but no tears came. Her fairy-tale was turning into a nightmare, yet she could not shake herself into action.

Laurence squeezed her arm. 'My darling, it's best if you get this over with quickly. Tell Cutler to pack your things and I will take you straight away to my family.'

'Certainly not, you traitor. Stand by your kinsman,'

she said harshly. 'He'll want your report on my activities.'

'Let me explain. You see . . .'

But he got no further as Rosie and Bill, breathless from a brisk cycle up the drive, entered the courtyard. Bill dropped his bike in the courtyard and rushed ahead.

'We couldn't believe our eyes! Captain Cartwright! It's so good to see you! I can't believe . . . wonderful.' He couldn't continue, but Cartwright came to his aid, taking Bill's hand in both of his and shaking it vigorously.

'Dear fellow. Great to be home. Just this spot of bother and we will soon be back to normal. And Mrs Cook. How well you look.'

'Oh, sir,' said Bill. Joyce thought he had lost all sense. He never even glanced at her. Not so Rosie, who looked into her eyes with concern. Then Bill continued, 'We've been keeping the garden in good nick, except there was no-one to appreciate it like you used to do. And we've got a new rose for you, bred right here on the estate, and we've called it Helmingham.'

'Why that's splendid. We must grow a great many bushes of it. The Helmingham Rose shall be my way of announcing my return.'

Joyce found her voice. 'Oh, my poor Rosie,' she said. 'And no credit at all. Are all men cruel deceivers?'

Laurence looked at her, clearly puzzled. Rosie bent her head, but no-one else paid any attention as they listened to Bill describing the pale pink blossoms.

As they all stood outside, awash with sentiment and joy at Cartwright's return, Joyce suddenly dashed indoors, and locked and bolted the door. She would not leave. She would fight for her inheritance. He had been given his chance. He should have come home sooner. He should have married years ago and produced an heir. Now Helmingham belonged to her, was loved and lived in by her. Somehow, she must get a message to her dear friend. Marsha would think of a way to help. She must employ a lawyer. But how could she pay him? Would Cartwright demand the return of every penny she had spent? How she hated him and his ugly face. She hated him for the treatment his father had meted out to her mother, hated him for the suffering he had caused her, hated him for being alive.

From her bedroom window, she could see the people in the courtyard below, milling about, all talking at once. She saw Laurence guide Cartwright back into the motor car, saw him climb in beside his beloved captain, saw them drive away, saw the servants leave the courtyard to walk all the way around to the other bridge where they could enter the house.

She could, if she had the strength, nip downstairs and lock them out of the servants' entrance, but she had neither the strength nor the will. She sat down in the fireside chair, noticing as she did so that Cutler had lit a fire to welcome her home. The new trunk was standing open, its clothes half emptied. Such a fine wardrobe.

She closed her eyes, grieving more deeply than she had when her mother died. But then, Helmingham had never failed her as had her mother. The Hall had given her dignity, power, comfort and a purpose in life. The Hall had never deceived her. In return, she would devote herself to it. Twenty, forty, sixty years hence, she would be the mistress of Helmingham. She had been told that Cartwright had never lived at Helmingham from the day his mother died. He preferred d'Avranche House in London. Well, let him live there. She would have the Hall. She would fight him in the courts and prove that she had the greater right and the greater desire to preserve a national treasure. But how to pay a lawyer? She would borrow the money from her only friend, Marsha.

There was a tap on the door. 'Go away!' The door opened and Rosie came in. Joyce jumped to her feet.

'How did you get in?'

'The same way the servants did. I've been sent to plead with you, but also to tell you that Lord d'Avranche will allow you to stay here until December the first. That's very generous, you know. Laurence persuaded him not to make a scene.'

'Why didn't you tell me that Laurence was a d'Avranche?'

'How could I? Bill never told me about him. It seems he's very distantly related through his grandmother, and introduced himself as a kinsman the first time he met Lord d'Avranche. His lordship was amused and now always jokingly refers to him as a kinsman. Laurence loves you, Miss Joyce.'

'How can you plead for him? Or for any man, for that matter? Bill took the credit for your rose.'

Rosie sighed heavily. 'He did worse than that. He named it for all time "Helmingham". You know my secret name for my rose which I was going to reveal soon. I was going to call it Felicia after the daughter I will never have. Bill took away my rose and my baby's name, and I can't forgive him.'

'My mother always said no man can be trusted.'

'Your mother,' said Rosie with sudden ferocity, 'ran off with a poor crippled man who never knew a day without pain just to spite the old lord. She hoped for money and a title, but she didn't get them. She caused the most terrible suffering here at Helmingham. She is the cause of all your troubles, too. Her reputation has made life difficult for you. The captain's mother committed suicide. Did you know? Killed herself, never having recovered from the humiliation of having her husband's mistress living at Helmingham. And then to marry the next in line after Captain Cartwright! Yet, despite this proof that women can do horrible things to other women, I don't hate all women, nor consider that they are all devious. So why should I hate all men?

'We both have our crosses to bear. My father used to say, if you can't have what you want, you must want what you can have. You must prepare to leave the Hall. It will only make it worse if you wait until the first of December.'

'If you had awakened one morning to be told that you had inherited one of the most beautiful houses in England, would you be eager to give it up? Why, it's like winning the Irish Sweepstakes, then having to give it back.'

'Except,' said Rosie, 'winning the Irish Sweepstakes brings with it no worries and no responsibilities. Will you not be happy to hand over this great place to someone who can afford to maintain it?'

'During the last months I have planned my life and my future around this property. Laurence and I were going to marry and live here.'

'And now you and Laurence will marry and live somewhere else.'

'Oh, no!' Joyce shook her head vehemently. 'Do you suppose I would marry him now that I know he came to Helmingham just to spy on me?'

'If he hadn't,' said Rosie with maddening good sense, 'you two would not have met. He changed his mind about you almost immediately. He fell in love. I've never seen a man so quickly smitten. He realized straight away that he couldn't tell you why he had come here, or the truth about himself. He still hasn't. Have a little compassion. Give him a chance to explain.'

Joyce looked down at her hands, clasped tightly in her lap. 'I'll try.' She wouldn't meet Rosie's eyes, being no longer capable of feeling any sympathy for her. What was the naming of a rose compared to the humiliation of losing one of the grandest houses in Suffolk? Rosie had made her choice. Joyce had made hers. She had nearly two months in which to hatch her scheme.

'I will be ready,' she said softly. There was no question of trusting Rosie with her secret plans, yet Joyce did need her help. 'Rosie, will you wait a moment while I write a letter to my friend, Marsha? She is expecting to come here for a long visit. I must tell her what has happened.'

North Lodge was quiet. Rosie was all alone. Laurence, who had talked himself hoarse persuading Lord d'Avranche to wait until Joyce could come to terms with her loss, had gone home to Hadleigh. Bill had done no work this day, not since his beloved captain had arrived to stun them all. Oh, the rejoicing! Oh, the fawning and manoeuvring for position. There were going to be winners and losers in the coming struggle for possession of Helmingham Hall. Already, poor Mr Finch had been told he no longer represented the d'Avranche family, and Cartwright was scheming to have his revenge on a young woman he had never met until this very day. How ironic that Joyce had longed for a family, only to acquire one suddenly and to be plunged into the worst aspect of family life – the feuding.

Yet Rosie had little time for Joyce. Her own grief and sense of betrayal were choking the life from her. The kitchen door opened and Bill entered, drying his hands on a towel, drying the water from the back of his neck. He had splashed water from the pump onto his hair, and it was now combed back harshly, giving him the sleek look of a weasel.

'You took the credit for my hard work,' she said in a

low voice. It was difficult to swallow. She couldn't clear her voice or speak in a normal tone. She couldn't hide her rage.

'I'm sorry for that, my love. I'll make it better. I'll tell the captain that it was you what bred the rose. He'll tell you how good it is. He saw it today and said it was a beauty. He wants to buy dozens of bushes from your father. That will bring them in a few bob.'

'You had no right to name my rose without talking to me first. How could you?'

His face registered his incomprehension. 'But what better name than Helmingham? Why, the captain wouldn't be buying so many if it had some other name. What did you have in mind? Harley, after your old man?'

'Felicia,' she said quietly, 'after the child I'll never have. I named the rose for the baby. You stole my baby's name.'

He didn't tell her she was being foolish, because he was well aware of her superstitions and little rituals. So he knew full well what crime he had committed and his regret was plain. 'Oh, my God, Rosie. I didn't know. You are always so secretive. I thought you had some plot hatched with your dad. You know how you two get together and I'm always the last to hear what's going on. I'm sorry. I'm really sorry. I'll tell the captain. I'll say to him we aren't going to name it Helmingham. I'll tell him, I promise.'

'What? And risk your job? You know what a temper he has. It doesn't matter anymore. It's done with. I'll get over it. But why, in God's name, must you bow and scrape to him? Why, you tie yourself in knots every time you see him. Surely it's not important that he's a lord. It's just a title. We are all equal underneath, and you shouldn't lick his boots. It's undignified. None of this would have happened if you had some self-respect. But

343

just give you the sight of a title and you can't get your nose off the ground.'

With great care, he slowly folded the towel and put it on the rail in front of the range. 'I've lived with titled people all my life. I'm not so tied up with the nobs as you think. Cartwright and I were just a few years apart. In the old days, we used to play together in the summer. But then we went to war. Him and me have been through some terrible times. The war was just about over, and young Laurence had joined us at the front. The captain, he'd seen his young officers dying around him for years— well, we all had. Death was in the air, and the only way you could keep your sanity was to make jokes about it. Jerry was bombarding us, and the captain was busy rallying the men, keeping our nerve. Laurence and me were trying to advance, out beyond the wire and trapped in a crater. No way out. A shell landed nearby and we were both hit. I knew then that the next shell or the one after that would kill us. I was almost ready to die. The strain of seeing your mates go one by one was becoming unbearable. I had just begun to think death would be a blessing. All I wanted was to get it over with.

'Then suddenly, down on us swoops the captain, pulls me to my feet, picks up Laurence like he was a sack of potatoes and starts back with us. More shells. Laurence and me both got a few more bits of shrapnel rammed into us, but the captain, he took more. In the head, the arm, the leg. God knows how he got us back to the trench. Or why. I've asked myself that question most days for the last ten years. Why would a man risk his life to save two others? Why? I was his batman. Laurence was so distantly related to him that it didn't count. And after this brave deed that saved both our lives, he was in hospital for months. His gongs, and they gave him a few, didn't help one bit. He's still in pain after all these years. You can see the way he'll move and his eyebrows sort of go together in a frown as he gets a twinge. He's in pain, all right, and probably has even worse nightmares than I do. So, you see, it's not his title but his guts I'm bowing and scraping to. I'm licking his boots because I'm glad to be alive, to have met you, to be able-bodied.'

She was silenced. What could she say to Bill about his idol? Eventually, when the pain of her own small loss had lessened, she would be grateful to the captain for Bill's life. But, it was all a long time ago, and meanwhile the dear captain had come between her and her only female friend, and he had taken away the name of her baby. She'd not be able to look at that rose in future. All the pleasure in the breeding of it was gone. In fact, she wondered if she ever wanted to breed another rose.

'I understand,' she said at last. 'I do understand, Bill. It's over. We must get on with our lives.'

That night in bed, Bill turned to her and said that the quarrel could not go on. He would do anything to make it up to her. She must forgive him, for otherwise he'd never sleep again. She took him in her arms and made love to him fiercely, as if to block out her resentment that simply would not die. She loved him, no other. She forgave him. She understood. Still the pain continued, except for those few moments of passion in the chilly darkness of their bedroom. She did love him. Eventually, she would be able to remember why.

There was no denying the rector. Mr Crow announced him and he entered the small sitting-room before Joyce had a chance to say she wouldn't see him. He wore a thunderous expression. 'When you advertised in the *Church Times* for a rector for the Helmingham church, I assumed you had the right to do so. How deceived I was in you.'

'Aren't you grateful I refused your offer of marriage?' she said quietly.

'Yes, I have to say I am. I presume that you refused me because you knew you were living a lie. I have received a letter from Lord d'Avranche telling me that he is not entirely sure he wishes to have me at Helmingham. My entire life has been thrown into turmoil.'

'So has mine. Have you no words of comfort for me, Mr Catchpole?'

He drew in his breath, affronted. 'I think you would do well to consider the trouble you have caused, the friendships you have betrayed, and the spectacle you are making of yourself by refusing to leave this house immediately.'

'Good day, Mr Catchpole. It's possible I will be living at Helmingham long after you have married some gullible titled lady.'

Stunned by her rudeness, the rector left without saying goodbye.

She thought he would be her last unpleasant visitor, but she had forgotten about the schoolmaster.

'So, you are one of us after all, Miss d'Avranche. It was all a dream. Do you suppose these people will treat you kindly? They have no sympathy for the likes of you. If you were better educated, I would suggest that you take up a life of teaching. However, you are young and still have time to learn. You might consider joining the struggle.'

She actually laughed for the first time since Cartwright's return. 'I have my own struggle and therefore have no time for yours. Your kind words are most comforting. I had hoped you would wish to be employed by me rather than by Lord d'Avranche, but I should have known better.'

'I think he has broken your heart, and for that I am

deeply sorry. But this is not your property, Miss d'Avranche. There is no getting around that fact. It is best for all of Helmingham that the new lord should take on his old responsibilities. He has the money to make life easier for everyone. You might at least consider that. It has been an interesting experiment, this sudden elevation of yourself. Perhaps in time you will come to see that there has been some benefit to yourself. I wish you all the best.'

Joyce had no other visitors during the following week. There was no further communication from Cartwright, but she was still afraid to leave the Hall. After the draw-bridge was lifted at dusk, she would wrap up warmly in her new clothes and walk round and round the Hall on the ramparts. Betsy, who seemed content with her company, accompanied her until the old dog was tired.

Joyce had cancelled the daily newspaper, fearing that Cartwright would demand she pay for it. The wireless batteries had run down, and she knew she must not spend the little cash she had left. As no-one called and she never left the Hall, her isolation was complete. Yet, she scarcely noticed. Her thoughts were turned inward as she tried to think of a way of thwarting Cartwright. Her only hope was Marsha. Marsha must lend her some money.

Chapter Sixteen

Marsha was stunned when she received Joyce's letter. For a few very human moments, she revelled in the news. Joyce and she were equals once more and she need no longer be envious of her quiet English friend. Then she remembered that Joyce was depending upon her now as never before, and Marsha was determined not to fail her friend. Images of Joyce's gratitude and happiness filled her head for several moments. Dressing carefully in a navy costume with matching fur-collared coat, she hailed a taxi and ordered the driver to d'Avranche House.

A splendidly terrifying manservant ushered her into the library of a house that was much grander and in much better condition than Helmingham. No wonder the new lord preferred his London home. It obviously had electricity, proper bathrooms and even some central heating. This house, she knew, had never been part of Joyce's inheritance. Perhaps Lord d'Avranche would be willing to let Joyce remain in the crumbling Suffolk house while he made himself extremely comfortable in London.

Lord d'Avranche entered the room. Marsha turned from inspecting some old leather-bound books and met the tortured blue eyes of a tall, round-shouldered man. He came forward hesitantly, attempting a smile which was hampered by a scar at the corner of his mouth that prevented him from stretching his lips too far. There was another scar on the outside of his left eye which slightly drew down the lower lid. Still recognizably the

Cartwright of the photograph in Joyce's bedroom, she saw that his battle wounds had destroyed his good looks. No longer one of the handsomest men in England, but a mature man dogged by daily pain.

And her second thought was: he needs me! Here was a man who needed the loving attention of a woman, someone who would restore his faith in himself, give him a reason for living. Butterflies filled her stomach, and she felt the strength in her knees beginning to disappear.

'Lord d'Avranche, I am Miss Marsha Grissom, the good friend of Miss Joyce d'Avranche.'

'How do you do?' His handshake was strong, his voice very deep.

Unable to blurt out the reason for her visit, she looked about her. 'I was just admiring the painting over the mantel. Fantin-Latour?'

'Why, yes it is.'

'And are you a rose lover, sir?'

'It is a family weakness,' he said, watching her as she studied the painting of a bowl of luscious, pale roses. 'Helmingham has been famous for its roses since my great-grandmother began collecting them, and many of the old bushes from her day are still alive. At least, they were the last time I visited Helmingham in the summer.'

'How fortunate that your gardener's wife is so knowledgeable.'

'Truly fortunate! She has bred a rose to be called Helmingham.'

Marsha thought this would be the perfect way into a discussion of Helmingham, but he changed the subject. 'What do you think of this pair of hunting pictures? Hasn't the artist caught the horses perfectly?'

She peered at the pictures, wishing she could impress him by her knowledge and taste. 'I'm afraid I don't know this artist's work.'

'Oh, he isn't famous or anything like that. Major Godfrey Giles. I knew him slightly. Poor chap died a few years back.'

She turned. 'This is a beautiful room, sir. Filled with exquisite works of art.'

He lifted an eyebrow, apparently not sure where the conversation was leading. 'Ah, here's the coffee. Won't you sit down? D'Avranche House does not have as many treasures as Helmingham.'

She helped herself to sugar, surprised that her hand was not shaking. 'But so much more comfortable.' She looked up from her cup and discovered that he was grinning. 'I am not going to give Helmingham Hall to Joyce. Is that your mission?'

'No, of course not.' She took a swift sip of her coffee and scalded her mouth. He was an intriguing man, intelligent, dignified and yet exciting. She felt that such a man could provide her with all that she wanted: security and a sense of worth. 'I was only hoping that you might see your way clear to allowing her to continue to live at Helmingham. She does love it so much.'

'Miss Grissom, you are a charming advocate and a selfless friend. I doubt if Joyce deserves your devotion.'

'Oh, you don't know her. She's quiet, but dependable. I'm rather scatter-brained, but she is steady. And very scholarly—'

'As any shorthand typist would be.'

'Lord d'Avranche, that was unkind. Joyce has catalogued every book at Helmingham and every painting. Why, it's all beautifully written out in a big book. She has wonderful handwriting.'

'I'm staggered. More coffee?'

She frowned at him. 'You don't even know her. How can you hate her so much? Besides, Helmingham has no happy memories for you, has it?'

He sighed, rather bored by the discussion. 'You're

trying your best and you must write to Joyce and tell her what you have done on her behalf. But I could never bear to think of the daughter of Thora Jefferson living at Helmingham.'

'Well, I don't see what her mother has to do with it. She's dead, after all.'

'Has Joyce never told you her family history? Well then, you must ask her to do so. For I think you have been deceived into championing this young woman. You are too trusting, too kind. Someone ought to protect you from your own good nature. Now, if you have finished your coffee, allow me to show you the drawing-room. I have a couple of Stubbs of which I am very proud.'

Marsha opened the letter from her father with trembling hands. It was the first day of November, and she already knew that her father must have been badly hit by the Wall Street crash on the twenty-third of October. She simply didn't know how much of his fortune had disappeared.

His letter gave her some comfort. He had sold the remainder of his shares in September, fearing the market was over-heating. And he had received a good price. Leading industrial stocks had gone from an average of ninety-three dollars in 1923 to three hundred and eighty dollars when he sold out. He had put his money in the bank, intending to reinvest when the market was calmer.

Despite his foresight, he was deeply worried. Store managers, believing that people would have less money to spend on Christmas, had begun to cancel their orders. This in turn put men out of work. Unemployment was rising. President Hoover was unable to reassure the public, and people were clamouring to take their money out of the banks. Mr Grissom now had some of his money under the bed, and felt that the nation was heading towards an abyss.

Marsha was of an optimistic nature. Since her father had removed his money at the best possible moment, she was not inclined to worry about the United States, believing that everything would be all right soon.

The news of the crash brought her an unexpected but very welcome benefit. Lord d'Avranche, having read his newspaper about the crash, had telephoned her with expressions of sympathy and concern. Within the hour, he had called round and her anxiety and his understanding and sympathy had set their friendship on a new and deeper level.

Marsha and Cartwright had seen each other every day since their first meeting. In fact, on that very first occasion, she had been invited to stay for luncheon. Since then, visits to the theatre, the opera, museums, restaurants and nightclubs had filled her days and evenings. These occasions were light-hearted and fun-loving, but during quieter moments they had occasionally spoken of more serious matters. He had treated her to a brief history of Thora Jefferson's involvement with the d'Avranche family, and Marsha had not been as shocked as Cartwright had hoped and expected. She had said how sorry she was for the grief his mother had been caused, but had added that it was time he put all his hatred behind him. All the major players in the tragedy were dead. Cartwright, she said, must concentrate on the future.

She was taking a chance by speaking so plainly, because she hoped with all her heart to become Lady d'Avranche. Yet, to her great surprise, Cartwright had seemed to appreciate her earnest little lecture.

The day the news broke about the crash, he insisted on taking her to the Savoy for lunch, where they were directed to a table in a quiet corner. Here, in a rather unromantic fashion, Cartwright had proposed marriage. He even had an exquisite diamond ring of his mother's in his pocket. The ring fitted her perfectly. They were both deliriously happy, and an orgy of buying had followed.

But in reflective moments, her conscience had begun to bother her. It took very little imagination to understand how Joyce would feel when she discovered that Marsha would be living in the house from which she, herself, was going to be evicted. It would seem like a betrayal to Joyce. How could it not?

Love had changed Marsha; she knew she had matured. Certainly, she had come to appreciate her father's wisdom. If, as he always said, a woman's destiny was to marry and make some man happy, then a woman's greatest achievement must be to marry a wealthy titled man like Cartwright who needed to have his interest in life restored.

And she knew she made him happy. That was the most wonderful part of it all. His injuries, especially the ones to his face, had robbed him of much of his confidence. Accustomed to being spoken of as the handsomest man in England, he had wanted to hide away from the first moment he saw his changed features in a looking glass. Marsha understood his feelings, but pretended to have no sympathy. What was the matter with him? she asked. Did he not know that she found him immensely attractive, and that she feared some other woman would take him away from her? Didn't he realize that he was mature, dignified and wise? Her reward for all this extravagant praise warmly spoken was a smile of pure joy. His face lit up whenever she came into his presence. Was this not the role for which she had been trained all her life?

Cartwright had for years neglected his duties as a landowner and had wasted his life and ruined his health with alcohol and life-threatening pursuits, but all that had come to an end. She understood him and knew how to control him for his greater good. Marsha intended to be the perfect wife, and only wished that they gave prizes for clever wives, because she knew she would win the prize every year.

Reassured by her father's letter, she felt strong enough for any trial. That evening, after she and Cartwright had dined at the Ritz, and she had made him eat all his spinach and refused to allow him to order a second bottle of wine, she offered him a petit four and spoke gently. 'Cartwright, dearest, you know I love you and I can't wait to be your wife, but I feel so guilty about Joyce.'

'You have no need to be. She and I would never have married.'

'Now, don't make jokes. I'm serious. Could you not lease Helmingham to her for a peppercorn rent?'

'No. My— *our* children will be born and brought up there!'

This Marsha had assumed, so she said, 'Then give her an allowance. Jobs are awfully hard to get and Joyce gave up hers when she moved to Suffolk. After all, you are making an allowance to Rupert.'

He sighed. 'There are some things, Marsha, which I must decide for myself.'

There was a chill in the air and she knew she was on dangerous ground. How easy just to let the matter drop. How dangerous to annoy the man on whom all her hopes for the future were pinned. 'Of course you must decide this for yourself, but I cannot and will not stay silent. I must make you see what Joyce is, apart from being the daughter of Thora Jefferson. She and her mother lived in great poverty. Joyce began to work at fifteen. She was the only comfort her mother had, and was forced to endure Thora's bitterness. She asked for nothing from her high-born relatives, and would have loved to be able to thank Lord d'Avranche in person for his kindness in sending her to Paris. She has lived a blameless life, and one day she thought she had become an heiress. You tell me the estate has no money to support it, but Joyce didn't know that. She believed herself to be not only rich but important for the first time in her life. Now, it has been snatched from her. And I, of all people, her American friend, will be living in the home she cherishes.'

Marsha knew he was upset for he picked up his fork and began to draw lines in the table cloth. After what seemed like several minutes, he looked up and gave her a wry smile. 'I'm putty in your hands.'

'Oh, Cartwright, I don't want you to be putty in my hands. I want you to think it through and do the right thing.'

'My father and I knew of their financial circumstances, because he hired a detective to check on Thora. Father even stationed himself in the road one day so that he could see them pass. He was besotted with Thora and beside himself with rage when she ran off with Nicholas and had a child. When Thora died, he sent Joyce to finishing school. He said it was to prepare her for inheriting Helmingham, but it was really a gesture to punish me for not having married. We quarrelled and as a result of that quarrel, I eventually went off to Brazil.'

'So even her year abroad was given in spite.'

'I'm afraid so. Father said Joyce was a scheming young woman who looked exactly like her mother. But that day when I confronted her in the courtyard of Helmingham, I was surprised to see a small, gentle, very pretty young woman. She looks nothing like her mother. I will give her two hundred pounds a year. Is that sufficient?'

355

'Oh, yes! Very generous. Thank you so much, and I promise not to mention the subject again. I must go to her and explain about us.'

'But don't apologize. You have nothing to apologize for. Tell her about the allowance. That may make the meeting a little easier. Laurence Ballard is determined to marry her. He's a distant cousin of mine, you know.'

Marsha had not known this. 'But then what was he doing acting as a chauffeur at Helmingham?'

'Sentimental chap,' said Cartwright, smiling. 'Thought he would arrive sort of incognito to see if Joyce was a worthy owner of the estate. He soon decided she was and promptly fell in love with her.'

'Oh, I hope he's rich—'

'No, I'm afraid not. I will give Joyce two hundred pounds, partly because I'm quite fond of Laurence. You might go so far as to tell her what a lucky person she is to have won a chap like Laurence. Salt of the earth, even if he has found it hard to settle down. God knows I'm hardly in a position to criticize.'

Joyce stood up and brushed the cobwebs from her face. She had spent the past three hours cleaning out the cupboards and cabinets in the Great Hall. There were large glass cases filled with stuffed birds and small creatures. No-one ever opened the cabinets to dust them, and no-one had thought to name the contents so that visitors could see what rare forms of animal life had been preserved for their information. Some of the birds were so rare that she had to look in several illustrated volumes to find out the names. Small cards now rested in front of each one, and they all looked rather better for having had years of dust removed.

As for the contents of the cupboards, she found a few more old books and twenty or more board games. Each game had been checked for contents, and missing pieces enumerated on the boxes. Possibly no-one would every play them again, but her passion for the Hall had taken new directions in the past weeks. If, God forbid, she had to leave, she wanted to be sure that Cartwright could not criticize her caretaking efforts.

Joyce was pleased to see Marsha, if somewhat surprised. She had sent an invitation ten days earlier and received no reply. Now here was her friend looking absolutely splendid in a smart tweed suit, while Joyce looked at her very worst.

'Don't give it a second thought, Joyce. I'm sorry not to have given you any notice, but I was sure you would be glad to see me. You are glad to see me, aren't you?'

'Of course. Let's go into my sitting-room. It's cold in here. I'll finish another day.'

Marsha looked at the boxes of board games, the dusters, scissors and polish. 'But whatever have you been doing? Surely, the servants do all the cleaning.'

'I am straightening the cupboards. And I've put labels on the stuffed birds.'

Marsha frowned as she followed Joyce to a seat in front of the sitting-room fire. She waited while Joyce ordered coffee, looking about her as if she had never seen the house before.

'Oh, do sit down, Joyce. I have good news for you.'

'Cartwright will give up the Hall?'

'No, dear. He feels very strongly. We . . . he intends to live here most of the year.'

'Oh, Marsha, I have been so anxious to see you. I wonder if your father will lend me a few hundred pounds. I wish to take Cartwright to court. I think I can win the right to keep Helmingham—'

'Are you mad?' Marsha collected herself and spoke more quietly. 'My dear friend, you have got this thing all wrong. It's terribly sad, but you really have no right here. It belongs to Lord d'Avranche.'

Joyce flopped down into an armchair and put her hands over her face. 'I can't leave. I just can't. It's too awful. Please tell me. Will your father lend me some money?'

'No. How could he after the stock market crash? Don't you read the papers or listen to the wireless? Americans have lost their money. The whole country . . . my father says America is falling into an abyss.'

'I didn't know. I don't have a newspaper and my wireless batteries . . . so this is the final act. I've lost.'

'I said I had good news. Oh, Joyce, do cheer up. Cartwright is to give you—'

Joyce's eyes narrowed as she faced Marsha. 'Cartwright? You seem to have become very good friends.'

'We are to be married. Now, Joyce, don't go thinking I schemed for this. I didn't. I asked him to give Helmingham to you, but he won't. I did try, and Cartwright said he will make you an allowance of two hundred pounds a year.'

Joyce said nothing for several seconds, but she stared at Marsha until the American had to look away. 'Well, well, haven't you been busy? I should have suspected, but I didn't. Does he know how close you came to—'

'Oh, please don't tell him about Rupert. It wouldn't do you any good. Joyce, listen to what I'm saying. Two hundred pounds a year!'

'Yes, I heard. How galling. As I have nowhere to go and no income, I shall be forced to take Cartwright's charity.'

'He says Laurence Ballard is mad for you. He says to tell you that you are a lucky girl to have won him.'

Joyce smiled wryly. 'So Laurence is to be second prize. I can't have the Hall but I can have Laurence. Well, I don't need Laurence and I don't need you. I will not send you away immediately, because you will want to look around your new home, but I will hate you for ever, Marsha.'

Marsha was distressed and tried to comfort her old friend, knowing that she was the last person able to do so. She did, also, want to look over the house that would soon be her home. She wondered if she would ever love it as Joyce did, and decided that she would not. In fact, wherever she and Cartwright lived would be home to her; what did Joyce see in the old place?

Dinner was extremely painful. Marsha rose very early the next morning before Joyce was awake and, refusing any breakfast, asked the butler to arrange for her to be taken to the railway station. On the way, she told the driver to stop so that she could speak to Mrs Cook. Rosemary agreed to send Laurence to Joyce as soon as possible, but Marsha didn't mention her engagement to Cartwright, believing that Joyce would soon tell everyone.

Laurence shone his torch on the ramparts and, after a few minutes' search, found Joyce leaning against the wall of the Hall. As it was half-past seven of a moonless night, the torch blinded her.

'Joyce, let down the drawbridge! I must talk to you. Joyce! Do you hear me? Let down the drawbridge now.'

She lifted her shoulders from the wall, shielded her eyes from the torchlight and began walking towards the drawbridge as one in a dream. He was standing on the bridge as it fell in place and crossed quickly.

'My dear, I came as soon as I got Rosie's message.'

'And what message was that?'

'Miss Grissom said you wanted to see me.'

'Oh, Laurence!'

She seemed so despairing that he pulled her to him and, discovering that she was inadequately dressed for such a cold night, opened his top coat and pulled

359

her inside. 'What is it, my dear? What has happened?'

'Marsha is to marry Cartwright and they will be living here and he is to give me an allowance of two hundred pounds a year.'

He sucked in his breath, trying to imagine his captain married to the American woman. He found he could not imagine it and wondered if Joyce had misunderstood or if Miss Grissom was simply playing a spiteful joke. But no, it must be true. Joyce would feel this as another betrayal. The two young women had enjoyed a certain rivalry in their friendship, and Marsha Grissom must be judged to have won the contest. He held Joyce tighter and murmured sympathetic nothings, to which she did not respond. With one hand, he lifted her face and kissed her, but she gave no sign of displeasure or of wishing him to continue. Much as he felt sorry for the series of blows that had befallen her, he began to be irritated.

'The captain owes you the money. You have kept his home in fine order. You will be independent, able to buy whatever you choose without reference to me. I have always loved you. I believe you love me, although you're rather upset at the moment. It is time we began to lead a real life. No more fairy-tales for you. No more refusing to take on responsibilities for me. We will be happy together.'

'If you love me, you will help me fight for what is mine. Lend me some money, Laurence. I need to find a lawyer who will take my case to court.'

He stood back, leaving her shivering and exposed. 'You have no case.'

'You've been a soldier. Never say die. Fight to the end. There is a chance, so I must hang on. Cartwright doesn't seem to be in good health. He might—'

'Stop that! You have chosen the wrong man to be your champion. I am the sort to consider first if the battle is worth fighting. Cartwright, on the other hand, will fight to the death for what he believes in. You have chosen a formidable opponent. Can you not accept that the rightful owner wants what is his?'

'But all these beautiful things! I know all about them now. I've earned them because I love them. Listen. There are six Van Dycks in the Great Hall. There is a Ming vase in the large drawing room—'

'Joyce, please.'

'I can't leave. I am to give a Christmas party for all the village children. It will be such fun. I've planned it with Mr Goodenough. And on December the fifth I am to hold a supper in aid of orphans. The tickets have gone out. I must be here.'

Gently, he pulled her to him again. He could hear her teeth rattling. 'I know that Cartwright will honour the commitments you have made.'

'No, Marsha will take my place if I don't fight. She's going to live here and I can't bear it.'

'I hate to think of her in your place, but can't you be happy with me? I own Boscomb House. We could—'

'How could I give up Helmingham for Boscomb House? I have no intention of marrying you. You deceived me. Everyone has deceived me and I will not have it.'

Although he knew she was slightly deranged and desperately in need of comfort and support, her words wounded him deeply and his patience was at an end. Thrusting her away from him, he said, 'I've had enough. Send for me when or if you come to your senses.' She made no reply as he walked back across the bridge. Shortly afterwards, he heard the drawbridge creak as it was drawn up.

Chapter Seventeen

By common consent, the rosarian's year begins in October. It is a month of dreams, of plans for the glorious displays of the future, of new varieties, new beds, the removal of old ones, the discarding of useless plants. Normally Rosie loved this month, which was often very pleasant during the day, though the days were short and the nights often chilly. This year she had gone through the month mechanically.

One of the rose beds outside the walled garden had shown signs of rose sickness. She had burned every rose in it and removed the soil two spits deep, wheeling the bottom spit right away, setting the top spit aside. This went into the space left at the bottom of the bed and new maiden loam was brought in to fill the top.

In several of the beds, fungus had been a problem, but she had waited until the first frosts when the topsoil could be removed more easily in its frozen state.

Several roses had been potted on into eight inch pots, ready to bloom under glass. Those greenhouse plants would provide blooms for the new Lady d'Avranche, and this irked Rosie. She wondered where Joyce would be when the bride arrived. In fact, she wondered if the bride would care to live in comparative discomfort at the Hall when so luxurious a residence as d'Avranche House was available to her. No doubt, Bill would be required to send great boxes of fruit, vegetables and flowers to the town house, and they would scarcely ever see the happy couple in Suffolk.

During the third week of November, now fast

approaching, she would plant the new varieties ordered by mail. There was nothing new from the Dobson Nurseries, but she must have new varieties at the Hall, because Bill demanded them.

Having finished her day's work, she walked back to the lodge, feeling sick with worry. For several weeks, the American crash had been the main topic of conversation. The tragedy across the Atlantic was sure to have dire consequences for all Britons, and now word had arrived of hundreds of banks closing, of Americans losing all their money, of suicides. Wherever people met and talked, the mood was gloomy.

Rosie planned to serve cold beef and pickles this night for supper. She had baked a treacle tart, but felt too tired to eat anything. The truth was, she could not forgive Bill for naming her seedling Helmingham. He had taken something precious from her, something that could not be replaced. Yet, common sense told her that she and this man would spend the rest of their lives together, come what may, and she had better learn to forget her sorrow and resentment.

She wanted to scream at him. Sometimes, when he was talking about the garden to his men, she wanted to tell them all that they needn't look at him as if he were some sort of god, because he had done a terrible thing to his wife. And the strange thing was, this urge to speak, to make him suffer, which was warring with the need to keep quiet, made her feel sick. Her throat would close so tightly that she had trouble swallowing. Occasionally, her anger would rise up in her and she would feel physically sick, as if she wanted to vomit her anger.

She was just placing the hot plates on the table when he walked in the door, his cheeks rosy from the raw day, his hair slicked back. Like a weasel. *I hate you*, she thought, and all of a sudden her stomach lurched.

363

Running from the room, she was violently and repeatedly sick in the lavatory, feeling exhausted but strangely light-headed, as if this act had purged her hatred. Shakily, she returned to the kitchen where Bill was waiting with a worried expression.

'What's up with you, then?' he asked. 'Best sit down and let me make you a cup of tea.'

'I don't want a cup of tea.'

'Hot water?'

'No! Leave me be.'

'I hope it's not the influenza. There's a lot of it about.'

She sat down, put her arms on the table and cried.

Laurence parked his motorbike and knocked on the door of North Lodge, and was swiftly ushered inside. November had come in with a roar, sending the last leaves swirling to the ground. One or two trees, their shallow roots resting in sodden soil, had toppled to the ground, and slates flew from roofs, causing further damage as they hit windows or animals. The safest place after dark was indoors on this last day of November.

'It's good to see you, Laurence,' said Bill. 'Come into the kitchen. You don't mind if we eat in front of the range, I'm sure. It's bitter out there.'

'Several roads are blocked. We're in for a night of it. Good evening, Rosie, how are you?'

She smiled as she indicated his place at the table. 'Braised beef in your honour. I'm fine, but I have no news of Miss Joyce. She stays indoors and has done this past month.'

'She has answered none of my letters, but I hope that when she leaves tomorrow, I will be allowed to take her to my parents' home. She has nowhere else to go. It's a bad night, but she will be safe enough until the morning. I understand the servants have all left her. Oh, my goodness, this looks wonderful, Rosie. I have to confess, I have not been eating too well recently. I must find another cook, for this one can't carry on for much longer. I had hoped that Joyce—'

'How's your business?' asked Bill quickly. He had heard enough about Joyce to last him a lifetime.

'At the moment, it seems to be holding up. I confess, I am amazed. Two new contracts this month. Life goes on, even if the economic situation continues to worsen.'

They ate in silence for several minutes, but when Rosie had cleared the plates, she said, 'It's true the Crows have left. Mrs Able's already in her new house, so there's no-one indoors. The Yankee Doodle has been round, although she didn't go into the Hall, nor attempt to speak to Miss Joyce. I understand they've taken on a new cook, some fancy woman will come from London when they are married. They plan to live here most of the time. I can hardly wait.'

'Marsha Grissom is an unworthy successor to Joyce. I can't bear to think of her lording it around here and I feel profoundly sorry for you both.'

'I've heard enough of this,' said Bill, surprising the other two by his vehemence. 'It's not disloyal to your Joyce to say that the future Lady d'Avranche will make a fine wife for the captain. She's got some plans for the garden, nothing that I can't deal with, but good ideas, you know. She's got style and confidence and the captain is as happy as a flea. I know you love Joyce, Laurence, but two people can be decent. It doesn't have to be one or the other.'

Laurence put down his fork and wiped his mouth before speaking. 'I'm sure you are right. If, as you say, Marsha Grissom will prove to be a good manager of Helmingham, then I feel even sorrier for Joyce. If only she wouldn't mind so much about leaving!'

'She shouldn't have been so rude about Boscomb House,' said Rosie. 'That was unkind.'

'Yes.' Laurence smiled ruefully. 'And I wish I hadn't told you about that. Unfortunately, I was still furious about it when I returned here. But now I've had time to see that she is very depressed and hurt. Why is it that everyone has been so critical of Joyce? What did she ever do to hurt anyone?' When no-one offered an opinion, he went on. 'I think it was because she was so anxious to please. She longed for privacy, yet she was the subject of vicious gossip. Her every action has been noted and criticized. In the pub, her name was on every lip, I swear.'

'It will be the same for the new Lady d'Avranche,' said Bill. 'Bound to be.'

'I'm not so sure.'

Bill smiled at a sudden recollection. 'The captain was a bit miffed that old Sparrow had not been as welcoming as he should have been when my lady-to-be was introduced. "Well," says Miss Grissom later, "we just won't invite him to the summer party, or if we do he shan't have a second helping of ice cream."'

'You've made my point, Bill. Miss Grissom is confident and she doesn't care if people dislike her. She is the much-loved daughter of a successful man and his intelligent wife. Her confidence silences her critics. Joyce, on the other hand, has been desperate for acceptance, desperate to put behind her the scandal of her parents' marriage. And sensing weakness, society has moved in for the kill.'

Bill laughed, but said, 'Steady on. We've not treated her badly. She's a queer one, begging your pardon, Laurence.'

Rosie stood up quickly, fearing a quarrel. 'Time for dessert. We've got—'

But at that moment the wind suddenly began to gust.

A dustbin lid flew up and crashed against the side of the house. They all rushed to the window where the rain was lashing fiercely against the panes. There was a flash of lightning, then another. A third flash seemed to connect with the Hall.

'My God, did you see that?' asked Laurence. 'I think one of the spires went. I'll have to get Joyce out of there. It might have crashed onto the roof, might have come through. Do you suppose it could start a fire?'

Bill grabbed two ponchos from the hook in the hall and handed Rosie's poncho to Laurence. 'Let's hope we can contact her. The drawbridge will be up and there's no way of getting her attention.'

'I'll think of something when I get there,' said Laurence. They fought their way out of the door and started up the long drive. The wind snatched at their breath. The drive was littered with small broken branches and running with rivulets of rain and gravel. To walk down an avenue of ancient trees was not the safest of occupations in a gale. Bill swung his torch this way and that, and whirled round when he heard a huge branch crash to the ground.

By the time they reached the footbridge, they were both soaked, despite the ponchos. Even by the light of both their torches, they couldn't see for sure if one of the tall spires had toppled through the roof. They could tell, however, that it had not landed on the ramparts.

'Might have gone into the moat!' shouted Bill into Laurence's ear.

Laurence shone his light across the façade of the house. 'There's no point in trying to call her. She'd never hear in this noise. The drawbridge is up, but if I can get across to it, I can climb over the top.'

Bill grabbed Laurence's shoulder. 'We haven't got a ladder long enough, and I doubt if we can raise enough men to devise some other scheme. She'll be all right. Let's leave it until morning.'

'Here.' Laurence handed Bill his torch. 'Hold this and train both torches onto the drawbridge. I think I can jump across.'

'You idiot! You'll land in the moat.'

'Perhaps. Now, will you shine the light onto the drawbridge?' Without waiting for a reply, he slipped off the restricting poncho and walked back from the gaping hole where the drawbridge should be, calculating the distance, trying to get up enough speed to make a satisfactory leap.

Bill, certain that he would be trying to fetch his friend from the moat before the water in his boots dragged him down, shone the light on the entrance to Helmingham Hall. The opening that accommodated the drawbridge was extremely small. If he made it at all, Laurence would have a job to scramble through the small space. He heard Laurence's pounding feet behind him and held his breath.

Laurence leapt the moat and managed to cling with the tips of his fingers to the drawbridge. Bill took a deep breath. Laurence hitched up a leg, got a toehold and was suddenly through to the other side; the drawbridge began to descend. Bill helped it into place and crossed, handing Laurence his poncho and torch, with a muttered, 'Well done, you fool. I hope I never see a trick like that again.'

Fortunately, the door was unlocked. They let themselves in and ran to the hall and began climbing the stairs, calling for Joyce.

The worst noise of the storm did not penetrate the ancient walls. The comparative quiet of the hallway left them feeling as if they had suddenly gone deaf. Then they heard the clicking of Betsy's toenails on the uncarpeted upper passageway. She barked frantically, and Laurence began to call Joyce's name.

'In here,' she said when she finally heard them. 'This way. There's a hole in the roof. Have the men come to repair it? In here. The rain is coming through. They'll have to get up into the attics.'

She was moving furniture into the middle of the room, throwing small rugs over precious artifacts to protect them from the rain.

'The men can't be expected to come out at the height of the storm. They can't see to make repairs in the dark anyway,' said Laurence. 'Come on, Rosie is waiting to look after you. Come on, Betsy. Let's be going.'

'No.'

'Don't be a fool, Miss Joyce,' said Bill, exasperated. 'Laurence has just leapt the moat for you. The least you can do is show some gratitude.'

She seemed totally incapable of making the decision to move, so between them they swept her down the stairs and soon had her rigged out in a waterproof coat and gum boots. Bill saw that he was going to have to carry Betsy who was terrified of the storm.

Joyce clung to Laurence, stumbling repeatedly. 'All evening, I've been listening to the tiles clattering to the ground, and there's no money to rehang them! Then the storm began in earnest and I went upstairs to the attics to see how much water was coming in. There was a terrible flash and the thunder deafened me. I fell down. The lightning struck on the south front, and I was in the north front, but it was still amazingly loud. Now everything will be ruined, and I had wanted to leave it all in good order. There will be terrible damage from this night everywhere on the estate.'

'We saw the lightning strike. That's why we came.'

'Poor old thing.'

This was too much for Laurence. 'It's only a bloody house. Have some sense of proportion.'

'No,' she said with surprising calm. 'Some houses are only houses, but Helmingham is different. It has stood here for five hundred years. Plots have been hatched, alliances made. Once it was a powerhouse, the centre of political intrigue, then the heart of a community, a residence for the exalted rich. Now it's needed by the villagers for the jobs it provides. What with prices collapsing and everything going wrong in America, the village will need whatever Helmingham can give. And I wanted so much to be a part of it. I just hope that Cartwright and Marsha do what is expected of them, and they can't do their duty from London. They need to be here.'

Laurence knew that what she said was true, but he was more interested in the way she seemed to have accepted that she had lost her fight for Helmingham. Reality at last.

Rosie took her straight upstairs to her own small bedroom where she urged Joyce to remove her wet clothes and put on Bill's dressing-gown.

'I'm all right. Just my hose,' said Joyce, 'and I'll need a towel to dry my hair. I'm not wet otherwise. I've lost the battle, Rosie. I'm defeated and there is nothing for me. What is there about me that I always lose out?'

'First you have to decide what battle it is that you fought, then you can decide whether or not you lost it. You fought against the ill-will towards your mother. You fought to learn to manage a great house and to meet hundreds of people and to be what all of them expected you to be. Isn't that a battle won? You'll know how to manage a smaller house better than anyone. You'll know how to help others. Doesn't that count for anything?'

Joyce shook her head, smiling sadly. 'My mother was

right. Women lose. You're a brave woman, but you and I have both lost our battles. Look what Bill took from you.'

'Yes,' said Rosie. 'I hated Bill so much I thought it was making me sick, but I was wrong. When one door closes another opens and sometimes we get what we really wanted all along, instead of what we thought we wanted. What I'm trying to say is I'm expecting a baby. I wasn't sick with hate after all. It was just morning sickness like any woman gets. So I don't care if the rose is named "Helmingham" when I can have a baby named whatever I want. Bill has said I shall choose. The midwife says everything is going along just fine. What more could I ask for?'

'Oh, Rosie, I'm so happy for you. You deserve to have everything you want in life. You are such a good person. Believe me, I think your news is wonderful, but it's different for me.'

'And you, why you've lost a cold house that can't speak to you when you're lonely or give you a family or be there when you need it.'

'I wasn't lonely. There were people—'

'No, those were strangers, like ships that pass in the night and hoot their fog horns at each other. There was no loving, just distant politeness. You were in danger of forgetting what really being with friends and loved ones is like.'

'I never knew.'

'No, I don't suppose you did before you came to Helmingham, but Bill and I have offered you friendship. We liked you as soon as we met you, but it was difficult. And Laurence loved you from the moment he first saw you.'

'For a very few minutes I actually thought I would be able to have Laurence and the house. I never thought I would have to choose between them.'

'Oh, Joyce, leave the ghosts of your unhappy parents here at Helmingham and turn your attentions to a new house. Boscomb House is—'

'I know. It belongs to Laurence, doesn't it? I think I always knew that he wasn't some casual labourer, but I didn't want to like Boscomb House, and I didn't want him to love it. You see, I can't love a new house yet. I'm still grieving for the old one. On the other hand, I am ready to give up the ghosts of my parents. They have truly haunted me. Laurence leapt the moat tonight, did you know?'

'He loves you and he's willing to risk his life for you. You're rich if you have a man willing to do that.'

Joyce smiled. 'He says he only fights for what he thinks is worthwhile. I hope I deserve him, but oh, Rosie, it hurts so. My mother used to say that we were invisible. If we dropped down dead in the street, no-one would notice. Then out of the blue, I received a letter from Mr Finch. For a little while I was somebody. I was Miss d'Avranche of Helmingham. Now I'm nothing again. Who will I be in the future? It won't be the same. Cartwright has robbed me of my identity and I've lost my place in history. When they write about Helmingham a hundred years from now, I won't even be a footnote. What makes me feel especially bitter is that Laurence was willing after all to come to live at Helmingham. We would have been a good master and mistress of the Hall. We would have done our duty. I want to be his wife, but I could have been so much more.'

Her shoulders sagged and she covered her face with her hands. Rosie, never having considered her place in history, didn't know what to say.

After a moment, she went to Joyce and laid a hand across her shoulders. 'Come downstairs. Tell Laurence you love him and take him out of his misery.

He's been round here every day since Captain Cartwright came back, just waiting to carry you away.'

'I wouldn't answer his letters. I thought he must hate me, so I burned them.'

Laurence had been sitting before the kitchen grate, nursing the pain in his shoulders. The strain on them had been immense when he clung to the drawbridge, and he reckoned he was no longer as fit as he had been in his youth.

Joyce smiled at him shyly. 'What is to become of me tomorrow when I must leave Helmingham?'

'I shall take you straight away to my parents' home in Halstead. You can stay there until . . . until we sort out a few things.'

'Thank you.' Her voice was scarcely above a whisper.

Bill managed to get the wireless tuned in and they listened to news of the gales off the East Anglian coast. Many ships and small boats had failed to reach port in time. The lifeboats were out in high seas. Already several fishing boats were known to have gone down with all hands.

Joyce, it turned out, had not eaten any supper, so Rosie served up a heaping plate, then they all had dessert. The evening passed soberly as the storm's toll began to mount. Bill said he would have a lot of work for the gardeners, but expected Mr Trimble to want all hands to help clear up at the house. Rosie kept the fire burning brightly, and finally said she thought the best plan was for Bill and Laurence to share the family bed, and for Joyce to share the guest bed with herself. This idea was unwelcome on all sides and served to rouse Joyce from her lethargy.

'I must go back to the Hall tonight. It's unlocked and the drawbridge is down. Think how awful it would be if something were stolen.'

Laurence nodded and set his mug of tea on the table. How small and vulnerable she looked! Captain Cartwright (Laurence could not think of him as Lord d'Avranche) could not be brought to understand her plight or to sympathize with her. He could have allowed this sweet young woman to continue living in the home for which he had no love. She would have made a very good caretaker. Laurence had incurred his wrath by suggesting it. The new lord wanted revenge for an incident in his childhood that had plainly scarred him. For this reason, a man who had risked his own life on the battlefield to save others was perfectly prepared to destroy the happiness of a harmless young cousin.

He brushed a few strands of wet hair from her cheek, allowing his hand to linger on the warm flesh. 'Well?' he said lightly. 'Are you going to marry me or not?'

All the tension in the room evaporated with her laughter. 'Of course, sir.' Her smile teased him. 'What choice do I have?'

When Joyce and Laurence had wrapped up warmly and gone out into the dying storm, Rosie reached for an old coat. 'I must see what damage has been done in the greenhouse. I'm sure most of the glass has been broken. I do hope I haven't lost everything.'

'No you don't,' said Bill, taking the coat from her. 'Remember your condition. I'm as concerned as you are, but it's still dangerous out there. We have someone else to consider these days. Wait until morning.' Then he laughed. 'You gave me a terrible fright tonight. I thought I was going to have to share my bed with Laurence!'

The next morning, Laurence was waiting with the estate workers when the drawbridges were lowered. He crossed quickly and found Joyce in the kitchen. The room was bitterly cold. He had stayed long enough the previous night to build a fire in Joyce's bedroom. Old Betsy had been unable to stop shivering. Joyce, on the other hand, had seemed immune to the cold. He had not stayed long, preferring to talk to her about their future once he had removed her from the influence of Helmingham.

Her possessions were quickly packed into one of Laurence's lorries which had arrived from Halstead at half-past six. He and Joyce would ride in the cab with the driver, while the motorbike joined the trunks. It was too cold to travel thirty-five miles on the bike.

'Rosie says she will be in the glasshouse if you want to say goodbye to her. If not, she will understand,' he said when she announced that she was ready to leave.

'I must say goodbye to her, of course. And to Bill. But I won't look back at the Hall.' She blinked away her tears and took the hand he extended.

He was prepared to stay silent, but she seemed determined to talk. 'Laurence, I want to say that I do love you. There has never been anyone else for me from the day we met. That's just how it is. The trouble is, I can't seem to feel anything very much except a strange numbness, as if a part of me has died. Can you forgive me?'

'There is nothing to forgive. I will always love and cherish you, even if you never love me, even if this numbness never goes away. I don't mind being second in your affections to an old house. I don't understand it, but I can live with the knowledge that you feel something almost mystical about Helmingham Hall.'

She was too moved to speak, but squeezed his hand, then straightened her shoulders to face the ordeal of saying goodbye to Rosie.

The two women smiled sadly at one another. Rosie extended her hand, and suddenly they were in an embrace. It lasted for mere seconds, each of them embarrassed by this display of affection.

'Rosie, I expect you and Bill to visit us often at Boscomb House. And what is more, I expect to be given half a dozen bushes of "Helmingham". To me, the rose will always summon up memories of the place. I will smell the fragrance and think of the home I once had, but I don't intend to cross that moat ever again. Goodbye, my dear friend. Keep well and write to me often.'

Epilogue

Joyce stood at the front door of Boscomb House and waved goodbye to her visitor, Aurelia Kent, who lived on a large farm three miles away. The hot June sun bathed the house in brilliant light, showing up the rotting window frames, the broken pane in an upstairs sash window and the freshly weeded gravel drive.

Leaning against the door frame, she sighed with deepest pleasure. Joyce and Laurence had been married in a quiet ceremony at the Trinity Church in Halstead, and had come directly to Boscomb, promising themselves a proper honeymoon when Laurence's business made them millionaires.

On their wedding night, Laurence had put his foot through a rotten floorboard in the bedroom. Soot, which had lain undisturbed for a generation, had chosen that moment to descend onto the grate, covering Joyce's wedding gown with black specks.

The next morning, they found the kitchen extremely cold because the old cooking range had gone out. Laurence had to search out an old spirit lamp to heat water for tea, and the milk was frozen.

However, a month of hard work for six grateful local men, plus a variety of building materials, paint, wallpaper and wages had cost them only seventy-five pounds and given new life to a tired house.

So radical was the change that Joyce felt she had reinvented Boscomb House. She loved it dearly because she had helped to create it. Nor did it take her long to appreciate Mr Micawber's recipe for happiness. She could not afford proper repairs for Helmingham, which caused her to worry all the time. At Boscomb, on the other hand, she and Laurence could manage to pay for whatever was necessary, even if they had to wait a few months between projects.

That laurel is going to cut out too much light in the study if it's not cut back, she thought. *What will Bill say when he sees it?*

On December the first, 1929, it had taken them over an hour to reach Halstead, but by the time she had been welcomed by Mr and Mrs Ballard and all Laurence's sisters, the sickness that had been her love for Helmingham had begun to dissipate.

The weight of her responsibilities had been lifted from her shoulders. She was once again young and carefree, with the added pleasure of a large, loving, ready-made family. There had been little time to brood over a lost inheritance.

Marsha and Cartwright had attended their wedding, had given them a large cheque and departed early.

A month later, Laurence had insisted that they attend the wedding of Marsha and Cartwright. She had been reluctant, dreading the sight of her beloved Helmingham Hall, but to her surprise it had been all right.

Joyce was about to go indoors when Laurence came round the side of the house and saw her. It was five o'clock of a Saturday afternoon, and he was dressed for work in old trousers and a collarless striped shirt.

'What, still here? I thought Aurelia left ages ago.'

'She did. I was just thinking. I believe Helmingham Hall cast a spell on me. And this spell made me act in a very strange way. And a handsome prince carried me away in a big black lorry and the spell was broken and—'

'The prince and princess lived happily ever after.'

She laughed. 'Exactly. You know, I was afraid to leave Helmingham Hall because I would no longer be Miss d'Avranche of Helmingham. But now I am a different person. I am Mrs Ballard Who Used To Live At Helmingham.'

'An intriguing title.'

'Yes,' she said, 'it is, but an easy one to bear. Half an hour ago, Aurelia said, "You used to live at Helmingham. What sort of curtains should I hang in my sitting-room?" And yesterday, Mrs Pease asked my advice about what to serve at her garden party. She thought I ought to know, because—'

'You Used To Live At Helmingham. No experience is wasted, I suppose. And the knowledge you picked up has certainly benefitted Boscomb.'

They heard the sound of the motor several seconds before Bill's motorbike and sidecar came into view. Bill was buying the vehicle from Laurence by twenty-four payments, and was extremely proud to own such a handy form of transport. He climbed off the saddle and helped Rosie, who was holding baby Robert, to get out of the sidecar.

'Bill, I'm so glad to see you!' called Laurence. He chucked the baby under the chin and greeted Rosie warmly, before leading Bill directly to the garden.

'Is "Helmingham" in bloom?' asked Rosie.

'Yes, and looking very pretty. Oh, do let me hold him. What a splendid boy you are, Robert. You look just like your papa. Come indoors first, Rosie. I've something very special to show you. Are the rose trials going well?'

'Yes, I've heard from the National Rose Society and they say the signs are good. It's going to be a great rose for many years to come.'

Joyce led the way to the drawing-room, now brightened with pale cream paint and light fabrics. She pointed to the space over the mantelpiece and waited for Rosie's gasp of surprise.

'*Stuart Child* by Van Dyck!' she cried.

'Yes,' said Joyce with quiet pride. 'I wrote to Marsha that I was expecting, and my cousin Cartwright sent me the painting!' She laughed. 'Of course, it's more valuable than the house!'

Rosie reached out to touch Joyce on her shoulder. 'Surely nothing is more valuable than Boscomb. This is your home.'

'Oh yes. But I shall treasure this painting because it is a gift from Cartwright. I'm doubly blessed, you know. I have Laurence's family and I have a family of my own after all. And as if that weren't enough, Cartwright has the money and the will to put Helmingham in perfect condition as well as to help those who need it.'

Neither of them said anything for a moment, then Joyce said, 'Come on. Let's go outside and join the men.'

The hot sun glinted on the clear water of the newly refurbished pond. Bill had his sleeves up and his pruning knife in his hand as he tackled a small cherry while Laurence hovered anxiously.

'We'll make gardeners of you both one of these days,' said Rosie. 'I'll have to breed a Boscomb rose.'

THE END

CAPEL BELLS
by Joan Hessayon

Charlotte Blair had worked hard all her life. Raised amongst the porters and street sellers of Covent Garden, she had achieved unusual success for a woman in 1911 – her own flower shop. It was unfashionable, in a poor part of London, and made only a small profit, but Charlotte had a secret ambition, to become one of the great floral decorators of the period, transforming the ballroom and grand houses of the aristocracy.

When she was bidden to Capel Manor for her first floral assignment she fell in love with the house, but – cruelly – fate snatched the commission away from her before she had even begun. It was several weeks later that she learned Capel Manor could be rented and, borrowing every penny she could, she moved her business to the beautiful old house, believing that this would give her an entry into the great families of the neighbourhood.

Beset with every problem, cheating gardeners, the crooked plans of her old friends in Covent Garden, and the return of Matthew Warrender, the owner of Capel Manor, Charlotte fought to realise her ambition to become the most famous floral decorator of her time.

0 552 14220 4

THE SECRET YEARS
by Judith Lennox

During that last, shimmeringly hot summer of 1914, four young people played with seeming innocence in the gardens of Drakesden Abbey. Nicholas and Lally were the children of the great house, set in the bleak and magical Fen country and the home of the Blythe family for generations; Thomasine was the unconventional niece of two genteel maiden aunts in the village. And Daniel – Daniel was the son of the local blacksmith, a fiercely independent, ambitious boy who longed to break away from the stifling confines of his East Anglian upbringing. As the drums of war sounded in the distance, the Firedrake, a mysterious and ancient Blythe family heirloom disappeared, setting off a chain of events which they were powerless to control.

The Great War changed everything, and both Nicholas and Daniel returned from the front damaged by their experiences. Thomasine, freed from the narrow disciplines of her childhood, and enjoying the new hedonism which the twenties brought, thought that she could escape from the ties of childhood which bound her to both Nicholas and Daniel. But the passions and enmities of their shared youth had intensified in the passing years, and Nicholas, Thomasine, Lally and Daniel all had to experience tragedy and betrayal before the Firedrake made its reappearance and, with it, a new hope for the future.

0 552 14331 6

FOOL'S CURTAIN
by Claire Lorrimer

For three generations Rochford Manor has dominated the lives of the women who lived there. Willow Rochford became its chatelaine at seventeen. Her daughter, Lucy, taken from her mother and her home as an infant, fought long and hard to return to the life that should have been hers within its walls. For Zandra, Willow Rochford's young niece, the house became a place of sanctuary after the tragic death of her parents.

But when the Rochfords' family business falls victim to the Wall Street Crash, the future looks bleak and Rochford Manor itself is threatened. Zandra could never have imagined that she might be the unwitting saviour of her family's fortunes when her beauty and vivacity capture the desire of Anthony Wisson. The wealthy tycoon swiftly concluded a deal which bought him a bride as well as a new business, but for Zandra the price of her family's happiness meant the sacrifice of her own.

The long-awaited concluding volume of *The Rochford Trilogy*.

0 552 14002 3

A SELECTED LIST OF FINE NOVELS
AVAILABLE FROM CORGI BOOKS

THE PRICES SHOWN BELOW WERE CORRECT AT THE TIME OF GOING
TO PRESS. HOWEVER TRANSWORLD PUBLISHERS RESERVE THE RIGHT
TO SHOW NEW RETAIL PRICES ON COVERS WHICH MAY DIFFER FROM
THOSE PREVIOUSLY ADVERTISED IN THE TEXT OR ELSEWHERE.

14060	0	MERSEY BLUES	Lyn Andrews	£4.99
14229	8	CEDAR STREET	Aileen Armitage	£4.99
14309	X	THE KERRY DANCE	Louise Brindley	£5.99
13313	2	CATCH THE WIND	Frances Donnelly	£5.99
14382	0	THE TREACHERY OF TIME		
			Anna Gilbert	£4.99
13686	7	THE SHOEMAKER'S DAUGHTER		
			Iris Gower	£4.99
14140	2	A CROOKED MILE	Ruth Hamilton	£4.99
14141	0	PARADISE LANE	Ruth Hamilton	£5.99
14529	7	LEAVES FROM THE VALLEY		
			Caroline Harvey	£5.99
14297	2	ROSY SMITH	Janet Haslam	£4.99
14220	4	CAPEL BELLS	Joan Hessayon	£4.99
14390	1	THE SPLENDOUR FALLS		
			Susanna Kearsley	£4.99
14045	7	THE SUGAR PAVILION	Rosalind Laker	£5.99
14331	6	THE SECRET YEARS	Judith Lennox	£4.99
14002	3	FOOL'S CURTAIN	Claire Lorrimer	£4.99
13737	5	EMERALD	Elisabeth Luard	£5.99
13910	6	BLUEBIRDS	Margaret Mayhew	£5.99
13904	1	CSARDAS	Diane Pearson	£4.99
10375	6	VOICES OF SUMMER	Diane Pearson	£5.99
14123	2	THE LONDONERS	Margaret Pemberton	£4.99
14124	0	MAGNOLIA SQUARE	Margaret Pemberton	£4.99
14400	2	THE MOUNTAIN	Elvi Rhodes	£5.66
14466	5	TOUCHED BY ANGELS	Susan Sallis	£5.99
14513	0	THE LAST SUMMER	Mary Jane Staples	£4.99
14296	4	THE LAND OF NIGHTINGALES		
			Sally Stewart	£4.99
14118	6	THE HUNGRY TIDE	Valerie Wood	£4.99

All Transworld titles are available by post from:

Book Service By Post, P.O. Box 29, Douglas, Isle of Man IM99 1BQ

Credit cards accepted. Please telephone 01624 675137,
fax 01624 670923, Internet http://www. bookpost.co.uk
or e-mail: bookshop@enterprise.net for details.

Free postage and packing in the UK. Overseas customers: allow
£1 per book (paperbacks) and £3 per book (hardbacks).

Also by Joan Hessayon

CAPEL BELLS

and published by Corgi Books

Joan Hessayon was born in Louisville, Kentucky but grew up in Missouri. In 1949 she went to Paris where she met her husband, Dr David Hessayon, the creator of the bestselling *Expert* series of gardening books. They married in 1951 and share a love of history, plants and writing. Joan Hessayon's first novel was published in 1983; her tenth and most recent novel, *Capel Bells*, is also published by Corgi. She lives in Essex and has two daughters and four grandchildren.